The Great Carry
Francis J. Smith

ISBN: 9781985100510
Edited by Bill Smith and Ann Tanyeri.
Special thanks to Micah Labatore and Stella Dwyer.

Map Blockhouse courtesy of the Florida Center for Instructional
Technology and the Educational Technology Clearinghouse
(ETC.USF.EDU)

Cover Photo courtesy Cloudia at Can Stock Photos

More Books at: http://www.centervillebooks.com/

Editor's Note: This is a work of fiction. The author has made an effort
to portray all historical characters and events as honestly as possible
in the context of fiction. There never was a North Fort at the Great
Carry, at what is today Fort Edward, NY. The conquest of Louisbourg
and the destruction of Saratoga are real events.

For William Wood, an ancestor who epitomized for Francis the perseverance and grit of the early Adirondackers. Lost in the winter woods and nearly frozen to death, William was rescued by Native Americans who saved his life by amputating his legs below the knees, and who later showed him how to construct the customized snowshoes and wood and leather braces that allowed him to continue indulging his love of the woods. William once trekked on those shoes and for reasons unknown to us, from Raquette Lake to Elizabethtown, eighty-four miles, a two-hour trip today. 2/19/2018.

Table of Contents

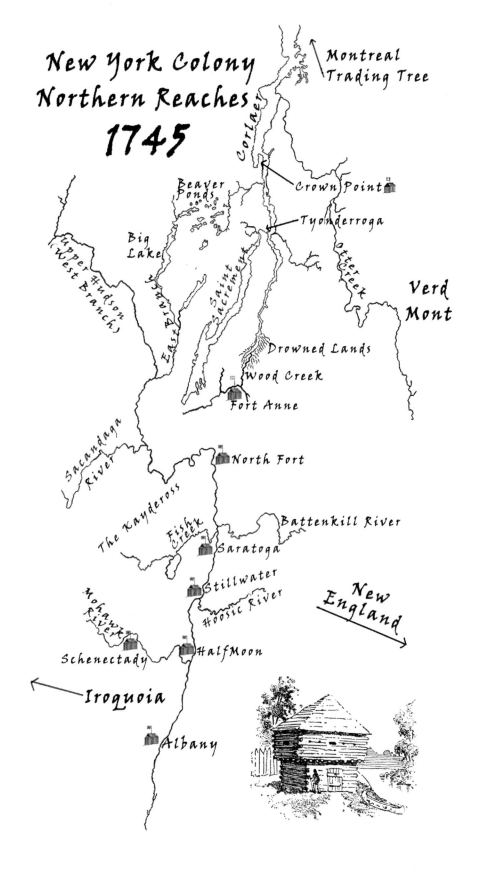

New York Colony
Northern Reaches
1745

Montreal
Trading Tree

Corlaer

Crown Point

Tyonderroga

Beaver
Ponds

Big
Lake

Otter
Creek

(Upper Hudson
West Branch)

East Branch

Saint Sacrement

Verd
Mont

Drowned Lands

Wood Creek

Fort Anne

Sacandaga
River

North Fort

The Kaydeross

Fishk
Creek

Battenkill River

Saratoga

Stillwater

Hoosic River

New
England

Mohawk
River

Schenectady

HalfMoon

Iroquoia

Albany

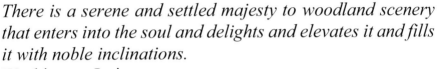

There is a serene and settled majesty to woodland scenery that enters into the soul and delights and elevates it and fills it with noble inclinations.
Washington Irving

Chapter I – Scalp Point

The French were raising a castle at Crown Point. Word of this treacherous breach of the treaty between England and France came to my folks' Albany tavern one summer day in 1731, brought by smugglers back from Montreal. I remember when it came, how the men began congregating in the common room. Father was swamped with business. A fresh batch of beer made only days before was quickly gone, the tension and worry in the room obvious to an eleven-year-old boy.

Mother sent me off to bed but no way would I miss hearing the talk. I climbed out the window and shimmied up the tree which grew there, crept across the roof and got back in through the trapdoor over the common room. I watched from up in the rafters. And listened. The puffs of smoke and the odor from the Dutchmen's long-stemmed clay pipes rose up to where I was hidden. My eyes burned.

"Damn the Assembly for allowing it to happen," said a beefy, red-faced farmer from across the river, dressed in brown homespun and with a skunk-skin hat cocked off one side of his head.

"Not just the Assembly, that rat-faced son-of-a-bitch of a governor is to blame too," a tall, skinny riverman from Halfmoon said loud, a tankard of beer in his hand. The room always reeked in summer and on this night, along with the sweat and tobacco, I smelled something else. Fear.

"T'is the goddamn cowardly Dutch who cry for neutrality so they can deal in their bloody fur," said a fat Englishman in beaver hat and fancy suit, remembering as he spoke just whose place he was in. All attention in the room shifted to my father.

I heard the Englishman's chair scraping as he tried to rise. With my sight obstructed by the height of my perch and the rafters, I could just make out his try for the door. Father got there first. Pops, though not tall, is a beefy man who knows how to use his fists. Years spent at sea in charge of the foc'sle of a navy ship makes for a hard Dutchman. The fight was short, the laughter loud as Pops tossed the beaten man into the street. Pops went back behind the bar. "Any odder Enchlismans here thinks dis Dutch iz an couvard?"

None did.

There was plenty more for me to see and hear. Men coming and going, shouts and curses, fists and bodies thrown over rum punches and cold beers. Pops and Mother and our serving wench worked without letup. Late into the night, the mayor, the high aldermen and others of the prominent men of Albany passed through the doors.

"Where in hell is the British army?" a man demanded of the mayor. Pops sneered. Those near paused to hear his words. "Der gotterdam English ish too busy fighting der Scotch und der Irish to take care of der business here."

Everybody agreed, and with the Canadian Indians having now a base just three days' travel from our gates, men said we were no longer safe, not even in winter. It was getting on toward dawn afore I snuck into bed. My dreams were of this new and terrifying fort up in the northern wilderness. I awoke early and rushed to tell my friends what I had seen and heard. They didn't believe half of it, at first.

A scout was sent north to investigate. The entire town, indeed, the entire colony, awaited his return. Our intrepid spook was back in little more than a week. He reported first to the officials, word spread he was back, folks gathered at the tavern.

He came by as soon as he left the fort at the top of the hill. I was present when he came. The rumor was true. The French had moved south of Split Rock, the boundary on Corlaer between them and us. "They's at Scalp Point, erecting themselves a log palisade a standin' out to the far point a the east shore," the scout said, "and on the west shore, they's building in stone, not wood. And with plenty a Injuns. I had a good deal a trouble slippin' by 'em."

"What will the British do about it?" someone asked. The men, the Dutch, anyway, which was mostly what frequented the tavern, agreed the British would do nothing. The scout could not say with certainty when the forts would be completed. For a few days, our scout was the biggest man in Albany. Pops' customers toasted his courage, shook his hand, slapped his back, bought him drinks and supper.

How I admired his woodcraft, spooking the enemy forts, sliding past Indians in the woods. For the next days, in our boys' games played with toy guns, I refused to play any part other than the scout, sneaking past my friends in the woods and fields outside the stockade, lifting mock scalps.

With attention on him waning, our scout's retelling of his exploits grew more heroic, his embellishments more bold. He was sent back north for what more he could learn and was never seen again. All summer our officials tried to contact the Montreal authorities, to demand the removal of this unlawful threat. They met with no success.

We boys talked of nothing else and we felt the tension in town. By fall, our games included scaling the walls of Albany and sneaking past the sentries, who would have boxed our ears did they catch us, and we heard talk of yet another problem the French incursion would bring. "Them black-robed priests'll surely be there," was how one man put it. "Sneakin' Papists'll be turnin' the heads a our Iroquois. They'll use Scalp Point ta worm their way inter the Mohawk keeps. Connivin' bastards'll be causin' trouble, mark my words."

That fall, a man's flintlock pistol accidentally discharged in the tavern, narrowly missing injuring a farmer. Men said it was an omen. Said Crown Point would be troublesome, if it be allowed to stand.

Indeed, it was not long before the troubles started. A number of the Iroquois, who hitherto had been our staunch allies, were lately convinced by the Jesuits to take up the cross. Word had it they moved to a newly established post along the upper Saint Lawrence River. That winter of '31 into '32 was a long dreary one, folks afraid to do much outside the gates for fear of the blow to come. No smugglers or scouts ventured north. An uneasy peace held. We wondered for how long.

Mother feared to let me out of her sight and she nearly fainted when the sergeant of the garrison, a lobsterback Britisher, came to the tavern with a stern warning. If I didn't desist in sneaking around the palisade walls with my friends, Pops would be paying a stiff fine. If the already nervous sentries didn't shoot me.

In the spring of 1732, with our scouts reporting the completion of one of the French forts and steady work on the other, a conference was called in Albany at the insistence of our Iroquois friends. The governor of the colony, come up from New York Town, held the first place amongst the whites at the council. Originally set for the fort at the top of the hill, the unexpectedly large number of people, both white and red, necessitated it be held in a field outside of town.

Pops kept me busy hauling in supplies and helping with making batches of beer, which we stored in kegs specially made by one of the local coopers. Days before the conference opened, the Indians began arriving. Representatives came from most of the Iroquois tribes, the sachems and chiefs leading long files of tribesmen. They camped just beyond the city walls. Old and young, male and female, they roamed the streets and entered people's homes. "Not a whit of understanding the idea of private property," I heard one stuffy old bag of an English lady snort. Indeed, Indians were looking, touching, taking, and with so many arriving, it was one of the busiest times I remember. Day and night our tavern was filled. Men hollering, spilling beer for me to sop up, a great beam of drinking and confusion, heady excitement for a frontier lad, even if he be working much of the time. Mother was very grouchy for all the cooking and cleaning she had to do.

Many of the white men who came were dignitaries from around the colony. We could tell them by their expensive suits and beaver hats. And with how they pushed past people and demanded things be just so. Pops said with a sneer and in his gruff way, "Vot it means, one tinks he iz un important person, ya." Pops didn't mind, he just raised his prices according to how important a man thought himself. These Lordships, as Pops called them, had personal manservants, older black men, slaves who must constantly attend their master's needs.

When Father could find nothing for me to do or when I could sneak away, I was with my friends out to the meeting grounds. Indians was everywhere, drinking, arguing, trading curios, furs and horses. Rum flowed in a raucous bevy of color and noise. We seen a fancy-dressed Englishman arguing with an Indian through a Dutch translator, the Englishman so mad I thought they must fight but the Indian remained stoic in the face of the harsh treatment. The argument had to do with furs, the white man feeling cheated.

Indian men and boys hawked wares of every sort. Horseraces run dangerously close to the crowds, games played with sticks and bones. We seen a squaw at a shell game emptying a drunken sailor's purse. Gangs of Indian kids dashed about, hurtling into people and getting into fights with the white kids, even us, we had ourselves a couple of nice brawls.

****

Roaming the camp the day before the pow-wow began, us boys gaped hungrily at a skewered ox turning on a spit, juices popping and snapping, grease splattering noisily into the fire below. The scent of the meat made a boy powerful hungry. We were wondering was there a way to filch a taste of it. The two men turning the spit cussed and told us to move along.

A giant of an Indian chief a little way off had also been looking at the meat and was looking now at us, as if deep in thought. He wore simple buckskins, his only ornament a bear-tooth necklace. His hair was in two long thin braids down his back. He looked right through each one of us in turn, starting with Eric, who about peed his britches. Whilst the Indian was staring at Abner, then Ben, I recalled something my father had once told me, how one man will try to own another by gazing steadfast into his eyes. If ever a man tried this with me, and did I want to be a man, I was to fix my gaze on his and keep it there. And what else Pops said, and he always laughed for saying it, "Vatch out der man don' kill you for it." So when the chief's gaze came to me, I met it straight on, looking into his gnarly face, so stony and hard. So ferocious, his intent could not be good! I dared not move. He drew a knife which appeared in his hand as if by magic, a wickedly long and sharp affair which he pointed directly at me.

Eric, quivering fearfully, said the Indian was going to scalp me on account of an Injun boy I had whupped upon. I, without moving my gaze from the Indian to Eric, said I didn't think so. "He wuzn't hurt so bad as to get a chief after us." Abner said as how the chief looked fairly riled. Eric was shaking and iffen his feet hadn't a been frozen to the ground, he'd of run for certain. "He ain't a gonna hurt me none," I said. "He's on our side." Ben said he didn't appear to be on our side.

With panther-like gait, the big Indian strode, not toward me, but instead toward the roasting ox. The men working the spit had been watching our encounter with the chief and as he came toward them, they backed away. With his scalp knife, the old warrior cut a slab of meat. I watched the sharp edge slip through the meat and I wondered how many scalps the knife had removed in the same manner. With meat skewered on the deadly blade and with the slightest movement of the knife, he bade me come forth. I did, still eyeballin' him. He further bade me with a gesture to take the meat from the tip of his knife. I took it and began chewing, still gazing into his eyes. His stern visage melting into the wrinkles of a grin, he reached out and tousled the hair on my head, the way the men did sometimes with the boys. Then he cut a generous piece for himself and strode away.

****

To any who might chance upon my journals, I should introduce myself. I am Ken Kuyler, born in Albany, New York Colony, in the year 1720. My father was an ex-Dutch-navy sailing master, some say a pirate, who swallowed the anchor and came ashore. He had a discharge paper dated 1715 in a heavy metal box in his sea trunk. I had seen it myself.

My mother was also Dutch, from the same town in Holland as Pops. Mother's first husband sailed with my father. Pops was with him the night he washed overboard and was lost in a violent storm in the North Sea. After this, Pops retired from the navy and returned to the homeplace, still a young man in full health and vigor. He and Mother married and came to the New World, which he had visited. The money they held between them was enough for passage and for an investment, should the right one come along. He knew this new land to be one of opportunity for any man willing to work hard. She believed in him.

They landed in New Amsterdam, which the English called New York. This city was too English for their taste and they went north to the city of Orange, or Albany, on the upper Hudson, a growing settlement with decided Dutch leanings. Albany sat one hundred and fifty miles north of New York Town, just below the junction of the Hudson with the smaller, though not insubstantial Mohawk River, which came in from the west. Our palisaded town was situated on a hill on the west shore of the Hudson. Scattered around on both sides of the river were other small settlements.

Mother and Pops found Albany more to their liking despite the dangers of the frontier. Here, the Dutch influence was slow to die. It lingered in the politics and commerce of the town. Below Albany were the patroons, vast plantations carved from the heavily timbered shores of the river. The proprietors, almost all Dutch to this day, were rich and influential.

Father worked as a cargo super on the docks of our small, bustling port, unloading fast sloops from downriver and coasters from the other colonies. On the return trip downstream, they carried furs and hides, farm produce, rough lumber. Mother assisted the teacher in the Dutch school, and a year after their arrival in Albany, a popular waterfront tavern, the Hitching Post, came up for sale. They paid cash money for it. Father renamed it the Full Sail and had a large sign hung, a sailing ship with all sails a blowin'. A year later, I arrived, an only child.

My earliest boyhood memories were of trappers, soldiers, bateauxmen, Indians, all passing through the tavern. We lived in a cabin behind the kitchen and joined to it by an enclosed passage used for the storing of kegs of beer and salted meats. From the rafters hung carrots, squashes, corncobs, the makings of suppers. Our beer was considered the best in Albany but the men who crowded in at noon and at the end of the day came as much for Mother's stews as for the beer. The stews, with a secret sauce, were raved over, as were Mother's breads, which too were delicious. I have heard sailors tell Mother they would come from the other side of the world for the pleasure of dunking her breads into her stews. Above the passage was a second floor with sleeping chambers for boarders and a third floor, a straw-strewn attic loft for transients.

Most nights the common room was full. I often listened, fascinated by the boasting of the men who hunted and trapped north of the Mohawk River and of the boatmen who, in the employ of the Albany merchants, hauled trade goods out to Oswego and came back with furs. The Full Sail was the first stop for these men on their return from the far country. They came reeking of the woods and of adventure.

Mohawk chiefs came too, from the west, trading salt and furs and to meet with the politicians. In their feathers, paint and beads, the chiefs were colorful, exotic, sometimes terrifying to a boy. The chiefs were stern and unsmiling. Mother said this was an act put on for the white man. She said it was easy to tell the Indians' affection for any and all children.

The most interesting men to my ears, the ones I most wanted to listen to, were the fur smugglers. Their tales of excitement and danger on the waters of Corlaer the most fascinating of all. These were furtive men who turned toward the door whenever they heard the latch and who sized-up other men, weapons close to hand. They talked only to each other. Sometimes, when I could listen in, I'd hear them speak of the richness of the north, the wildness of the mountain country. Their talk, hard to hear for it was quiet talk, was of lofty peaks and endless forests, turbulent streams full of fish, woods with deer and elk, turkey and bear. Pirates and Indians.

I remember my friend Eric and me sitting by the fire in the evenings after my chores were done and before Mother would run him home and me to bed. We would listen to the stories or to the news of the day. We dreaded grim retellings of the burning of Schenectady by the French and their Indians in the last century, during King William's War. Most of New Hampshire was destroyed in those old wars and it always made me shudder to think the same could happen to Albany.

The raids, most often by way of Corlaer, hit the border settlements of our colony and of neighboring New England.

We grew up on stories of our friends, the mighty Iroquois, their attacks on the French and Algonquins. In times of war the Iroquois struck without warning or mercy, often in the dead of winter. Entire tribes, even the European-style cities of the north, felt the united wrath of the Six Nations, as the Iroquois tribes were known. The French had ample reason to fear the dread cry "Iroquois!" In the late years of the 1600's, the French erected strong fortifications at the mouth of Corlaer to prevent the attacks, which forts did little in buttressing against the Iroquois.

Corlaer was the setting for stirring tales of yore, deeds of valor and of unspeakable cruelties. Many a battle had been fought on the shores of this lake, which the French called Champlain and which had borne continual witness to the passage of armies and raiding parties, sometimes going north, sometimes south, summer and winter, the raids often successful, many times not. Up there, the hunter of men oftentimes became the hunted. The hazards of the route, both natural and man-made, were many.

****

I grew up with a love of reading and writing, instilled in me by my mother. I learned to speak and write both Dutch and English. Mother fiercely cherished the education she had been fortunate enough to have received. According to Father, this was because as a child she was so stubborn that when she was told a girl did not need an education, she decided no one would stop her. Her determination she passed on to me. From my earliest days, she taught me the importance of books and writing. To her, and thus to me, any book was a most valuable item, almost beyond price.

On rainy days and sometimes at night, by candlelight, I penned childish stories about fighting Indians or of adventures set in the far-off places my father had told me about. Mother said I had a flair for writing and insisted I put down the things which occurred in my life, a record in my own words of what went on. My efforts were mostly feeble but she pushed me to improve. She said it was important, to keep the mind active.

The folks sacrificed to put me into the English Language school. I could not tolerate listening to the drone of the schoolmaster. He often put me to sleep then whipped me for it, as if it were my fault, not his.

Nothing made Mother so mad as the schoolmaster coming through our front door. She knew I was truant before he said a word. Much as I hated to displease her, I never could reconcile myself to sittin' all day in a stuffy classroom whilst the old goat droned on, putting half the boys and even a few of the girls to sleep. At the time, my attitude and poor performance did not mean much to me, except it got me into trouble with Mother. I realize now she had been more disappointed than angry.

Despite my aversion for school, I was a reader, devouring any book I could find. Books were scarce on the frontier. We had half a dozen, more than most families. I read and reread all of them and borrowed others when I could. Sometimes, in the woods or on the river, I might spend an entire day reading instead of hunting or fishing. I read some of the Shakespeare stories this way. These were Mother's most prized possessions and I was always most careful with them.

Father begrudged the time I spent with books but he never complained about it to Mother. He dared not oppose her in this regard. I used this sometimes to advantage by playing her against him. I helped her to learn English. We had many sessions and arguments about what was the right way to put things down. That way, we both learned.

Father preferred I didn't go to school for then he could put me to work. There were always more than enough chores. Chopping wood, hauling slop buckets, fetching water, handling kegs, sweeping and mopping the floor. Sometimes, to get him mad, I would speak to him in the high tones of Shakespeare's Elizabethans. This always made him furious, I was never sure why. Maybe because Shakespeare was English. To get back at me, he would have me read the newspaper. Papers were scarce but whenever one came in, either by post or under the arm of a patron, Pops would stand me on a chair in the common room and I had to read aloud for the benefit of those men who either didn't know how to read or wouldn't spend a penny on a paper. The men would cheer or snort, depending on what they thought of the news. Bad news was always my fault, the men hissing and jeering, and sometimes, when the news was particularly irksome, they threw things at me. Father thought my loathing of this business hilarious and would ask why I could possibly get so mad about it. He'd say as how he thought I enjoyed reading.

****

I grew up big 'n hard. Not so tall as my friend Eric but stronger.

My shoulders bigger than his. In our wrestling matches, I most always throwed him. When I could get away from the tavern, I hunted with the old firelock Father gave me. Fresh meat was money for the folks and a welcome change from salt pork and beef. They didn't say much about my missing school when I came home with meat. By the age of twelve, I had already taken a number of deer and turkey.

And had decided tavern-keeping was not for me. I reckoned it to be as bad as going to school. The more distance between me and the inn, the better. I often camped out overnight, not daring to come home until I bagged enough game to keep Pops from being too mad. Better not to face him without something to show for my absence. He complained most bitterly when I came home emptyhanded yet he never beat me, which is uncommon. Mother said it was because of how often Father got thrashed as an unruly child.

A lad grows up fast along the frontier. By the age of thirteen, as soon as I could raise a little money, I bought traps. Father found someone to show me how to use them. I took to trapping and collected fair amounts of fur. Trapping here meant muskrat, weasel, fox, coons. The biggest demand was for beaver, which was not to be found hereabouts.

One time, I was amazed at how a smart wolf stole my bait. I could read his sign, how his tail eagerly swished the snow as he sat on his haunches, and how he circled my set. He wanted the bait but sensed the danger. For the longest time he must have pondered, wary yet determined to have them fresh deer innards. Then he somehow sprung the trap and retreated lightning-quick before it clamped down on him.

Deer were plentiful, particularly over to Rennsalaerwick, across the river. The lakes and creeks supplied plenty of ducks and Canada geese. Partridges grew fat in the berry bushes and grapevines and were best taken around sunset when they roosted in the lower branches of the trees. My father slit their necks and hung them by their feet over a tub until the blood stopped flowing. Only then, he said, was they ready to cook. They was ripe to my nose but delicious the way Mother prepared 'em.

By the age of fourteen, I was spending less time at home, more time farther afield, hunting and fishing. I'd build lean-tos in the forest and camp for three, four days. Sometimes, when the hunt was good, I had to borrow a horse to carry home all the game. Most of the meat I gave to Pops for the tavern, a little I might keep aside and sell.

Eric and me took out our leaky rowboat in the evenings to fish for giant bass in the backwaters and swamps of the Hudson. In summer, did we see trappers or smugglers coming downriver, canoes piled high with cargoes of furs, we'd hurry to the wharves for a closer look. By the time we could get there, the men would have their bundles under cover. These are hardy, buck-skinned adventurers, users of hard language, sharp of eye. The next day after we'd see the men on the river, they'd be spending their fur money in the Full Sail. Many times, one or more of the men did not return. Did anyone ask after them, the answer was a shrug of the shoulder or a finger drawn across throat or topknot.

If the fur buyer was one I knew, I might get work and many a night, after a full day of scraping and cleaning, stretching and sorting bales, I'd sit in the common room and with pine knots snapping in the fire, I'd listen to the stories. Tales of Indian fights, of trapping beavers in the swamps and flows, of competition for fur with the coureur-des-bois, French half-breeds who had chosen forest life over civilization. These were the influences and the hard surroundings I grew up in, heady to a lad of tender years.

****

We had lately begun to hear of the French intruding into the Ohio country, using the dangerous western Indians to throw the English back east of the mountains. The French were rumored to be building a chain of forts along the Ohio River. This would hem in our colonies and, men say, it would swing the entire western area over to French dominance. The English, pushed back and surrounded, were weak and unable to counter the French thrusts.

Men spoke of our own fort, built near Scalp Point by the stout Dutchman, DeWorms, in the 1690s. If not for the untimely loss of an English fleet going onto the rocks entering the Saint Lawrence River, DeWorms might a taken Quebec and we would not have our present troubles. He and his Dutchmen fought winning battles in the wilderness but no Englishman ever had any success. So our Dutch say.

As always, there is friction between the English and Dutch. One or two of the old Dutch who frequent the tavern were with DeWorms. More were with Nicholson when he built Fort Anne up at the Drowned Lands then burnt it because his men would not stay the winter. They left more'n a hundred and fifty graves. Bad water in the Drowned Lands took those lives; some say Indians poisoned the waters.

One old farmer from Schenectady told me the English had captured Quebec and other major Canadian towns then made a treaty and gived it all back. "A mistake," he sagely predicted, "which will cost us one of these fine days, I kin till ya." He bragged to me of the good work he performed in the assaults. I figured out how old the man would have to be, to have been there, it was not possible. Pops says when men talk about all they have done, it can usually be understood they have done little. "Vatch out for der silent ones," he always said.

The men bragged in their cups what they would do to the French and what they had already done. Pretty ferocious deeds to a lad but still and as always, it was the fur smugglers who most interested me.

Trade with Canada was forbidden by law but the lure of Canadian fur was a strong one. Even in perilous times, the smugglers were eager to face the dangers. All winter they made their plans by the roaring fire in the tavern. How I envied them. How my soul burned to go!

Chapter II – Captain Hugh

Last summer, 1735, the Iroquois tried to intercept the fur carried by the western Indians to the rendezvous at Montreal. The result was humiliating for the Iroquois; they came home bruised and without furs. They were mad and looking to avenge their honor. Tension ran high in Albany. The shady merchants who had backed the Iroquois worried over the loss of their expected profits. Others, more prudent, prepared for defense, for fear the Iroquois might lash out at us, we were so close. Then we heard the Iroquois had raided some Delaware Indian towns along the Pennsylvania border and things settled down.

The rewards for fur smuggling would be especially high this year, as not much fur could be had at any price. In normal years, Albany, with its location and the superiority of English manufactured goods, held a near monopoly on the western and northern fur. Only the best fur went to London and most went by way of Albany, coming down Corlaer or along the Mohawk River from the trading house at Oswego. Now and with last year's ruinous attempt by the Iroquois, fur was in demand.

Rumors of war with Spain over the ill-treatment of English sailors or with France for invading a province in Germany, or with both, increased the risks and thus the profits in the fur-smuggling trade. Despite the rumors and always with the danger of trying to slip by hostile Indians and even with the French now at Scalp Point, word got out. The French were interested in doing business, providing it went through their governor. No other contact would be allowed with Monseignor's Indians. The governor of New France must have his cut, same as our Albany politicians.

I listened to the talk all winter in the Full Sail, three or four parties were readying to go a smugglin', the expected profits outweighing the dangers in the minds of the men. I, in my innocence of youth, felt I was thoroughly familiar with all aspects of the smugglers' trade and I yearned to be included.

****

Spring began to show. The white blossoms on the shadbush, the first colors of the year, were starting. Within a few days, the shadfish appeared in the river. I fished the run, but my heart lay elsewhere. I wanted to go smuggling. To see the far north I had grown up hearing about.

One night at the tavern, I got up courage enough to ask a bearded smuggler would he take me along. He rocked the common room with his laughter. To think he'd take a rawboned kid such as me. Then his laughing stopped, his face turned cold, the room turned silent, and with everybody watching, listening, he asked loudly did I know what awaited the man or boy who insinuated he was a fur smuggler, which he was. With his eyes bulging as he looked around at the men, he ran a finger across his throat; the men roared, my hopes for adventure were dashed.

The shad run was good. I worked hard and took enough fish to supply Pops. My fingers was cut and stinging from cleaning all those damn fish, my back ached from the bending. We filled seven barrels which Pops salted down, and with two barrels for me.

I peddled mine along the wharf at the bottom of the hill, amid the prows and gangways and tangles of rigging hanging over the docks. I admired the sloops in from New York, the coasters from Boston, Hartford, Philadelphia, Charleston, the Indies, and I wondered if I might someday follow in Pops' footsteps, see the world as he had. Cathay, India. The Congo!

I called up to a shipmaster, offering my catch for sale, "Fresh salted fish, Cap'n, fresh as kin be." I sold at a good price for me. His sloop was bound for Philadelphia on the tide; indeed, his sailors was casting off lines and he asked did I want to sign aboard and learn the seafaring trade. "I'm short a men," he said, and looking me up and down, "ya cu'd make a fair tops'. Come along and ye'll 'av more of a time than stayin' 'erabouts in this stinkin' town. An make a fair more shilling than hawkin' fish, eh?" He grinned, sure he had me. I was tempted, remembering my father's stories of adventure, and because my prospects looked bleak for the summer. I could learn a trade, make some money. When his men came to take the casks from my cart, they were sure they had me. "Comin' along, friend?"

I declined, realizing out loud how my interests did not lie with the sea. Returning home along the dark streets with the captain's silver jingling in my pocket, I was approached out of an alleyway by a man in buckskins, Hugh McChesney, a fur smuggler of ill-repute, the same bearded man who had caused an uproar when I asked could I go a smugglin' with him.

I knew from my eavesdropping on the smugglers' conversations this McChesney was the best damn smuggler in all New York Colony. A respected woodsman and water pilot, a shrewd bargainer, be it French, Dutch or Indian on the other side. Hugh McChesney would trade or fight with any of them, didn't much matter, and now he asked in an oddly polite manner could he speak a moment. I said yes, he swore me to secrecy with a look I did not mistake for a second. His narrow eyes held me in a grip of iron. His lips, too, I watched 'em moving as he spoke from behind his thick, bushy black beard. "Ye be interested in big money, bucks?" I said yes, my heart pounding for knowing what he meant. "I have need of one or two stout lads to fill up my party. Ye knows to keep your mouth shut, eh?" His eyes burned holes in my head, his hand on my shoulder like the talon of an eagle. "Tis hard work, lad," he said. "Nay so much adventure as ye thinks, just hard work. An' dangerous. I know ye be a bit of a buddin' hunter an' woodsie." He grinned and added, "It be your choice, laddie, to go along with me or stay home an' haul yer daddy's slop buckets."

I asked could I bring along a few things for trade. "Give me what money yer got," he said, "an' I'll see ye gets best value fer it. Plus ye gets a mites share a yon profits be there any, same's all the men." Not hesitating a moment, I gave him my money and dug around in my sack and pockets for what loose coins were there. Told him I had more money at home. "Fetch it to me tonight, to your daddy's place, eh?" I asked when did we leave. He did not answer, he just strode off. I went home elated, my chance to see the wild country!

I walked up to the bar where Father was dispensing drinks to thirsty men. "Unt' ow much schillings chou got for mein fish?" he asked in his thick Dutch. I told him how much, and unhesitatingly announced what I had done with it. I never seen such a mad Dutchman! He surely took the puffery out of me. "I vill hear uf no such ting. Youse vill stay here and help mitt der tafern dis summer, ya. It vill be busy." I said I was not asking permission; I was telling him what I intended doing.

"Is dat so? Ve zee about dat."

The argument got heated enough so I thought Pops might hit me. Mother got into it, terrified at the thought of losing her only son to the northern wilds. "There is naught but death up there for you," she said. There was no dissuading me and one telling point for my going, which

I pressed upon Father, "You know I am going sooner or later, and you know Hugh to be a stalwart man. You have often said so yourself. He is experienced in the woods." I argued wasn't it better to go with Hugh and learn the right way of things than to go with a fool who would get me killed. "Ya," was all Father said and "ya" didn't mean assent. It just meant my argument was maybe a sound one. I said what I thought would win Pops over, the profits would be huge, which, and with my mother already crying, put Pops into a rage. He said there was more profit in the tavern than in the woods, which was maybe true enough but there was no adventure in the tavern, only drudgery. This I didn't point out, not wanting to insult them. I never did convince 'em to let me go, nor did I wear them down. I just proceeded along my chosen path, same as Pops had done when he was my age, fifteen.

That night, when I seen Hugh come in, I was scairt him and Pops might get into a fight over me. Instead, Pops corralled him and they huddled for a long time in a corner. I am not sure but Father invested some money of his own. He never did say. The next two days saw me feverishly preparing for the journey of a lifetime. The folks, though it hurt them, would do nothing to help me get ready.

Anxiously I waited. Checked and rechecked my gear, all was in order. Eric said I was going to wear things out checking so much. Mother said little, only, "This will be the end of you. Do you somehow survive, you will be as wild as those ruffians who loiter here, unfit for honest labor."

Unfit for honest labor? I hoped so!

Hugh kept our departure date entirely to himself. Days passed with no word from him. I began to worry I was being left out. Were they fixing to leave without me? Would Hugh steal my money? I thought my mind would explode with anxiety. None of the other smuggling parties had departed yet, as best I could tell. We could be the first ones away did we leave now. Going first was important. Pops said it would be best if we had already gone. Indeed, none of Hugh's men had I seen for days. I was feeling mighty low. That night, the first of the full moon, Hugh came by, late. Said, "In thee mornin', bucko, three hours before ye sun rises. Upper landing. Tell nobody 'ceptin your pappy."

On this night of departure, Mother got me alone for what I expected would be her one last attempt to dissuade me from going. Instead, she presented me with a leather-bound book with blank pages, quills and ink included, and told me to put down my experiences. Her look was both sorrowful and stern. I was not to come back with blank pages. I wrapped the book in a pouch of sealskin and wolf's fur.

No way could I sleep. Up just after midnight, checking everything again. Way ahead of time, Pops and me hurried down the street, I with my too-heavy pack and my old musket over my shoulder and with powder horn and possibles across my chest, the possibles a leather bag containing things small and necessary. Gun grease, a tinderbox, fish-hooks, needle and thread. The moon was going down. In the dark we met the men with whom I would share the rigors of the journey. Hugh held a paper for our inspection and showed us by candlelight the total amount of goods, and what was my small part. Bolts of stroud cloth, steel traps, boxes of wampum beads, mirrors, rum. Father said the fig-ures were in order. The share of goods Hugh obtained for my money was not much but he said it would bring a fair return. I was as burning with anticipation to be moving as ever anyone could imagine.

Pops and me spoke for a moment. I saw excitement in his ruddy face, his eyes shining in the dim lantern light. He said the morning felt like the half-hour before a ship weighed anchor and hoisted sail. All 'round us was silently hustling men who spoke in hushed tones as the loads were packed smartly into the canoes. Lashings secured, checked and double-checked.

Hugh gave each man his place in the line. When he told me mine, the reality welled up inside of me. I really was going. Then and whilst he changed some things around and spoke to all of us, I thought I must burst with impatience! An hour before daylight, we shoved the canoes into the river, and as we were lining up how Hugh wanted us, I looked at Pops. He stood alone with a lost look about him. I couldn't help wonder was the look for a son he thought he was losing or for the old warhorse too old to go. I looked him in the eyes and raised my paddle in a salute to him. He glared back, the lines of his wrinkled face set hard. Cold. A look I shall long remember. He lifted his hand briefly, turned and walked away.

We pushed off north and were swallowed up by the early morning mist rising off the water. The adventure had begun. When the first rays of the morning sun showed, we were far upstream, twenty men in six elm-bark canoes, trade goods piled high. It was a cool fresh dawn but the constant exertions had us peeling off buckskin jackets and vests. The mist cleared, the day was bright and sunny.

Hugh had put me in the center of his canoe. As we moved into the current, he, behind me, said, "High up in yon mountains ye'll find spring 'as barely commenced." He then explained what he expected of me, the youngest member, the many chores I was to do without question. He instructed me to move my eyes constantly, to watch the water for dangers, the riverbanks for trouble. "In yon woods, laddie, the heedless man comes up amongst the missing. Caution an' common sense is thee key. No sign a trouble to be o'erlooked. Danger'll come from anywheres and at any time. Mo' likely when ye least s'pect it."

We went up the Hudson with a speed surprising to me. These were powerful men who never seemed to tire. I paddled hard all day. By nightfall, my muscles ached. There was little sign of life on the river, an occasional clearing with a rough cabin, the roof of a barn showing out of the trees, smoke rising from an unseen chimney. Some small outposts we passed, Stillwater, Halfmoon. Hugh always knew when a town was around the bend and made sure we passed hugging the opposite shore. Less chance of being seen.

Saratoga, the last outpost of civilization along the river, was naught but a cluster of houses along a street close up against the fort. Beyond was wilderness. Someone whispered as we passed, "A slow-budding blossom on the tree a humanity, a growin' outta the forest." Someone else retorted, "High smellin' fer blossoms, be they not?" This attempt at levity the men repeated down our line of boats. "Quiet!" Hugh said.

At the lower landing of the Saratoga portage and on both sides of the river were abandoned palisades. We went to the eastern shore and debarked just below the palisade. I stared at the wooden wall, what I could see of it in the dark. It had a ghostly look to it.

Hugh had sent two men on a day ahead to Saratoga, they met us in the dark with a wagon and a team of horses. We would carry most of the trade goods and gear along the portage road, the horses would haul the boats. Elm-barks are heavy, even when dry. Now they was wet, it was difficult enough just getting 'em into the wagon. We could not have carried 'em far. "Worse portages be ahead," a man said, "and there be no hosses waitin' fer us." The men appreciated Hugh's planning. It took three trips to get everything up and around to where we could reload the boats. Even with the horses and wagon, the portaging of heavy loads around rapids and falls too dangerous to be challenged was hard work.

By the dawn we were underway again and with one canoe staying ten minutes ahead. The river narrowed and shallowed, the current was swift. There was no sign of human life, other than our own.

Hugh forbade unnecessary talk and warned against dropping any-thing over the sides which might give away our presence. Information concerning our passing, if put into the wrong hands, might cause trouble for us farther up. According to Hugh, "Might'n be a spy 'round what's working 'fer pirates who be a waitin' yonder." A flotilla such as ours would be quite a prize, our cargo a most valuable treasure.

Hugh had us passing by the more dangerous places according to a schedule inside his head. Be at a certain place at a certain time of day so to pass the bad places at deepest night, see how the current dragged the water over the riffs, how the clouds skiddered across the moon. Here were the things I must learn, the knowledge to help me. Unlike school-learned book things which are all right for tame men. I had no intention of being tame. I would liked to have written it all down at once but with the unremitting paddling and with all the work Hugh and the others put on me, I had no time for it and tried to remember everything for writing down later.

I managed a single notation in my book. *There is much drudgery.*

Near dusk of a clear day and as we worked our way upriver, past a couple of islands, one of which was very long and narrow, the roar of cataracts became audible and grew louder. The Great Carry. We seen our scouts ahead, waving, signaling the all-clear. The cataracts were the highest, widest falls I ever seen, the entire Hudson River pouring down over a twenty-five-foot drop. Spray and mist reaching a long way below the falls. Here on the north shore, the Great Carry began. A well-marked portage trail led twelve miles to the northwest, to the head of Saint Sacrement. Another trail led off to the northeast, to the ruins of old Fort Anne and to the head of Wood Creek, a dangerous watery path winding north for over forty miles, the south entrance to Corlaer. Up there was the much-dreaded Drowned Lands, a swampy morass, a dangerous route which Hugh said was to be avoided.

We spent the night camped on the big island below the falls. Before sunset, one of the men, just a few years older than me, asked did I want to have a look at the mountains to the north, those we'd soon be getting into. I said I did, he told me to come along, and I seen the other men was watching whilst seeming not to. The lad scampered up into a towering spruce, as tall as any tree I ever seen, and he commenced climbing. I watched him and after a moment, I clumb too, on account of I had to, with all the men watching. I got up too high and made myself scairt to look down from the height I had attained, I never having been so high up before. Thought I might spend the rest of my life up there! The other lad, in a tree close to me and seeing my agony, laughed. I said to hell with it, resumed climbing and made it to the top, the tree swaying with my weight and with the wind.

"There they are," I said with awe for the wonderful aspect of mountains higher than any I ever seen before. "Aw, them's nothin' 'pared to what we's gonna see on Corlaer," said the lad from his own perch a little above mine. He spit, his stream of tobacco juice blowing past me on the wind. I found out later the men had bet amongst themselves would I go all the way to the top and would I make it down safely.

Supper was fresh fish caught by members of our company. The evening we spent before a fire, the men telling stories and swapping lies. Out on the river and without fear of being overheard, the close-mouthed men, who uttered nary a word in town, opened up. The need for camaraderie amongst men who must depend on one another in the wilds was not lost upon me. It was akin to what my father called good shipmates.

Hugh reminded us we would cross tomorrow into truly dangerous country. He warned us all, even the most seasoned, of wolves, fast water and rattlesnakes, and of pirates and Indians. About the Indians, and to me and the other youngsters, Hugh said as how they played by no rules known to white men. "Don' never s'pec 'em to act thee way ye would and report any sightin' tuh me damn fast, even if ye be not certain."

"They be no declarations a war hereabouts," he went on. "Keep yer musket close and keep 'er primed. Pay attention ta thee woods and whet's goin' on 'round'bouts." He sent a tall, skinny man, not much older than me, Bill Morrissey, on ahead with an older man to scout the trail to the head of Lac du Saint Sacrement. "Keep your noses to thee wind," our captain said. How I wished to go with them and not be stuck gathering wood and hauling water and cleaning cookpots.

We spent the morning a half-mile below the lower end of the portage, stashing our canoes for the return trip. Left them well hidden in brush where nobody should find them. Then we moved off a ways and dug a hole. When it was deep enough for the captain's liking, we put in some of our gear, to lighten our load.

The captain reminded us about leaving as little sign as possible. He put out scouts, right and left, front and back, we shouldered our heavy packs, grabbed our muskets and paddles and headed for Saint Sacrement. It was an arduous trek, more than ten miles over a stony trail worn smooth by countless generations of moccasin-clad feet. Hills rose high and steep around us. Sheer ledges, sometimes on both sides, boulders as big as houses. The men told me these hills were nothing to what we would see farther on.

We walked through a forest of pine and balsam. A few tamaracks. I asked one of the men if Montreal was at the other end of Saint Sacrement. He laughed and as it passed down the line of men, what I had asked, I could hear chuckling. My ears burned for acting like a first-tripper. We met Morrissey coming down the trail. He reported the way was clear as far as the height of ground. We plodded on and with all the rock formations, it was like going up stairs. At one place where we rested, we had a view of magnificent peaks rising in the distance. I could not tell if what I was seeing atop the mountains was clouds or snow and I didn't ask, for fear of getting laughed at again.

The trail led up through a steep pass, high mountains on both sides. Captain Hugh called it a hill. Some hill! We attained the height of ground and started down the other side, into a valley set amid rugged mountains of the most delightfully craggy sort, stretching for miles on either side. The valley and the surrounding ridgetops looked to run off endlessly to the north. At the foot of the mountains lay the sparkling blue waters of Saint Sacrement. So often had I heard the smugglers talk of it and now there she was, spread before me, a jewel of a lake.

As we made our way down, the lake showed in and out of the trees, dipping behind boulders and higher ground and re-emerging more dazzling, more spectacular each time we rounded a ridge or climbed out of a depression in the trail. I stumbled on roots and rocks for not watching where I was going. So enthralled was I by the view, I was not able to take my eyes off the lake and the mountains around it.

We reached the shore. The lake sparkled in sunshine, a refreshing feeling to the whole aspect. The air especially tangy. A panorama of pines and blue water, pleasant to behold, soft on the eyes.

The lake valley was rugged beyond the telling. Dramatic, mysterious, the water cold and clear, a drink from the lake proved mighty refreshing after the hard walk. Some of the men grumbled for not having a nip of rum, but Hugh would allow none to be taken from the trade goods.

"Jes' mix in a bit a gunpowder with the water ta make up der difference," said one rude old member of the party. I will not write down the other men's replies.

Hugh led us to some flat ground a little southwest of the lake and tucked partway up the side of a mountain. Here we constructed a camp of bark huts just big enough for crawling into. The camp was carefully chosen. "Safer," Hugh said, "and the air is better up high. Men have more spirit here." He was right.

The chores of portaging were split up. Whilst some of us went back down the trail to fetch the rest of the trade goods, one group of men got to stay in camp each day to construct the birch canoes we would use for the rest of the journey. That took six days. Everybody got to spend at least one day in camp except me. I made all three trips down and back to the Great Carry. The moon rose later each night, the last night it did not rise in time to assist us and we about ran the trail to get in before dark.

When we'd get in, they'd put me to fetching water and wood. One day I was sent to find just the right trees for the task of canoe building, of which I knew nothing. But do now. The men gave me a hard time whenever I did things wrong. My ears stung but it was rough, not mean, and I didn't care, for I was learning. When Hugh could not find anything for me to do, he'd send me to relieve the watch at the lake-shore. He warned me to keep a sharp eye. "Don' fall asleep."

I'd get up into a tree to watch the lake and the wonderful country which surrounded it. The view of the lake, of the ledges and bare rocks among the pine trees and cedars of the high mountains off to the north was an aspect most pleasing to the eye, if trepidacious and foreboding. Splendid May sunsets over the western mountains held my eyes until full dark.

When I did finally find time to write in my journal, the men kidded me about it. When Hugh learned of it, he ordered me to stop. "God-damn it, I cain't have my knowledge and 'speriences wrotten down. Suppose'n some snake-minded fella finds 'er. What then, eh?"

I didn't dare protest but I was downcast at his decision. He did not soften at the look of anguish on my face. However, he did keep the men from harassing me about it and a day later he said I could put things down. He had done some thinking on it and reckoned it might be a good idea. "Jes' don't be sayin' the McChesney name in there."

Smuggling was against the law and if he was ever taken to court over it, he didn't want his own words read out against him. Even with little enough time for writing, I was happy with Hugh's decision and was surprised to discover how much writing meant to me. Hugh was not long on the written word but he did seem to appreciate its value. Once he changed his mind, he started giving me pieces of information about the country. He always finished by saying, "Put 'er in your book right, bub."

Tried to make notes and sketches on the construction of the birch-bark canoes. These vessels are remarkably light and rugged and are capable of hauling big loads. "Tis the one advantage the Algonquin holds over the Iroquois," Hugh remarked. "Lighter and faster than elm-barks or dugouts, easier for portaging and last just as long, iffen they be built right." I asked why the Iroquois didn't make them, since they were superior to all other canoes. Hugh gave me a bug-eyed stare which got the men around us laughing. The birch tree does not grow in Iroquois country.

The men making the canoes shared their knowledge with me. They explained all they were doing and why, and they seemed pleased, not disturbed, with my writing down what they said. One man asked why I scribbled things instead of just remembering 'em. Writing it down, I told him, helped me to remember. He thought on it and said as how not being able to read or write maybe helped a man such as him to remember better.

Hugh was getting nervous about the coming moon. Kept telling us to hurry with making the canoes. He said we were running late if we were to pass Scalp Point at the first dark of the moon, which, he said, was critical not only to our success but to our survival as well. So narrow was Corlaer at Scalp Point and with fortifications on either shore, nothing less than total darkness would enable us to sneak past. The French commander might be under orders to let us pass but he would expect us to be discreet and did his men raise an alarm, he might have to arrest us. The bigger danger was Indians. Undeterred by either the French governor or the English and on the lookout for smugglers to rob, the Indians might try to grab our trade goods and our scalps.

The days warmed; the blackflies, which the men called longjaws and the French called brulets, came out. A most disagreeable pest, to tell it in the kindest of terms. They are savage and unerring in their accuracy, relentless in pursuit. Their sting, most unpleasant, leaves a bit of poison each time, for the redness and the swelling which follow. Morrissey concocted a potion to keep 'em off us. The potion smelled and as more of the men availed themselves, our camp took on a most repugnant stink. A more foul odor had never crossed my way. Even a polecat would turn up his nose and make tracks. After trying Bill's potion for a few days, I decided the old way worked better and I kept my exposed parts well-smeared with mud.

Most of the men took a liking to me. They sensed Hugh was putting many of the worst chores on me, testing me, and they did some testing themselves, but with I not shirking nor complaining, they began offering advice and encouragement and even they helped me out some, though not much, they had plenty of their own work to do.

The last afternoon before our canoes was ready, Hugh took me and Morrissey hunting. We sat for two hours at a place where it was likely deer might pass. "Hunt Injuns same's you hunt deer," Hugh said. A deer came by, Hugh shot it with his bow. He went back to camp, me and Morrissey dressed out the deer and dragged it in. After supper, I went for a swim in the lake. Surprised at how icy cold was the water.

After dark, we got around a fire. Pipes came out and were lit. The only sound was the slap of hands against skin at the incessant bugs as the men waited for Hugh to get started telling one of his stories. He hesitated whilst the men urged him to get on with it. The buildup to the storytelling seemed almost a ritual. "T'was up to Lake Memphremagog with my partner," he said. "H'ed a hard go at finding fur and dodging goddamn Saint Francis Injuns. A tough winter, aye, an wi' nary good result. Toward yon end thee wolves commenced ta slinkin' around us. They wuz bold for being so hungry. Well, thet day Jeb were out on yon ice 'ere a pond where we 'ad get some fur. He set to hauling in our traps, ta keep from losing 'em. Fell through black ice, he did. Shudda knowed not to be out on thet old ice. I went through too, aye, but in shallower water where's I could walk to shore but not without ther ice breakin' so's I walked with cold feet an' with them wolves a waitin' and a yappin' fer me on thee shore. I jes' did get myself up'n a tree 'fore they wuz at me. Spent 'siderable time up'n there. My piece were soaked. No ways would she fire."

He paused to stuff tobacco in his pipe and he smoked in silence, a long, thoughtful pause, as if he were sitting there by his lonesome and not with us all crowding around. "Jeez, pard," one grizzled old-timer said. "Don't leave us hangin' like thet. What'n hell happened efter, eh?" He is an old friend of Hugh and same as the others, had probably heard the story many times. The captain puffed some afore continuing.

We leaned forward from seats of stone or from the ground.

"I be freezin' cold up'n thet tree," Hugh said. "Jeb, he crawled 'round onter the ice, trying to sneak by them wolves without 'em seein' 'im. Jeb were so froze he couldn't do much ta save hisself once they commenced to get after him and there was naught I could do fer him with them wolves 'round my tree, tryin' ta git at me. He wuz trying ta get ter shore an' they wuz a runnin' for him and they catched him and begun tearin' at him somethin' fierce. He tried ta fight 'em off wi' 'is knife but they kept on comin' back. We said our farewells whilst they was chewin' on him, then he commenced ta hurtin' so, he wuz screamin'. T'was a longish time afore they finished him. Weren't much left a him when the devils departed. I clumb down an' gathered what I could a traps an' possibles an' struck out fer home."

The men were all looking at me. I tried to show no emotion though my insides were churning for knowing the same fate, or something worse, might await me too. Or was Hugh joshing and was it all made up, the purpose of which was to goad me into saying something foolish so they could roar their laughter? More likely it was true and they was looking at me to see did I have the stomach for it.

"Yep, sonny," Hugh said to me, whilst I was thinkin' on it. "This here be's tough country." His face showed tight in the firelight. "Turn in, boys. Who's got the next watch?"

Chapter III – Majestic Splendor

Next morning before sunup and with the men readying our boats and gear for the trip up Saint Sacrement, Hugh said to me, "C'mon over here and sit n'under this here pine tree." We sat. "The Drowned Lands," he said, "be bad country and are to be avoided." I had asked him about the Drowned Lands, the swamps around the lower end of Corlear and which the men cursed whenever it was mentioned. We would avoid the Drowned Lands by traversing Saint Sacrement. The men busy around us, Hugh told me about the Drowned Lands.

More than a half-day's journey from where we were, it was danger-ous country with rattlesnakes. As he told me about it, I watched him closely. Hugh is big, a giant among men in every way. Easy to laugh, slow to anger. When he gets riled, he prefers settling matters with fists or a knife. "I don' much care fer trouble, this way it's over quick," he says. Narrow predator eyes danced behind the fullest, thickest, black-est beard I ever seen.

They say he is from over Massachusetts way and has spent his life on the frontier. Lucky for me the captain was blessed with a good nature, though, same as my father, Hugh was gruff. He drank in the Full Sail, a hard, rough man, but not a troublemaker. More than once had I seen him wade in to assist when Pops was removing ruffians from the common room. Hugh was respected by all, a leader of men in the wilds, a top-grade smuggler.

"Ye' never heard about the army a English and Dutchmen in 1698, eh?" he was saying now. "Went inta the Drowned Lands and lost a hundred and more good men w'out firing nary a shot. Ain't nobody never been able to find the mass grave dug fer 'em."

****

After breakfast and still before dawn, we were away. I was in the middle of a canoe with Bill Morrissey and a grubby old fellow with long hair and beard unkept, Alpheus Bush. We started along slowly, trying as best we could to keep all our boats together in a heavy fog. Then the sun burned off the fog, the morning turned bright and we increased our speed and moved along pretty good, even with the weight of the loads we carried, all those trade goods. It was idyllic to me, the chill of springtime was gone, the air sweet and fresh smelling, the sunlight sparkling bright on the water. A warm day with the promise of hot summer coming.

The view from out on the lake was stunning with each succeeding rugged peak seeming to rise up more beautiful than the last. Hard to imagine anything prettier, and the deep-blue waters of such clarity, I marveled at how deep down I could see. Alpheus told me Saint Sacrement was so clear because it is partially fed by underground springs.

To the east were pine-covered mountains faced with bald ledges; to the west and after we had paddled a ways, lower country quickly clumb back again to steep-sided mountains. With each paddle stroke taking us farther north, I thrilled to it all, raptured by the rich aspect of the land and by the pristine mountain air, permeated by the scent of hemlock, tamarack, the nose-clearing fragrance of cedar. A grove of chestnut trees extended for miles along the east shore, all the way to the tops of the highest hills.

Some of our company broke into an exuberant song, the rest joined in, even Hugh. We could not help it, though Alph said it was at such times as these when one must be on the lookout for trouble. When all seemed quietest. When a man's guard might be down.

According to the old Dutch legends of Albany, the earliest white man to see this lake is said to have been a Jesuit black-robe, a prisoner of the Mohawks, in about 1634. His capturers were taking him home with them, to be brutally tortured in every village they passed, as was their custom, and to murder him when they got home. So fervent was the black-robe's faith in his god and so taken was he by the beauty of the lake, he named it the Lake of the Blessed Sacrament. The priest was saved by a Dutch trader at great danger to himself and was taken to Albany. He was sent back to France but insisted on returning to Iroquoia. Imagine the astonishment the heathens must have felt when he came back to preach to them again. They put him into the cookpot.

I am not given to thoughts of God but I could appreciate the black-robe's reverence for whatever deity carved this lake valley, whether said deity was in the sky above or beneath the waters, as the Indians would have it.

The lake, more than thirty miles long, was dotted with islands, some of them of a good size and heavily wooded whilst others weren't much more than rocks sticking up out of the water. Along both sides of the lake, the forests came down to the shore, the limbs of the trees hung out over the water. Clumps of the slender, white-barked birch trees glistened in the sunlight and I seen boulders, some of great size, back under the trees.

Then came the first narrows. Here, the lake, formerly wide to the length of a mile, funneled to a bottleneck dotted with more of the small wooded isles. The surrounding hills were high on both sides. The trees were evergreens, which gave to the air a most agreeably pleasant odor. A pretty place but one Alph said was dangerous. Ambush here would be hard to fend off.

As we traversed the narrows, our company watched on every side, alert for trouble, our muskets across our laps. Primings checked and protected from the wind by tight-fitting leather pouches easy to slip off. We moved along in silence, watching for signs of trouble. Some of the islands we passed so close, the pine branches nearly scraped our shoulders and any of us might have got hisself brained by a tomahawk. Hard paddling without letup and we were through and to where the lake opened to a wide expanse, and with the peaks rising higher than before, even those of the men who had been this way before enjoyed the spectacles.

We saw a snapping turtle, four feet across its shelled back. One of our boats took off after it, the others of us cheered them on, the turtle submerged. Then some of the men trolled fish lines behind the canoes. The deer-hair-covered hooks caught colorful, red-bellied trout, fat and sassy. Full of life for chasing an early hatch on the lake, the trout leapt clear out of the water in pursuit of mayflies. With the men playing and landing fish and bragging who got the biggest, our order of march became ragged. Hugh got mad at the straggling and made us put away the fishing gear.

Mid-afternoon and after we had stopped on one of the islands for a short rest, Hugh put me in his canoe. As we moved along, I gushed over the beauty of the lake. He appreciated it too but said it could lull a man to another danger. "These mountain lakes are becalmed in thee mornings but come afternoon, the wind blows up. I've learnt it thee hard way to git my arse ashore soon's she starts. She'll whip up four-foot waves on thee wider parts. Come from outa nowheres to swamp a boat."

"Especially like ours, so heavy burdened," I added.

"Come sunset," he said, "the wind dies down as quick as she came up, in yon meantime, beware!" He looked hard at me. "Good lesson for yer book."

Late afternoon, the wind did indeed start to blow out of the western hills. Hugh called a halt right away. Birch canoes, if built right, will not wander. Ours were good ones but no birch canoe can challenge wind-whipped waves on the exposed portions of a big lake. With the waves rapidly building, Hugh took us in toward the western shore. We were taking heavy spray before we got behind the lee of an island. One of our boats didn't get in and was having a hard go, in trouble of swamping. I thought they were going over. Hugh got more canoes along the windward side of the distressed boat, this helped to steady her and we all got to shore. "Ol' Hugh, he ain' about to lose a boat full a trade goods, ye kin believe thet," Alpheus said.

"Quick thinkin' an' damn faster actin' than most a youse farmers," old Duckwith said. "Course, most of youse needs a wettin' anyhow."

Hugh decided we had come far enough and would stay the night where we had come ashore. Just north of a rocky gap which, when we had passed it, Hugh said it was a rattlesnake den. Whilst we were making our camp, I asked about the rattlers, though it did give me the shivers to think on 'em. "Them snakes," Alpheus said, "kin only habitate where there be a large rockslide. So's they kin git down below the freeze in thee winter. Otherwise, they cain't survive. Fella I know says they gits wrapped round like a living ball of twine down n'under there. Hundreds a snakes, all ta once."

Hugh said the snakes should just be coming up now outta their winter sleep and when I said I had heard the snakes were good eatin', Hugh said, "A taste a their own." Then, "C'mon, bub," and with me and him each carrying heavy sticks, we walked back toward the rockslide. I was more than a little careful where I stepped, same as when I had fetched water for the cooks. Got into the rocks and seen plenty of rattlers. They were drowsy for just having awoken, most didn't even shake their rattles as they slithered away from us. Hugh knocked two big ones on the head and put 'em in a sack, and when we seen another big one, he told me to go ahead. I whacked it and back at camp, Hugh showed me how to skin 'em and they went into the cookpot. I tied the rattles on a leather thong for wearing around my neck, the skins I gave to one of the men, and as we were bedding down, another man told me to give my blanket a shake afore I got under it. I did, they laughed, but I wasn't the only one who did it.

Early next morning, whilst fetching water for the cooks, I saw a family of baby mink. Momma scowled, I backed away lest she bite. Then, and before we set out, a massive flock of pigeons flew low over the lake. The small but delicious passenger pigeon. So many to the flock they darkened the sky as they passed, their wings making a loud clatter. They roosted in the trees, we threw sticks and stones and killed plenty. Some we added to our breakfast, others we would hold for the night's supper.

Back on the water, I was in Hugh's boat with him and another oldster, Hambone Rush. We seen flocks of ducks and geese and an otter. We had been forbidden to fire our guns but the amount of game was surely tempting. A big buck drinking at the shore looked up, seen us and bounded away. That time Hugh almost broke his own rule, so big was the deer. The great stag was without its horns but no doubting its majesty. We saw bears, a mother with a yearling cub.

More hard paddling and by early afternoon and as we approached the end of the lake, a flat-topped, slab-sided mountain rose up on our left. This the men called Bald Mountain. I could see why! The side of the mountain facing the lake was a sheet of rock, must a been a thousand feet high and a quarter-mile or more across. It wasn't a straight up and down cliff, it had an outward slant from the top to the bottom but was surely precipitous. Hambone said the slant was sufficient so a crouched man could walk to the top, just the man couldn't come down the same as he'd gone up. Here and there along the bare cliff were small trees, twisted oaks, birches and pines growing out of crevasses. We passed close under the mountain's great heights. Hambone told me the water here was so deep, they were not able to touch bottom once with more than a hundred feet of fish line with heavy weight attached.

Hugh said to me as we paddled a little way ahead of the others, "Don' tell a soul, laddie, and don' point, jes answer. But see on yon Bald Mountain where the little birch tree grows on yon south side, sort a toward the middle?" I did, and said so. "Don' let 'em see it in your book but there be a cave on yon side o' the tree. Right now she be's underwater. Is possible to keep things dry in there even when the mouth be under cuz inside she slopes up so much. In the fall, they's a chance she'll be out. Water's too high now with the spring runoff."

Past Bald Mountain, we came to extensive clay banks along the eastern shore. These marked the end of the lake. The water along the banks was muddy and shallow. Behind the banks were high ridges and unseen on the other side of the ridges, Corlear. We had reached the debouchment of Saint Sacrement, the mile-long descent of the waters through steep cataracts and gorges, Portage Crick to Corlear. I was excited to be at this place which I had often heard talked about in the tavern. The Iroquois called it Tyonderrogha, which meant the noisy place. Indeed, the roar of the cataracts was loud, even at a distance.

We went ashore, Hugh got us gathered around him. He told us we was a little ahead of ourselves and with us needing the dark of the moon to get past the French at Scalp Point, we would stay the night here, spend tomorrow moving our boats and gear down to the lower portage and tomorrow night we'd get onto Corlear and get past Scalp Point in the dark.

Hugh sent two men on foot to scout the portage. When the men got back, they said the way ahead was clear, though they said there was fresh sign of a party having passed in the last few days. Somebody said it might have been one of the other trading parties out of Albany. Hugh said no. Said we was the first party to come through. He asked was the party going north or south. The scouts said north, walking. "French, I reckon," Hugh said. "Checkin' for smugglers." Intending to jump us? A shrug of the shoulders. "Any sign of any others?" Hugh asked. "One or two, alone," our men said.

We got our camp set up, got settled and had our supper. Pigeons, salt beef, potatoes, dried corn, fish. After dark, we carried the trade goods to a cave on the side of the mountain, three-quarters of a mile north of the lower landing. Here the goods would stay whilst we portaged our boats. We left a man there to watch from hiding. When we bedded down, Hugh posted a stronger guard than usual and he gave orders for changing the guard frequently. He spoke to his most trusted men, told them to make sure none of the watchers fell asleep.

The stars shone bright, the black sky seemingly full of holes which let in the light, this on account of we were nearer to the roof of the sky, what with us so high up in the mountains. Around midnight, the northern lights unfolded in the sky. Here was a phenomenon of origin not known to me. I had seen this Aurora Borealis before but never like this night. I woke Bill so he could see it too and before long the entire camp was up and looking upon the spectacle. The stars so bright and close, it made me feel frail and tiny to see such majestic splendor. I thought the heavens gone amok, the colors a frenzy to behold. Wide bands of four or five colors flashing and shimmering across the sky in wave after wave, green, red, orange, white, yellow. Then the bands of colors would reverse and go dancing the other way. Back and forth in exuberance. At first only in the west and north, then spreading to the east and overhead.

The night was cold, and watching the illuminations, I shivered, wrapped in my too-light blanket. A wolf howled mournfully across the valley, audible above the roar of the falls. He seemed to be calling out his own wonder for the supernatural delights. He was answered by three or four others in turn, one sounded to be close by in the brush. Alph said the wolves wouldn't be hungry or desperate enough this time of year to try anything with us.

Whilst we was watching the lights and without us hardly noticing, Hugh and another man snuck out of camp. Two hours before dawn, they came back. Hugh cautioned us to silence and we got into our boats and snuck away. Two men were left behind to build up the fires. We set up another camp a ways farther north, posted the watch and no fire lit. The men grumbled at all the extra work but Hugh did not seem to hear.

Alph said something must a convinced Hugh there was prowlers in the night. Alph said iffen there were, they might sneak into camp, steal a gun, anything, or, and if there was enough of 'em, white men or red, they might try to wipe us out. Hugh, Alph said, never took chances.

****

The dawn was cool and refreshingly pure. Hugh gathered us again. He didn't tell us what had got him spooked during the night but he said any danger out there wouldn't have gone away just because of the daylight. He told us to get our chores done and get some rest. We'd be on the crick at dark. Hugh had calculated tonight would be the first night of the dark of the moon. Once afloat, we must hurry to make it past Scalp Point.

Hugh took me and a few others down along the portage trail, which is rock-strewn. It was two miles from the upper landing at the narrows to the bottom of the steep gorge, the trail worn down over the centuries by the passing of copper-colored feet. The trail went through stands of tall pines and copses of impenetrable brush, briars, berry patches, and in places, soggy, swampy ground to suck a man's feet down into the mud. Massive boulders were strewn about.

The trail was ringed south and north by ridges, dangerous vantages where an enemy might lurk, then it wound under steep hills and under the rugged slopes of Rattlesnake Mountain. The ledges along the side of Rattlesnake stood one atop the other like bastions.

At the lower landing of Portage Crick was a wide, tall waterfall. An impressive affair, and hard it was to hear anything over the constant noise of the wildly foaming waters. Hugh said the French called this place Carillon, for the falls sound to them like the ringing of bells. "They must have bats in their belfry," Bill Morrissey quipped. Made a man feel small to stand beneath it.

At the bottom of the falls was a deep pool teeming with fish, some of which were trying to scale the falls. Hugh said the leapers were salmon which had come in from the ocean. They faced a daunting task in ascending the heights. The strength and volume of the water looked a tough barrier, yet the salmon, determined and powerful, might find a way. They was certainly willing to have a go at it.

We went down along the crick to where it narrowed. Hugh dispatched one of the men to go to a point five or so miles north on Corlaer, to where he could watch far down the lake. Hugh warned the man about the old trail which ran to the point. "For damn sure ye best avoid it. Don' even check 'er for sign. Follow 'er but keep right the hell off. We'uns'll pick ye up ternight three hours afer' dark sets in. Shoot your gun to let us know if Injuns is after ya." We others watched with guns at the ready whilst the scout crossed over in calm waters. Astraddle a large log, paddling, his musket lying in front of him with his possibles.

Hugh then sent me and Morrissey back up to the falls, Bill to fish the pool, me to stand guard. Hugh told us to be damn careful and to stay no more than a few hours. Bill made himself a spear and in just the short time we were there, he got six fat salmon, a pike and a muskellunge. We raved over the size of his catch, he wrapped the fish in wet moss.

We returned to camp and with little enough to do right then 'cept wait for dark, I asked permission from Hugh to go on an explore, out across the west side of the crick. The men were talking about the Valley of the Trout Brook, I wanted to see it. Hugh told me no. Said, "Ah ain't a goin' ta have ta tell thet badass pappy a yours thet somethin' happened to ya an I don' even know whet. Stay here!"

I snuck out of camp anyway, promising myself to not be gone long. I couldn't find a way across the crick until I was almost back at the outlet, where the water started its descent from Saint Sacrement. Here was a natural stone bridge. I crossed over and went west, around the base of a long mountain, through a beautiful, if barren, forest of pines. Ahead lay the mouth of a steep-sided valley, a quarter-mile across at the bottom, more than a mile across to the hill on the far side, straight across from where I was.

Both sides were quite steep. The brook ran through the bottom and drained into low swampy ground outside the valley. I could see the slight cut where it ran through the trees and I figured it emptied into the lower crick. I stayed to the higher ground so to better see where I was headed. There weren't no path to follow and with thick brush and boulders of every size, the going was difficult. After a bit, the valley opened, the trees were hardwoods; maple, oak, beech. The edges of this grove extended to the near slopes, where it was mostly pine. I got down to the brook and reckoned it must flow out of the western hills. Took a cool drink from the refreshing waters and followed the brook upstream, staying at a distance from the noise so I might hear any movement in the woods. Walked another mile and came to a gorge where the water poured down over the rocks as if out of sundered, foot-high spouts. All round was soft, luxuriant moss on the rocks, an inch or more thick. Deep green and wet. Huge ferns fringed the banks, some head-high, a pretty place for sure. I skirted the gorge, clumb a high-backed ridge where, from the top, the rolling hills ran off in every direction. It'd be easy to get lost in this country. To my unpracticed eye, the hills were all too much alike. Might already be lost and not know it.

The stream ran next through groves of pines with more rocks and boulders strewn about, the pine needles a soft brown carpet. I came to a succession of gentle waterfalls splashing down one after the other, creating deep pools, the water seemingly catching its breath in each of the pools afore plunging on.

I watched a red fox pass by with a fresh-killed partridge in its jaws. Then picked myself up and continued on. The brook curved around a hill and ahead, the water flowed down at a steep angle and through a quarter-mile of bare rock. The forest close on the west side looked as though much more water once ran through here.

I came across an old camp, a fire-hole and a piece of busted leather. This valley was more traveled than one might suspect. I sat on a rock in the sun, a foolish thing to do, and imagined how it might have been to trap here when there was beavers. There was no sign of 'em now, they were trapped out.

I would have explored farther but Hugh would already be madder than hell at me. Never had intended to go this far. Before I got up, I saw an otter splashing in the stream. The otter saw me but didn't seem to care. He dove under a big rock and came up with a fish in his mouth. How I envied his meal, hungry as I was. The otter lay on its back on the water, holding the fish in its front paws, eating it from the head down, the hard crunch of its teeth cracking the fish's skull and bones.

I headed back. By now the sun was setting and I hurried, unheedful of danger, too worried about catching hell. I crossed the stone bridge over the crick in deep shadow and as I approached camp, somebody hollered. "Here he be!" Hugh was furious and with a terrible mean look in his eye and with his fists clenched as he strode toward me, I was sure he was going to beat the hell out of me. He didn't, but with how roughly he grabbed my shirt and shook me and with his face up close to mine as he chewed me out, I reckoned to not ever disobey him again. "You ain't gonna last long up here, bub, iffen yer don't foller orders. Aughta whip your arse good. I just might'n, iffen I takes a mind ta. Next time I will fer sure." After he calmed down some, he questioned me closely on what I had seen, he askin' mostly about any recent camps. I showed him the piece of leather. He said little about it. The men were plenty bothered for me breaking Hugh's orders, missing work and being gone a dangerously long time.

One man said pirates and vagabonds from the frontier backwaters roamed here in search of easy plunder. "Ye surely be'd easy, laddie, iffen they'd seen ye in yon forest." He spit a plug of tobacco juice. "There's plenty what knows tradin' parties be afoot in the land. Too easy for an unseasoned lad to run afoul a them. We be smugglers so we can't go to the high sheriff 'bout robbers."

"Some years back," another man said, "after Queen Anne's War, a band a ruffians up from Carolina held this here portage hostage for an entire summer a fightin' an stealin', robbin' any what passed by. In the fall they wuz jumped by a big party of Mohawks and Cayugas. Fifteen cutthroat bastards wiped out in ten minutes, an' nobody the sadder fer it. Thet's thee law hereabouts." Later, Bill said they weren't trying to scare me, only were they telling me how it was.

Hugh put me to hauling water for the cooks and when supper was ready and without a need for more water and with all the men getting around to eat, Hugh told me to keep on with what I was doing. None of the men laughed nor showed any sympathy for me.

After the men had finished eating and were preparing to move the boats, Hugh brought me a dish of grub and sat down with me. He asked what did I think he and the men should have done, did I not get back before it was time for us to leave. Go looking for me and thereby endanger the lives of all of them by not getting past Scalp Point in the dark or just leave me to my fate. I had no answer for him. He said pirates or a war party might have taken my hair for me being out there by myself. Scalps and plunder was what mattered to them. Peace between the English and the French meant nothing.

What else he said, there were always fledgling warriors out on their lonesome, lookin' to prove themselves. Young bucks eager for anything to give 'em recognition around the home fire. Hugh said such a buck might a stepped out from behind a tree or a rock and took my scalp before I knowed he was there.

****

Just after full dark and with our canoes in the water downstream from the falls, we shoved off. The current carried us swiftly along the narrow crick. I was in with Bill and Alph. Piled high between us were bundles of trade goods. Alph was in the stern. Listening. Sniffing the wind. "Might'n be the scent of a campfire afore a sighting of it." The peepers were in a chorus of thousands, singing away the night. Here, below the falls, Portage Crick wended through a narrow gorge cut out of the bedrock by the steady action of the waters. The banks loomed ominously on either side; tall willow trees shrouded us in eerie shadow. The twisted branches in the dark and the rising mist made me uneasy. The back of my neck was prickly as we ghosted along.

In some places, we had to lift our boats over snags and downed trees. These can be dangerous traps in a high-water current did a canoe get caught up broadside against them. The crick opened into a channel through a swamp. We followed the channel through swathes of tall marsh grasses. Ground mist sprung up and quickly spread into a dense fog. The mosquitoes were thick enough to drive a man crazy if he would let them.

The night was moonless, just as Hugh had planned, though the stars shone. Enough light to see by if the damn ground fog would blow away. The nighttime noises of this swampland, spooky in the gloom, conjured images of dangers harsh and unforgiving, from sources both known and unknown. I had the feeling one could never learn all the mysteries hidden in this country. It was so vast and wild.

"The Indians say their gods move the mountains in at night here," Bill said, more to himself than to me or Alph. I could hear the awe in Bill's voice. In truth, the black-shadowed mountains did seem to press in over our narrow ribbon of water, an omnipresent feeling of dread.

We came to where the crick debouched into Corlear. Rising up on our left was the Tyonderrogha point, a rocky knob of land. We swung around the knob and facing north, we dug our paddles into the water and moved single file into a steady north wind which eased the bugs considerable. Little sound did we make as we moved along. The word was passed to keep up close. A few short rests with no pipes lit, no talking.

The fog lifted to reveal low shores on both sides, neither more than a good musket shot away. The northern lights came out for a while, a spectacle we had no time to ponder. As if offended by our lack of interest, the lights died down and snuffed out.

Even in the dark, Hugh knew exactly where to meet our man who had been sent ahead. Swooped in and picked him up. He hadn't seen anything on the lake, nor along the shore, neither, and we were soon approaching Scalp Point, the lake narrowing to less than half a mile. Hugh had warned us before we departed from the lower portage about the French, sure to be here in strength and maybe active, even at night, with boats out and patrols on both shores. They might grab us and turn us over to our own government. Jail and stiff fines for us smugglers, a show of upholding the law for the politicians who put up the money for our trip. Or, as Alpheus so pleasantly pointed out, the French might give us to their Indian friends for sport.

The original stockade, built in 1731 and which had caused so much consternation in Albany, was on the east side. A much larger structure, a four-story limestone rock castle with cannons on each of the levels was to the west. We approached trepidaciously. Some few lanterns were lit along either side and we could discern the dark outlines of the shores and the forts. We passed almost in the shadow of the four-story donjon; close enough to hear sentries calling out as they made their rounds on the dark ramparts. From the east shore, a dog barked and kept at it. After a tense moment, every damned dog over there seemed to be yapping. Then those from the near side of the lake. Pursuit was not forthcoming, which didn't mean we weren't getting watched, and grateful we were to be led by Hugh, who had calculated days ahead to ensure we passed by here on a night without the moon.

Past Scalp Point and with the lake widening, we eased back over toward the eastern shore. Less traffic likely over there, is what Hugh said. At intervals through the night, he slowed the boats to take a count and each time, he warned us to stay together. Any boat which became separated from the others would surely find itself in trouble, come daylight. We pushed hard until near dawn. Hugh allowed no rest. I dozed off a few times and whenever I did, Alph, who was behind me, woke me with his paddle. Not gently.

Still in darkness, we arrived at Hugh's secluded bay on the eastern shore. An island a short way out shielded the bay, two small cricks flowed into it. We paddled up the second of the cricks. A perfect stop-over for pirates or smugglers. Hugh kept us moving upstream until we were well away from the lake.

First off, set the watch. Then came the dawn of a bright spring morning. The sun rose up over the eastern mountains, its rays striking the high peaks beyond the western shore, peaks higher than any I ever seen. This land had surely captured my imagination and as wild as was this country down here in the Corlaer Valley, I wondered how much wilder must it be up in those mountains. What manner of man could survive up there? Could I?

We spent the daylight hours in camp, fixing gear, patching holes in the canoes, making new paddles to replace ones which had got busted. Hugh had us rearrange some of the loads in the boats and he sent Bill out to get us a deer with bow and arrow. "Fer an hour er so n'more," Hugh told him. "We leaves here at dusk an' there's plenty a work twixt now'n then. You'n better git back fer to git some sleep. Ye ain't gonna git any ternight." I wanted to go with Bill but was too scairt to ask Hugh. He still scowled every time he looked my way and he had me doing more chores than even before.

I was still at my work and was hard-pressed to stay awake when Bill came in with a small deer. The few men who were awake razzed him quietly about the size of the animal. He said any who objected to venison veal could excuse themselves from the repast he set to preparing. I helped him with the butchering, we not doing a neat job, just a fast one. Alpheus and another man got Hugh's permission to dig a shallow pit and got a hot, nearly smokeless fire going. When all was ready, they put the meat and Bill's fish in on a layer of sticks and clay atop the coals, then covered the hole. Hugh told me to get some sleep.

I got into my blanket. "Sleep fast, Kenny," Alpheus said, amused with how tired I must be. "Yer looks as though ye needs it."

What joy to get roused from sleep by the aroma of fresh-cooked venison and fish. No more talk was there of how small or thin the deer; the entire animal was devoured, the fish too. This was the first time I had ever tasted salmon; they were surely delicious.

We started out again just after full dark, still along the east shore. Every stroke of our paddles seemed to push Polaris farther out of the forest and higher into the sky. I asked Alph was there a place where one could stand directly under the North Star. "Isn't never been there," he said. "Dunnow." He chewed on it, then he said for me not to get my curiosity up too much, else I might go looking for it, same's I done down to Trout Brook. He considered this to be a fine joke and I could hear him suppressing his mirth in the darkness behind me.

All night and the following nights we paddled. Mostly were we going into the teeth of a north wind which kicked up dangerous waves but kept the mosquitoes and blackflies away. Each morning, just as the sun was coming up, Hugh got us into one of his hiding places.

The lake widened considerably, more than ten miles, enough so the western shore was entirely removed from our sight. Often, during the days and whilst I fetched water out of the lake, I'd stop and look out over the grayish expanse with its white-capped waves and soaring gulls, and not seeing the farther shore, I'd get a notion of what Pops meant by a sailor's courage for seeing naught but water, day after day.

Our last night on Corlaer, we slipped past the French garrisons at the outlet, called Ile Aux Noix, and got onto the Richelieu River. More hard paddling and we came to shore, hid our canoes and made camp. This was as close as we would come to Montreal. I was disappointed, I never having seen a city before, and I said I would have liked to seen this one. The men joked, said for me to go for a look, my only look, ever, at a city. Or anything else. When all was settled to Hugh's satis-faction, he said he was goin' to contact the French. "Nobody leaves here for no reason whilst I'm gone, hear?" Three men were chosen to go with him. I was one. Hugh said, "So's to keep an eye on you'n."

We walked to the Trading Tree, a magnificent spreading oak in a clearing. By its size, the tree must have seen two-hundred summers. Names and dates carved into the tree in English, Dutch and French. Hugh showed us a faded date. 1641. He had me write a message on birchbark and tack it to the tree. Then we returned to the river.

39

Two days waiting, all of us edgy as no Frenchmen showed. Was we being set up for ambush? Hugh calmed us, kept us busy. We did some fixing on our canoes and built two new ones. We kept a strong watch posted; I used the time to write down in my book some of the things Hugh had said on the way up.

Chapter IV – The Devil's Pageant

The governor's agent, a snaky little man, arrived with a handker-chief over his nose to indicate plainly how foully we stank. "In the pay of the governor hisself," said Alpheus, his own disgust evident. The Frenchie was accompanied by helpers and two wagons. During his talk with Hugh, and with us looking on, Frenchie showed further disgust with everything connected with us. Except for good tobacco, which he asked did we have and which he grabbed out of Hugh's hands as soon as he seen it. Whilst we loaded our trade goods onto the wagons, the teamsters spoke jovially about what the Indians was sure to do to us. I watched with anticipation and dread as our goods were driven away by those sour Canadian teamsters. Could these French, of whom I have heard so much evil, be trusted?

Frenchie told us the Indians, painted and feathered, were arriving, their flotillas of canoes streaming in along the Ottawa and Saint Lawrence Rivers. Frenchie escorted us to a hidden place deep in the woods where we were to await the trade fair. He told us not to leave camp for any reason. Said there were plenty enough Indians around to take the hair of any what wandered. What he meant was, the French governor didn't want us to be seen by the peasants, His Excellency not wanting it generally known he was dealing with us.

That night, our men mixed their concoctions. Terrible mixtures to severely test the strength of any who drank it. Gunpowder, pepper and tobacco, sugar, molasses, water from a muddy crick, a little tea, a generous amount of rum, even a sprinkling of dirt. Hambone and others of the men regaled us with tales of this annual rendezvous of Canadians and Indians, their celebration of imminent summer when the furs from the north woods around Hudson's Bay and the Great Lakes were delivered downstream.

"With the drunkenness," Hambone said, "things gets out a hand and plumb dangerous. A more savage assemblage will not be seen on this Earth." He told of fights and games. "Lacrosse!" he said. "Now, there's a game for fools. In lacrosse, the players sometimes get killed." Another man said he once saw a game with one tribe agin another.

Huron and Montagnais. Said the beatings they served up were surely somethin' to see. No white man could survive a minute of it. "And them two tribes," Hambone said, "is s'posed to be friends." He said the Indians loved to gamble on the ballgames. "I seen 'em bet an entire winter's fur on an outcome," Hambone said, and as a warning for me, "Don' never gamble agin a squaw." A lesson he had probably learned the hard way. "See, them squaws likes playing the bone game cuz they can make the bones do 'bout anythin' they wants. She'll lure ye on 'til ye thinks ye got a bull right by the arse. When ya comes to, it's too late. Come to find out, yer the arse."

Alpheus, with a wicked gleam in his eye, said of the trade fair, "Scenes right out o' Hell, 'specially toward the end, when the whiskey stops flowin' so freely." He declared there was nothing as treacherous as a hungover Indian. "By the time they gets started on sobering up," someone said, "I reckon ol' Hugh'll have us down the lake and headed like the bloody dickens for Albany."

We waited two more days and Hugh, exasperated and maybe more worried than he showed, left camp with another man. Whilst they were gone, the drums started, and when Hugh returned, hours later, he said the fair was getting going, no more than a few miles from where we were encamped. Next morning, the greasy little bugger who had so greedily partaken of our tobacco returned and he and Hugh and two of our men went off to barter. Us others waited nervously and were thankful for the work Hugh laid out for us before he left. Necessary chores, no doubt, but intended to keep us from thinking about all those Indians close by, if such be possible. Hugh didn't get back until after dark and didn't say much and the next day, early, he and the same two men were gone again. Fear and anxiety worked on me, fear for the loss of my profits turning into fear for my life but the men who had been with Hugh the longest didn't seem overly concerned.

Late afternoon, Hugh got in, and before dark we received our first bundles of fur. Prime beaver with some beautiful otter and mink, finer than anything I ever seen. Wolf, bear, mountain painter, even some few sealskins, all sure to fetch a good price in Albany. We looked to do well for our troubles.

Whilst I was admiring one beautiful beaver pelt and remarking on its size, Hambone told me about the giant beavers of the Great Lakes. "Bub, a hunnert years ago they existed a race a mammoth beaver, six-foot tall, weighing over three-hunnert pounds. Wasn't never many of 'em, an' by thee time thee white man had been 'round some, why they wuz trapped out slicker'n rain by the Indians."

"I'd like to see one of those, Mister Rush," I said. "I bet they could bring down a tree faster than could a man." Thought on the size some more and asked Hambone had he ever seen one. "No," he said, "but I cralt inside a one a their houses oncet to scape from Injuns what was hankerin ta scalp me. Out past Oswego in '21 it were." He winked at the men; they'd got me again.

Two more nervous days passed with Hugh gone each day and with our fur arriving each night. Early the third morning, before Hugh left for his palavering, the mousy little fancified French rat came into our camp with dire warnings. The Indians was drunk and wanted English scalps. "Ze ask to be turned loose by zer father." He grinned slyly. More rat than fox. "Ze Mesieu does not know can he control zem." He advised us to leave our trade goods and depart at once with what fur we had. Hugh wasn't cowed and spoke to us loud enough so's the Frenchie could hear him. "It's what they always say. Figuring to run us out of here afore we get all of what we's got comin' to us."

That night, Hugh didn't get back until well after dark and told us the last of our furs would be arriving in the morning and we'd be loading up and shoving off. He overheard three of us, me, the other first-tripper and Bill, saying we'd like to go for a look at the goings-on in the Indian camp. "Too dangerous," Hambone said, but Hugh, looking at us with hard eyes, said he'd take us if it be what we wanted. He warned us to stay in the shadows. "Keep damn close and don' do nothin' stupid. No matter what. Hear me, Kuyler?"

****

Hugh was cautious gettin' us there, I was scairt enough to turn back but I kept on, lured by the Satanic draw of what Alph said was a Pageant to the Devil. An hour's walk, the pounding of the drums and the raucousness of the festival growing louder, Hugh got us to where we could see it through the trees. The smoke of a massive bonfire stung our eyes.

Alph was right, what we seen was straight out of Hell, for the devil himself could have done no worse. The Indians' native modesty, said to be considerable under normal circumstances, was lost in a haze of whiskey and rum. In light and shadow and to trills of ancient passion, a thousand painted savages swayed in seductive rhythm. Men, women, even children, all naked or nearly so and all howling, leaping, carrying on, each in their own way, doing whatever suited, some in deep shadow, others bathed in the glow of the fire. Sweat-glistening bodies swayed in accompaniment to the primitive rhythm of the drumbeats, a Stone Age ritual aflame with whiskey-fueled emotions and carried on without dignity.

Hugh, as he moved us around the darkened periphery to different vantages, pointed out not all the revelers were Indians. "See them over there?" He indicated two men in buckskins. One wore a fake beard which kept falling down his chin, the other's face was blackened with burnt cork. "Look close et 'em," Hugh said. "They's Frenchies alright, and the dandified snob what looked down on us for us smellin' ripe t'him, I reckon he be amongst 'em. I reckon them Injun squaws don' smell so bad to him as us did. Lots a Frenchmen joins in just so they can chase the squaws. Even some said to be gentry or nobility. They say in years past thet governors, politicians, soldiers, even the priests, gets caught up in yon fever." Indeed and now it was pointed out to me, I saw what looked to be other white men who had donned Indian garb and painted their faces to avoid being found out.

In the short time Hugh kept us there, we saw an astounding number of lewd and violent acts. The worst we seen was where naked squaws, young and old, was passing a jug whilst hopping in and out of a circle. A buck come along, threw a girl to the ground in the middle of the circle and got on top of her. The buck's eyes gleamed in the firelight. The girl resisted coupling with him but he was too strong and she, poor thing, was slipped down too far.

My Christian mind shuddered, I felt shame for the amorousness aroused in me. Hugh sensed my unease. "Goddamn it, you young whelp, stay put." He dug his fingers into my arm, hard, and made me promise not to move. "Easy prey," he said, his tone making plain he didn't care to see it neither but there waren't nothing to be done about it. "Law o' thee woods, bucks."

A stout woman, might a been the young girl's momma, at close range and to the amusement of those Indians what seen it, blew the buck's head off with a dragoon pistol.

We returned to our camp, a scant distance away and which I now feared was too close and too poorly hidden. Before turning in, we told the men some of what we had seen. The leers on their faces said they'd liked to have seen it too. Or joined in.

Hugh pointed out how easy it was to destroy Indians through the mighty weapon of rum. "Ugly to ruin a way o' life," he said, "jest for cash money." I reminded him we had brought rum for trading. "Shet yer yap, bub," he said, and when I marveled at how a people could become so debased, he said he hated to see it happen. "Near bad 'nuff," he said, "to make me cease hauling the spirits. Remember, bub, rum and whiskey be powerful good tastin' but don' never let 'em get aholt a you." A pause, then an admission, "It do pay good." He grinned at the thought of so much profit. After I and Bill got settled beneath our blankets, I vowed never to smuggle whiskey again, no matter the gain and did I have a say in it. I slept fitfully for those drums beating their cadence and I kept jerking awake with visions of all I had seen. Sights to stick in my brain forever.

****

Next morning, Hugh had us up and moving our furs back to the river even before the last of it had come in. This was risky as it meant splitting what men we had, with some carrying the furs and guarding them once they were down to the canoes and some staying in camp to guard what hadn't been moved and to receive what was yet to come. Hugh feared the last batch might be delayed or might not come at all and if it didn't, I don't think he intended waiting and would just get us out of there with what we already had. I was with the men moving the furs and how relieved I was when we got back to the camp and I seen the last of the furs arriving.

We hurried it along, fearful for our very lives. The warriors among the Indians surely numbered in the hundreds, and just twenty of us. With our canoes loaded and manned, Hugh warned us, "I'm hope'n their pageant keeps on here at least a few more days. With all this here fur we needs a head start case'n they decides ta foller us. When they be done carousing, the woods is gonna be plumb full a angry savages lookin' ta recoup losses from the drinking an' gambling. They'll be buzzing 'round like a swarm a angry bees. Me and the lads seen plenty a fresh scalps'n the camp a their'n, an' I don't aim to be 'round these parts when they wakes up an' goes huntin' fer more." We all agreed.

****

The rising sun saw us well on our way south. Hugh drove us hard. We did not stop all day, our rest breaks few and short and taken without going ashore. We just pulled our paddles out of the water, took a drink, closed our eyes a moment and were gone again. "There be a world a territory 'twixt us and safety," Hugh said. "Lots a places for ambush 'tween here and there." He said our cargo would make a princely haul for anyone bold and strong enough to snatch it.

Late afternoon we were exhausted but nobody wanted to quit, the men glad, I think, for Hugh's pushing us to ever more effort. We kept on until the men were played out and darkness came. Hugh called a halt. We went to shore and unwound stiff, weary muscles. Our respite was a brief one. Hugh had us moving again. We paddled all night and in the early morning, we passed by Split Rock.

This, a magnificent edifice extending out from the western shore, was the ancient boundary between Algonquin and Iroquois territory and was by treaty the current boundary between the English and the French. A treaty which is now broken by the French occupation of Scalp Point, thirty miles south.

It was here, the old tales have it, that the good Dutchman Corlaer, founder of Schenectady in the 1600s and leader of the Dutch colony, drowned whilst on a peace mission to the French. When Corlaer's Mohawk guides sprinkled tobacco on the waters to propitiate the cranky gods who dwelt in this place and kept the wind, he bared his arse to the deities, an act which cost his life for a brisk wind came up and blew him overboard. He sank like a stone.

Just north of Scalp Point, we pulled in to shore and hid. Here we waited until dark and in the time between full dark and the rising of the moon, we got past the Point in the shadows of the east-shore palisade without arousing the French sentries. North of Tyonderrogha and still in the dark, we went to shore where a swift, spring-fed brook emptied into Corlaer. One boat went ahead to scout the portage. "Rest yourselves fast, fellas," Hugh said, "and don' get comfortable. It be a damn short rest. Fill your canteens afore we leaves."

Here, one of the men told me, was where the Frenchman Champlain had his famous fight with the Iroquois, more'n a century ago. That battle marked the first time the Iroquois had ever seen white men and their guns. The loss of many chiefs and warriors in a shocking defeat turned the Iroquois away from any friendship with the French ever since.

When our scouts returned, it was with word there was plenty of fresh sign around the portage. Mighten be a large party of Indians in ambush. Hugh thought on it and decided we would stay on Corlaer and go out through the Drowned Lands. The notion of going through the dreaded swamps might a caused a mutiny under other conditions but now, none of the men spoke against it. They trusted Hugh.

Hugh took me and Bill aside and gave us instructions on our next duty. One of our boats had lagged behind in the dark and in the time we waited for our scouts to get back, the boat hadn't showed. Now, and whilst we headed for the Drowned Lands and did the missing boat not catch us afore we got to Portage Crick, me and Bill was to go to shore there and watch for the boat so to intercept it before it headed up the crick. Hugh warned us about Indians maybe showing up instead of the missing boat. Alph laughed, said did we see a boat, not to go rushing out less we was sure it was ours. I asked what we should do if Indians came down the lake and kept on past the crick. Hugh thought this unlikely but said did it happen, we were to go a few miles down Corlear, to another portage. Hugh told us how to find this other trail and said it was difficult as it went up and over a steep hill. Once onto Saint Sacrement, we were to go only at night and either meet up with Hugh at the Great Carry or get ourselves back to Albany as best we could. Hugh said if he didn't see us again, he'd figure Indians got us. What else Hugh said, and this was to all the men, not just to me and Bill, did Indians get onto Saint Sacrement and not find us, they'd figure we had gone through the Drowned Lands. They'd stay on Saint Sacrement and try to get out ahead and ambush us somewhere between Fort Anne and the Great Carry.

Me and Bill moved our furs to the other boats, reboarded, and with the rest of the men, we struck south. As we passed Tyonderrogha Point and with the missing boat not having caught up, me and Bill veered to the west shore. We stashed our canoe behind a brush pile and got up onto the knob and into a position from where we could watch the lake, north and south, and watch too the debouchment of the crick out of the swamp. With the others gone, I had feelings of dread for the possibility of seeing the very thing I was not wanting to see. War canoes filled with Indians out for scalps and furs.

It was a hard watch. The mosquitoes were ferocious and we was cramped for not wanting to move around too much. The sky was clouding up bad, fixin' to storm. I said to Bill, "If Indians come down and split up, some to Saint Sacrement, some staying on Corlaer, they interpose between Hugh and us and block both ways for us gettin' away." I asked what would we do then. Bill said he didn't know and a while later and because he'd been chewin' on it, he again said he didn't know. I said if the missing boat didn't show in the three hours

Hugh had told us to wait, we could save ourselves some portaging, more'n ten miles with a few hundred pounds on our backs, if we didn't get up with Hugh 'til after they carried the furs from Anne down to the Great Carry. "Think the black-bearded son-of-a-bitch won't have somebody waitin' with big loads for us?" Bill said.

Our talk went back and forth, all of it dire, but we saw no sign of trouble and soon as we saw the missing boat coming down the lake and made certain it was ours, we shoved off and headed south, two boats, five men.

Only too glad to be on our way, we took our nervousness out on paddling. Me and Bill's canoe, smaller than the other and not laden with furs, boiled through the water, maybe fast enough to outrun Indian war canoes. More than a few times, we had to stop and wait for them others to get up with us.

I was trepidacious for being exposed on the water. Kept looking behind and at the nearby shores, watching for what I was sure was going to be the end of me. I thought on all Hugh's talk of the Drowned Lands, now I was goin' in there and without the safety of the rest of the party. Bill and me both checked our guns a few extra times.

We were cautious as we moved down through the South Bay, for we had to make certain we got onto Wood Creek and not some other crick which might take us deep into the Drowned Lands and get us lost in there. There were so many creeks, it was easy to be confused and we let the other men, more experienced than us, do the deciding. "One mistake," Bill said, "and we might not ever see Albany again." We came to what we considered to be the first big stream and recalled Hugh's words. "Don't take thet first big one."

A mile or more and we came to another large crick on the east shore. Here was a portage around a falls and on the shore, a pile of stones, a cairn marking Wood Creek, which would take us to the ruins of Fort Anne. We remembered what else Hugh had said. Watch fer rattlesnakes and don't drink the water.

"T'ain't fit for man."

Up the twisting, narrow channel we went. Thick brush overhung both banks. Rattlesnakes and bad water in a land cut by innumerable cricks and holding fetid black water in stagnant pools. The man who drank from the pools would get sick and would most often not recover and over the pools were swarms of mosquitos and brulets. The little biters, even more than the rattlers, ruled here.

There was plenty of sign the party had gone up this way, our own passage made easier by Hugh and the others having hacked their way through. We passed between rocky overhangs, tree-covered slopes with hardwoods along the shores and with pines on top of the higher hills. Harsh country and foreboding; an ambush might a been sprung on us from anywheres. There was not a breath of wind. The air warm and humid, the sky darkening, the clouds dropping lower. The air was heavy, we heard the crash of thunder out beyond the western slopes.

We passed an area charred black from the ravages of a fire which must have been started by lightning. The pungent smell of burnt wood was present, though the fire was not recent. The forest seemed hesitant to retake the soot-covered slopes, as if it no longer wanted the land. The blackened stumps and logs were scars on the east side for miles and in patches on the west side, in those places where the fire had jumped the water.

The sound of axes became audible ahead and grew louder until we got up to our party, the men sweating and swearing profusely whilst chopping and sawing their way through. We reported to Hugh. He was cranky for not having made good time since getting onto the creek and within an hour of our rejoining them, he sent the men to shore, to make camp. A miserable night on swampy ground, the biters pestering, the men slapping and cursing. Toward morning, it began raining, too hard to get the cookfires going. Nobody said much, tempers were short, any man who spoke got cussed.

By sunup of a foggy, rain-soaked day, the mugginess as bad as ever, we were back on the creek, hacking our way south. Moving laboriously through the fog, it was hard to see the canoe ahead, then we'd come to where a dead tree or a snag lay across the water and we'd bunch up whilst the lead men cut away the obstruction. A naked feeling, sittin' whilst a passage was cut, the men giving wary looks toward the close-up banks, thick trees and overhanging brush, all shrouded in gloom. The rain stopped, the weather stayed hot, dripping with mugginess. The air was hazy, the visibility into the forest was poor. Our powder would be damp, we doubted its effectiveness.

Hugh would not say so, but I figured he was sorry for coming this way, with the slow going and with us chopping a path for any pursuing Indians to use.

Hugh called Bill and me over. "Drop back. Watch yon backtrack. One to each bank." We walked down the creek, one along each side.

The season was advanced into June, a time of unsettled weather, so the men called it. The transition from spring to summer was not placid. Thunder-boomers and lightning, wicked winds shifting and abruptly ceasing, the air steaming when the wind died. Bees and longjaws in my face. The most aggressive deerflies I had ever known.

The rain came in a great deluge. How the mighty heavens did roar! Sheets of water; thunder rolling down through the valleys as loud as cannon fire and climaxed by spectacular cracks of lightning. The wind shrieking fiercely. The summer storms seldom lasted long, extreme though they be. This one turned to hail; chunks of ice pelting us stung like blazes. I put a hand across my face against the worst of it and stumbled on. The storm continued for half an hour, then stopped.

After the weather passed, I saw a lot of game I would liked to have shot. A couple of deer, a flock of turkeys coming out of a brush patch where they had taken shelter from the rain. I killed a rattlesnake with a stick, surprised at its weight, and soon came across another, a six-footer. Got him, too, though he tried to crawl away. I took them along for supper.

Then more rain, soft and not too bad, just it was steady. The mist thickened off the stream, the streambed became damn near impossible to follow. I lost sight of it a few times then lost it altogether. With the sun going down and the mist rising, I had to find the stream before dark. I hurried, scairt of encountering Indians or snakes in the gloom. I wouldn't see an Indian until he jumped out from behind a tree nor a snake 'till I stepped on it. Hoped the rain had driven 'em to shelter, Indians and snakes both, if they be about. Couldn't find the streambed, the rain came harder, great sheets now and showing no sign of easing. I was soaked and miserable and I cursed Hugh for having sent me on such an errand but I did find the creek, to my great relief. Thinking now I might get into camp afore dark, I wondered if there might be a little supper waitin' for me. I had eaten nothing all day.

Walked on, slipping on the wet ground, the woods too dark to see, I lost the creek again and knew if I tried to find it in the dark, I would be entirely lost come morning. Resigned myself to a cold, miserable night in the woods and looked for a big rock or a dead tree to shelter against or crawl under. Two shadowy forms appeared out of the foggy night. I was terrified for certain it be Indians.

"Bub, ye wanna stay out all night?" Hugh and Alph, looking for me. "By god, I am surely glad to see you," I said, the relief obvious in my voice. "Jesus Christ, bub. I didn't mean fer ye ta walk the whole durn ways back to Scalp Point." I asked about Bill, they said he was already in. They guided me to the stream, which weren't far, and into a canoe. I asked how the hell they found me in the dark and with the rain and in such an awful place. They shrugged.

We got to the camp at Fort Anne. In the dark and with the fog and the rain, I saw the shadowy ruins standing up on the charred, rotten remains of logs. The palisade, built and abandoned before I was born, looked as if one more strong wind might blow 'er over. Most of the fort had been burned by the English during a retreat from this frontier. The land for a long way around was originally cleared of trees to provide a proper field of fire. Now it was overgrown with small trees and brush, the forest fast reclaiming the land for its own again.

The men seemed glad to see me in safe. They had worked straight through until they got everything under cover of the fort ruins. We spent the night waiting out the storm beneath the crook of a crumbling roof and the adjacent side of the palisade. The men had thrown a tarp over the roof and it did not leak too badly. It felt good to be out of the rain. Hugh's plan was to hide the birch-barks somewhere around the fort ruins and portage our furs to the Great Carry, where we would finish our journey in the elm-barks we had stashed on our way up.

I got into dry clothes and got up close to the fire. They had saved a generous portion of supper for me, good stew and still warm. I gave over the two snakes from my sack to Bill for cooking. Ravenous, I devoured the stew and my share of the snakes, which wasn't much.

Morning it was yet raining, hard. We stayed there most of the day. Hugh would not let us remain idle. First, he had us work on our guns until he was satisfied each one would work properly. Bill, ever the good hunter, set snares and got us turkeys.

Hugh had sent two men to the Great Carry, to see were our elm-barks still where we had stashed them. The scouts came in drenched and with bad news. Our elm-barks were gone. One of the scouts held up an arrow. Hugh studied it a moment and said it was Abenaki. Now, besides lugging our furs from Fort Anne to the Great Carry, we would have to portage our birch-barks as well. More'n ten miles. Plenty of hard work, and we would need be watchful. Them Abenakis might be waitin' fer us.

We was all somber, thinking on it. Hugh wouldn't allow us to feel sorry for ourselves and got us building travois for transport'n the boats and making sure the furs were well hidden, and about the time we finished, Hugh said, "Fellers, look what I found in my sack. Damn!" Grinning, he held up a rum jug. "Coulda got four 'er five more beavers fer it." He grinned some more. "Git yer cups out." And to me, "Ye too, bub. Ye've worked as hard as any of these here rascals." Now we was all grinning. "Ta ward off thee shaky bones," Hugh said. It did warm my insides. Like a fire in there. Reminded me of when Eric and me had used to sample Pops' booze when I cleaned up the tavern on Sunday mornings. We sipped and talked quietly. Not enough rum to get us drunk but enough to make us feel better.

Before first light we were up and ready for the hard labor ahead. Hugh pointed out again the possibility of danger to come from any-wheres. With scouts out, front and back, left and right, we commenced dragging our canoes on the travois. The canoes, soaked through, were heavy but not so heavy as they might a been had Hugh not insisted we put 'em under cover as soon as we got to Fort Anne. He had done this to dry 'em out some, for iffen we needed them.

The portage trail had not had much use the past few years and we suffered for getting up and down hills and for the thick brush. Our buckskins and homespuns already worn out, now they were torn by thick brambles, berry bushes and thorn apples. Our faces, arms and legs were scratched and bloodied. This was the only time I heard any of the men really bitch.

At the Hudson, we skirted the lone settlement, John Henry Lydius' trading post. Hugh said he was friends with Lydius, and said Lydius wouldn't bushwack us, as he was rumored to do sometimes to others, but best to avoid him. There were always shady characters around the post. If those Abenakis was lurking and were there enough of 'em, somebody from the post might take word to 'em in hope of sharing in the rewards of a bushwack.

We stashed the canoes, Hugh left two men to watch and ordered the rest of us back along the trail. By the time we got back to Fort Anne, it was dark. It was too late to cook supper, and with nothing much left for cooking anyway. Hugh broke out another rum jug and passed it around until it was gone. We slept three hours and he had us up again. Somebody griped about needing more rest, Hugh would not let up. "We rests when we gets to Albany, damn it." He is tough. Some of the men had been talking it over and now they told Hugh they were for carrying the furs and gear in a single trip instead of the two trips he was intending. Hugh was doubtful, as was I, but he was in a powerful hurry, not only because of the dangers but because the end of the journey was in sight and him impatient to collect his money. "First ones in with fur fetches ye best price, lads," he said. We lifted heavy loads onto each others' backs and off we went.

Our line quickly became strung out, with hills to climb, boulders to get around, low, swampy ground to trudge, slippery rocks and mud, it all made for hard going. We were banging elbows and knees. Some of the men suffered hard bruises in addition to us all being bad cut up. Lucky nobody got hurt bad.

Hugh pushed us along all day, working us when we would have rested. My shoulders hurt awful from the load on my back. Tempers flared. It started to rain again, which made for even worse going, and still he refused to call a halt. The men was getting mad. His constant harangues about the dangers of ambush and the expectations of best price were true enough and also true was his reminding us it had been our idea to shoulder double loads, although I think it was what he had intended. Only did he want us to suggest it rather than him order it. Still, we were all in for more rest and only kept on because nobody dared challenge his authority. We trudged through the fog and mist of a cold and rainy afternoon, the men soaked through. Hugh's strong goading and his seemingly endless supply of rum kept us moving. I will say Hugh worked harder than anyone else, he leading by example.

When Hugh produced yet another rum jug, I said to Alph, "Where in the hell does he keep getting 'em?" Alph shrugged. Too wet and miserable to care. Unbeknown to all but a few of the men, Hugh had kept back a few jugs from the trading and had also arranged back when we first got up from Albany, to bury some jugs at the Great Carry. Little else would make us move on a day as lousy as this and for the time we portaged, we had a jug going. We were grateful, and in a most incredible display of strength and endurance, about which I still sometimes shake my head, we got in before nightfall. The men left behind to guard the boats had built a shelter big enough for men and furs, and when we came in with double loads on our backs, they didn't think it unusual, what we had done.

The rain had stopped and as deserving as we were of rest, Hugh first made us dry off our guns, clean 'em and change the powder. He inspected every gun. Most of the men had extra clothes in the cache left here on our way up and we shucked our wet clothes. One of the

53

men left behind, Bill Morrissey, had shot two deer with his bow, the deer already getting butchered when we got in. "Green meat, boys," Hugh said, "and raw. Eat too much and you'll get the drizzles." He said this so we'd think he wasn't going to allow a cookfire, and after a pause, he grinned. "Get 'er goin', jest keep 'er smokeless."

Hugh took me aside for some private talk. "Ken, ye be a sharp lad an mebbe cut out fer some kinda life up here'n these woods. Fer so long as ye can survive, which ain't never fer long. Always remember, when Injuns buys your beads an' ye thinks ye be gettin' rich off'n 'em and thinkin' 'em for dumb Injuns what do'n know better, 'member, them beads is for keepin' their'n tribal history. T'is writin', jest thee same's your'n. More valu'ble'n a few furs could ever be. If ye's goin' to survive, ye's gots ta see things from your foe's point a view. Don' git trapped by your'n own. Yu'll live a little longer thet way."

The wind shifted and began to blow harder. The air turned cold. Bill cooked up a stew, rough stuff but hot. Chunks of venison, ribs, bones and all, a couple rabbits, some not so ripe ground nut, a rattlesnake. Wild onions, fresh greens picked by one of the men. New buds from the birch tree. The stew went some toward comfort.

We set to with the rest of Hugh's rum and enjoyed knowing we were very near to the end of our trek. Hugh reminded us what we were doing was illegal, said the law now became a factor in it but with our situation secure, our powder dry, which would likely not be true for any Abenakis which might try to jump us, the men razzed Hugh some.

These men, true men of the north, be a silent lot by nature. They speak volumes with their eyes and with the way they stand and move, and it is hard to get to know them. Now, having shared the rigors and dangers with them and having learned not to ask stupid questions, I joined in the talk and the laughter. I felt as if I were one of them.

We all mostly slept, except for Hugh. He regarded the wind closely and soon as it shifted and eased a bit, he had the watch wake everybody and we were on our way. The river was treacherous in the dark, a spill would have meant disaster, still, we would go only at night, to avoid detection by our own people. Down the river, drawn homeward by the swift current. One thing for sure, the biters were less bothersome on the river than they had been up north.

Early morning, we got off the water and hid. Whilst we waited for dark, I took a bath to wash away the terrible smelling concoction we used to keep the bugs away, as well as the dirt and grime infesting me.

When I returned to the company of the others, I realized how bad was the stink of the bug juice and of the men too, for none of them had bathed. "Youse all stink, y'know it?" I said. They laughed and made raucous remarks about my cleaned state.

One more night and we got in to Albany. We deferred our load of contraband furs in secrecy to the barn of a prominent Dutch politician who, in his fiery speeches, was against trading with the French of Canada. He wanted them driven out. He even spoke against his own Dutch, accusing us of sympathy or worse with the French.

His animosity did not extend to French peltry.

We were the first smuggling party to get back, thus gaining an advantage, just as Hugh had said, and we all benefited from having him do our negotiating for us. He got us what all say is a terrific price. I was thrilled with my share. Everybody was.

Pops and Mother were joyous to see their only offspring walk in through the front door of the busy tavern. Home safe, and when I told Pops who it was who'd received our furs and asked why, since said politician was opposed to smuggling, Pops was scathing.

"To dat man der Schillink, der zource iss not important." Pops said der Schillink's speeches about fur smuggling were meant to drive up the price of fur and his tirades against the Dutch were to ingratiate hisself with the English. Pops also warned me against telling anybody about der Schillink and the furs. The skunk would have me arrested.

The men spent a few days around town, mostly drinking in the Full Sail. They were once again a close-mouthed bunch. Couple days later, I shook hands with Hugh and said goodbye. He and some of the others had bought more trade goods and were headed west to Oswego. He invited me and Bill to join 'em, if we were of a mind. I declined, as did Bill. Hugh promised to be back in the spring to go north once again and said he'd have us along. Bill and me kept two of the birch canoes for ourselves.

Chapter V – Arnold and Priscilla

Into the summer, Bill and me spent our time mostly supplying meat and fish for the tavern, which kept Pops quiet, although whenever I was around, he wrangled me into doing work for him. I didn't mind helping if he needed me but to listen to him, he always needed me. Calamity would surely strike unless I wheeled kegs of beer into the common room or fetched wood from the woodpile or did whatever else and right away. He called it honest labor. I called it something else, just not when he was around. Bill went home to New England, he saying he'd be back for the fall hunt and to do some fishing.

The tom-toms from the Indian pageant haunted my sleep. Nights when I lay down, they started in just as real as when I had heard them. The drums and the picture in my mind of the drunken buck dragging an Indian girl by the hair and mounting her. I tried different things to rid my sleep of the dreams, even went to Eric's father at his apothecary to see what he might have but he had no powders I dared try.

When Eric could get away, we fished evenings for the pike which lurked in the weed beds of the Hudson backwaters. We took 'em a yard long. They are vicious and have nasty rows of teeth. When we went for them, I carried a stout hardwood club to give 'em a mortal whack afore hoisting them aboard. No other way would I bring the savage monsters into the boat. Careless men have lost fingers to 'em.

Out on the river, I told Eric about my recent adventures. The beauty of Saint Sacrement, the grandeur of Corlaer. Riding in a frail canoe piled high with furs, laughing at the danger, although I don't suppose I had laughed so much at it. I talked about seeing those tall mountains where no white man had yet trod and where I would one day go. "Hugh says I'll get scalped before I'm twenty," I almost boasted. "I see my future in the wild, beautiful country."

Eric seemed distracted and uninterested in my adventures. We were so different from one another yet we remained the best of friends. He spoke only of someday running his father's shop. "I am studying hard to learn the trade," he said. "I spend long hours at the store every day. Our business is growing with the town. Father says I can run it myself soon." Proud of being always shut in and serving old ladies!

I suppose most people would approve of Eric's way, he is practical and smart-headed whilst I am a dreamer, a wanderer who will come to no good. Probably Hugh is right, I will end up scalped under a tamarack tree in some nameless part of the country.

Eric was setting himself up with the prettiest girl in town, Sarah Moncton. Short, vivacious, brown-haired and with an ambitious head on her shoulders. I must admit to being jealous. Eric and me were sixteen years old, Sarah was fifteen and she already had the rest of their lives planned out. "She reckons I will be a great success," Eric said, he filling up the way a male partridge did in the spring, puffing his feathers to flaunt his importance. Drumming his wings. "Reckon most hens are easily impressed," I sneered, and I said as how she had the hook buried so deep in his gut, he might as well give up the fight. "We are going to get married next spring," he said, and he got mad enough to fight when I asked had he poked her yet.

He caught the biggest pike of the night, a three-footer, stomach full of baitfish. Right after he caught the fish, he said he had to go home. I got mad for him not staying all night but he said he had to get his rest to open the store in the morning. Afraid to stay away too long. "Next time tell me afore we leave the damn dock," I said. "You know the best fishing don't come 'till after dark."

Eric could hardly get away the rest of the summer. Sarah kept him at short tether. She never seemed happy when I was about. I was a distraction, a threat. One she did not feel comfortable with. Eric must spend all day in his father's shop, and when he was not working, Sarah kept a wedge between him and me.

About this time a pretty girl took a lively interest in my future well-being. New to Albany, come over from Boston with her mother and father, demure and well mannered, two years older than me. Lydia Pryor.

Her father was a shipping merchant. I followed Lydia's lead, even did I let her get me into church one Sunday in the late summer. That August morning when I appeared at my folks' breakfast table, spruced up like even I couldn't believe and announced I was going to church, my poor mother, pleased but amused, asked me not to scare her so again. "Please, son, next time a little warning." Pops had plenty to say about it and truthfully, I felt a little silly.

I went to Lydia's father's house, a stately brick mansion along

Market Street, where all the rich Englishmen lived. Lydia presented me, her father looked me over as if I were something he had purchased and wasn't sure why. In front of the church, he greeted all who entered whilst we stood modestly behind him. We sat in his pew at the front, listening to the sonorous preaching. The church was the English High Anglican but it was not so high to keep me from falling asleep when Ol' Sol's rays came through the window and warmed me.

Lydia nudged me awake more than once. I followed the flight of a droning bee, hoping it'd alight upon a sleeper's nose and sting 'em. The preacher rambled. Halfway through the service I recognized my partner in crime, the fat politician, der Schillink, glowing in pontifical splendor. That finished church for me. A hypocrite Dutchman in the English Church, and when I told Pops about it, he laughed.

Lydia's intentions were to straighten me out. Get me into something with a future. Such as clerking in her father's business. A proper life according to the way she set her sights. Soon as she realized I would not surrender to her as Eric had to Sarah, she moved on to more fertile fields, afraid of ending up an old maid, driven to rid herself of the stigma before it could attach to her.

She corralled another fellow, they got married and moved to Saratoga. Married to a man whose father was a land speculator. A crook, I always heard, and the son just like him. Too bad, for I was fond of Lydia and think it might have worked out differently had I succeeded in getting her out from her father's influence. Her future seemed assured with her husband involved in his family's land business, which was profitable and growing. Sarah chastised me for letting Lydia get away and for my refusal to settle into Pops' tavern. Sarah said, "You could make a good living if you worked at it."

Luckily, Bill returned about the time Lydia left me. He took a room at the inn. Mother's boarding house was most always full but we found a place for Bill. Me and him had much in common, having shared the dangers of our trip and with our fondness for the woods.

I showed him plenty of good fishing and coon hunting and we hired ourselves out as hunters. Albany folks were always eager for the meat we brought. We found buyers in the smaller settlements on both sides of the river, men too busy with their farms to hunt for themselves. We shot plenty of big bucks. Always seemed to be plenty of them near the cornfields. The trick was to get them before somebody else did. The competition for winter meat was tough, there were plenty of good hunters around Albany. We decided to spend the winter trapping the Sacandaga country, west of Saratoga, and come spring, we would go north again with Hugh. We commenced gathering all of what we'd need. Traps and gear. Axes, more traps, skinning knives, pack baskets, wooden buckets.

****

One afternoon I was walking along the bustling docks. Having just sold a side of venison and a barrel of salted herring to the captain of a schooner in from New York, I stopped to watch as some immigrants disembarked. I was accosted at the foot of the gangway by an absolute shrew of a woman who demanded the direction of "The most prominent inn of this dirty, filthy, smelly town!"

She was tall and stout and was dressed in the fanciest traveling clothes I ever seen, her hair done up in a conical hat and getting blasted by the wind. She continued her jabbering and with a long finger waved in my face to punctuate her words, there could be no doubting her perceived authority. She made one understand immediately her breeding and station in life was considerably above theirs.

She looked me up and down and pronounced me unwashed, dirty and unclean. "Not the worst I have seen." She sniffed. "You simply must help us." She didn't consider the possibility I might have affairs of my own, which might preclude me from assisting her.

A small man was just emerging at the head of the narrow wooden gangway. He was wrestling with a heavy trunk and was perilously close to dropping it into the water. Whilst I watched him, she prattled on, oblivious to his predicament. "We have just come from England to this godforsaken, wretched, uncivilized place. My stupid husband has purchased a manor house and slaves and one hundred acres of land at a place called Saratoga. Is Saratoga as horrid as Albany? If so, it is certainly barren of civilized people and is most certainly barren of culture. Where is Saratoga, up the hill?" She didn't ask so much as she demanded.

"No, ma'am." I laughed. "Saratoga is thirty miles north, and did you say a big place with a manor house? Must be some mistake. Your manor must be downriver somewheres. There be no such a thing up that a way." I was still eying the chap who was having trouble on the gangway. Three sailors stood leaning over the railing of the ship, they weren't going to help him and were smirking boldly in anticipation of the trunk sliding into the water and maybe the man going with it, as there was no railing on the gangway.

"You cannot be serious, bumpkin," the woman said. "It cannot be so. Have you ever been to Saratoga? Ever seen the place? Surely you know naught of what you speak." She eyed me fiercely, like a hawk on a tree limb watching a mouse.

"I'm certain, ma'am," I said. She said they had been swindled, "All because my lout of a husband is incapable of making a living proper for one of my breeding and standing in our own country."

The little man who by the suit he wore and with the way she eyed him, could only be her husband, was losing his battle with the trunk. It was poised to go over. "Yes, ma'am," I said, even as I moved to help the man. She didn't even pause. "Where are you going, bumpkin? You must help us find shelter in this godforsaken place." Indignant I should leave her whilst she was talking, she was more willing to lose the trunk than to lose my ear to bend.

I tried to assure her I was listening, even as I grabbed the trunk. Only then did she notice her husband's struggles, which caused her to start in on him. "Arnold Baldwin, you are a clumsy, stupid, good for nothing oaf. Now you have been swindled." Then to me, "Don't just stand there, you moron, help him." I said I was, and we soon had the trunk safely on dry land. "Thank you, lad," the man said. "I am Arnold Baldwin." He stuck out his hand. "What be your name?" We shook, his grip was weak. "Ken Kuyler, sir. Pleased to know you."

"Yes, thank you, Ken. How far is this Saratoga? Is it as big as what Mister Langston says?" Langston! So Lydia's father-in-law was the swindler. Arnold looked around. "It certainly must be bigger than this. There are comforts, are there not? Mister Langston spoke glowingly of the amenities we would find."

"No, sir," I said. "Saratoga has only a few hundred people inside of a palisade. Shops and houses along one street leading from the fort gate. Small farms around. A mere tenth of Albany."

"And this is Albany? A tenth the size of this? Oh, my goodness, this will never do." He looked worried and avoided his wife's eye. It didn't matter if he looked at her or not, she was going to give it to him. The lady had one sharp tongue. "Oh, my goodness, indeed," she said. "You miserable bumbling fool. Now we are stranded in this wretched place." And to me, "When is the next boat to New York? We shall be on it."

Told them of Father's tavern and offered to escort them there. I helped Arnold with his burden, it being obvious his wife would not help. "How much farther is it?" she asked, when we had gone only a short way and with Arnold and me struggling with the chest. "Just along the quay," I said, wishing now I hadn't offered to help them.

"You seem to be an enterprising lad," he said, to which she added, "For a bumpkin," and she never stopped jabbering. She had a sharp eye, missed nothing, and kept up a running patter about the town laid out before her, and the "dirty despicable, feckless folk." Her poor husband just plodded along with his burden and said little 'cept, "Yes, dear, whatever you say, dear."

To my relief we were soon at the inn. I was getting highly perturbed with this womanly monster. We set the trunk inside the door. Early morning, the place was empty except for my folks. I introduced them. Mother showed the woman, whose name was Priscilla, too much deference at the first. We all thought Priscilla really was some sort of fancy nobility. Mother took them upstairs to show them the room they might hire. I stood with Father at the bar, relieved to be free from the woman's blather and the spineless behavior of her husband. He had said little against his wife's onslaught and simply endured, a man beaten down by the constant harping.

"Bah! Englichmans!" Always a curse when Father snorted it. Soon the Baldwins came back down, she complaining still but resigned to renting the room. Mother gave me the dirtiest of looks. Then she was scurrying to the increasing demands of the harridan.

They were settled in a day, and we went looking for Langston, to try and get their money back. We had a hard time to track him down, more so with Priscilla's incessant hounding of Arnold. We finally got ahold of a clerk for the land speculators and tried to coerce him into returning their money.

The amount offered was a mere pittance, not nearly enough to get them back to England. The clerk said the person they needed to see was Lydia Pryor's father-in-law but as he was presently in New York Town, I took them to see Lydia's husband, a thief, same as his father. He refused to do anything for them. They had signed a paper and he would hold them to it. Arnold threatened legal action, Priscilla and me threatened much worse. Richard knew we weren't to be put off and he offered Arnold the job of schoolteacher up to Saratoga, in the school he was building. Arnold accepted, over the protestations of his wife.

Whilst Arnold and Priscilla were in Albany preparing to go north,

I got to know them. Arnold was actually a clever fellow. Educated in what he called the Classics, he had, along with his book learning, practical business experience and was capable enough, if she would leave him be.

Priscilla had money from an inheritance, an aunt who, Priscilla said haughtily, was royalty, a duchess or countess, I never could figure out which. "Light-fingered chamber maid," Arnold would say, when it was safe for him to do so. Then he would laugh and the briar pipe he always smoked would twitch between his teeth. His laugh would get out of control and he would get hysterically loud, the braying of a donkey which often caused the lighted contents of the pipe to dump onto the floor.

Bill and me took Arnold and Priscilla to Saratoga, which settlement is the last town on our northern frontier. Beyond, there are just a few isolated homesteads and trappers' cabins and up at the Great Carry, Lydius' trading house. When we showed them what they had bought, Arnold was dismayed, Priscilla was outraged. Their baronial manor was uncut forest overgrown with grapevines and berry bushes, which would be mighty tough to clear. "Cannot someone be found," Priscilla said, "to buy our land so we may realize a good profit and leave this wretched land?" Arnold took the school-teaching job and they found a place to live. Bill and me helped them move. Soon after, Arnold found additional work as records keeper for Lydia's father-in-law. Working for the crooks who fleeced him! I chided him about this.

****

Summer turned to fall. The leaves changed color and dropped, the nights were cold, sleet mixing with the rain, the season for trapping was at hand. Bill and me moved into an abandoned cabin west of Saratoga Lake and ran our traplines. Sacandaga fur was not so prime as the Canadian fur we traded for when we was with Hugh. We didn't expect to get much of a price. We found no beavers. I shot a bear and borrowed his coat for the winter. Winter bearskins are the warmest coverings known to man, if he can persuade brother bruin to part with his.

We worked hard all winter but come spring, when we went to one of the Albany fur-buyers, Mister Burnes, we were angry with how little money we were offered. Bill called Burnes a thief and threatened to beat him up. I pulled Bill aside. Told him Burnes was a crochety old buzzard but he was honest. Leastways he was less a crook than the others of the fur-buyers. I told Bill to have a look around at what fur was there in the shed. This calmed him some. The other pelts, even those from nearby New England, was better than what we brung. Our rewards so poor, I determined never to trap around Albany again.

Burnes offered us jobs and we went to work for him. Cleaning fur in his smelly shed. Burnes was hard to deal with, we were most always arguing with him. He bitched loudly about us in the tavern. We heard about it from Pops. Then Bill and Burnes argued, Bill punched Burnes in the jaw and we quit him before he could fire us.

Next came the shad run. They came early and in good numbers. Here was a way for us to make up a little for the disappointing fur season. We sold salted fish to Pops at a good price, for him. The rest we sold around town. Three barrels to the captain of a schooner in from the Bahamas with sugar.

By the time the run was over, a little fur was starting to trickle in from Oswego. We took jobs with Burnes again, skinning and readying the fur for market. He and Bill clashed daily over most everything but we held onto the jobs.

Bill and me pooled our money to see where we stood. "If we do good enough at the Montreal rendezvous," Bill said, "we won't have to work the rest of the year." We anxiously anticipated Hugh's arrival, it was past time for him to show. Our cash was draining away as it always did in town despite our best efforts to watch it. We worked hard and waited.

Bill came into the tavern one night, excited. He had found a bargain in trade goods, come off a ship run aground in the Hudson just below Albany. In anticipation of Hugh's arrival and another sojourn with him, we decided to take advantage of the chance and purchase our trade goods. It was a big demand on our poke, it about cleaned us out but the returns in Montreal would be many times the amount of money put down for it. Father was on to our plans, saw there was no chance to dissuade us and decided to invest some few coins of his own. We were excited for the killing we would make in Montreal and wondered where the hell Hugh was. He was overdue.

In early May, Hambone Rush came into town. He had been out to Oswego with Hugh and coming into the Full Sail, he told us Hugh was dead. "Got hisself crushed by a tree blown over durin' a plumb wicked windstorm 'bout a month back."

Me and Bill were stunned, and saddened, and for the longest time, we three sat silently at a table. Hambone had known Hugh for many years, had shared many an adventure with him, and for Bill and me, two lads with nothing to offer except eagerness and a willingness to learn, Hugh had been a true mentor.

I remembered how mad he got when he found out I was writing things down and how he had changed his mind and encouraged me to write. He had told me I was not to put his name in my journals, which I did not, for as long as he was alive, but I think he knew I would use his name, did he pass on before me, and it was what he wanted. His vast knowledge of the north, his success at getting smuggling parties in and out of French territory were things he was very proud of, and I think it had always bothered him, knowing how at his passing, his legacy would vanish. He saw in me and my journals a way for him to live on, same as I hoped the journals would do for me.

Breaking our silence, we raised our tankards. "Hugh McChesney," I said. "Best teacher who ever bestrode a classroom." Bill called Hugh a captain "Who kept his men alive in the woods and kept his hair 'til the end." We banged our tankards in tribute. "Aye," Hambone said.

Hugh's death put Bill and me into a most precarious situation. With all our money invested in trade goods, we'd be ruined if we did not go north. We discussed the possibility of going out to Oswego and trying our luck but neither of us knew the way and we had doubts about the profits to be gained. "Competition be tough out there," Hambone said. "I don' reckon ye youngsters oughta try 'er alone."

Pops sold his goods the next day. He took a loss but better than losing all. Advised us to do the same. We tried to find another party to get in with but with the legal pressures, everybody was quiet about their plans. Besides, the smuggling captains said their parties were already made up and they did not have the need for additional men. What they meant was, they did not know nor trust us. We thought about going alone but decided it was too risky. "Too deep in for gettin' out, no way to finish the job right," Bill lamented. Hambone headed out for New Hampshire.

****

One night, Pops asked me to get behind the bar. He did this sometimes, saying he had important business. I never knew was it the truth or not and once he was gone, he might stay gone for hours. I did not complain, I knew how hard he worked. This night he was not gone long and with me pushing slops from behind the bar and Bill grousing in his beer, both of us thinking on our predicament, which was getting more desperate, Pops came through the front door proudly bearing a brand-new shiny rifle smelling of grease. He said he had been down to the docks to see the captain of a coastal sloop just come in and he gave the gun to me. Not a smoothbore musket but rifle-barreled for best shooting. A new kind of weapon, a new idea. Made in Philadelphia by an old navy friend of Pops, a gunsmith from their sailing days. He and Pops had always corresponded. I had met this Heinrich in my childhood. The men in the tavern all got around us for a look-see.

The barrel of this beautifully balanced weapon was ten inches or more longer than the standard British military rifle. Inside the barrel were four rifled-grooves, which, by causing a ball to spin rapidly when it came out, meant the gun could be fired accurately a longer distance than could any smoothbore. Up to two hundred yards. My old musket was never accurate at any distance. The rifle had front and rear sights, the back-sight hinged to allow for raising and lowering. All of this was according to the accompanying letter which Pops had me translate from Dutch into English so Bill could understand too.

The letter said the gun had been copied from the German Jaeger rifle, the first grooved barrel in existence in Europe. We had heard about these guns but none of us had ever seen one. The wooden stock was ornately carved, a giant stag with a magnificent rack and some smaller deer, an idyllic woodland scene. The letter said the barrel could be shortened seven or eight inches to allow for better use in the woods.

Pops said he had ordered the gun last summer when he seen the direction I was headed. He knew the north woods to be a tough path, similar to his own youth spent at sea, and he wanted the best chance for me, since he could not shake me of my druthers. I am eternally grateful to him.

First light in the morning and after Pops gave me another stern lecture about caring for the gun, him, Bill and me headed out through the gates to a nearby pasture. I was excited, my hands shaking as I poured powder down the barrel. The gun was awkward to handle because of the added length. I fired and missed the mark by quite a bit. Pops laughed and took the gun from me after I reloaded.

He hit the target, on the outer edge, then the three of us took turns shooting. Once I had fired three or four shots, I was comfortable with the gun and was fast accustoming myself to it. And discovered Pops was a marksman. Time after time we hit blazes cut on trees. The gun would hit dead center. One thing we noticed immediately was the difference in the sound of the shots. The smoothbores are a flat boom, this gun had a distinctive crack, as if the sound was more concentrated. It also had a stronger kick than most.

Some men just arriving to do some target shooting of their own laughed at how far back we were from the blaze, a much farther distance than a musket could shoot with accuracy. Pops fired, the wooden target splintered, the men came over to admire the gun. This was some weapon!

The gun burned powder more thoroughly than the smoothbores and would not require such frequent cleaning. Even with the long barrel and the extra weight, she was well-balanced. It was almost noon afore we left the pasture for having expended all shot and powder. I made my thanks obvious to the old man.

"Ya. Goot." He grinned and reached into his pouch, took out a sheet of paper and handed it to me. The bill. He said laughingly, "Ya is good gun, nein, but youse pays for. Youse got der bush-fur money, ya?" Which meant that although he wanted me to have the best there was, he had no intention of paying for it.

I appreciated his thinking enough of me to get the rifle, he got the best there was, but just as surely, he was a skinflint. Bill laughed so hard he almost fell down. Pops would not wait for his money, which put a further burden on me. He said, "Iv youse go'n get scalpt nein will it be vid mine money in youse pocket."

Right then the money did not seem to make much difference in Bill's and my scheming. We tried to find partners who would put up money but to no avail. Eric refused when I talked to him about it. We about got into a fistfight over it. He was a bit too harsh in his criticism. I got my ruffles up and would have whipped his arse had he not backed down. For Bill and me the time had come. We had to make a decision as to what to do.

Chapter VI – Reckless Gambit

Discouraged, me and Bill spent nights in the common room, at a heavy oak table by the fireplace, quaffing beers, about having given up, certain our plans and our pocketbooks were doomed to failure.

Until one night, through the door came another of those Dutch politicians who, whilst publicly opposed to the fur-smuggling business, was invested in it. Accompanying the fat Dutchman was a big, brash, fancified young man in his twenties. I paid little attention to them until they came over to us. The politician, whose name was Van Schaack, nodded a curt greeting and asked, "May ve sit vi you?" Bill was in his usual foul mood and told Schaack to go to hell. Schaack pulled up a chair and sat. The other man proposed rum and beer all 'round, and with neither Bill nor me objecting, the man went over to the bar. I was situated as to watch him as he came back with the drinks on a board.

His long legs had a wide gait, like a seaman just come ashore from an Atlantic crossing. He wore new buckskins and a white silk shirt. His long hair he wore clubbed in back. He sat, Schaack introduced him as William Johnson. He was no American. Scotch or Irish by his thick brogue in which he told us he had arrived from Ireland a year ago. "To manage an estate out beyond Schenectady. The estate of my uncle, the famous English seaman, Admiral Warren. Peter Warren." Johnson was as puffed as a peacock. "Surely you have heard of him?" We hadn't neither of us ever heard of Peter Warren and I asked what had Warren done to make hisself famous. Johnson smiled ruefully. "Not much yet," he said, "but great things are expected of him, as they are of me. My uncle is a captain in the British Navy. He has married into the Delancy family and is becoming one of the richest men in the colony." Bill sneered and said the Delancys were naught but thieves. This was said to goad Johnson. The big Irishman and the fat little Dutchman had interrupted Bill from doing what he did most nights, brooding whilst getting roaring drunk, and Bill had apparently decided to pick a fight. Johnson's talk, as smooth as his silk shirt, and his brashness, did not sit well with my friend. Johnson was aware Bill was looking to start something, and Johnson's smoothness I judged to be intentional, as if he'd fight too, did Bill insist and I was sizing 'em up. Bill, though thin almost to gauntness, was a tall man and was wicked fast with his fists. Whenever Bill got into a fight, I was sure he would win. This time, I wasn't so sure. What I did know, these two gettin' into it was something I'd want to see.

"I like this New World," Johnson was saying. "I have established good relations with the Mohawks. I am learning their language as well as their ways." Bill said what he thought of the Mohawks; Johnson remained unflappable. He talked about the virtues of Indian culture. "Indian culture, schit," Van Schaack said. "Indian women, you mean.'

I studied Johnson whilst he talked. He had a commanding presence, as if he knew his words would be listened to, and he was right, for had it been any other man annoying Bill the way Johnson was, Bill would already have gone for him. Johnson said he was only twenty and he proved himself no stranger around a tavern. He declared my old man's beer to be the best he'd ever tasted. He repeated his claim, more matter of fact than boastful, of being destined for great things. "If the French don't scalp me first." He grinned. A cocky one. "Or an irate husband, more likely," chuckled old Schaack.

"Chrissake," Bill said, and he started to get up, slowly and backing away even as he stood so Johnson would know Bill wasn't coming for him. "We would like to talk to you about going to Montreal," Johnson said before Bill could get to an empty table where he might get further soused in peace. Johnson looked around, to ensure no one else was listening and to give Bill time to sit back down, which Johnson was certain he would. Bill sat and our talk, or rather, Johnson's, shifted toward the possibility of money to be made up north. Johnson was as informed of our last year's trip as if he had made it himself. How he knew so much about it was from Van Schaack, who was one of the men who backed Hugh McChesney. By their conversation and familiarity with each other, Johnson and Schaack were pretty thick. Whatever they were intending, I was sure it was not the only scheme they had on the fire together. The hard questions Johnson asked showed he got what was important and what wasn't. And showed he had a mind like a steel trap.

Schaack informed us the same governor was still in Canada, same offer for English trade goods still stood. For as long as the peace held between the two countries, a profit could be made. Bill said as how we had been looking for a way to go north to trade but had about given up. It was too late now to get there in time for the trading.

"Iv you leaf viddim der next two days," Schaack said, "youse can get there in time. Ya?" I could tell Schaack did not understand the difficulties involved in moving along the river and the lakes. "Be iffy," Bill said. "The moon is almost at dark. By the time we could get to Scalp Point it would be near to full." I agreed, it was too dangerous. "Perhaps there is un way," Schaack said, and with the way he said it and with him leaned back, smiling, we knew he had some sort of plan a brewin'.

"We have the trade goods and we can supply the men," Johnson said. Bill gave each of them a scornful look and asked Schaack, "You fixin' ta come along?" Schaack, a round-bellied, short-legged little man with a flabby pink face, in his Dutch accent, "I am too old for a trip such as dis." Bill asked Johnson if he was coming. "Neidder of us," Schaack said, "know der vay around der voods. Nor can eidder of us spare der time from der odder business to go. But I vonder if you could consider un arrangement. You see, I have der official clearance for mine party to go vidout trouble from der French, und it is signed by der minister of all Canada." He pulled a paper from the pocket of his fancy vest. "Ah, der moon is wrong, but you vill be safe iff youse carry dis letter." Schaack paused for a draught of his beer and intimated the Montreal authorities would be expecting his representatives. A sanction which would be crucially important. "You'll want an extra cut of the profit for having your letter," Bill said. "Vhy not," Schaack said with a shrug and with just the merest hint of a smile, as if the answer could not be more obvious.

"Ve haf der cash for der possibles unt der goods iss sitting in der varehouse packed unt ready. How many canoes has youse?" I told him we had two fifteen-footers. Schaack warned, "Prompt action iss der virst necessity. I vill fait one day vor der answer. I already vaited too lonk vor McChesney and most of my men iss gone to Osvego." Bill told 'em we'd think on it. He was tempted, easy to tell. "Only thing is, Mister Van Schaack," I said, "I won't carry any spirits up there. Not after what I seen last year." Van Schaack and Johnson grimaced at this but I was resolute, still haunted by the rememberence of a wild-eyed buck having his way with an unwilling girl. I told them if they insisted on spirits, they could carry it up there themselves. We argued, they only relenting when they seen the uselessness of trying to dissuade me.

Schaack talked a bit more and left soon after. Johnson stayed and drank with us long after Pops closed the bar. Blathering and spinning yarns. We talked about the lakes' country, which, though Johnson had never been up there, he seemed to know much about it.

"Any beavers up there, boys?" Johnson spoke casually the question anyone would like to have answered. Smooth and slippery. "Wouldn't tell ye iffen there were," I said. Bill looked Johnson right in the eye. "Ask your Indian friends."

Bill and me were pretty much of a mind to try out this partnership. It seemed our only way out. If Schaack and Johnson would pay the wages and expenses of two more men, we could take two canoe-loads of goods, which would include our own stake. We reckoned the fair would start ten days from right then.

The three of us were still there drinking in the common room when my old man woke up with the sun and kicked us out the door. We went for a walk to clear our heads. Up the hill to Schaack's big house. The fat Dutchman was up and waiting for us. His black man brought us coffee and small cakes. Johnson told Schaack we had agreed to go. Schaack offered us powder, food, utensils, possibles, and a one-sixth share of his profit, to be split between us upon our return. The alderman said, "Der cost of der goods comes out of der first returns. Your profit vill be from der remainder." We argued the details. I wanted a better percentage. They again wanted to include rum. I refused; Van Schaack got on me about it. Watered-down rum meant more profit. "If it's what the boys say," Johnson said, "it's how she lays." This silenced Schaack and angered him too.

I said two more men must be hired to help with the work, yet any who were of a mind to go smuggling were already gone. I doubted our chances of finding any worthwhile men. Schaack agreed to hire two men and pay their wages. He mentioned a pair who often worked for him and who were, he said, inured to the hardships of the trade and the ways of the wilds. He swore they could be trusted. I knew them, too. I didn't care for 'em and doubted either had ever been smuggling.

Finally, with everything smoothed out, we switched from coffee to rum to celebrate our partnership. We signed an agreement and after toasting to our success, Schaack added, "Jakop, my son, is going alonk to oversee der trading. He speaks der French."

Jakop, whom I knew mostly by reputation, was a few years older than me, built like his father only shorter and fatter, a prissy, overbearing weakling with his fancy clothes and airs, his powdered wig and a snuff box detailed in silver. He would be naught but a useless encumbrance on so hard and dangerous a journey. Worse than useless as he'd need to be cared for and watched after so's not to get hisself into trouble. All this was true, and what else was true, the reason Jakop was going was for him to learn enough so they could do it next year without Bill or me.

I told Schaack his son wasn't goin'. Bill got the drift of why I didn't want Jake along and he, Bill, got mad. He said he was of a mind not to go at all. "Goddamn it," he said. "I ain't takin' along no fairies nor step-lighties. This here's dangerous work, and hard. You think it's just gettin' into a canoe'n and goddamn paddlin'. Bullshit, it's damn hard work. Ta hell with it." Bill's face was red, the veins in his skinny neck all purred up.

"You gave your word, shook hands on it not five minutes ago," Johnson exclaimed, incredulous, yet still as smooth as silk. Schaack said, as he poured more of the rum punch, "Vat about your moneys? Youse have put all dat you own into dis venture."

Bill took the drink in a gulp and smashed the fancy-stemmed glass by hurling it into the fireplace. "Goods and profits be damned," he said. Schaack insisted, lifted the paper off the table and waved it at us. "Your names is on der agreement," he said. Johnson tried to keep us all calm. "You will get in and out all right, lads," he said. "You are certainly hardy enough."

I couldn't see taking such a loss upon ourselves if it could be avoided and I kept talking, lest Schaack take us to court. I reckoned we might find ourselves in the debtors' prison. At one point I had to grab Bill to prevent him from leaving. We argued a while longer and finally worn down, Bill assented. "Two days to get ready," he said. "Otherwise I and my partner are goddamn going alone, understand?" Pure bluff on Bill's part.

We broke off, Bill and me walked down the hill. I was dissatisfied with the details but excited to be going. We began at once preparing. That afternoon, Schaack sent for us. He showed us a list of the goods we would carry and the prices we were to ask. We went over in detail what there was. Then we signed another paper.

My father, when we told him about it, tried to talk us out of going. He was harsh in his criticism of the situation as it then stood. "Der papers youse signed iss no good und dat damn Schaack is un snake.

How can ant agreement for der smuggling be legal?" Pops, then, and to Bill, "I don van to loss der son, dunderhead dat he iss." Pops' face, set hard, reminded me of when I had looked at him on the morning when I had departed with Hugh. "Youse schmart vello," Pops said, again to Bill. "Gotterdamn vuy comes youse don schmarten upp? Bah!" He gave us a stern warning of the probable outcome of our venture. He about convinced Bill we should not go, even did it mean ruin for us both. Still, Pops had to concede, Van Schaack was a powerful man and nobody to fool with. Bill said afterward, "Your old man is pretty rough, when he sets his mind to it, ain't he?"

I didn't care, for I was determined to carry on despite the problems. Worried sick, and tired as hell I was. The next morning, we met with Schaack again. Prepared our cargoes for transport. The two hired men, I was sure, would be useless. Ben and Joe. English river rats. In truth, Ben did look like a little brown rat. The other, Joe, was a hulking man with sloping shoulders and a protruding jaw of immense proportions, his jaw more exercised than his brain as he was always mumbling to himself, not a good habit to take into the woods. Lesser men than what we had gone with on our last trip. Johnson oversaw our preparations and seeing more of him, I told Bill I wished Johnson was going along instead of them other three.

Our time for departure came and went. Jakop and his father were twenty-four hours late. Finally, they were ready. Or so we thought. Whilst loading the canoes, Bill and me were forced to throw out much useless gear. We had to go through every pack of Jakop's and the other two, and judging by the things we tossed, they had no notion of what they were getting themselves into. I found rum stashed in Joe's pack. He told me Schaack had insisted he take it for trade. I poured it out on the ground.

Bill and me got into one canoe, the three of them in the other, they about tipping it over getting in and we were immediately exasperated by their clumsiness and ineptitude. They struggled to go upstream against the current, we outdistanced 'em before we had gone a mile. Finally, so far behind were they, we could not even see them. We went ashore and waited and when they got up with us, the men complained. Said Jakop had paddled only so far as the first bend in the river. Then, and out of his father's sight, he laid aside his paddle and sucked on his pipe. Jake complained too. Said his legs were cramped from sitting and he demanded we take a rest.

"No way, fat ass," Bill said. "We move. Now!" Jakop commenced explaining to Bill how he, Jakop, would be making all the decisions. Bill and me ignored him and we got one of us into the stern of each canoe. The two hired hands got in the bows. "Jake," Bill said. "Either join us now or walk home." Jake got into the middle of my canoe, so he was more afraid of Bill than of me.

The soft hands and weak shoulders of the dandy would not allow him to do any real work, even if he had been of a mind to, which he was not. He simply sat idle in the canoe, taking repeated pinches of snuff and complaining because each time he tried to light his pipe, I splashed water on him or rammed him in the ribs with my paddle. At the first portage, we got him to work some by threatening once again to leave him behind, which to my and Bill's thinking would have been preferable. Bill did everything he could to upset Jake. Trying to make him give up and turn around. "Go home," Bill said, looking Jake in the eye, a short foot from his face. Bill had no tolerance for clumsiness or laziness in the woods or on the water, and with the lizard-look of Jake's face, his squat body, Bill got to calling him Toad.

The two hired men proved to be useless and stupid.

Toward evening of our second day and as we approached Saratoga and the portages there, Toad demanded we cross over to the west side of the river and stay the night at an inn. Drink some beer and sleep in a bed. "And tell everybody where we are headed," I said, then Bill got on him. "You lazy son-of-a-bitch, you can sleep when you get home." Toad ordered us to stop; Bill told him did he give one more order, we would take his scalp back to his father on a stick. Bill then steered his canoe up alongside mine and whacked the back of Toad's head with a paddle. I laughed, nor did the other two hide their amusement.

We disembarked at the lower end of the portage, Bill and me hid the trade goods, and when it was full dark, we moved off with one of the canoes, leaving the other for them. When our boat was portaged and with no sign of them coming up behind, Bill said, "The fools kin either catch up or go to hell." Bill is a tall, lanky man and when he is angry and stomping around, he reminds me of a spindly-legged water bird. "Let's take ourselves away from them," he said. "Go it alone. They can find their way home from here." He meant it. "Think we could just leave them?" I said. I was undecided too but tempted. Bill was worried about the more dangerous country ahead. Rightly so!

Late in the night, whilst portaging the trade goods, Bill and me realized Ben and Joe were drinkers. Them and Toad had fallen behind, we stopped to wait for 'em, they came up and I never saw three more clumsy oafs. Two drunk, one pitiful. Ben and Joe were played out and stumbling beneath the weight of their trade goods, in heavy packs over their shoulders. They had been sipping from hidden flasks. Bill was going to skin them, and Toad too, for not watching them. Bill set down his pack, shook his fist in the faces of the drinkers and demanded, "If you be hidin' more whiskey, git 'er out, now!" They insisted there was no more. "Iffen I catch you taking one more drink," Bill said, "I'll be lifting some hair."

When Bill and me had finished portaging and with the others not having come up yet, I suggested we get some sleep whilst we waited. Bill was most unhappy. "I don't want to wait, damn 'em, anyway. I don't want to go one more step with the useless sons-a-bitches. We can punch a hole in their boat and just go on with what goods is ours." I asked did he have a letter from the governor of Canada and did he speak any French. "No, goddamn it, you know I don't," he answered. I lay down; Bill bitched, I shut my eyes.

We were awakened hours later by them others struggling in with their sacks. They were scared for having been left alone in the woods. Even Jake was carrying a load, though his was less by far than what the others hauled. "They're gonna get us killed, pard," Bill warned. They needed to rest; Jakop wanted to sleep. When Joe, the big one, got too near the edge of the riverbank, Bill bumped him off balance enough to send him into the river and make it seem as if it might have been an accident. Joe knew better and came out of the water mad and sputtering. I thought Bill might have to fight him. No doubt did Joe want to get into it, Bill would oblige. Joe knew it too and was cowed by the knife which appeared in Bill's hand. "Least maybe we got one of 'em sobered up," Bill said with a snarl and turning to the other, "How 'bout it, you skinny, rat-faced polecat. You need sobering too?"

"Something more to tell Father when we get home," Jakop said to Bill. No need to write Bill's reply.

We proceeded to the Great Carry of the Hudson at a too-slow pace. Bill said, "I don't see how we get to Canada before the fair is over and all the fur is gone." He said he should a gone home to New Hampshire for the summer. We lifted our too-heavy packs up over our shoulders and going along the trail to the landing at Saint Sacrement, we saw sign of smugglers out ahead of us.

We were three days portaging, which included pulling our canoes on travois whilst carrying loads on our backs. We had always to be warning our town boys about lighting fires at night, and shooting at game, which they probably couldn't a hit anyway. They complained most bitterly whenever they saw a deer or some other meat and Bill forbade their shooting. Another danger was Jake's prattling, the sort of unnecessary talk which can get a man into trouble. Nothing could shut him up except the threat of the scalp knife. Bill put it up against Jake's throat more than once and I think Bill finally just gave up and suffered Jake's whining about food, or rather the lack of it, and about the bugs and everything else.

Finally got everything portaged and even with still a long way to Montreal and with but a few days before we reckoned the rendezvous would start, me and Bill decided our travel on the lakes from here on must be at night. Thus and on our third day of portaging, we lost plenty of daylight hours at the Saint Sacrement landing.

I insisted everybody bathe, especially Jake, whose odor of sweat, fear and bug juice made it most unpleasant to be near him. Jake was reluctant and after disrobing and testing the water with his foot, he declared it too cold. Bill tossed him in. After our swim, we donned another coating of Bill's repellent. I wasn't sure it was not an attractant, though it did smell bad enough to maybe have an effect. Even with the concoction, the bugs was awful.

Toad spent most of the day in his blankets, sucking on his pipe. Bill mostly ignored him except for an occasional kick but when Bill decided we needed more paddles and told Toad to see to it and Toad ignored him, Bill exploded and in a flurry of vicious kicks and slaps, he had Toad tumbling and rolling around on the ground, to the delight of the other two. I had to pull Bill away. Jake grudgingly carved paddles. Bill let him alone until, inspecting the paddles and deeming them unusable, Bill hurled them into the brush.

Just past dusk we boarded and were on our way down the peaceful waters of Saint Sacrement. Bill told Toad to paddle hard if he wanted to keep his scalp. He did, for a half-hour, then his strength gave out and he was useless. The two hired men were a little better. Not much. Schaack had assured us they were accustomed to the rigors of the trail but they showed little promise. Toad held sway over them with the threat of his father's wrath. The littler one, Ben, kept out of the way, like a sneaking ferret. I didn't trust him at all.

Jake lit his pipe on the lake, in the dark. I smashed his hand with my paddle. Stupid on my part for the ashes might have set the canoe on fire. The birch canoe would burn quickly, did it catch, but the pipe, small as the glow might be, would be a beacon on an otherwise dark lake. Toad complained for the pipe embers burning a hole in his fancy shirt. Said I owed him the cost of the shirt.

Bill or me had to be all the time watching him for fear of what he might do. What he didn't do was his share of the work. Only what mattered to him was his comforts. The pudgy fool thought he was on a lark which had somehow got out of hand. I tried to get through to him the seriousness of our position in this dangerous land. He insisted his father's letter of protection with the French seal was all we needed. I could not make him see just how wrong he might be.

It took us three nights to cover Saint Sacrement, a distance which should only have taken two. Our lack of speed was exasperating and on our last night, when we got to the north end, Toad said we had earned a full day and night of rest. Bill said, "Slow as we are, we need all the dark there be." He said the trade fair might be over by the time we got there. This had no effect on Jakop until Bill pointed out, "Your daddy will take away your fancy living iffen you don't bring back his profit."

Whilst the others got some sleep, I spooked the portage trail. Along the crick, downstream from the falls, I found the remains of a camp, white men and Indians, no more than two days ago. Smugglers, or bandits looking to prey upon smugglers? The Indians were Iroquois, by the sign, which didn't mean they were friendly. Our Iroquois had relations who had taken up the hand of the black-robes and lived along the shores of the Saint Lawrence River. These renegades were foes of the English, and even our own Iroquois, in these times of uneasy alliances, would be tempted by the chance for fresh scalps and plundered trade goods. I returned to camp. Bill was on watch, the others were sleeping. I told Bill what I had seen. Me and him talked it over and even in as bad a shape as we was for the phases of the moon and for darkness to cover us when we got to Scalp Point, we decided we better stay off Portage Crick. We would use instead another portage trail, the one Hugh had told us of when we were coming down Corlear and had got down almost to Tyonderrogha. The trail went up over a hill from Corlear and came to Saint Sacrement at the clay banks, which was where we was now. We found the trail without too much trouble. Bill grimaced at the sight of it. A hill, not a mountain, but plenty steep. "Hard going," I said, "but safer." The others, when we woke 'em and they seen it, said they reckoned the portage trail would be safe enough. Bill told 'em to shut up, and Toad, still gaping and remembering the rigors of the earlier portages, tried to avoid this one. Or make it as easy on himself as he could. "As my father's representative," he said, "I do not have to do the work. It is for the hired men." He pointed at Joe and Ben, sure of having his way.

Bill pulled me away for some more talk. "Going any farther with these fools," he said, "is plain nuts." He was for leaving them. I was too but said we'd need Toad's letter when we get to Montreal. Bill said we could just do our own bargaining. "If we leave Toad," I said, "Schaack will get us somehow with the paper we signed. I know him. We'll be ruined, all our effort for naught. He'll put the law on us for smuggling." Bill was still not convinced. "If we scalp 'em," he said, making sure they heard him, "and swear it was Hurons what done it, Toad's pappy can't touch us." I shook my head. There wasn't nothin' for us 'cept to persevere.

A terrible hard climb over the hill which we had to do twice, first with the boats, then with the goods, awful burdens for men to carry on their backs up and over such steep ground. The trail was narrow where it existed and we had a time getting around ledges and boulders. We were a full day at it.

Just across the top and starting down the other side was a grotto, a bubbling spring set inside a cave, like the altar of a church. Around the cave were rocks and with how they were arrayed and with their flat tops, they might have been seats around the altar. A place of the utmost peacefulness yet dangerous, for the Indians would know of it. The water out of the spring was a thin brook, a mere trickle which flowed down alongside the trail and emptied into Corlaer a mile below the mouth of the Portage Crick.

At sunset and this after having paddled all night and just a short rest, we got onto Corlear. Big fishes spooked noisily around us. A splash in the murky waters close by, a thump against the side of the canoe, startling in the windless night, the scrape of something sliding along the hull, our canoes swaying to the bulk and power of these monster fishes. Some must a weighed fifteen, twenty pounds. I feared they might do damage to the fragile birch-barks. All down this narrow part of the lake, we seen the fishes as vague shadows ghosting near the surface. Some were slender, four-foot-long and with razor-sharp bills. Last year Alpheus Bush told me these were gars.

It began to drizzle, then a steady rain. Toad was for going to shore and seeking shelter. How I and Bill saw it was as a godsend. The dark sky would cover us from the moon, the rain would keep Jake from lighting his infernal pipe and would deaden the sound of our passing. "Might drive in the pickets," Bill said and he demanded we go all out for the Scalp Point narrows. Toad started to protest some more, Bill told him to shut up or he'd toss him out of the boat, then, and to us others, Bill said, "Let's go!"

****

Got to Scalp Point whilst it was still raining and as we got into the narrows, we slowed some for the quiet it would give us. I was jumpy with every splash of a fish but we saw no movement along either shore nor heard any shouts of alarm. Soon as we got past, Toad was for stopping. I called for more speed. We pushed hard for a few hours and went ashore before daybreak. Not at the well-hidden campsite Hugh had used and instead on the west shore above the northern end of the shallow bay which, with the lake, makes of the Point a north-south situated peninsula. We slept the day through. Bill woke up first and explored the creek. He found a waterfall which dropped forty or fifty feet into a pool among boulders. Said it was most pleasing. The pool held spawning salmon. He got us enough for supper and baked 'em in a small hole.

****

We tried to travel by Hugh's clock best we could remember and accomplish. My journal was a help but I wished I had been able to put things down immediately when I had seen them, rather than having to wait days. Surprisingly, we did move fast, driven by a strong, hot, south wind that brought with it haze and a constant threat of rain. We did not see nor hear anyone. Still traveling only at night, we got up the lake and past the island forts at the mouth, then up the river and a hike to the Trading Tree where we posted a message for our contact.

The place showed sign of recent activity but we could not find anyone, French or English. Whatever trading parties had come up from Albany were either in hidden camps around or more likely had already started for home. Might be we had passed 'em on the dark lake without seeing 'em. The drums were loud in the night. Bill said, "At least the redskins is still here." Our contact showed up on the second day. The same despicable little creature who'd met us when we was with Hugh. First thing, he asked for tobacco. Then he told us the festival was still going on but not for much longer. He said there was no fur left and advised us to give up our trade goods and get away whilst we could, he making ominous gestures about the Indians. Toad showed him the letter, they spoke together in the French tongue, then Frenchie spoke to all of us, in English, "There is a little fur left, mostly ze poorer stuff zat nobody vants. Ve had been expecting you. Vy are you so late?"

Toad said something about poor leadership on the part of Bill and me. Said we didn't know what the hell we were doing. Bill tried to stop him. Too late. The Frenchie grinned, looked at Toad and the other two. Frenchie understood only too well our weakness. He told us there mighten be some little fur left but said there would be no bargaining, we must simply take whatever he could get for us. He departed with a promise to return soon. We were all scared. "Toad has his letter from the governor," I said, trying to steady them. Bill said, "I reckon there's no way out of the frying pan now." I said Frenchie had made the same threats last year and nothing came of it. Said his talk was for driving up the price. "We'll be out of here in a couple of days."

Teamsters came and took away our trade goods in a wagon. We waited another day and when Frenchie came back, he was haughty, and despite his earlier insistence about us taking whatever fur was left over, he engaged us in long bargaining sessions. The weasel knew our need for haste and used it against us in haggling. The fur was poor and Bill and me twice caught him trying to short us. We could not get anything close to a fair price yet there'd be profit enough and through two days of anxious wrangling, our main concern was with getting the hell out. Frenchie kept telling us the Indian camp would soon break up but each time we tried to hurry the bargaining, he slowed it down for one reason or another.

One night, after our companions had gone to sleep, me and Bill went for a check on the Indians. There were fewer than what we had seen last year, many had probably already departed. Most of those we saw were still drunk and carousing but not all of them. Some was sobering and looked mean as hell. Then our trading was done and whilst we hurried to move our furs, the drums stopped. Fear lent wings to the feet of even the slowest and clumsiest. We all felt the need to get as far away as fast as we could.

There were no complaints of weariness or lack of food. All energy was put toward getting down the lake. We stayed close to the western shore and paddled all day and most of the night. Toad gave out early and about upset my canoe when he fell asleep. We were still going well into the next day, hardly resting at all. We were about done in but I insisted we keep going. Bill laughed, called me Hugh. I was in hopes of meeting up with other smugglers. If we could find another party to get in with, we'd all have a better chance but no others did we find.

By late afternoon, we had slowed enough so we knew there was no sense continuing without rest, and having come to where Hugh had shown us a creek with thickets screening the mouth from view out on the lake, we figured to stop. Sleep until dark then push on during the night. We had been sitting cramped up for so long, we were five bone-weary travelers.

Our canoes shot through the brushy opening into the turbulent waters of the crick. We wound our way upstream to a rock falls and went to shore. Our camp would be more than a hundred yards up from the lake. If there was pursuit, they would need to come in close to find us. Jake beamed for the distance we had made. He reckoned we were safe now. "Hell's bells," Bill said. "We ain't even ta Split Rock yet."

We dropped to the ground without any watch getting posted nor any precautions for waking up at sunset so's to travel all night. We simply went off to sleep, slept the rest of the day and all night too, not awakening 'til dawn. Jake was the last to awaken, we had to rouse him, he grumbling for no fire nor tea. Bill would have no nonsense and said so. They argued, I did not care to listen and I walked out to the point of land for a look onto the lake. It was a goddamn good thing I did!

Chapter VII – Flight!

I could see Indian war canoes off to the north and coming at such a pace we could never hope to outrun 'em. I eased on back to the others, who were about to pull our canoes out of the brush and get on the crick. "Shut up and stay down," I said. "Keep hidden and check your primings." Jake near peed his pants when I told 'em the danger. "Father said I would be safe," he said, his voice quavering. We all felt it. Our only hope right then was for the red men to pass by without seeing us, a possibility with us concealed back away from the lake. Unless they knew the crick as a regular camping place for smugglers and stopped to see if we were here. Bill snuck down to the water and when he came back, he said he had watched until they were gone 'round the next bend. He confirmed they were war canoes, four of 'em, each with seven or eight warriors. A mix of Ottawa and Huron, by their face paint. Bill said they were close enough to shore so they was scanning the bushes as they went past. He said one Indian seemed to look right at him, though the Indian gave no indication he'd seen Bill. Toad said Bill's rashness in going down there was going to get us all killed. Bill said he had been hidden well enough. Maybe, but there weren't no way of knowing and it might be the Indians had just kept past after seeing him so's to sneak back on us. As relieved as we were for them having gone by, we understood they were now interposed between us and the way home.

We had a hurried talk. "They will soon know we have not got to the carry at Saint Sacrement," Bill quietly pointed out, "and they'll split up. Some'll go down to Wood Creek to see are we down there, others will come back this way." Toad interjected hopefully, "Perhaps they are not coming for us and are only going to Crown Point for some other reason." Nobody else thought so. Bill said he reckoned we had just a few days and further reckoned we best use the time to advantage. "Else we'll all be minus our hair, for sure in hell them Indians, when they come back, will check all the places where we might a gone off into the woods."

Me and Bill talked about crossing the lake and heading for New

England by way of the Connecticut River Valley. Follow the big river south. Bill knew the country over there but said it would be too risky for it being Abenaki hunting grounds. We decided we'd go west into the mountains. The Hudson had its source somewhere out there. We could find the river and follow it down to Albany.

We weren't any of us hopeful of our chances. Those nimrods of the forest, soon as they figured us out, if they hadn't already, would fan out far and wide and there'd be no outsneakin' nor outrunnin' 'em once they got onto our trail. It'd be the end of us and with nobody the wiser.

We began making our preparations. First, we went through all the packs and loaded everything except weapons, food and fur into the canoes. We put heavy stones in too, then me and Bill stripped off our clothes and floated the canoes into deep water. Tore open the bottoms with our knives and sank them where we hoped they would not be found. Cookpots, extra powder and shot, clothing, blankets, all went to the bottom. We swam back to shore, the others were engaged in inept efforts to hide any sign of our having been there. Bill shook his head, we got dressed quickly and me and him finished the bungled job. Our packs were made up more to what each might carry rather than to an even split, which meant Toad carried little and the rest of us too much.

We shouldered our packs, took a bearing off a tall mountain which stood to the west and a little south. I seen Toad's knees knocking with fear and I spoke to steady him. "Jakop," I said, "we are a hell of a long ways from home. We either move fast, all of us together, or none of us is gettin' out."

"Hey, Toad," Ben said. "Might'n as well throw away thet paper a your'n. Isn't worth nuthin' now." The way Ben spoke surprised me. I didn't think he would talk so to his boss. I tried to be mirthful, which I did not feel. "Reckon them Injuns can read?"

"It be a long walk home," Bill said, his face darkly troubled; he was not hopeful, nor was I as we plunged into the forest. We walked an hour on mostly level ground beneath tall trees then clumb a rocky escarpment up and onto another nearly level shelf where the going should have been easier, a respite from the climbing, but was instead a horror of thick underbrush. This was for there having been a fire long enough ago so the clumps of undergrowth which had sprung up after the burning had spread and merged into a massive thicket of thorns and vines. Unable to immediately determine how far the thicket extended to either side and anxious as we were to put distance between us and the redskins, we plunged in and hacked our way through. When we came out on the other side, we were scratched and bleeding, our pants and shirts ripped. Toad carped as if it were Bill's and my fault. Bill threatened to cut him into quarters and have each of us carry a piece home to his father.

For the rest of the day we trudged and were mostly silent 'cept for Jake's griping and me and Bill's fretting over our too-slow pace. We reached the first of the tall mountains, which I had hopes of getting up and over by nightfall. When I said this to Bill, he pointed at Jake, who was struggling to keep up.

The mountain, once we got onto it, was nigh impossible for ones such as Toad and them others. Truthfully, me and Bill wasn't doing much better. Damn near straight up was how it was and us with heavy loads on our backs. Rocks overlaid with wet leaves made for slippery going and for bruised ankles and shins. I remembered some of what I had heard in the tavern about the dangers of lonesome country. Not just redskins, there were other things fatal to a man. A broken ankle, even a bad sprain, could mean death.

Not until noon of the next day did we approach the crest of the mountain. Bill and me, ahead of the others and as we neared the summit, were hopeful though doubtful for what might be on the other side. What we wanted to see was a valley and cutting the valley, the Hudson River. Or at least a stream deep enough to float a canoe which might take us to the Hudson. What we seen instead was a thickly wooded valley and on the other side, mountains taller than what we had just climbed. Behind these next looming highlands were the tops of taller peaks, indeed, there seemed to be many more ranges arrayed one behind another, each rising higher than the last. We could not see the tops of some of the farthest ones, so hidden were they in clouds. "That be a long way out there," Bill said. The others couldn't believe it, when they got up to us. "Shoulder ta shoulder, elbow ta elbow," Ben said. "We'ns'll never get over thet."

I feared Ben was right. It looked a far piece. Toad was for leaving the furs there on the summit, so the Indians might find them. If it was furs they be after, he reasoned, they'd maybe go home once they got 'em. Bill looked at Toad, who cringed for thinking Bill was going to whup on him but Bill was thinking on what Toad had said. I was considering it too. It might be our best chance. Drop the furs and hope it satisfied our pursuers. I talked it over with Bill and we decided the Indians wanted our furs but were just as surely coming for scalps. Abandoning our furs would proclaim our weakness. Bill suggested, only partly in jest, we leave the furs and three scalps and run like hell, him and me.

We plunged down into the valley. Straight down, and with the steepness and the weight on our backs, we was lurching and had often to grab onto a tree or rock to keep from falling forward onto our hands and knees, or faces, and when we did stumble thusly, we had to get helped back onto our feet.

The valley floor, when we got down to it, was cut by a stream flowing northeast, toward Corlaer. Too bad, for the stream held water enough to float us out. We waded across and began ascending the mountain on the other side, which was damn near straight up and with plenty of bare ledges to be got around.

Toad, each time we stopped to rest, said we had no chance of getting over the mountain and even if we did, then what? Climb the next one too? Partway up the slope and frustrated by our slow going, I called a halt and dropped my pack. Toad cringed for thinking I, in my anger, was going to beat on him for his incessant carping. Truth was, and not for the first time, what he had been saying was no more than what the rest of us was thinking. If we was going to outrun those Indians, this wasn't the way to do it.

I spoke to them of something Hugh had told me when me and Bill were with him. A few miles up from the south end of Saint Sacrement, a trail led off to the west, up and over a mountain which abutted the lake. Seven miles from the lake, the trail came to where the Hudson River was joined by what Hugh called the East Branch. Hugh said this East Branch weren't much of a flow but how I figured it, with all the rainwater and snowmelt it'd be bringing down out of the mountains, it'd be plenty big enough to float a canoe or a raft. I said with how close it got in to Saint Sacrement, the East Branch must lie to the east of where we was now. I proposed we turn away from those unscalable peaks and proceed south and a little east and look for this lesser river. I was certain the East Branch existed. Nothing Hugh had ever told me about the north woods had ever proven to be false and I had sometimes heard men in the tavern, men who had probably never been out here, talk about the East Branch as if they had seen it.

Toad and the helpers agreed at once. Bill was leaning toward it but pointed out the dangers. Firstly, he said, we might walk right back into our Indian pursuers or back to Corlear. I said did we go more south than east, we'd loop around any Indians which was after us, and did we overshoot the East Branch and find ourselves on Corlear, we'd be well south of where we had got off. We might even come out on Saint Sacrement. Whichever lake we came to, we could stay hidden along the shore whilst we hoofed in to Albany.

What else Bill said, men looking for the easiest way in the woods could convince themselves they were going in a particular direction even when they knowed they wasn't. Anxious to avoid the tall peaks and the lakes and did we not find the East Branch, we might get into Iroquoia, to be welcomed one way or another. I said did we get twisted around so's to get as far west as Iroquoia, we were dead even did we not blunder into Indians. I insisted the risks was worth taking. With Bill admitting the impossibility of getting over them western peaks, we emptied our packs and satchels of things which had earlier seemed important and covered it all with rocks and brush. "Let's go," Bill said, and with Toad and the others slow getting goin', he said, "Get god-damn movin'. Now!" My own nerves rattled, I said, "Come on, Bill. If they don't want to follow, to hell with 'em."

Bill and me shouldered our packs and started off, the others coming along behind. Once back down into the valley and still going a little west, we began what was a steady uphill climb south along the north-flowing crick. It was still hard goin' but not nearly so bad as heading straight up into them mountains. Bill's pace soon had Toad and the helpers strung out behind. They could either stay with us or get taken by the Indians, Bill didn't give a damn, nor did I. They knew what we were thinking because as much as they griped, they came along.

****

The ground generally descending to the south, we were finding the passes and gaps we needed for making our way whilst the peaks, the farther south we got and though we still avoided them when we could, weren't so tall. The flatter lay of the land made for faster going yet it was hard enough with those furs on our backs and there was a hard going of a different sort for us staying in the bottomlands. The ground was often swampy, spruce and cedar bogs formed by the rivulets of water which flowed down off the sides of the mountains. Pools of fetid black water and muck to pull the moccasins off a man's feet. Impossible to wade in some places, we had to retreat back up along the rocky hillsides, often into thick brush. Brambles slapped us as we walked and we saw patches of blueberries too green for eating, just it was something to remind us how hungry we were. "A damn shame them berries t'ain't ripe," Ben said, his first words in days.

We struggled over downed trees, moss-covered and rotting; stately ferns rose up out of the dead wood to present strange images of life and death; tumultuous waters rushed through rock-glens perilous to cross. These crick beds, in a few months, would be cracked and dry. Now, and augmented by the last of the winter snowmelt, they were roaring creeks. The water was cold and good tasting.

We were on the lookout for blazes on trees, which often marked old paths. Trappers or Iroquois or even the occasional lone hunter might wander this country from time to time and any trailblazers of yore passing through would have felt the same as we did about the mountains and would a found the best way through 'em with the least amount of climbing. Any trail we found might lead to the East Branch or to a tributary which would take us there.

Each night, when we bedded down, we slept fully clothed, guns primed and to hand. We'd eat a meager meal, a mouthful or two of dried corn and some too-tough jerky meat or half-smoked fish, did we have any. Toad would whine for wantin' a smoke fire for driving off the bugs. I wanted a fire too. The blackflies and mosquitoes, wicked during the days, were worse at night but there would be no fires.

Most nights we heard wolves. Sometimes they were close, more often they were out along a far-off mountain ridge, but even at a distance their howls carried across the valleys and same as when an owl hooted and another answered, we listened intently. Wolf, owl, or the prelude to an Indian attack?

One night as we were settling in, Bill pointed at Toad, sittin' on a log, removing torn moccasins from weary, swollen feet. Rubbing his aching toes, Fat Boy was utterly worn out. Bill said, "I don' reckon Jake'll come back up here again, no matter what his daddy says." I couldn't help laugh. "A month more of this," I said, "and we'll make a mountain man out of him, by god." Bill shook his head. "Not even in a year," he said.

****

Seven hard days had passed since we turned south. We still hadn't found a stream flowing our way and our food was about run out, just we stopped sometimes so's me and Bill could catch fish out of ponds and streams. We were stumbling and without sun or stars to guide us, I feared we were sometimes walking in circles.

We had thrown away our furs. First to do it was Toad. Always was he lagging behind and once when we stopped and he came up, he was without his cache. Bill and me screamed at him but we didn't neither of us send him back to get 'em nor go back ourselves. Then, sometime over the next few days, the two hired men came up without theirs, then me and Bill dropped ours. We didn't make any attempt to hide 'em, we just walked away. We didn't really have any choice, or maybe we did have a choice, our furs or our lives. With as little as we'd had to eat and with the rough going, no longer did we have the strength for staggering beneath the weight. Told ourselves we would come back for them when it was safe. This was delusional. If the Indians didn't find them, the critters surely would.

Come an evening, when we stopped and bedded down, Bill taunted Jake, same as he did most nights. "No fire tonight, Jake." Bill then added, "And naught to eat 'cept the last of the corn." We split the night into five watches, gave Toad the first one. I had the last. Sometime during Jake's watch I awoke and saw he was asleep. Lying on the ground, snoring loudly, his gun barrel pointing at his own damn head. I stayed up the rest of his watch. Hard to sleep with him looking out for me. On my own watch and with the sun coming up over the eastern mountains and with more light showing, I roused them. The day came in bright, Jake complained of an aching back, said he needed more rest. Who didn't? We prepared to go, they were all grumbling, even Bill. I couldn't blame 'em. I was pretty damn played out myself.

Hardly had we got started than we came to a pond down inside of a valley. We didn't see an outlet to the north or east, which was usually how it was with the ponds. This raised our hopes we had at last come to something with a southwest flow and as we circled 'round the shore to the south and still without finding an outlet, our hopes rose even more. A few hours getting around the pond and there was the outlet. No more than a trickle, partially held back by a mound of sticks and brush but surely going to the southwest, by the sun. "Here's your goddamn East Branch," Jake said, about spitting the words. He was most always vicious now with hunger and fatigue.

"You may be right, Jake," I said. The crick maybe wasn't the East Branch but, and with its southerly flow, it just as probably went there.

We all of us felt our spirits lifted. We knew we still had a long way to go, maybe farther than what we were capable, but we at least weren't lost anymore. Bill pronounced our chances improved, said we might soon put this nightmare behind us.

Whilst the others of us rested, Bill went ahead for a look. He wasn't gone long before he returned with more good news. The creek held to a steady southwesterly course and walking alongside of it wouldn't be too bad. He said there was another, bigger pond just below where we were and said this next pond was held back by an abandoned beaver dam, inactive for a long time but still holding plenty of water. I said the detritus which blocked the pond we were alongside of might also have been a beaver dam. "Sure as hell," Bill said, after looking at it and for us finding the stumps of trees with the unmistakable look of having been gnawed many years ago by rodent teeth. Out on the pond was a rounded hump of branches and mud which might once have been a beaver house.

We followed the stream, steady walking now for the easier going and for the hope we were feeling. Not only had we found our way but we must surely be getting close enough in toward Iroquois country so them others, if they still be on our trail, would needs be careful. Did the Iroquois get after 'em, the hunters would become the hunted! Of course, an Iroquois hunting party out here could be a danger for us too, so mired in the forest. The Iroquois were our friends but we could not depend on them.

****

Two more days and the creek, which had been fast plunging down over rocks and small waterfalls, had flattened with the land into a navigable watercourse with ponds, marshes and meadows created long ago by beavers. Abandoned remnants of bygone times. The beavers were trapped out of this country but the dams, even with gaping holes and entire sections collapsed, often held back plenty of water.

We followed Bill's lead and with the volume of the creek growing for all the rivulets entering into it, Toad began insisting it was time we built canoes and floated out. He said he was damn sick of walking. Who wasn't? Bill said, "Soon enough," his voice without the vexation it usually held for Toad. Bill was surely feeling the betterment of our chances. We all were. "Toad," Bill said as we walked, "you might get back after all to Albany and to your easy way of living."

Toward evening and about in my ear, there came the crack of a rifle. We all jumped for cover, except for Jake, the damn fool was wreathed in smoke for having shot a deer. The gut-shot doe, a small one, bounded, careened, and fell over. Joe finished her with his knife; Bill and me were rough on Jake for having fired. He said he was hungry. "Hungry, hell," I said. "We wanna stay alive." I went for him, Bill grabbed me. "Don't let go a me or I'm gonna whip his arse," I said. Bill laughed. "Have at 'im," he said and he let go of me. I hit Jake on the jaw, knocking him down. He stayed on the ground, I stood over him, my fists clenched. I'd have hit him again did he get up but looking down on him and with him crying, the anger went out of me and I felt only pity. His crying was for the hurt I had put on him but it was also for all the nightmarish days we had spent in the woods. All the fear and futility and now and with the pressure easing, it was as if his own dam had burst. Our powder-puff got up, rubbing his chin where I'd hit him. "We have to move from here, now," I said. Jake said the deer was his to do with as he pleased and he was going to eat it right there and now.

I lifted the deer up onto my shoulders. We walked away from the brook and in half a mile we stopped. Whilst I dressed and quartered the deer, Toad tried to dart in and grab some meat, to do what, I wasn't sure, eat it raw, maybe, for surely we were starving. I waved him off, he backed away but kept coming back and each time, Bill chased him with his knife. Toad, crouched and lurching, evaded the blade and giggled and carried on as if the knife-wielding was naught but a game. We were all laughing heartily as much for our own feelings of relief as for Toad's antics, he having most surely gone 'round the bend.

We packed as much of the meat as each of us could carry and after covering the head and guts with branches and leaves, we walked some more until Bill decided we had gone far enough. Jake began gathering kindling for a fire. I told him Bill would be making our fire. Toad defiantly struck a match, I about leaped for his throat, to stop him afore he set his sticks to smoking. City boy reckoned the only way to cook venison was with the biggest fire he could get going in the shortest time. Bill dug a hole for a smokeless cookfire. "Got to watch you every minute," I said to Toad. "Can't never turn my back on you."

I headed up our backtrack, afraid for who might a heard the shot. This near to sunset the birds should all have been trilling their last songs of the day, yet they were silent. I got back to the brook and followed it upstream, staying off it. Came to a pond. The flock of ducks which had been there when we'd come by was gone. Maybe on account of the rifle shot. I reckoned I was getting a mite spooked but the gray squirrels and reds often searched for food this time of day and now there were none. Everything quiet 'cept for the wind through the trees. Then came the cry of a blue jay, a sign of danger or just the strident cry of a puffy old male? He was surely agitated about something. He kept at it and was joined by others. Figured the jays were arguing with crows or a raven.

I started back toward camp. The smell of the roasting meat wafted my way, my stomach roiling, hunger and nerves all in a bile. Bill came along with a venison haunch, well-cooked. "Grabbed it afore there weren't none left," he said. "Them boys was eatin' 'er, fur, bones, and all." We sat down to eat and talked quietly.

"Green meat," Bill said, "will give 'em the infernal thunderbums tomorrow, no doubt." We laughed. "Course it'll slow us down," he said, "with them all day cleaning themselves." Bill said he had warned them about eating too much to once, said Jake had ignored him and had the meat half-eaten whilst it was yet raw. I said as how I figured Jake was about done. Weak as his body had become, his mind was worse. Bill agreed. Jake was fast losing the last of his sanity and didn't figure to make it out of the woods, even if us did. "Only thing keeping him going," Bill said, "is how mad he is with me'n you for the way we been treatin' him. Right now he's telling Ben what he's gonna have his father do to us when we gets to Albany." I ate slowly, mixing the venison with my last handfuls of dried corn. Not saying much, still bothered by the worries of what might be in the woods with us. I finished what meat Bill had brung and wished I had a shot of rum. Hell, I'd have settled for tea.

We got back to camp. Jake was lying on his back with his legs crossed at the ankles, his hands clasped behind his head, which was propped up against a pile of spruce branches. He was picking at his teeth with a sharpened twig and had a look of contentment. I spoke of my uneasiness and said we should move again. Jake, feeling brash for having fed himself and us too, laughed at me. Said he wasn't moving and said they were going to get started building canoes first thing in the morning. I warned them all again. One of the hired men said I was spooked at every shadow and even Bill, who should a knowed better, sided with them. They would stay where we were. Nothing I said could get them to see things my way and mad as I was, I got more mad for Bill siding with Jake.

Bill said any pursuing Indians would have got us by now and since they hadn't, our only concern was to get to hell out of the woods and the fastest way out was boats. Ben said as how Indians didn't have perseverance enough to have followed us for so long. "And don' forget," he said. "They had to find where we got off Corlaer afore they could commence looking."

I fumed, Jake amused himself and the hired men by describing all of what his father was sure to do to me when we got back to Albany. "I'll whip your arse again iffen you say another word," I said. His two idiots laughed, at Toad, or at me, I didn't know, nor care. Bill said we'd all do better in the morning for a good sleep. He said we were far enough from Corlaer and close enough in toward Mohawk country so's not to have to worry about Hurons. I said we had at least better get farther from the crick before we bedded down. Bill asked, "How could we find our way in the dark?" Indeed, it was almost pitch black.

Jake said if I didn't want to join them in the morning in making their canoes, I could keep on walking down along the crick and they'd give me a wave when they went past in their shiny new boats. They all laughed at this and I got even madder. Especially at Bill, who should have knowed better. "To hell with all of you," I said. "I ain't staying here, for damn sure." Bill sneered something at me, and I, never having been so cross with him, nor him with me, stalked away. I walked up the crest of a hill and in a fairly open area among some bushes, sixty yards from camp and high enough so I could see down into it, I lay down and fell off to sleep. I tossed fitfully and kept waking up, too mad to sleep. To come so far only to get damn careless for thinking we were out of the soup. What little sleep I got was bothered by nightmares of those Indian drums pounding loud in my ears. I dreamt they was beating for my scalp. I slept some more, then awoke again.

The weather had turned cooler, the wind moaned. I was thankful for not having tossed away my wool blanket. Even in summer at these high altitudes, the nights are cold. The stars shone sharp and clear through the treetops. Promise of a pretty morning with no clouds to hold in the Earth's heat. I fell asleep and was awakened by the smell of smoke. Jake had got hisself a fire going and had curled up alongside it and gone to sleep. I saw the faint glow then the flare of the embers stirred by the wind in the moonless night. I went down, to kick and rail at Jake, then, and deciding to hell with it, I put out the fire and walked back up the hill.

The hunting wolf howled and I recalled Hugh saying the forest animals would warn a man of the presence of danger if said man would but listen. Another wolf answered and an eerie chill ran along my spine, all the way up my neck. My hair stood on end. The howling sounded nearly the same as any I had ever heard, yet something was different about it. Heard 'em a few more times and could not convince myself what I was hearing was something four-legged.

I thought about what Bill and the others had said, about having outrun the Indians. I wanted to believe it but didn't. Those Ottawas or Hurons, or whatever they be, was born to the woods. They might have been slow in cutting our trail but once they got onto us, they would hunt us with the ease of wolves running deer in deep snow. I would not feel safe until the gates of Albany banged shut behind me.

The others of my party did not stir. Nobody stood guard through the night. They thought us perfectly safe. Even Bill. The green meat running through Jake and the other two should a had 'em up and down all night but I didn't hear 'em moving around. Waiting for the first light to show in the east, I lay listening; then, closing my eyes again, I drifted into fretful sleep.

I awoke suddenly and with the certainty something was prowling the darkness along the edge of the camp. I put my back against the ledge, musket primed and ready. I listened but only the one sound had I heard. A rustling of leaves on the ground or maybe the wind through the branches. The glow of morning brightened in the east, first light filtered down, making shadows, and still with nothing to see, no sign of movement among the trees and rocks. The sleep too slow in leaving my brain, I couldn't shake the drowsiness.

I heard the wolf howl, closer in now. Told myself it really was a wolf which must have followed the smell of the meat, and finding the entrails, the wolf was calling the pack in to dinner. Or had the smell emboldened the wolves enough so they were coming fer us? I was shaking with the cold and with the dread creeping into my heart. The sun was not yet fully up over the eastern mountains but enough light was penetrating the woods so the birds should have been stirring and yet they weren't. No blue jays shrilled in the treetops. My companions, in their camp below, slept on.

****

Shots rang out, war whoops pierced the air, the camp was swarmed by painted redskins screeching and swinging warclubs. I got on my belly and raised my rifle. Reckon I was too scared to fire but with so many of 'em, must've been twenty, and all jumping around, I couldn't get my sights on any one of 'em. I lowered my rifle and watched in disbelief as Bill and the others struggled to rise from sleep and defend themselves. Two of the dirty snakes were holding Bill, one on each arm, a third was shaking a tomahawk in his face. Toad was shouting in Dutch and French about the letter in his pocket. Toad's men were yellin' for me to come down and save them.

Bill shook off the Indians what had ahold of him and slashing with his knife and with as tall as he was, them Indians looked like boys dancin' around a man. They were reaching for Bill's hair but couldn't none of 'em reach high enough to grab it. Until one got up onto Bill's back and locked his legs around Bill's waist and began carving his scalp whilst Bill was yet fightin'. Blood poured down Bill's face and he dropped to his knees and they kept him there, an Indian twisting each of his arms whilst a third drove the spike of a warclub down into his head, damn near splitting it in half. Then and with how they was all over him, I couldn't see him and one come up waving Bill's hair and dancing around with it. My boon companion executed, the Indians carving his flesh with knives whilst others was tying Toad and the hired men to a tree. Ben and Joe were still calling out to me, Toad was waving his letter and screaming what it meant.

I was hunched down, unable to move. The Indians were not coming for me. They must have missed seeing me when they had scouted our camp in the dark. Hoped they didn't know I was there but for as long as they had been tracking us and probably having collected our furs, they would have known how many we were and would surely be after me. I could not save the others; I could only save myself.

Chapter VIII – Bad Trip into Paradise

I grabbed up powder horn, possibles and pouch, threw down my blanket and fled through the forest. Behind me were Indian whoops and the high-pitched, ungodly shrieking of my companions, hard to believe men could cry out in such voices.

I came to the brook, or a different brook, and ran alongside it, the whoops and pleadings fading, and realizing staying with the rocky watercourse would make it easier for the Indians to trail me, I veered off into the denser woods. Running, stumbling through the thick June forest, I couldn't see more than a few feet in front of me for the leafy growth and for the sun not yet up enough to penetrate the deep glades through which I ran. I tore gasping through brush and low-hanging branches, all of it slapping me as I went, and when I got myself tangled in a thorn patch, I clawed through as if I were a man gone mad, which I reckoned I was.

I ran all day, west with the sun, and didn't stop for nothing 'cept gulps of air, which were sobs as much as gulps. I was slipping and stumbling and getting up and running some more. I should have been keeping more quiet and should have been doing things to cover my sign but I could think only of flight.

After a few hours and with my mind unnumbing, I realized how abject flight could cost my life. I needed to keep my wits, else I might run right back into the clutches of the Indians or box myself in a way which would hold me until they came up. If I would get away, I must use good sense. Easy enough to tell myself but a damn hard thing to do and on I ran with no thought to my direction nor of quiet.

Only did I run where I could go the fastest. This was stupid but my brain was chilled by the remembers of what I had witnessed. Savages slashing with knives and tomahawks and my last glimpse of Bill, the poor bastard shorn of hair, the spiked warclub coming down, splitting his head, brains and blood splattering, and the screams of the others. Two of 'em or maybe three, tied to trees for the infliction of unspeakable Indian deviousness. Our path to a quick fortune turned to ruin and death. I saw laughing demonic faces in all the shadows and I kept on even as my overworked body and mind demanded I stop.

Late morning of this worst of possible days, I finally had to stop. I sat down on a rock, my head in my hands. I was gasping for breath, retching; then, and fearful of the sounds I was making, I took gulps of air meant to suppress it. Now and understanding the need to go more smartly, I seen I had boxed myself, just as I had feared. I had got into perhaps the worst situation for a man getting chased by Indians. A level tableland situated between mountains. Probably not too big an area but with towering hardwoods leafed-out so their canopy allowed no sun's rays to filter down and with an unbroken sameness on every side of me, I was entirely bereft of any sense of direction. Panicked, I began going in short bursts, first in one direction, then another and all whilst knowin' the Indians could easily navigate the gloaming and would soon be upon me.

Now, and as fearful as I was for the expectation of the quiet around me erupting with warcries, I did what was the hardest thing for a man in my situation. I took slow, precise steps in what I could only hope was a single direction. I did this for what seemed an agonizingly long time but was only minutes, and seeing a shaft of sunlight, I went toward it. Then another shaft. The thinnest of beams but with more of 'em and guided by the angle of their slanting, I kept on in a single direction. I went at a steady walk even as my mind urged me to precipitate flight. Didn't know what direction I was going. Mighten be back toward the Indians. It didn't matter. What mattered was gettin' out of the flat, half-lit sameness, and with more of the light streaming down for the trees not so dense now along their tops, I got glimpses of the sun. I felt the ground rising slightly beneath me and I burst out from under the trees and into sunlight along a rocky hillside.

Now and chastened, I began taking the precautions necessary to keep myself alive. Paid attention to where I was going and blurred as best I could the traces of my passing. I walked in cold streambeds and along the lengths of downed trees. I jumped or stepped from one dead log to another and from rock to rock. I used pine branches to sweep where my feet touched the ground and when I came to potholes or mudflats, I skirted 'em for how visible my tracks would be.

By sundown, I had got over the top of a mountain and down onto the open ledges on the other side. Scrub oak and granite boulders. The sides of the mountain falling away sharply to west and south looked too steep for scrambling down. I walked the ledges in search of a way off the slopes and was startled by a sudden thumping from a bush. Scairt for thinking it was an Indian, I realized I had flushed a partridge. Just as I got calmed, a second bird flew off and with the same startling effect on me, then another. A cover was roosting in the trees and it struck me, here was a place for stopping. Not even Indians could sneak in on me without spooking the birds. I could rest and be off at the first part of the day. I made my bed on a grassy spot under an overhanging rock ledge.

The wind blowing cold, I shivered, too scared to sleep. I watched the woods around me, what little I could see in the dark, my mind filled with sad, despairing thoughts. I dozed some whilst waiting for the dawn, when I could maybe get me a partridge with a stick. Probably not, for the birds would be wary and would need to be cooked and I could in no way risk a fire.

Before morning, rain came in. At first it fell softly, not too bad in my exposed bed. Then it came harder and the wind began whipping it in on me and the water poured down off the ledge. I tried to burrow deeper into the granite and though soaked, I was grateful for knowing the rain would erase whatever sign I had left. I finally got up and moved to shelter beneath a pine tree.

The sun rose, the rain stopped, I clumb down off the slope, the descent not as difficult as it had looked yesterday. I headed west, into the deepest mountains, those which we had heretofore avoided. As daunting as it might be, I would put as much of those heights as I could between me and the Indians. They, already with scalps and furs, might decline pursuit for a single scalp. They'd maybe just laugh and shake their heads for knowing the mountains would finish me.

For days I kept to my westerly course. The sun mostly stayed hidden behind dark shifting clouds, the rain was on and off. I traversed mountains and forests of massive pines, and not getting jumped by Indians, I began to hope they had maybe miscounted the number of our party. Or maybe all of what they had done or were still doing to Ben and Joe and maybe Toad had sated their savage lust. I remembered some of what Hugh's men had told me about what it meant to get taken by Indians. Torture, which the Indians called caressing. Poor souls made to dance and sing whilst enduring unspeakable horrors, and were the inflictors skillful enough, it might go on for days. This had always amused Hugh's men. Maybe Ben and Joe's caressing was what was keeping me alive. For a short while longer, anyway.

I doubted it. No distance between me and the Indians would be enough. Savagery such as theirs could never be sated and they had already shown themselves deviously clever and relentless in hunting us. More likely some of the Indians had stayed for the caressing whilst others pursued me. Did they get up with me, I would fight to the death. Better to go the way Bill had, as horrible as it was, than get tied to a tree for the amusement of the savages.

As I got in toward the highest peaks, the country took on a more wilder aspect, if such be possible, and had these mountains ever before witnessed the footfalls of a white man? High rocky cliffs, the ledges barren of cover except for the lone birch or stunted pine, hardy little things growing out of crevasses and exposed to the constantly blowing wind. Rivulets rolled down through rocky cuts, bogs in flat bottoms between the mountains, ravines too sheer for climbing in or out but which must be got across and always those awful mountains, steep and treacherous.

I trekked hard in the daytime and at night too, if there be sufficient moonlight. I had left my blanket when I fled the attack and without it and without a fire when I hunkered down, I'd get the shakes. Better it was to go on in the dark, tracking with the stars. I about froze when it rained and reckoned fever and chills would take me if Indians didn't.

Any time I stopped for more than just a breather, I set out snares, strips of rawhide and sticks, and I was delirious whenever I got me a rabbit. I'd get a smokeless cookfire going and before my rabbit was much more than singed, I'd get scared of the fire and put it out.

I got fish, too, at those creeks where small trout were tucked under the banks or against the sides of rocks. Using my steel fishhooks and line, and grubs which I dug up or found under rocks for bait, I caught plump little seven-inchers. They were pretty things, and as hungry and scairt as I be, I'd stop to admire their colors which sparkled when I held them up to the sunlight. Their dark backs were speckled white, blue and orange, and with the bright red slashes of their bellies, they were as pretty as the June sunsets.

****

I worked my way up into a range of mountains taller than any I had yet ascended. From the top of one peak and so high up was I, patches of cloud swirled below me. The mountain was part of a range which rolled in parallel lines to the northwest, a daunting vista, and with the afternoon sun reflecting off the farthest peaks, I realized the white-capped tops shining against the backdrop of the blue sky was snow. Snow-covered clear into summer.

With naught for me out there 'cept death, I turned to the southeast, more south than east. I walked through pine forests with scant underbrush. The pines were devoid of branches to a height of thirty feet, this made a man feel small but enabled me to move along swiftly. The going was nearly soundless for the brown carpet of dead pine needles layering the ground. Easy walking but these pinelands were as barren of game as a desert. Just there was the overhead chatter of squirrels and birds, mostly jays.

After many days of this and following a crick which flowed south and east, I got down into where the mountains, whilst still craggy and steep, weren't so tall, the forests a mix of hardwoods and pines. Plenty of oak and chestnut, and around the ponds when I came to 'em was more of the white birch than I would a thought could grow in any one place. Groves of the majestic white-barked trees in clumps of three and four long slender trunks slanting a hundred feet skyward. The color and sturdiness of this tree, which is not much seen below Saratoga, was most amazing.

Came into beech groves too, the gray-barked trunks ancient and magnificent. I seen one tree which, even amongst trees so large as these, stood out for the immensity of its girth and its height too, as I got up close and tilted my head all the way back so's to look up into it. Initials and a date were carved into the smooth gray bark and I thought on who might a done the carving. English, Dutch, French, no way of knowing. The date was 1680, and had some earlier solitary man, in the same straits as me, lost and despairing, stopped to make a record of his passing? Proof of having lived and died? Funny to think a doomed man could leave a record of hisself and all these years later, along come another doomed man, to take note of the first.

I came to a pond and saw two small deer along the brushy shore of the far side. Fork-horns just into the velvet. They were of the same size and horn growth and might have been twins. They seemed peaceful at their ease and I felt it too. Finished drinking, one deer pawed the ground in front of the other and they engaged in a mock combat, rising up on their rear legs in a dance which would soon be real fighting in their quest for harems.

As hungry as I was, I thought about shooting one of 'em. So many days had passed since we was attacked and without any sign of pursuit, I had in no way discounted the possibility the Hurons were after me but as much as I feared bringing them in with a shot, same as Toad had done, I needed meat. Besides, and again same as with Toad, any Indians close enough to hear a shot wouldn't need help finding me. Surely they had not ever been in pursuit, else they'd have taken me by now. The two deer sniffed me and bolted before I could get around to where I could shoot. Just as well, for with the distance, I couldn't a held steady on 'em. Rather have a turkey, anyway.

****

Farther south, I was deep into what had been beaver country. Low-lands inundated by water backed up by long-since departed beavers. I could only marvel at the transformed landscape, the size and length of the dams and at how solidly they was put together. So many years must have passed since they were built and still they held back water though in places the water had opened gaps and washed out entire sections. Must a taken generations of beavers to make dams such as these.

All those dams and ponds meant the most infernal of bogs. These I avoided when I could by getting a short way back up the slopes and looping around, same as what me and my companions had done, back afore they got taken. Sometimes I'd convince myself a swamp was passable and instead of gettin' up on a slope, I'd get into wet stinking boneyards of tall grasses, dead cedar trees yet standing and the rotting trunks and stumps of those what had fallen.

The worst about the bogs, worse even than the ankle-deep muck, was the swarms of bugs. They hadn't been so bad up high with the colder nights and a steady wind out of the north but here they were infernal. Blackflies attacked my exposed parts; clouds of mosquitos rose up each time my feet sank into the ooze. It all had me swollen. To prevent the worst abuses, I kept myself smeared with bog slime. This served to keep the devils off some but they were always probing for ways to get me, and with my clothes not much more than threads, they got down inside my hunting shirt and up my pant legs. The con-sarned infernalness of the little bastards cannot be overstated. They must be met to be truly known, so ferocious and constant were they. I had heard of men driven crazy from the torment. One might believe everything ever been told about the misery inflicted. It seemed the lowly biters would be my demise.

At night, I'd find a dry place for hunkering down. Nighttime in the

99

summer swamps was an unending clamor, noisier than Albany on a Saturday night. A concert of life and death. Bullfrogs, tree frogs, owls hooting, the hum of longjaws buzzing at my ears, a bear gruntin' and carryin' on. Coons in a spat over a meal; the exultant yip of a coyote snatching a bigfoot rabbit; the rabbit's cries like those of a babe. Then the howl of the wolf silences all others. The howl brings me terror and thoughts of my companions, dead and unburied. Somber of mind, I listen carefully to determine if it really is a wolf.

****

Always was I ravenously hungry. The few rabbits and trout I was taking were not going to keep me alive much longer and now I was into the hardwoods with so many acorns and beechnuts, the deer and bear spoor was plentiful and I decided I would shoot the next deer I saw. Get me some meat.

First, my gun must be cleaned, the old powder replaced. I got down inside a rocky gulch where the sunlight got in but the wind didn't. Using a strip from the tattered remains of my hunting shirt, I dried and cleaned my rifle in the growing heat of the sun on the rocks. This task consumed most of a morning. Cleaning a gun is a tedious job but must be done frequently else the barrel will become pitted and useless. I got the gun apart on a flat rock and after I got 'er cleaned up, I dumped the last of the powder onto the rock. The powder was damp and caked. I separated out the parts which did not seem the worst, broke up the clumps and spread it out for the sun to dry it.

The overall look of the powder, its poor quality, evoked a bitter remember. The powder had been advanced to us by Toad's father against the expected profits of the trip. Van Schaack had assured Bill and me the powder was top grade. From the best manufacturer in the world, an outfit in Spain. More likely poorly-made colonial powder from right there in Albany. Bad as it was, I knew, did I get home, I would have to pay Schaack for top-quality powder. I had signed the smuggling agreement and legal or not, the conniving Dutchman would have included the inflated cost of the powder against our profits, of which there were none. I only hoped I might get home to confront him about it.

I had enough powder for just two shots, maybe three, iffen the powder and flints would spark. Might be dangerous to try. But if she did go off, the shot would be a hard one, and still fearful of Indians, I'd feel better for knowing did they strike, I might get one of 'em.

That same day, clomping noises, footsteps from a stand of pines drew me up short and I was grateful for a loaded gun. Enough noise to be a man, or men. My fears returned at once. Hurons! Or Iroquois. Or Toad. If there'd been a Frenchie in with the Hurons, Fat Boy's pleadings about his letter for the French governor might have saved him and he had maybe convinced Frenchie I'd bring enough of a ransom to be worth saving too. Maybe the four of us, me and Toad, Ben and Joe, was to get took to Montreal. Irrational to think it but bitter to contemplate my more likely fate, to be caressed by the fiends after having eluded them for so long.

I stayed still and watched. Nothing more did I hear or see and just as I was thinking I had imagined it, I heard it again. Footsteps back behind the trees. Branches pushed aside. Sure as hell somebody was in there. Stinging sweat ran down into my eyes. Face to face yet again with the horror I had striven to drive out over the last weeks. Figured this was the end and whilst fighting back the bile rising in my throat, I checked the priming and hoped the gun would fire. I held steady for who might be in there.

Through a small opening in the brush, I seen a patch of buckskin. No feathers or paint did I see. Whoever it was, he, or they, had stopped moving. Must have got wind of me. I did not think from the hard footsteps it could be a red man but couldn't be sure. The steps and all the rest of the noise might a been ruses to get others in behind me. Kept watch over my shoulder. My nerves about done in, from out of the trees stepped a small moose, a yearling calf unsure whether to freeze or flee. My stomach growled for meat. Got my sights behind the calf's shoulder; I could not miss. Whilst I further considered the wisdom of a shot, the calf began to move off. I watched 'til it was a step from getting back into the shelter of the trees. That was too much and I touched off the trigger and waited whilst holding my aim. There was a delay which seemed a misfire. Goddamn Schaack and his cheap powder, then Kerblam! The gun bucked against my shoulder. I could not see for the smoke, and as it cleared, the moose was down. Meat! My stomach quivered with anticipation. Reloaded my rifle, hoping nobody was around to have heard the shot. I commenced work on the carcass. I drained the blood and began skinning and carving the animal. I would retain enough of the hide to make a cover for my gun and a mantle for draping over my shoulders. So keen was I at my bloody task, I was unaware of Momma in the bush until out she charged, straight for me. Bent on mayhem. I couldn't get to my rifle. The only escape from those flying hooves was to shimmy up the nearest tree, a thin spruce. Got up in time but with the tree not stout enough to hold me, I was helpless whilst the tree bent me ever closer to the ground. Momma alternately licked her calf, to bring it back to life, then she'd stomp her feet, snort, charge and ram the tree, which ramming nearly brought me down on top of her. I hung on grimly, easy prey for anybody coming to see about the gunshot.

The cow gave up and moved off into the brush. I swung down from my perch and whilst mindful she might return, I resumed my work. When I finished, I circled the kill at a distance. Only when I was sure nobody was spooking did I return and begin a small cookfire among some rocks. The smell of sizzling veal about had me in a frenzy, the meat not long cooked before this young hoss was into it. As hungry as I was, I tried not to eat too fast and make myself sick. Fresh venison can be troublesome. I ate my fill, drank from a stream and resumed the skinning work. I set more of the meat over the smoking coals, covered it with moose skin and left it overnight. In the morning, I wrapped my gun and powder horn in moose skin and packed the cooked meat into a bag of skin and hoisted it over my shoulder on a leather strap. Had to leave most of the meat, no way to carry so much, nor any sense in it, with how quickly it would spoil in the June heat.

****

Two days later, a day cool and cloudy and whilst climbing a steep escarpment, chills was running through me and I was having a spell of dizziness, which I was feeling more often. I came to the top, onto a sheer ledge. The wind had shifted and was out of the west, the air heavy, a storm was coming. I stood along the edge of the precipice. Mantled in my moose skin and with the wind in my face, I gazed out toward the approaching storm. Lightning flickered off the bellies of the clouds and I had sad thoughts of Bill, my partner and friend, dead in the mountains. And of Toad and the others, caressed, their remains to hang on trees until their flesh rotted away and their bones slid to the ground. All dead and me soon to be. Then came thoughts of Pop's tavern. Of rum, and of meat roasting on a spit. Such thoughts as these always sank my spirits and stirred the fatalism which was a constant pall over me.

I remembered something Arnold Baldwin had spoken of once. The gods, he said, often gave a man what he desired but they delighted in giving it in a fashion other than what the man anticipated. So it was with me. I had wanted a life in the mountains and here was the rest of my life, as long or short as it might be. The Wild Man of the Mountains, forever doomed to wander, a legend to be glimpsed and to chill men, red and white, around their fires.

I thought how easy it would be to foil the gods who had visited this cruel fate upon me. Two steps forward, a leap off the precipice and a screaming plunge hundreds of feet onto the trees and rocks below. It wasn't something I would do, but, and though the feeling of hopelessness was unrelenting, there was comfort in knowing I could end my travails whenever I decided I'd had enough. I would not abandon my efforts to get home, just it didn't much matter did I die in the trying. I had chosen this life and there were Hugh's words to consider.

"A man don't live long up here."

I got back into the trees behind the cliffs and constructed a shelter down in some rocks, a hut half as tall as me, branches overlaid with slabs of elm bark. I got in and got a small fire going. Darkness fell, the storm came in. My night was mostly sleepless for the wind and rain rattling and pounding my hut, the thunder and lightning crashing around.

Chapter IX – Beaver!

In the morning and with the rain having stopped, I commenced walking. I had the shakes for being so cold and wet. I needed sun and warmth but with Old Sol staying wrapped in thick clouds, the day was cool and blustery. I gnawed on the moose meat, ripping it from the bone with my teeth and spitting most of it out. It was fouled for the bugs having got into it and I tossed it aside. The foxes and mice could have it.

I came onto a deer run and followed it over the top of the mountain. The going was rocky and with patchy fog sometimes above me, other times below. Coming to the other side, I stepped out onto an open, rocky crest and there, spread before me was a sight of the most startling and eye-catching beauty. Deep below and showing in and out of swirling fog and with tall mountains enclosing it on every side was a lake. Flat, blue, peaceful, stretching to the west, this was no mere pond and was instead a true lake, dressed in a quiet and serene beauty for being nestled down inside its mountain fastness. Here harsh nature had become a gentle lady. A feeling of peace came over me.

My first thought was this must be Saint Sacrement. This elated me. Despite the danger in having got so far east, I at least knew where I was and I now had a chance, however thin, of making it home. But this lake wasn't near wide enough to be Saint Sacrement, unless I was seeing the inside of a bay, which I was fairly certain I was not. This was some unknown lake, which meant I still had no idea where the hell I was. Yet I was hopeful, and intrigued there could be such a lake as this in the mountains. All thoughts of hurling myself off a cliff or of the eternally wandering wild man were forgotten for here was a lake of a size which might go to the East Branch.

The clouds began to burn off and to rise and the sun, which I had not thought I would see this day, broke through, and I could see more of the lake. To my left a couple thousand feet, was the east end. There, a strip of sand built up by the action of a constant west wind had made a horseshoe curve around to the south shore. Behind the sand was a bog of dead standing trees in brackish water. The outlet might be through the bog, which would mean an easterly flow but I didn't think so. With how the land rose up around the swamp, the outlet must be to the west. How far down the lake, indeed, how long was the lake, I could not tell for the mountains blocking my view. Or the outlet might lie along the south shore. I would get over there, to begin searching but I had first to get down off the heights.

I paced the mountaintop looking for a place to descend. Cliffs too sheer for trying, I'd have to use one of the wooded slopes which were interspersed with the cliffs. Whilst I was determining where best to go, there came a shrill cry from overhead. T'was the great fisher of birds, the osprey. He was naught but a speck against the clouds but with me already so high up and him gradually lowering, we were soon on a level and I seen he was a bigger fellow than the ospreys commonly seen nesting along the Hudson. Each time his orbit brought him in toward me, I heard the faint whistle of the wind through his wings. His gaze, fixing on mine, showed he was aware of my presence and didn't much care.

Then and sighting a fish, he abandoned his seemingly idle soaring and dropped down out of the sky with such speed and force, my eyes could scarce follow. His splash when he hit the surface sent up a spray of water and he was away in a single motion. As he clumb higher, drops of water fell from his feathers and I seen he had a large fish in his talons.

Often, in this harsh land, things are not as they appear, for another was watching, the ancient robber of the fishing bird, the bald eagle. Larger than the osprey, he dropped down at a terrifying speed, talons thrust forward like unsheathed daggers, beak at fighting ready. The osprey, disadvantaged with its burden, cawed in protest but did let go of the fish. The eagle, with an even greater cry of its own, dove past the osprey and gaining speed, if such be possible, the wild devil of a bird snatched the fish an instant before it hit the surface. Rising again, the eagle went west, probably toward his own aerie, somewhere up along the rock ledges. I was short of breath for this avian thievery. The osprey, not seeming overly put out despite its earlier protest, resumed circling and soon had another fish. This time, unbothered, he rose into the sky and flew off down the lake. I yearned to travel this country as effortlessly as the great birds. They could go down to Albany and get back again in the time it would take me to climb down off the ledges. But I was a man and had not wings to soar. I had only what remained of my grit and sanity, slender reeds against the wilds.

I found what I judged to be the best way down, or the least-worst, a finger of tree-lined ridge which, steep though it was, looked as if it didn't stop abruptly at a cliff nor sink down into a steep-sided pothole. I got started, the footing was treacherous with the steepness and the slipperiness of wet leaves, moss and bare rockfaces. I couldn't have managed it if not for the small trees which I grabbed on either side as I went. These kept me from going too fast and getting thrown on my face. Through the trees, I got glimpses of the sparkling blue water and farther down, there was the fresh, idyllic scent of balsam and cedar.

I attained the lakeshore. Here the ferns grew taller than a man and there was a narrow shelf between the cliffs and the water. I walked the shelf to the east end and going around the curve of the lake and with the sand crunching beneath my feet, I decided I would have a bath. If this were truly my way home, I would rid myself of stink and grime. Then I seen two snakes skimming the lake for water bugs. One, a black snake, was near six-foot-long. The other, a true water snake by its color, a reddish-brown, might a been poisonous. I threw stones to drive 'em off. I did not care to swim with 'em, no matter how urgent the need nor inviting the waters. The littler one raised its head and hissed. Not entirely idyllic after all. Too bad, for I surely did need a dousing.

I got around to the south shore, a short walk for the east end being so narrow. The cliffs were recessed back from the lake, same as on the other side, which made for more easy walking along the shore. Over here all was brilliant for the sun's rays peering over the mountains along the north shore, where I had first come onto the lake. Back over there everything was yet in shadow.

Where a point jutted into the lake, I was brought up short by a most amazing discovery. Fresh beaver cuttings! I picked up a chewed stick, judged it no more than a few days old. Studied the lake from the tip of the point. Over toward the other side were what looked to be naught but brush piles raised up by the action of the waves. Or was I seeing beaver lodges? I couldn't tell for the shadows, and if they were lodges, were they abandoned years ago, same as others I had seen in my wanders? Or, and with the fresh-cut stick in my hand and more fresh sign around, were the lodges yet occupied?

I came to where a small brook flowed out of a copse and into a bay formed by a point of land which, thin and curved like a claw or a fish-hook, swept out and around and came almost all the way back again to the shore. Just off the tip of the claw and partially blocking the entrance into the bay was a hump of rock, a small island with a few skinny trees and aligned with the point so it might once have been a part of it. A peaceful, serene little bay with nary a ripple on the water.

On the other side of the bay, the cliffs came all the way down to the lake, pinching the shelf. Here was a formidable obstacle, heights without a shelf for getting around and precipitous enough so I had to step away, lean my head back and look straight up to see to the top, the heights enhanced by the spiraling pine trees up there. No way could I get up and over these cliffs. I would have to see about getting around them, trudge around through the woods or put logs together and bind 'em with strips of rawhide for a raft. Decided I better not get onto the lake. No telling who might be around the next bend.

I seen a turbulence just beneath the surface of the water. A school of minnows had been driven into the bay by some large trout which were jumping out of the water in the pursuit. The smaller fry tried to escape by schooling up in the shallows and weeds along the shore and were set upon by a swarm of bass. Then trout, bass and the lesser fish scattered as a three-foot pike cruised in. He prowled the weeds in the shallows at my feet. He got a bullfrog by the leg and dragged it into the deeper water and shortly, the pike came back and in repeated attacks, killed a too-curious bass.

The bay not so tranquil as I had supposed, then a flash of white behind me. A deer had come out of the woods unaware of my presence and startled for seeing me, had darted into the copse out of which the brook flowed. Here was something better than a bath for celebrating having found my way. Meat. Backing up some and bringing my gun around to the front, I had both ends of the copse covered and with the rockface behind it, the deer was boxed. Hearing nothing further and certain the deer must yet be in there, I tossed stones, to flush it. I heard naught but the stones swishing the leaves and rattling on the rocks. I stepped closer but stopped short of going in, for iffen I did, the deer would surely bolt out one side or the other. I waited and not hearing anything, I entered the copse. The deer was gone, which puzzled me considerably. I was certain I had seen it go in and just as certain I had neither seen nor heard it come out again.

The copse, from the outside, was a tangle of brush and small trees but when I got into it, it was open and spacious, like the inside of a wigwam. My deer was not there. Must have imagined it, and if my deteriorating senses had me conjuring deer, what might I see next, ten-foot Hurons brandishing tomahawks? Yet, and as I checked the wet ground for deer tracks, I seen plenty. The freshest were from my deer having come in and having paced for knowing I had him trapped, yet no sign showed the deer had gone out again.

With my eyes adjusting to the gloaming, I followed the deer tracks to the back of the copse from whence the brook flowed. I expected the beginning of the brook would be a mere splashing off the rocks and what I saw instead was a mighty gash cut into the cliffside. A passage carved by the water over eons of time or sundered by an angry god in a moment of divine vexation? From where I stood and with how the passage rose up and curved 'round out of my sight, I could not see whether or not it went to the top but I figured it must, for by the sign, deer went in there plenty. The cut, though narrow and did I follow it, could be my way to the top and there might be a way down the other side.

Still, though, I hesitated for the notch having the most unpleasant aspect, like the mouth of a trap. A most deadly trap were there some-one waiting to greet me in there. This was unlikely. Any trouble up there would come not from a man, or men, but from a bear or one of the big cats, or a rattlesnake, the snakes favoring rocky places. It didn't matter. I would go up the staircase, for staircase was how it looked, though there be no stairs.

Cautiously and not without trepidation, I entered the fracture. I went slowly, it was rocky and steep, and as I proceeded and with the narrowing, I became even more constricted and had to walk in the water which fortunately was no more than stagnant pools where the ground flattened, and with a measly flow from one pool to the next, it seemed I would soon be scraping both of my shoulders. My way to the top might be thwarted and was this what the gods had prepared for me? Enticing me on with the possibility of a way over the cliffs whilst using my own anxiousness to wedge me into a tomb? Sobering yet irrational, to die in such a manner, not able to go forward nor back, and what would the wolves think, did they also use this portal and find me blocking it?

Still I went on; it was an arduous climb, and I saw daylight ahead, the defile breached up there. The constriction eased some and I no longer felt as if both my shoulders would soon be scraping rock.

Abruptly and with relief, I stepped into sunlight and here was another hidden wonder of nature, perhaps the most amazing discovery on what had become a day filled with amazing discoveries.

A sky canyon with walls rising a hundred feet on every side from an already considerable height, the cliffs mostly sheer with scant brush or the occasional sapling which had gained a foothold. Enclosed within the walls was a place of seclusion, a flat grassland with trees old and weathered.

Stood there for the longest time, drinking it all in, then I walked to my right, toward where I judged the wall must rise up over the lake. Found a deer run which might go to the top and this I ascended, a mere thread of trail narrow and precipitous and with switchbacks. I arrived sweating and short of breath at the rim of this north-facing ledge.

I had attained as high a point as there was around the lake and again I stood in wonder for I could see nearly the entirety of the lake and could see well beyond it to the north and west. The sun was fully up over the cliffs on the other side. It penetrated the woods along the south shore and shone down on the lake which sparkled in its bastion of rock. The lake was wider toward the middle and narrowed to a mere slit at the east end. The west end I could not see for the cliffs farther down.

What else I saw, or realized, I was under no cover, the rim bare 'cept for some few small, wind-twisted trees, and yet and with the out-ward curve of the wall as it rose up, a man passing below, unless he chanced across the cut up from the lake as I had, would entirely miss seeing it.

The deer runway went down the other side, the back door I had been seeking but instead of following it, I returned down into the canyon for another look. Down off the rim, I walked the length of the ground whilst staying close to the wall opposite the side of the canyon where I had entered. Got to the south end where the cliffs were not so high and saw another runway which came in through trees and brush and just past the runway, a box canyon.

This lesser canyon, a few acres or more, was much the same as the other. The ground was level and grassy and with stands of brush and trees. The brook flowing out from here, I followed it deeper into the canyon, to where the water seeped out from cracks in the rock wall and collected in a pool which, surprisingly broad and deep, was the source of the brook.

I got back into the bigger canyon and continued walking. I got entirely back around to where I had come in and found no more places other than the cut and those deer runways where a deer or a man might climb in or out.

I walked out to the center of the canyon, to a grove of pine trees. The red squirrels chattering in the branches over my head were angry for my having intruded into their sanctuary. I thought how at first this canyon had looked too dangerous to enter. With more sense I would have stayed out of it, yet, having walked it and sitting now with my back against a tree, the canyon gave me a sense of safety and ease, of security, as if the seclusion did not shut me in so much as it shut out all the dangers of the outside, even those murderous, thieving redskins who might still be spooking me.

I had seen sign of rabbits, the flattened grass of nesting places and runs, and I put out snares. I went back down through the defile, to the lakeshore. I made a spear by notching the end of a hardwood stick and lashing one of my remaining steel arrowpoints into the notch and fastening it with rawhide. Speared a few small bass in the shallows and when a big pike cruised in, I speared him too. Mighten have been the same pike I had seen feeding earlier, he probably never realizing a bigger hunter than him might one day come along. I went back up into the canyon, the snares were empty. I got into the smaller canyon, to cook my pike, and I seen the pool was brimming with trout. Small they were but plentiful and I got five or six. I wrapped them with my pike in a covering of clay and leaves and buried 'em deep in the ashes of a hidden campfire. When the clay split open, the fish were done, the meat fell away from bones and skins.

Night came on, warm and humid. I sat under the stars, belly partly full. I kept the fire burning with not too much smoke, just it kept the bugs off some. I had often heard it said the beavers, once plentiful in the Adirondacks, were entirely wiped out by the greed of men. White men coveting the red man's furs, red men anxious to acquire trade goods, but what if the talk was wrong? What if there existed a hidden valley with beavers and nobody knew about it 'cept me? Was this possible? I was pretty sure there was no beavers to the east of where I was, surely not on Corlaer or Saint Sacrement, but what about to the west? I aimed to find out.

****

In the morning, refreshed by a good sleep and a cold bath in the icy

110

waters of the pool and a breakfast of trout, I decided my quest for the East Branch would have to wait one more day whilst I further explored this wondrous land.

I went back up to the rim and walked it, like a lord of old Europe around the walls of his mighty turret, such as I had read about in books. Surely none of those lords ever knew such splendor, for all the lands they called their own. The walking was treacherous for the narrowness of the walkway and the precipitous drops along either side but I wanted to see how much was visible from up there. Not much, it turned out, as I got around to the south. At least not this time of year for the trees being leafed out.

I followed the deer trails down off the other side of the cliffs, which brought me into more cliffs but these scarps, craggy though they were, weren't impassable for being more broken and scattered. Here was a forest of tall trees and in amongst the trees, massive boulders strewn about as if scattered by Providence. The downward paths the boulders must have taken off the higher ground were thick now with fully-grown trees which spoke to how long it had been since the boulders had rolled off the cliffs.

Closer to the water were stands of poplar trees which were always the first to reclaim a forest after a burn and were the beavers' first choice of food. The beaver sign was abundant. Cuttings, dragways, chips and sticks, the stumps of downed trees.

Where fresh cuttings had floated down a brook and collected, I walked the brook up a hillside which was no more than a lateral hump of the bigger mountain alongside of it. Here in a saucer of ground was a small beaver pond with a shoreline thick with scrub oak and pines, juniper and blueberry bushes. The pond teemed with trout rising to flies.

I skirted the pond and following the upper reaches of the stream and attaining the crest along the east slope of this unusual flat-topped mountain, I could see almost the entirety of what I was calling my Eagle's Lake. It was two miles long, and to the west, close enough so my lake must flow into it, was another lake. This one, twice the length of mine, was wide at first then became a mere slit midway, and where it opened again, the western end was considerably broader than the eastern, the channel between naught but a ribbon. I dubbed these First and Second Lakes. Beyond the lakes to the northwest were more hills, "Elbow ta elbow" as Ben might have remarked, had he not died somewhere back to the northwest of where I was now.

I moved around the side of the mountain to where I could see south and west. A succession of valleys ran west and there was yet another lake out there, bigger'n the others. Nestled between rings of hills and laying north and south by the sun, this big lake looked ten miles long and it weren't hard to discern how the flows went. The Eagle's Lake into First Lake into Second Lake into Big Lake, and somewhere south of Big Lake, sure as hell, a connection to the East Branch.

I sat silent as a stone and with so much of the land spread before me, I saw no smoke nor movement on the waters, no sign of men, although most of what I was seeing was at a distance. There might be smokeless camps hidden along the shore. Interlopers, they would be as wary as me.

To the southeast as I moved farther around the mountain, I seen a mountain taller than all others and standing like a guidepost. Easy to mark direction from this peak for it's towering over its lesser siblings. Royalty gathering homage from its subjects, for the lesser mountains did seem to dip their tops in salutation to their majestic lord. I dubbed it the Pharoah's Mountain.

I was seeing how this high canyon was well within reach of a fair-sized trapline, with beaver colonies a plenty to the west and probably to the south too. By the sign, game was abundant, unlike the bitter land off to the northwest where it was mostly pine. Deer, bear, moose, flocks of ducks and Canada goose on the waters. Pigeons in a massive flight in the distance. I would have knocked many of 'em out of the sky had they not stayed away. This country was a hunter's paradise sure to be bountiful in the fall and with enough beavers in winter to justify a go at trapping.

With the sun getting down in the west, I hurried back to the canyon. I was struck by how my attention had got turned away from the East Branch, which had for weeks been the only thing which mattered. On the cusp of finding it, I had instead turned aside, for this amazing land having entirely distracted me from my purpose.

I got back to my camp with some little time before full dark. Two of my snares had caught rabbits, though one got snatched by a coyote before I got to it. All that remained was blood and fur, part of one foot. The other was big and fat. He would make a good meal, did I have about three more to go with him. I reset the snares, rebuilt my fire, roasted my rabbit on a stick and whilst I devoured it, and with the pleasing sound of the water splashing down out of the rocks and into the pool, I considered how the discovery of this land might alter the direction of my life. Heretofore, my future I had only contemplated with reluctance and for the badgering from Mother and Pops. There had always been the notion I must someday settle in at the tavern. Tending to drunkards, listening to their boastful nonsense, cleaning their filth, and the honey-wagon! How I loathed pulling the filthy, foul-reeking slops-cart down the street to the east gate. Heckled by gangs of boys and swarmed by screaming gulls, back the cart up to the river, open the rear and rake the refuse into the river so the current could draw away the stinking mess.

Given my age, sixteen, consideration of my future was something I could not have avoided much longer and now and instead of a life-time of drudgery, I was seeing another way, a most dangerous notion taking shape in my head. Gathering beavers in the wilds, for surely a fortune in pelts awaited the man who could survive the rigors of a northern winter in this land. Trapping this country couldn't be no more dangerous than trading in Montreal and with luck and in just one win-ter, maybe two, I could take furs sufficient to make me a rich man. Then retire to a life of ease, buy a ship with all my newfound riches and sail away to those far-off lands Pops so often talked about.

How much money would it take to grubstake for one season up here? More than what I had. I could maybe talk Pops into backing me but even were he for it, Mother would forbid him doing anything to encourage my affinity for the north. Thought about Eric. No. He was too controlled by his beautiful wife to risk money in an undertaking so foreign to both of them. I wished Bill were alive. He wouldn't of had money but he'd surely have been for it. I considered Schaack. He was greedy enough to be interested and was not daunted by risks, so long as they were taken by someone other than him. But Schaack was a crook and did I tell him I had found us a beaver canyon no more'n a hundred miles from Albany, he would use me to procure the furs and squeeze me out of any profit. Certain I was I must tell no one. Paradise Valley was to be mine alone.

Darkness closing down over my rocky glen brought a dampening of my heretofore unbounded enthusiasm and I thought more soberly about whether a man could survive a winter in these mountains. One consideration, I realized, was the distance between here and Corlaer. The Eagle's Lake must lie outside the Corlaer Valley and so was situated west of the heavily traveled route of French and Indian activity. Corlaer lay to the east. Probably not far, for all the trekking I'd done since turning away from those western mountains. But how far? Might be just over the next hill and though we were not at war with the French and it was them encroaching on us, not us on them, the right or wrong of my being here wouldn't matter, did I encounter them.

The Eagle's Lake, judging by the lack of sign, never saw men, and even was the valley close enough to Corlear for the French to come up, my secluded glen would be difficult for 'em to find. I laughed to think a man sticking his head into the noose which was the entrance into this canyon would be as scairt as I had been.

But I must not be blinded. This country was dangerous. One could not avoid forever the inevitable meeting with one of the hunting or war parties which must sometimes come along. Northern Indians from Corlear or Iroquois from the west, it wouldn't matter. The first time any of those Stone Age remnants cut my trail would be the end of me. I remembered a sketch from one of Mother's books, a representation of people before progress was made. Men and women living in caves, dressed in furs, hunting with sticks. The Dawn of Man. "The Indians," Mother said, "are not so far removed from their caves." My mentor, Hugh, had explained it thusly, "Indians live so differ'nt from us, we don' understand how they think. I reckon their backward life grows 'em thet way. A harsh winter in an Algonquin camp be mighty thin." I remembered the look in his eyes when he said this and I shuddered to think on it. Boilin' and eatin' the bark of trees, shivering for it being too cold to go outside to fetch wood, afraid of the dread cry, Iroquois! who often attacked in winter. Better to think on how the cold season grew the fur thick on the beavers.

I thought I better go east in the morning for a look-see. If Corlear be close enough, it might be my way home. The most dangerous way but the fastest, yet I decided I must go west. My only purpose for now must be to get home. Only did I decide to come back would I scout to the east.

And I had another reason for going west. The East Branch had become a sort of Holy Grail for me. In an odd way, I must find it, not only for myself, but for Bill and them others. Find it or perish in the seeking, as they had.

With thoughts of the riches to be taken from this wild, wonderful country, I wrapped myself in my moose skin, burrowed into a pile of leaves and slept. Where previously my sleep had been invaded by demonic Indians in pursuit and with me waking up in a sweat and reaching for my knife, this night I dreamt of prime fur. Beavers! And the other fur-bearers I had seen sign of; fisher-cat, raccoon, fox, otter, mink, muskrat. Visions of a fortune to be made, the life of the mountain man in winter, the Albany gentleman in summer.

Chapter X – East Branch

In the morning, I picked up my snares, of which one held a rabbit. I did not stop to cook it, I only hung it on my belt for later. I hurried up and over the rim and down to the lake. I again considered a raft. Surely the fastest way to get to the outlet but I decided I better not.

Got started walking west and even with the cliffs recessed back away from the lake, the going was hard for surely this was one of the damnedest places I had ever set foot. The shore would be easy enough for a time, then it would be cut up bad for walking or blocked by unscalable cliffs which, fortunately, I was able to get around. There were potholes to be avoided. Drop-offs into steep-sided ravines with sheer sides and without grips for hand nor foot. Get into them and I must fly like a bird to get out again. In other places the ground was swampy and I had to retreat farther back away from the water. It all might have put me into a foul mood except I knew the hard going which daunted me would daunt as well any man who would invade my newfound kingdom from the west.

Whilst back away from the lake, I came to where a crick came in off a hill. A beaver dam backed up the crick in the pass leading to the lake and had formed a sizeable marsh of water lilies and dead cedar. As I looked for the best way of getting around it, a beaver poked its head up out of the water, no more'n thirty feet from me. The beaver, with a stick in its mouth, climbed up onto the dam, which allowed me to see it in its entirety. It looked to weigh a hundred pounds and it stiffened for having got the scent of me, maybe his first-ever whiff of a man, surely the first time in my life I had set eyes on a living beaver. He sniffed a few times and scurrying back off the dam and into the water, he slapped his tail against the surface, loud as a gunshot. He submerged and with his alarm spreading, there came more slappings, some right there in the pond, others fainter and from ponds unseen. I strained for more sightings and though I saw plenty of ripples on the water, no more beavers did I see.

This raised my mood; so much pleasure was I feeling, I might, if not for my usual caution, have been whistling a tune, same as if I was sauntering along the Albany streets from one tavern to the next. Wondered how many men in Albany could boast without lying of having seen a real live beaver. Not many, I reckoned!

Past the crick and the dam, I came to the end of the lake, which was not what I had expected. Instead of a wide flowing creek, here was a marshland of dead trees and tall weeds. Discouraging, until I seen an outlet brook snaking through the marsh. My way home, and iffen it weren't, I might, a few days ago have sat down and blubbered. Now and if it weren't, I would go on to the next lake and the next, as many as it took to find my way home. I got up along the higher ground, skirted the marsh and when I could, I got down close again to the crick which widened and deepened for all the rivulets flowing in. Finally, ahead through the trees, I seen the shimmer of sunlight on blue water.

Here was First Lake and some scouting showed me all of what I would need for making a canoe was close by. Stands of birch; cedar and ash for the frame and ribs; spruce roots for sewing; spruce gum for sealing. With rabbit runs evident along the hilly shore, I put out my snares. Then started a small fire to cook the one I carried. Tried the stream with my spear and got some few small fish.

I did not have much to work with, just knife and hatchet. Lucky I still had my whetstone. I cleared an area of grass and underbrush and scratched an outline for the frame of my boat in the dirt. I cut strips of cedar for the backbone and ribs. I gathered vines and cut them into sinews for lashing the frame. I peeled sheets of bark from the birch trees for framing the sides and bottom. I made a pail out of birchbark and clay and used it to boil sap for sealing the skin of the boat. Awkward for a man alone to hold the frame taut whilst attaching the bark and securing it. My snares kept taking rabbits though a smart old wolf or coyote often got there afore I did. I carved three paddles. Crude, but they would suffice.

Took me five days to build my canoe, and to stay fed and maybe build up a supply of food for the days ahead, I'd go down the lake to where ducks was bobbing. I'd take off what was left of my buckskins and swim out underwater. Grab a squawker from below, the way me and Eric had used to do when we were lads. Pull it under by the legs and hold it there until it drowned or until I could get my knife into its belly. Fat mallards they were and strong enough to about drown me with their powerful wings. Roasted, they were welcome additions to my otherwise poor fare.

Evening of the last day of my tedious work and with the sun going down, the air blessedly starting to cool, the skin of the canoe was drawn up tight, the seams were pitched. It was time to go and all I could think about was lurking Indians. Not for the Hurons which were surely no longer after me but for any which might be ahead, for these lakes must draw attention. Out on the water I would be seen by anyone along the shore or up on the ridges. No telling how much trouble might lay between me and Albany and I had not come so far to lose my hair now, so close to getting out. Rash judgment, too much eagerness could cost my life. If I would get home, I must give Dame Fortune a nudge and traverse these lakes only in darkness.

I had a quick meal of cold fish and duck and put my canoe into the water. Unencumbered with my weight and as light as she was, she floated in a scant three or four inches. I got in and pushed off into the gloom.

The canoe proved immediately to be not the best of craft, nor the worst. She wobbled some and water seeped up through the bottom but she'd hold, did she not get bashed about too severely. I pushed on down the lake, the wobbling more worrisome than deadly, and though she shifted erratically, side to side, she wasn't hard to handle. I began to gain confidence, to think she might take me home, although I didn't fool myself; these were placid waters. Turbulence lay ahead.

The night was dark with the waning moon not yet up. I attained the narrows along the middle of the lake and got through trepidaciously for the nearness of the shores on either side and I was relieved to be once again out onto wider waters. The night was peaceful under the Milky Way of stars, bright for the moon not yet risen. The starlight reflected off the white birch of the canoe. So serene. So dangerous, if one did not pay strict attention at all times. "Trouble comes when you least s'pect it." That had been Hugh's caution, more than once. The awful fate which had befallen my companions might still await me if I be not vigilant. The terrifying image of Indians swarming our camp would never leave me. Listened to the night sounds and tried to separate and identify each from the rest. Never could really be sure.

I came to the outlet creek, the way made eerie by thick overhanging willows. Reminded me of Portage Crick over at Carillon. Getting onto the crick, the canoe banged against rocks and logs and I feared she might break apart but though she leaked some, she stayed together. Birch-barks often run one way or the other in a current if not built on an exact keel, mine performed well enough, especially once I learned her tendencies and adjusted for them.

The crick was easily handled at first then came whitewater where the one crick emptied into another. Downed trees and snags of brush to be got over or around whilst the current lurched me ahead. Fighting such obstacles didn't bother me, so long as it didn't bring destruction to my boat, for now, surely, I was on my way home. Poorer I would be, did I get there, but wiser.

This second crick was wider and deeper and with nothing much to hinder my passage, I moved along pretty good and soon heard water splashin' ahead. The drainage into Big Lake. I stopped to listen for any sounds which might signal danger. Heard none, and with the moon full up behind me, I edged my nose into the expanse of the lake. My paddle dug in, my stroke was sure and steady, the water boiling into a froth around the hull. A slight wind blew out of the western hills and ginned up small waves which slapped gently against my boat. Some few islands, half-seen in the shadows. Passing one such island a little way from shore, I heard the snorting of a bear, sounded close, then she rose up alongside me. She was snarling and waving her claws for my having disturbed her. I snarled too and shook my paddle in her face, she turned and run off. I heard her going through the brush then came a splash from the other side of the island.

I went by the light of the moon and kept close to the east shore. I did not care to be toward the middle of this wide lake if the canoe should break apart. But a ways down and making out a large bay on the eastern side and with confidence in my boat, I decided to forgo the shore and instead went across the head of the bay. This put me about in the middle of the lake but it saved plenty of time. Past the bay, I soon enough reached the south end of the lake. Massive brush piles broke the debouchment into three or four disparate channels, some blocked by downed trees and limbs which had washed down the creek. Some of the trees were freshly uprooted; older, rotted logs bobbed just under the surface. One channel had a five-foot waterfall. I chose what looked to be the most passable. A skinny down-chute flanked by piles of debris. It was fast water but was a straight run and narrow enough so I got jabbed on either side by branches mostly unseen in the dark, then I was through and onto the East Branch.

Here was steadier going with the river wider than either of the cricks, and with nothing to obstruct me and with the current, I moved at a nice pace. Farther down, the river meandered. First around one way, then back the other. The current was strong through the turns and I became adept at allowing it to do my work for me. For long stretches, I used my paddle as a rudder, along one side through one turn and then the other side through the next.

The land here was less mountainous. It was hills more separated than previously in my wandering. The shores and river bottom were sandy. There was scant sign of fur-bearers. Muskrats but no beavers. This was a good thing. Beavers this far out would get found and would draw men into Paradise. Saw a moose feeding on water lilies in the shallows. The big fellow lifted his massive head and watched me go by, his jaws working, chewing, as if he was pondering me.

I pulled up on the bank. Got out, stiff and weary and in the morning light, I inspected my boat. Cut and dented and with water seeping through a crease where I had scraped the rocky shore around a turn. I patched the boat with the extra bark and sap I carried and went straight off to sleep. And didn't realize my stop put me alongside of a swamp. Longjaws was king here. Sleep was difficult for all the attention they gave me but, and with how bitten up I was, and how tired, I did sleep some. Upon awakening, I carved a paddle to replace one I had lost and clumb a tree from where I might survey my situation both ahead and behind. Not a foolproof way to discern the presence of enemies, they would be well hidden too, but better'n being blind to 'em, iffen they was out there. From up in the tree, I seen the Pharaoh's Mountain, to the northeast of me now.

Spent another night on the water and with the river straightening, no more of those twisting turns, and the current strengthening, I was nearing the confluence of the East and West Branches. I had heard from men in the tavern about this meeting of the waters. Those who had seen it, or claimed to, said it was incredibly wild, with rapids both above and below a magnificent waterfall, all of which, fortunately, would not be at their worst this time of year. I listened for any sound which might indicate I was nearing the falls and when I heard it dimly, I got off the river. I stashed the canoe and found the portage trail along the west side of the river, a seldom-used path marked with notches on the trees. I followed along the trail. It started some few miles above the confluence. How much portaging a man had to do depended on the time of year, the force of the water from snowmelt and rain. Figured the trail was a few miles long below the confluence, same as

120

it was above. The sound of the falls hadn't been much more than a rumble when I got off the water; now and as I clumb a steep hill, it was a mighty roar which told me I was right alongside the falls. Went down the other side of the hill until I figured I was below the falls. I stepped through the trees and onto an outcropping and there she was.

The Hudson!

The mist of the cataracts heavy in the air, I stood for a long time in awe of the majesty of what I was seeing. Here at the funneling of the lesser river into the mightier, was the tallest, widest waterfall I had ever seen. Bigger even than those falls at Tyonderrogha or down to the Great Carry. The water had probably calmed considerable from what it would have been in the spring when the worst snowmelt came down out of the mountains but it yet frothed and heaved with white-water and bashing debris. One great snag sat precariously at the top of the falls, buffeted by the surging waters as it awaited the bump of one more log which might send the entirety over the edge. The logs which I saw go over, even those of twenty feet and more, plunged deep down into the pool and came thrusting back up again.

Downstream from the falls the river roared and spewed, a wild and foaming race which must go on for miles, the water rising in untamed spouts where it bashed against hidden rocks. I walked down, to see how far would I have to portage before it would be safe to get back on the water. Quite a ways, as it was, and with the day well advanced and feeling it would be too dangerous to try these waters at night, I would wait until morning.

I came onto a clearing beside the trail where men had camped only recently. White men and Indians by the sign, pairs of feet with heeled shoes, others with moccasins, five or six men. Probably not French, but I reckoned English or even Dutch a way out here might be trouble.

I saw a flock of mallard ducks in a backwater eddy and with hunger gnawing at my innards, I decided to try for 'em. I eased into the cold water and even staying close to the shore where the current was less strong, I was pushed swiftly down toward the eddy. I got under the surface and greedily took two birds by the feet and held them under whilst they drowned.

Got back up above the falls, made camp in the woods, away from the trail, and got a small fire going behind some rocks. With the ducks roasting, I stayed up close to the fire. When the birds was cooked, I pulled 'em away from the fire and put it out. I walked a quarter-mile farther, sat down and ate. Even did men come upon the remains of my fire, they'd have a hard time finding me, and with the roar of the falls not so loud here, I might hear did someone approach. I would not have uninvited guests.

I got into a place where the wind blew soft through sweet-smelling evergreens and I slept, my dreams this night unencumbered by my usual nightmares. Before going to sleep, I had set out snares where some rabbit runs crossed. Checked them first thing upon awakening, each snare held a rabbit, both of which I immediately skinned, cooked, and ate. I then returned to my canoe. It was still too heavy for hauling down the rough trail. I would have to wait another day and impatience tore at me. I was so thoroughly sick of the north woods, I considered hoofing it the rest of the way. I could start at once and with no way to get lost, did I simply follow the river. Yet it would be a mistake, a difficult trip through country I didn't know. Besides, and what was a surety, one day of canoe travel in this rough country was worth three days or more of walking.

I went in search of something more to eat, a deer or a turkey. Three hours of fruitless hunting, I returned to the snares, found them empty, robbed by a fisher. He left splotches of blood and fur all 'round. These were my last snares and he had torn them so they were not usable any further, even for combining into one. I would be hungry this night.

By the middle of the day and having built a travois and driven by impatience and despite the weight of the canoe, it was time to go. I got the boat onto the travois and set out dragging it along the portage trail. Slipping on wet rocks and leaves, I yet resisted getting onto the river whilst it was still too wild, or simply stepping away from my travois and canoe and walking home. I must needs be patient and as it was, I got down to where the rapids eased some, though the current was still strong. Here, I felt, it would be safe to launch. I would sleep the night and with luck, I would be in Saratoga by nightfall tomorrow.

Chapter XI – Tavernkeeper or Trapper

It was dark, a light rain was falling as I walked on unsteady legs past the wide open, unguarded gates of the Saratoga palisade and into the adjacent town. The main street was deserted, there was just the barking of a dog and even he didn't seem much impressed at seeing me. After barking a few times, he stopped.

I figured to go by Arnold Baldwin's place and see if I might not find supper and stay the night. Almost the first person I encountered coming up the dark street was Arnold himself, walking to his home on the far side of town from his work at the land office. He looked prosperous in a wide-sleeved frock coat and beaver hat. I stopped him and spoke. For a moment and with the darkness and the shadows, he didn't recognize me, then, peering closely, "Kenneth! Oh! Good to see you. How are you? You look a little peaked, eh, what?"

"Yeh, reckon I am a little peaked, pard," I said. He went on chattering, he not able to see in the darkness how truly bedraggled was my condition. Tattered clothes, face and arms cut up from brush and bugs. My beard ragged, I must a smelled some fierce, though Arnold kindly said naught about it. "Jumped by Injuns," I finally managed to say. "Killed my partners and took our furs. We had plenty of good fur, we surely did." I started to give him the story, not having talked to anybody for so long was affecting me. "You have suffered an ordeal, have you not?" he said, interrupting. I said I had, indeed, and he invited me to go along with him for some supper. I said I did not want to impose though truthfully, I wanted very much to impose. "Oh, my boy," he said, "do not be awkward. Priscilla will be glad to see you."

He laughed some. The pipe in his mouth got to jiggling, burning ashes spilled on the ground, blew away on the wind. "Priscilla asks about you often, if there is any news of her favorite bumpkin. You see, my friend, you are one of the very few people in this new world other than your wonderful Momma and Poppa she speaks well of. She has liked you since the first day you helped us. I have asked about you in the taverns and inquired of people passing through. Nobody has heard a word since you left Albany a month and more ago."

"Been out of touch," I said, my voice raspy. "Well," he said kindly, "tis obvious you are in need of refreshment before dinner." He insisted we stop at a tavern along the way and whilst going, he asked hadn't I been involved in skullduggery of one sort or another. "Come, come, tell me now. Where is Mister Morrissey?"

"Everybody's dead 'cept me," I said. I became upset, he was sympathetic, asked how many were we. "Five," I told him. "Indians had 'em good. Weren't no point staying." My voice cracked with the feelings. "No, I suppose not," he said. "Goodness no, I say." Right then I come near to being overwhelmed with emotion and with relief for being out of the woods. It was a struggle to stay afloat.

"All my money was tied up in those furs," I said. "I have nothing to spend." Forced my voice to be steady, still trying to get a grab on myself. "Your financial straits," Arnold said, "mean nothing tonight." He told me there had been a man around asking questions about me and about the alderman's son. We got to the tavern, Arnold said, "Step inside, watch your head, it be a low ceiling." He put his hand on my shoulder from behind as we went down the stone steps.

It was crowded and loud, until I stepped in and all the men and the few women stopped their chatter to stare at me. A man snorted for how fiercely I stank. I would a hit him did I have the strength, which I did not. Arnold announced I'd had trouble with Indians. They all got in close to ask questions and backed off for getting too close. I didn't say much. Arnold got beer and whiskey enough for both of us. He was no teetotaler anymore, and the men, understanding I wanted the rum more than the talk, let me alone.

By the greetings called out to Arnold when we had first come in and with the way the men were joshing him about the ferocity of his wife, it was plain he had made a quick adjustment to life on this harsh frontier. The joshing was all in fun, hard fun, for these are hard men. Rough farmers and soldiers, a trapper from the Sacandaga, a hunter, a British officer. And others, some familiar to me from Pops' tavern, although those I recognized surely didn't recognize me. It was quickly apparent Arnold was one of them.

Still curious as to my encounter with Indians and even with the smell of me, they got in close again and began pestering me with more questions. In as few words as possible, I told them of the tragedy and of my flight, only leaving out where I had come from and about the smuggling and the beavers. Drinks began to collect in front of me as

I told my story of woe and I thought we would never get out of there. Not having had a drink for so long, the whiskey and beer went to my head and I, damned near starved to death, was relieved when Arnold said it was time we got along to supper.

We got to his place, Priscilla was at the top of the porch stairs, her hands on her hips. She berated Arnold for her having worked so hard in the hot kitchen and him being late. Dinner was maybe spoiled and here he came home with "Another one of your drunken ragged scarecrows!" On and on she prolixed, a female colossus at the top of the steps. I hung back. "Come, my boy." Arnold pulled me along. "Don't be afraid."

"Arnold Baldwin, where do you find these stray dogs, anyway?" she asked sharply. "Ever since you started in drinking again, you bring home nothing but ruffians. If only you would listen to me and stay out of those cockroach-filled dens of iniquity." Frontier life had certainly not softened her rough tongue, she carrying on about as bad as I ever heard. "Will you never appreciate what I do for you? Nor understand what I mean when I say dinner is at dusk?" We got closer to where she was holding forth. I was in a quandary, whether to stay in the face of her wordy onslaught or flee. I hesitated. "Come, Kenneth." Arnold pulled me by my arm. I stopped ten feet from Priscilla, near enough so she got a whiff of me. She went for her broom, kept on the porch for such times as these, then she drew herself up short. "Kenneth. Did you say Kenneth?" She peered down at me. "Why, it t'is. Kenneth Kuyler! Goodness! I did not know it be you." She became apologetic and began asking all sorts of questions at once, a way too fast for me to answer.

I stammered for the drinks having thickened my tongue. Frustrated by my slow responses, she started in again on poor Arnold. "Why didn't you send word Ken was coming to supper? Blast you for an inconsiderate lout! I might have fixed a proper supper for the only bumpkin with manners and breeding." She never needed much excuse to start in on him. "Now I have made a great fool of myself in front of him and it is all your fault, Mister Arnold Baldwin. Do you hear me?"

I don't think he ever really heard her, he just mumbled, "Yes, dear, I am sorry but Kenny has only just appeared in town. He needed a stiff drink, for he has had terrible experiences. His friends are dead and he fortunate not to be so likewise. He is quite hungry, I am sure, and will eat your dinner be it hot or cold. I am sorry we kept you waiting." He gave her a mousy peck on the cheek which I thought she received in an oddly passionate sort of way.

She went inside and came quickly back with a stub of bread, which she gave to me, to hold me over whilst Arnold and me went round to the back, to the washtub. I stripped off what remained of my clothes and got into the tub. Arnold heated and dumped in pails of water whilst I vigorously scrubbed myself. Priscilla went to the neighbors and got clothes for me and she instructed Arnold to toss my buckskins into the fire. Finished bathing, I got into the clothes, not a good fit, slightly large and baggy but good enough, and feeling soft against my skin. I felt like my old self again except for my hunger and for having lost so much weight.

I combed my hair and beard, we went inside and supper was on the table, bowls of steaming cornmeal mush, slices of beef, bread and cheese, boiled potatoes and carrots. I dove in hungrily, my manners were not the best. A couple of times I noticed the amused looks which passed between them. I apologized for my boorishness even as I kept on, they not offended and pushing more dishes across the table to me. They asked many questions, I gave only such details as was safe to tell them, again not mentioning anything about smuggling or beavers.

According to her talk, Priscilla was not adjusting to the uncivilized ways of frontier life, though thankfully her cooking had not suffered. She was one damn fine cook. She complained of the summer heat and the mugginess. The lightning storms scared her. They did seem more violent around Saratoga than farther south, toward Albany. She said the mosquitoes and blackflies were insufferable. "Priscilla," I said, "you should go where I have been. Here they are a joy compared to farther north." I could remember how bad they were just yesterday. Worst of all for her were the red men who passed so frequently by her door. These Indians, Mohawks and Mohicans who came to town to trade or buy whiskey, knew Priscilla by reputation and it had become for them somewhat of a test of courage to be run off by her. To peer in through her porch windows for however long before she saw them and came out screeching perdition and damnation for their insolence and chasing them off with her broom. They took what bashing they could, then fled. I had heard this in the tavern.

Arnold ate little and said less during dinner. He is a most temperate man. Surely a lesson for me there, one I should undoubtedly learn. Priscilla started in again. "The filthy, ill-mouthed frontiersmen and farmers are boorish louts. Obnoxious know-nothings no better than woodchucks that might better be made to stay in the forest." She had words for everybody and everything. "Saratoga is a dismal pit of inhumanity, the inhabitants not fit for the company of proper folks." She bemoaned the lack of civilized diversions in this outpost.

"And the miserable wretch of a husband who has brought me to this low station in life." When he got the chance, Arnold pointed out how well they were doing. He was making more money than he ever did in England. "My services are much in demand here. In soot-filled London there were too many with my training who were willing to work cheaply. The only work I ever got was poor paying. Here, I am becoming a well-off man. Soon we will have money enough to go back to our English countryside and live in the style you deserve." This man never raised his voice.

"When I am too old and feeble to cross the ocean," she said. "Oh, I know I shall never again see the home of my youth, my dear sisters nor my mother. It is all your fault, you and your dreams of a new world and a new life. And your drinking!"

Arnold tried to tell me about his garden, of which he was very proud. Something else for Priscilla to carp over. "I have to do all the garden work whilst he sits in his office doing naught but shuffling his papers." Arnold said his work at the land office left him little time for the garden, or for teaching school, his other job. "I have a young lass helping out. She learns from me and is teaching the children." He then added proudly in his clipped tongue, "We have thirteen youngsters enrolled. Nellie does most of the day-to-day teaching whilst I oversee." Priscilla huffed at the thought of another woman around her man. Called her a mere bit of fluff. Having had a bath and a most wonderful meal, my interest was sparked by the talk of a young lady. An interest which the ever-keen eye of Priscilla noted. She quickly made clear the girl was spoken for. "Pull in your horns, boy." They laughed. After supper we talked some more but so tired was I, I was soon on the floor, rolled in a blanket, asleep.

Next morning, over breakfast, hoecakes smothered in honey, eggs, strawberries, cream and coffee, all spread on a linen tablecloth, I told Arnold where I had stashed my battered canoe. Told him to use it if he wanted, and finished with breakfast, I headed for the lower landing to see about a ride south. I got in with a flatboat hauling dried cowskins, as stinking a cargo as there was on the river. In return for the ride and a meal, I helped them move their cargo ashore at Halfmoon, well downriver. By nightfall, having got a ride on another boat, I was through the gates of Albany and walking into the Full Sail. Mother nearly fainted at the sight of me and declared me back from the dead. After she and Pops had welcomed me most fervently, she commented on my hair and beard and on how much weight I had lost. My haggard look justified her worst fears, her worrisome state of mind.

With the stories going 'round from other smugglers who had been to the Trading Tree and had witnessed the ugly mood of the savages, Pops and Mother had begun to despair of my ever returning. The smugglers said the Montreal authorities had encouraged the Indians to chase Englishmen, promising immunity from punishment for any who robbed furs after the fair was over. Father said others had problems getting home.

After I told them my story, leaving out the worst parts, Pops insisted I take a walk up the hill to the house of Jake's father on Yonkers Street, to give him the news of his son. Pops said Schaack had sent someone around almost nightly seeking news of me and my partners. I had already downed a few beers, and with my stomach full from all the food Mother put in front of me, I did not feel like moving. Pops kept insisting. I dreaded what I would tell Van Schaack but there was no dealing with Pops when he was adamant and truthfully, he was right. The alderman had lost his only son and needed to hear it from me, not from the street gossips.

I went up the hill practicing in my mind how I would break the news to Van Schaack and trepidacious for how he would react. Probably say it was my fault. I knocked on the door, a black servant came. He was not going to allow me in, the hour being late, and the look of me not altogether pleasing. I was glad enough for it. I didn't want to be there either. I was just turning to leave when the master himself came to the door. He gave his black man a scathing rebuke and with the black man having retreated, Schaack asked anxiously in Dutch, "What news have you of my son?" I answered him in the same language. "Sir, I am sorry to have to inform you, your son is dead, taken by wild Indians in the highlands. All our party except me are dead, all our furs are lost." His shoulders sagged and with him trying to get ahold of his grief, I told him I would leave and come back in the morning. He assented with nods and pushed me toward the door, which he slammed behind me.

Next morning, he met me at the door. By the handkerchief in his hand and the redness around his eyes, he had grieved plenty through the night. He clutched my arm tightly and leaned into me as he led me through the house to his office. He sat down behind his desk, I sat in a chair up close and over glasses of schnapps, we talked in somber tones and for a long time, he snorting away more tears. When he knew the full story, minus the parts about beavers, he was indignant I should have left his Jakop without trying to save him. When I laid it all out for him again and he had time to think on it, he said "Is not it possible some of the party, maybe my son, is alive unt prisoner in a campt to der nord?" I said it was possible. I hadn't seen Jake die and had heard him screaming about the letter in his pocket. If there'd been a French-man along, he might have intervened to hold Toad for ransoming. Possible though not likely.

"I vill send der letter of inquiry to unt friend in Montreal," Schaack said, and with a weary shake of his head, he raised his glass in thanks for my safe return.

I told Schaack good things about his son, of the deer Jake shot to feed us when we were starving. Schaack asked was the gunshot maybe what brought the savages down on us. I said no. If the Indians had been close enough to hear it, they'd have got us soon enough. I said naught of the nuisance Jake had been, a hindrance to us all. Instead, I let the old politician believe his son died a man. Which I reckon Jake did, right enough. There wasn't anything to be gained by deepening a father's grief. Had I known what was coming, I might have felt differently. First, the shifty old buzzard talked to me about the possibility of future employment or even a partnership in the fur business. Which meant the trade with Canada. "Young Kuyler, you iss der bright younk man, unt tough. I can zertainly use unt vellow like youse in der plans I haf for der vuture. Stay vis me mine boy unt I vill make you money. Enuff vor youse to repay all der goods I advanced youse party." Repay all? "Ya. I expect dat you vill reimburse me for der losses I haf suffered."

"Surely," I said. "You can't expect me to repay the entire amount. I will pay only my share, as one of five in the party." I was thinking it would take me years to pay back all the money advanced to us. By his smile, I knew I did not want to hear what was coming next. "Zertainly, mine boy, you do not vant to get into der trouble vid der debtors' court, do youse?" No sir, I didn't. My stomach was roiling. My plans for going north to trap would be ruined if I had to pay him back. There would never be enough money to grubstake a winter up there. "I haf lost mine only son. Der odder two vere employees. Dat leafes you unt your partner, Morrissey. Unt you say Morrissey iss dead. Which leafes you. So you can sees, you are responsible."

"Understand, mine chilt, dat I yam responsible to Mister Johnson vor his part also, vhich I must make good." I didn't say anything. Couldn't. I was numb. Downcast and miserable. Maybe I was in over my head but somehow I missed his logic. The debtors' court was not something to get involved with. Schaack would see to his money and there did not seem to be much I could do. He was a powerful presence around Albany. It would take working hard all summer just to begin paying him back. There would be no money left over for me. Told him I would stay in touch and try to pay him back but for now it would not be possible. He smiled for knowing there was no way for me to get out from having to pay.

I walked home kicking stones out of the street, despondent at the turn of things. The next day I wrote a letter to Bill's sister over to the Hampshires. I told her of my friendship with Bill and his death, again leaving aside the details. Found myself pouring out pent-up feelings to this young lady I had never met and probably never would. I sent the letter by way of a coaster headed for Portsmouth and hoped the address for Bill was right, for Bill never did tell me exactly where he hailed from. Never did say either whether his sister could read or not. Many females can't.

The rest of the summer, I worked for Pops and for Van Schaack. I pushed Pops' beer kegs around, made batches of beer, worked behind the bar, hauled slop buckets. I cut and stacked wood for the alderman. Dull, boring work, when all I could think about was the north woods, what it would be like to live and trap up there. Excitement was what I craved. There was none to be had in town. When I could, I hunted and fished and dressed out the meat for the inn or for peddling. Everything I made went toward my debt, nothing left over to put aside.

Before the summer was fair gone, my dear mother was trying her damnedest to get me married. She knew where my interests lay and would not abide it. For no, I would not see myself tied down like Eric, my gangly best friend. He had married Sarah Monckton, prettiest girl in Albany, blue eyes, golden hair in ringlets, but he was paying for it. He must spend his days in his father's shop, learning the apothecary trade. He couldn't go hunting or fishing. Not ever. I reminded him how he loved catching pike in the ponds, sturgeon in the river. Seemed he always caught the biggest ones. Between his wife and father, they would not let him spend time alone with me. I was a bad influence.

Father insisted I go back to the fur trader I had once worked for. Go back to skinning someone else's pelts. "Ya, unt maybe oben der vur-shed uf you own sum day if youse vorks 'ard enuff. Vor once." In his thick Dutch tongue. Pops laughed to think of me working so hard. "Youse tinks so damn much of der fur. Bah!" I stood my ground. "No way will I go back to Burnes. Damn Englishman! The crook held back most of what he was to pay me. Took my best skinning knives and ruined 'em, cussed me and tried to slap me when I didn't work fast enough to suit him. I won't put up with him again, not for nothin'.''

"Maybe jus' for a vile," Pops said. "Den you oben youse own business unt cheat zomebody else, ya!" Mother chided him for drinking too much schnapps before dinner. I recalled this past spring when Bill and me had gone to work for old man Burnes and quit and then gone back to him before quitting again to go north on our ill-fated journey. We had laughed at Burnes for leaving him in a big pile of fur. "He says youse is goot boy, but reckless." Father's face and tone said he thought the man was right about me. "Mister Burnes promise to pay you more dan bevor. I tink more dan you deserbe." Where had I heard that before? I would have to apologize for all the nasty things I said to him. "Ya, an' den youse take da tavern. I gif to youse for goot price." He chuckled at the thought of what was a good price.

By August, Sarah commenced lecturing me about the value of settling down. She turned the heads of one or two pretty girls toward me. I reckoned she was trying to divert what she called my wildness away from Eric. My own thoughts lingered continuously on the north woods. No one except me knew about the beavers flourishing in the interior valley. All my life I had listened to the talk in the tavern and never had I heard mention of any fur up there. And I was not going to tell one soul. Damn, if I could last out one season, I would be rich. What would Sarah and her friends say then? I knew the canyon would be safe, at least for a winter, and the beavers would be both plentiful and prime. I was determined to have a try at it.

****

My folks were glad for the help I gave them. Hoed Mother's garden until there was not a weed left, kept the woodshed filled for Pops.

Most days I went by the house of the alderman and worked with his crews loading freight on and off his coasters, sometimes hauling his goods in wagons to the huge plantations on the river below Albany or out to Schenectady. I worked long hours to get money ahead, yet I was not successful. All my money went for the alderman's bill. Each time I worked for him I made sure he marked down the money on a sheet he kept and I always checked the sheet against my own copy of the debt. I would tolerate no chicanery on his part and I fully expected him to try. He would keep me working off the debt for the rest of my life if he could. He had done so with others. One day he said he liked having me around. Said I remind him of his son. Damn!

Mother, ever the schoolteacher, pointed out the value of being able to write and cipher, otherwise Van Schaack would cheat me. She was right, for many of those who were bound in debt to Van Schaack could not cipher. The best times were when Schaack or Pops put in an order for a fresh deer or turkeys, or a mess of fish.

Sometimes, when he was not busy, Schaack would call me into his study and offer me a drink of lemon water or tea. Then he would ask to hear about his son. I hadn't the heart to tell him the truth. That his boy was a bigger fool than him and was naught but trouble from the first day of our trip. Toad's inability to keep up and to carry his share of the load surely contributed to his death and the deaths of the others. I could never tell Alderman Van Schaack the truth. Instead, I told him how hard and cheerfully his dear Jakop worked. The alderman asked sharp questions and I was hard-pressed at times to keep from tripping myself up. I never could tell if he knew the difference or not.

I still intended to go north in the fall, despite all the sound reasons for not going. And I would go without telling anyone. They would only try to dissuade me. Schaack might have me jailed or I might get bushwhacked. I had been putting money aside, money owed to the fat politician but he would not starve without it. I didn't have to give him all my money. To hell with the debtors' court!

There were so many things I needed. Bill and me at least had traps from last year and some gear. I inspected the traps, spent evenings cleaning them up. Took a tally. Way short of what I would need but the time was coming for me to go and I was gathering necessaries, including hammers and nails for building my cabin. A good Dutch carpenter can build a cabin or even a house or barn with wooden pegs, no nails. I am not so skilled and to obtain the necessary nails, I worked for the nail-maker in town, an Englishman by the name of Townes, who made them in his blacksmith shop. The work was hot and thirsty but I got all the nails that came out crooked when Townes pounded and shaped them. Traded loads of wood for the rest of what I would need.

Nights when I was not fishing or cleaning traps, I chased the young women of town. Even caught a few. Briefly. Stole a girl from one fellow. That part was easy enough. A nice lady, just not too smart. Her ex-beau's mother warned her about me. "Don't try to catch the wind." I suppose I knew what she meant. The girl did too, because she began pressing me about my intentions, as much to prove the beau's mother wrong, I think, as for any feelings for me. I stayed vague, we had a nasty spat, she went back to her beau and was soon married. I had earned a reputation of sorts and after this, I got discouraged and quit chasing. Women are pleasant enough in the ease of summer but with fall coming around, I could think of naught but the far woods.

All summer I had chewed on the notion of finding a partner. There would be much advantage in it but disadvantages too, and possible danger, and so I resolved to go alone. It shaped up to be a lonely winter.

By the middle of September and despite Mother's worriment, I was near ready. The sharper air carried along with it the usual improvement in hunting and fishing. I worked hard at both for there were good English coppers to be had selling hunkers of venison and stringers of fish. I had learned as a lad how the ship captains in port paid the best price for fresh meat to put on their mess. The debt to Schaack not paid off by half, I began to disappear more often. He'd grumble until I returned with meat, then the old windbag wouldn't say much.

As the time for departure came closer, I had doubts enough to about persuade myself not to go. It would be cold and bitter, I would surely freeze to death, if I didn't starve first or get my hair lifted. I couldn't possibly lug up everything I would need and did I want to trade the warmth and security of a winter in front of the common-room hearth with its sizzling roast beefs and hot rum for the frozen north?

The resistance from family and friends intensified. They didn't know what I was intending, they just knew it was dangerous, whatever it be. Schaack knew something was up and demanded I go see him. I went, he was furious. Said he'd put the sheriff onto me afore I could get away. I laughed in his face. "Try to stop me, you toad!" I said, and going down the hill from Schaack's, I realized the old skinflint had his claws into me for more than just money. I was a link to his dead son. Schaack could not bear to have the link severed and for this, I pitied him.

Pops, who had heretofore been mostly silent, pointed out the harshness of winter and the dangers I would face, and with his arguments not dissuading me, he began ruffling through my assembled possibles, tossing things aside and grumbling at how unprepared I was. "Vould a schipp go to der zea in zuch unready condition? Bah! I tink not" He was maybe right but I was his son and damn near as stubborn as him. Once my mind was made up, I was not easily swayed. Mother joined the argument and when she said I was too young for whatever I was intending, I would have spoken harshly but for the look which crossed her face. Indeed, it wasn't her words nor anybody's which most nearly persuaded me not to go. It was the sorrow in the way she looked at me. A mother's sorrow. Having thought to have lost me once, she could not bear to endure it again. Still, a man must find his own way, and I was firm. Pops had gone to sea at fourteen, I was sixteen. Old enough to make my way in the world. Pop's response, "Bah!"

The night before I left, I went around to the blacksmith. Townes had offered to lend me a horse to carry my pack as far as Saratoga. I promised to see it returned. He knew part of my plan but not where I was going or he too would have tried to talk me out of it. He gave me a bag of nails, good ones, not bent, and said he had a job for me when I came back. With the way he said it and with how he looked at me, I figured he thought he was gazing upon me for the last time.

Chapter XII – Adirondack Trapper

With just a few hours' sleep, I loaded my gear onto the horse and left silently in the middle of the night, slipping out the back door when I thought Pops and Mother wouldn't hear me. Walking up the road, I was scared and had plenty of doubts, yet I was determined. At Saratoga, I arranged to return Barnes' horse with a man heading for Albany with a packhorse much overloaded with sacks of potatoes for the market. The old swayback seemed grateful for the help. Spent two nights with Arnold whilst I effected repairs to the boat, not the most solid nor stable of crafts. I had built it under crude conditions and it had been banged about on my trip down and had to be made sturdy if it would carry me and my gear.

Priscilla chided Arnold for not having hired someone to repair the canoe over the summer. I told her it was not Arnold's fault. She said it was indeed his fault, I had asked him to watch over the canoe and he had failed. Again. I let it go. They thought me mad for what I was doing although they too had no clear idea of where I was headed. I lied and said I would see them again before the snow flew. Priscilla gave me a copper pot for cooking. Said I should boil water and stick my head in it for being such an idiot.

On my way out of Saratoga I encountered a young mutt wandering about in search, it appeared, of attaching himself to someone. A blackie with a patch of white on his throat and with ears that stood up straight and pointed when he was alert. I gave him a piece of jerky out of my sack. He followed me to the canoe, got into the bow and never looked back.

I kept careful watch going up the Hudson and saw no one, and with the current not too strong this time of year, I made it to the Great Carry in three days. I had already decided to avoid both Saint Sacrement and the Drowned Lands and would go instead out to the East Branch. Took two days to get around the mighty falls of the Great Carry, first with my canoe, then with my gear.

Continuing along the river, the trip was easy and exciting, the spectacle of the colors in the hardwoods beautiful to gaze upon. Beyond the Sacandaga, the colors were mostly gone by, the leaves had all mostly dropped. At the mouth of the East Branch, I portaged around the falls and past there, the current slowed. Had to get out a few times and pull the canoe at the end of a rope across the riffles, and where the river narrowed up and with too much water rushing through the defiles to paddle against, I portaged. I shot a turkey what was roosting along the shore. Slid right up on him. He never saw me coming. A tom with a long beard.

A few more days and I reached the Eagle's Lake and it occurred to me I hadn't seen anyone since getting north of Saratoga. Nor much sign, neither. I stashed my gear along the south shore and went to see how far or close I was to Scalp Point. Might be it was just over the next hill and if it were, I'd have to rethink staying or not.

Turned out my Eagle's Lake sat near the eastern edge of the last escarpment before Corlear. Three-miles walking, a gradual uphill, and I was looking down into the valley, not at Scalp Point but at Tyonder-rogha, which, seven, eight miles from where I stood, was ten miles from my Paradise.

I pondered why the French had built at Scalp Point and not at Ti. Might be they felt Ti would have been too south of an intrusion, even for the lethargic British to ignore. If the French wagered they could build at Scalp Point without the English reacting, they'd won their bet.

Or it maybe had to do with the smuggling. From Scalp Point, the French could close the door or leave 'er open, whichever suited 'em, whilst at Ti, with its location on top of the Portage Crick debouch-ment, the way would be more difficult to keep open without exposing the truth of the French conniving with the smugglers.

I trekked up to Scalp Point, staying on the escarpment, well back into the trees the entire way. I looked down on the French castle from high up on the mountain which overlooked it from the western shore.

The distance from Scalp Point to Paradise was fifteen miles, far enough so's I could stay the winter. The French and Indians, though close by, were orientated north to south along the Corlaer Valley. For them, my lakes and ponds, close as they be, were an alien land. A blank space on their maps. They were vague about how far west they might venture before blundering into trouble and they well knew the consequences, did they offend the Mohawks.

The Mohawks considered the entirety of the Adirondacks, Corlear and Saint Sacrement included, to be theirs. They had only grudgingly assented to English and French presence on the lakes and always made it clear they would not tolerate either side pushing west into the mountains. French adherence to this stricture was what might make it possible for me to survive up here.

Back at my lake, I made three trips up the incline with my gear and began preparing for a winter of trapping. Among my possibles were a couple of shovels given to me by Townes. "Guaranteed to see you through, lad," and grateful I was.

My cabin was to be in the box canyon, toward the back wall. Here was a hump of high ground of dirt for the digging. High enough so did the canyon flood in the spring, I would be above the water. It also put me close to the pond and the brook. These would provide for cooking and washing, even in the fall of the year when the water be low elsewhere, and at night, when I lay down on my bed of spruce branches in a frame of cedar, the water splashing down off the rocks and into the pool would be a lullaby for sleep.

I lined out for my cabin and commenced digging out a cellar hole. I raced against time for winter would soon enough be upon me. I could already feel it coming. Five days digging and I decided to make the hole bigger. Deeper, too, to get it below the frost line.

For a month I worked morning 'til night. The rocks I encountered in my digging I used to line the hole, together with the trunks of the small trees I cut down. Just about the time my shovels was broken to not being useable, I had my hole and an entryway of logs and rocks, three stairs leading down in. I made the walls four logs high above ground, supported by rocks and topped with a bark roof. I filled the chinks between the logs with moss and mud and screened it with the dirt I had dug. Except for the smoke out of the chimney, the cabin would be damn near invisible. With the wolves howling at night and sometimes prowling my canyon, I decided I better build a trapdoor in the roof and rig an inside ladder so's to get onto the roof and shoot 'em without goin' outside.

I felt a bit ashamed for living in a damp, low-ceilinged cellar hole. What would Mother say if she knew? My conscience told me I should build a proper cabin instead of wandering the country. Consoled myself with the thought scouting was a more valuable use of my time and besides, this boy possessed no great skill at carpentry. I knew naught of tools, just a rudimentary use of the saw, the hammer and the ax. Reckoned the cellar hole would have to do. Promised myself I'd build a more proper cabin next year.

By the end of November I was moved in and pleased with what I had built although truthfully, it wasn't much. More of a hole covered over than a true cabin but, and although I was not of short stature, I could get around inside without having to stoop much. The chimney of mud and rocks would make for good strong heat, at least for as long as the fire burned.

The dog and me took to being friends. He did not bark much and those few times when he did, I corrected him. A sharp whack with a stick will get the attention of a smart mutt. He was still in the puppy stage when I found him and was eager to learn. Taught him to communicate soundlessly, same as an Indian camp-dog. Barking at the wrong time could jeopardize the position of an entire tribe. Any dog which could not be broken of this natural habit got put into the stewpot. The tribesmen were fond of dog-meat. The hound seemed to know this and learned not to bark nor even growl. He spoke to me of danger with the movement of ears and tail.

Yapping when we was off chasing deer proved a harder instinct to break. After trying for a month to teach him how to approach deer, I shut him inside the cabin and went out and shot a doe. Fresh meat! Once he learned the right way to chase, he became a big help although he sometimes forgot what was the proper way of doing it.

I spent time learning the land and with beechnuts thick on the ground, the deer hunting was excellent. I glimpsed bucks with antlers such as no man had ever seen around the towns. Without anyone to brag to, I took only the smaller bucks, easier to drag home and better eating than those tough old stags.

A mile east of my lake, a sizeable crick ran down from the higher mountains and unlike the Eagle's Lake and its outlet which went to the west, this creek flowed east and north, through a strikingly beautiful gorge. The upper creek was dammed in some places by beavers although none of the dams entirely stopped the flow. I, proceeding most cautiously, followed the creek down into the Corlaer Valley. Between rugged hardwood-covered hills, the crick flowed over rapids and falls, including one magnificent sequence of seven or eight falls in quick order, each no more than two or three feet high.

In another place I saw springs which bubbled up out of the ground and often did the brook meander over swampy, moss-covered forest floor. Deep holes formed by boulders in the streambed, dead trees fallen into logjams. Water swirling in deep eddies. One set of rapids sent the water plunging a hundred feet into a shaded glen, into a pond where the first ice had already formed. The pool held trout and salmon. Around the glen were tall ferns.

I spent a comfortable night with a smokeless fire against the back wall of the overhang and in the morning, I continued down the creek and came to where it emptied into a swamp along the shore of Corlaer. I figured the French, did they ever come up to my Paradise, would follow the crick, though it was a daunting climb and no short distance. It was six miles from Scalp Point to the debouchment of the crick into Corlear and another twelve up to Paradise. A long walk for men terrified the woods around them might erupt with gunshots and Iroquois whoops.

On the way home, I stopped in the glen where I had seen salmon and filled my pack basket. Got home and smoked my catch and a few days later, I walked Outlet Brook the other way, seeking its origin, which turned out to be a large pond only a few miles from my cabin. And the beavers! This high-country pond sat in a natural depression with rugged mountains on all sides, the mouth dammed by beaver works of amazing size and strength. A dam flattened along the top for the forest critters using it as a walkway across the pond. Counted five beaver houses.

It was still too early for best trapping, the fur wouldn't be prime yet, and I kept busy chopping wood and fishing. Speckled trout were plentiful in the westward-flowing brook which served as the outlet for my Eagle's Lake. Big ones; eight, ten pounders. Easy to take with a spear around dark, when they began to move. I filled my pack basket each time I went down and when I got home, I salted the fish to preserve 'em. The sack of salt I brung up from Albany had made for hard lugging. A smoker would have been easier and smoking was a better way to keep fish but it would have been too dangerous to keep meat smoking long hours over a fire.

When I had eaten all my salmon and wanted more, I decided to go down to the Portage Crick, where Bill had caught so many when we were with Hugh. At the Saint Sacrement end of the portage trail, near the natural stone bridge where I completed my descent, I seen the body of a white man, nationality unknown. Mutilated in evil fashion, topknot lifted. Stripped even of his stockings, a grim reminder of the dangers constantly around me. The small critters of the forest had been feeding on the corpse. Mice, foxes, fishers and crows.

I took my salmon from the pool below the falls, and back up in my valley, I spent time preparing my traps, scouting the best locations for setting them, and chopping wood, always was I chopping wood.

****

Each morning, as soon as the night mist was risen off the mountains, I trekked the deer runway to the top of the cliffs which ran along the north rim of the canyon. This afforded me a view of the valley of the Eagle's Lake and beyond, a ways off to the north and west. High mountain country it be. Bare hardwoods made for dramatic views. I'd look for the smoke of campfires, see none, then trek around to the south rim where the view was not so expansive. I'd see distant spots of water, the ponds, but no smoke.

Often did I hear the osprey's exultant cry and if I was up on the north rim or some other high place, I might see him circling, plunging and rising again with a fish in his mouth. Saw the eagle rob the osprey a few times. When the lake froze over, the birds would be gone.

In late November I began putting out my traplines. This was hard work but I loved it. Tramping and learning the wilderness, thrilling at the endless small valleys so pretty to gaze upon. The Twin Lakes, or what I called First and Second Lake, for it had the appearance of being two lakes connected by a narrow channel, led from the Eagle's Lake to the East Branch and was four miles long. In some places, it was a mile across. The channel was long and narrow. I built a raft of six logs laid up together and used it to pole around the shoreline, checking traps. Within a few days of the lake freezing, which came in early December, I was able to walk the ice to get to my traps. Up in the hills surrounding this lake and emptying into it were smaller ponds which sent their waters down through rocky gulches. Some of these upper ponds were sizeable, a half-mile or more across. They all held beaver colonies and gave up many a fine pelt. And trout too, for the deep-water ponds were laden with fish.

I mostly worked the lakes and ponds outflowing to the west. There were beavers to the east of me. This was a bad thing as it seemed the beavers, however they might have got their start here, were spreading west to east. Left unchecked, they might announce themselves to the French in the valley with woodchips and gnawed sticks floatin' down to 'em. This I would prevent by trapping along the edge of the escarpment and using the utmost caution, for it wasn't just beaver sign which might alert the French. A float stick or a piece of English leather might betray my presence to some sharp-eyed Indian or bush-loper.

To the south and a bit west of my cabin sat another good-sized lake, bigger than anything I was trapping. The lake was nestled under the steep-rising slopes of the awe-inspiring edifice I called the Pharoah's Mountain which, with its thick base and mere point at the top, formed a pyramid. I did not trap the Pharoah's Lake, though there were plenty of beavers and I was tempted. It sat too far from my valley. Told myself I'd climb the mountain before the winter snows got too deep.

Also south of my cabin and closer to me than the Pharoah's Lake, were three ponds. One had a colony of otters, another had a big sow bear and the third was in the shape of a goose's neck. Thus, Otter, Bear and Gooseneck Ponds.

I started to gather fur in fair quantity, especially once I seen there was as much running through the woods as there was in the water. Fisher-cats prowled the land in abundance. I set traps for them under rock overhangs and downed trees. Wished I had more traps suitable for catching the vicious little meat-eaters. There was sign of bobcat and cougar. Came upon a lynx without either of us knowing the other was there, figure him to still be running!

My work went along fine until what I reckoned to be the end of December, when I discovered I had until now no notion of what winter here really meant. I was unprepared for the storms which dumped a foot or more of snow in a night's time and between the storms, days and nights of cold such as I had never known before. The wind howled and raised the snow in white spirals, as if all the banshees of Old Eire were out there exulting at what was surely going to be my death. I heard the iced upper-branches of the trees rattling in the wind and feared a big limb or an entire tree might crash down through my roof. I wondered why in the hell I was doing this fool thing. The dog stayed close to the fire, on a deer hide. When the fire died, he woke me with his nose. He liked the heat.

My fur gathering slowed considerably. For long days at a time, I could not go outside. Predators robbed my sets, which too often froze. I lost many traps and much good fur under the ice. Seemed my fingers were most always in freezing water. Numb. So much wood chopped and split in the fall proved not enough. My woodpile dwindled, I spent daylight hours chopping and stacking more instead of checking traps. My bold plan began to look a failure. The rivers and lakes lay beneath deep blankets of snow and ice. Scared to go too far from the cabin for fear of getting lost and freezing to death. The feeling of being trapped lay heavy on me. Went hungry when the storms raged. Nothing to eat for days at a time 'cept thin soup. Almost gave up at times yet it was what I wanted and so I persevered. The black dog stayed by my side, braving the worst of it; the comfort of his company helped keep me going through a lonely Christmas and New Year's, near as I could make the time.

Deeper into winter and with '37 coming in as harshly as '36 went out, me and the dog began sizing each other up for a meal. I feared waking up some night to him gnawing on my leg. When things got their worst and I was resigned to cutting him up for the soup pot, there came a break in the cold. I caught fish through a hole in the ice and shot a scrawny turkey. Got a few rabbits in my snares. Altogether not much but enough to keep us going.

I often had nothing to eat 'cept soup flavored with the bark of trees. Even the dog was too thin to look appetizing; the poor mutt, his ribs showing, suffered same as me. Ate beavers and small game, mostly. Shot a few turkeys. In February, I spent most days hungry in the cabin, the weather too awful for anything except dashing out to the woodpile.

When the weather allowed, I resumed work. It was man-killing. The beaver dams were strong put together and treacherous with ice. I'd set traps and go back the next day and hope a wolf or fisher had not gotten there ahead of me. Chopping places in the ice for the sets, I fell through a few times and near froze to death before getting to a fire. To increase my take of fur, I began chopping holes in the dams with my hatchet and setting traps for the beavers what came to patch the holes. My hands and fingers were most often froze before I could get the water gushing but oh! What prime fur!

I spent long hours over my stretcher boards, working the fur. The wind blew in through the chinks in my walls and ceiling and try as I might, I could not keep it out. I was always shoveling snow off my roof. Otherwise, when it got hot inside the cabin, the snow up there melted, the water ran down through the cracks. Then, did the fire get low or go out, the water froze again. Many nights I awoke to the splash of water on my face, many mornings I got up and my first step had me slipping and sliding on an icy floor.

When I thought I could carry on no longer and had about decided to give up and go down and surrender to the French at Scalp Point just so's they'd feed me, the sun saw my plight and came back north. The winter broke, the land came cautiously alive, and with the coming on of warmer weather, it was even worse for me. The pond ice often broke beneath my weight and into the water I'd go. Ice under the snow made for treacherous footing and where the snow was gone, there was mud, thick and clinging enough so I had to go wide around it.

But day by day the trees budded, the grasses showed between the patches of snow. I was excited for having survived the winter, and my cache, readied and packed in bales, would be worth a small fortune if I could get it to Albany. In addition to the beavers, some old bosses goin' upwards of a hundred pounds, I had a half bale of deer hides, a few wolf pelts, mink, and a dozen or so otter pelts. Three small bales of fisher-cat. The fisher was prime blanket and had been in demand when I left Albany last fall. Also a bobcat pair I caught in fisher traps. Preparing the furs, stretching, cleaning, sorting, bailing, though it be inside work, was mighty hard. I was not fast at it; care need be taken.

My old canoe I judged too battered from the winter weather to be useable on the rough waters of the Hudson and too small for the load it needed to carry. I repaired it for use on the Eagle's Lake. Kept it hidden there and built a bigger and sturdier one down to First Lake.

Spring came on slowly, the winter was reluctant to release its hold. March is the cruelest of months for it holds the promise of warmer weather and yet is bitterly cold and can turn without warning. Hot one afternoon, snow a foot the next. The new snow would be gone in a few days, except where it lingered in the shaded places.

By what I figured was the middle of April, the Corlaer Valley was turning green. But not yet up on the heights. When the ground thawed, I dug a hole, put in all my extra possibles and one small keg of gunpowder, things to be protected until fall. I smeared my traps with bear fat to retard rust. Before leaving, I planted corn, potatoes and ground nut in small patches of good dirt. Girdled a few trees for next winter's woodpile. These would save a lot of work, did I come back. I portaged my bales down to First Lake, packed it all into my new boat and was on my way. It felt good to be moving along the lake on a bright spring morning, all thoughts of the harsh winter forgotten. The black hound pointed the way, nose into the wind, ever eager for adventure.

The mouth of the sandy creek below Big Lake and the rapids where the East Branch emptied into the Hudson were wild. I portaged both, made a fast daylight trip as far as the Great Carry and made a hidden camp. From there I traveled at night and hugged the eastern shore, hoping nobody would see me. If they did, I might get bushwhacked for the fur or arrested for smuggling. Eased on down to Albany and went straight to a Dutch fur-buyer, thinking he would give me a fair deal. Turned out this man was as crooked as the English buyers. As bad or worse than Burnes. I'd known this man a long time. All my life he had come into the tavern. Last summer he told me to see him first anytime I had fur. Now and instead of treating me right, he was suspicious regarding the origination of my cache. He called over some of his cronies and they began throwing questions at me.

"Why is it so unlike any other?"

"How did you come by it so early in the year?"

"Did you come from Montreal?"

"This fur is thicker even than Great Lakes fur, equal to any from the north." This too was a question, or perhaps a challenge. All their inquiries I evaded. They tried to ply me with whiskey. I was sorely tempted. It had been a long time. When I saw them laughing amongst themselves and saw one man wink at another, I refused their drinks. Been around these fur sheds enough to know how they operated. We haggled awhile. Back and forth. Watching the Dutchman fingering the good fur, I knew he would not let it out of his shed at any price. It would make a killing in London. I was prepared, I knowing what I had right down to the last pelt, and what each was worth. We haggled long, he got closer to what I wanted, we agreed on a price. I was excited, the money would allow me to pay off my debt to Van Schaack and with plenty left over. When I understood it was all agreed upon, I had some whiskey. Palavering is thirsty work. Then the fur-buyer tried to dupe me. "My friend," he said, "here is my chit. Redeemable in any business in the colony." The crook would weasel me in a second if I accepted. I would present the chit to Van Schaack to cover my debt, the two of them would cook up a deal, I would suffer heavily.

"No, sir, cash money or I take my bales to Burnes or Van Braun." Stand fast or be robbed. "There are plenty of other fur buyers who will gladly pay cash money for my bales once they see the quality of these furs. You do admit they are good, eh, Mister Burger?" I was just as haughty as him. "Yes, yes," he said, continuing to admire my prime pelts whilst counting on his fingers and making notes in his ledger.

Then he wanted the agreed purchase price reduced for cash, saying the higher price was good only for a chit. "If the chit is as good as cash money," I asked pointedly, "why does there have to be a difference in price?" More haggling. I was exasperated, wanting to get it over with and get out of there. He came up some, nearer to the agreed-upon price but still short of what I wanted. His cronies were starting to close in a little too tight and the second glass of spirits went right to my head. He went up a little higher and I took the cash. Probably should have gone for a better price elsewhere but didn't do too badly.

Next stop, the Full Sail. I walked in jaunty as hell, and not for the first time, I heard my mother exclaim I was back from the dead. Quite the homecoming. Later the same day I walked up the hill to Schaack's big house. He started yelling as soon as he saw me but calmed down when I gave him the full amount I owed. He gave me a receipt, paid in full, and yet, and in the kindness he showed, I sensed a regret for the debt he could no longer wield over me.

He wanted me to stay for tea and some talk. I said as how my thirst would not be slaked with tea, and when he suggested rum, I again demurred. I suspected the old buzzard had known about my furs before I got to his house and same as the others, he'd try to get information out of me. I started for the door, he followed along, about begging me to come back the next day. I didn't, and he sent inquiries to the tavern, which I ignored. Finally, he came himself and asked for a meeting at a certain time.

Others were there with him when I arrived, the high sheriff and men I knew to be close to the mayor. Schaack offered me a drink, I took it. I was prepared to have to once again answer questions about my fur but this time the questions would be official government business. I knew how the men who bankrolled the smuggling, men such as Van Schaack, did sometimes use the law to intimidate those who did the real work, especially were the men uncooperative. I had information they wanted, and once they got it, I would be expendable.

The sheriff asked where my furs came from. "Sacandaga," I said, which they all knew was a lie. Mine were not Sacandaga furs. "Nobody saw you out thet a way," said the sheriff. "Ain't no such beavers out there and only a little fisher." One of the lackeys added, "Your'n fur is prime." Casual as hell, I said how it didn't take long for word to get around. The sheriff dropped a threat. Said he knew I had been to Montreal before for furs. Had I perhaps been up and back again? "Mighty fast trip," I said, "iffen I did." He suggested I had wintered with the French, a guest at their Crown Point castle. I wasn't sure how serious this was. We were not at war but scaring me with treason or consorting might have been a way to force me to divulge the source of my pelts. It didn't, and the questions and evasions went 'round until finally the mayor's man asked if I would lead a smuggling trip to Montreal. "No, sir," I said. "I will not go to Montreal ever again for furs. It is more dangerous than how I spent the winter, and isn't smuggling against the law?" Someone asked what was I aimin' to do with myself now. "Chase women," I said. They didn't laugh at my remark and with how the sheriff was looking at me, I figured I was in the soup. Schaack spoke for my trustworthiness. Reckoned he was just helping so's he could take advantage of me later and reckoned they was all thinking the same, then Schaack helped me further by telling me I could go, and before any of the others could insist I stay, Schaack diverted them toward some other business.

Chapter XIII – Trouble Around the Bend

I passed the summer spending my money on good times and gettin' ready for another season in the mountains. Determined I was to go again, despite the first winter being so hard and lonely. I felt it was a good life and was certainly justified by the profits. I tried to convince two different women to spend the winter with me. I was vague to them about exactly where we would be going and cited instead the money to be made in a winter's time and the fun to be had. Alas, no luck, which was just as well. The girls thought I was crazy, as did my folks, who couldn't understand my wanting to go off woods-loping when I could make a perfectly good living staying home and running the tavern.

Through the summer, we hosted a black-robe, an old man recently rescued from the harsh treatment inflicted on him by the Oneida Tribe of the Iroquois. The priest had gone from Montreal to a western castle on a mission to spread the Papist religion and draw our Iroquois away from their Sacred Council Fire. The Oneidas had made a prisoner of him. They tortured him and would have killed him if not for a Dutch trader named Handel who bought him to save his life. Handel put the priest up at the Full Sail a week or more whilst they awaited a ship to take him back to France. He was a destitute, hobbled beggar. All bent over, fingers and ears chewed to nubs. I watched as he paced behind the tavern in the afternoons, mumbling to himself. Wondered what he was saying. I thought him gone mad but Mother said he was making his daily compact with his god. Seemed funny to see him, stooped and moving so slowly, shuffling his feet and jabbering to hisself in a foreign tongue. I reckoned he did not look evil to me, only evilly done. He learned through his conversations with Van Schaack, who speaks the French, that I was a woodsman, and with Van Schaack interpreting, the black-robe tried to hire me to carry a message to Scalp Point, to inform his superiors in Montreal of his circumstances. "Send them a letter from France," I said. Eric said the old priest must a been a hundred years old but come to find out he was only forty-five or so.

****

Eric told me two men he never saw before had come into his shop asking about me. Right after, the same two men began coming into the tavern most nights. They would stay until I showed. Soon's they laid eyes on me, they'd vamoose. As if they were checking to make sure I was still in town. Father asked about the pair. When I told him I didn't know who they be, he inquired of Schaack. The alderman denied knowing anything about them or their purpose. He promised to try and find out. One of them looked familiar to me but I couldn't place him.

He was tall and rapier thin with slicked-down black hair, a black goatee and mustache, all perfectly trimmed. As though he must spend hours on it each day. He wore a brown greatcoat and brown pants. A deliberate and dangerous-looking fellow. The other was a woodsman. No doubt about it. Short, and thick as an ox. Polecat hat, wolf-fur shirt, deerskin leggings, beaded moccasins. Eyes darting ceaselessly. One tall man, one short, a most treacherous looking pair. We never could find out where they came from or who they were, but they caused no trouble. Indeed, they said little and just drank and watched. They became such regulars we ceased noticing them.

****

Mother's kitchen was a hot, busy place. There was a hominess to the aromas of roasting meats, fresh-baked cornbread and pies. She employed a succession of serving girls, most were newly come over from the Old Country, usually someone's cousin or niece. Mother took her responsibility toward them most seriously. It was hard to chase the girls whilst avoiding Mother, though I had begun to do better. Most of the girls were willing enough. My father was severe in such matters but usually with the merest twinkle in his eye. He always said, "Do not leaf tracks so dat your mudder vill tink dat you am up to zomesink. Ya." He always worked up such a mad when he thought of me getting into trouble with Mother. He'd glare with piercing eye, like some ferocious bird of prey. So hawkish, I had to laugh. Then he'd get mad at me for laughing and the words would start.

In July a new serving girl came to work for us, a middlin' pretty lass named Anneke. Tall and blonde, from a Dutch family just come over to the colony. Poor they were. Her parents and two brothers were working for a rich uncle on a patroon downriver. The uncle had paid their passage over, now they were paying him back. From what she told me, the uncle thought he just about owned them. Father paid most of Ann's wages to the uncle. I found the wench to be kind-tempered enough, not at all sharp tongued. She was sweet on me from the first moment I walked through the door. Got me worked up in a hurry. Trouble was, come to find out, she was sweet on any man who had a bit of money or a future, as is the way sometimes with women. We rendezvoused in the hayloft a few times but as soon as she realized I was not for settling down, she turned elsewhere.

Then it was September, the worst of the bugs would be gone by up north and off I went with a heavy load to add to my possibilities. Just before I left, Mister Townes, the nail-maker, came by the tavern with a warning. "Watch yourself, wherever you be headed. Thet fur you brung last year created more interest than you know." I thanked him and put the warning out of my mind, not realizing the value of the words.

The dog was glad to be back on the trail. Up north he was not under foot so much and received fewer kicks for his trouble. Approaching Saratoga around dusk, I decided to stop for the night. I stashed my canoe just below the lower carry and drank at an inn with Arnold and his boss, Lydia's husband, Richard. Not telling them where I was headed. An hour after we commenced drinking, the two fellows who had shadowed me all summer showed up. They acted as if they did not notice me but I seen the tall one looking my way when he thought I was too drunk to notice. That night I drank a gallon or two of beer, of not such good brew as Pops'. I left some pages of my writing with Arnold to read and correct. Next morning, I was on my way, hung-over, my head hurting like the blazes. Too sick to think of much.

****

All the way to the Great Carry, the air stayed thick and muggy, hard to breathe. Above the Carry, the change in the air was obvious. Vapors given off by the vast pine and balsam forests cleanse the lungs. The air cooler and sweeter smelling, the change alone worth the trip.

West along the Hudson, I went past the mouth of the Sacandaga, pushing up across shallows and riffles, which, tame now, would become boiling rapids in the spring. Used a rope to drag my canoe across many of the shallows. Glad I was to see ahead the high open ledges of the towering, rounded-off hump which landmark was at the joining of the East Branch with the main river.

All day something had been bothering the dog. He was nervous, which is dangerous in an overloaded canoe. He kept sniffing the air and growling. I put it off to a deer or a wolf but toward the end of the day I realized I had better find out what was making him act so queer.

I played a hunch, pulled to shore and stashed my canoe. I covered all sign of having got off the water and hid behind a big log. Whilst eating my dinner of peas and ham, along came a canoe, hard against the current. It was the sinister pair which had been watching me all summer and which Townes had warned me about. I watched them go to shore not far above my own camp. Then I remembered where I had seen the tall slick one with beard so trim and neat. He had been present at Burger's shed last spring when I brought in my furs. So! Burger's man, sent after me, to locate the source of my furs and neither he nor Burger would care what happened to me once they learned my secret. I tied the dog to a tree to prevent him following and giving us away. Then I snuck along the shore on foot. Crept up on them and from the bushes, I listened.

"Where'd he get to, Mike?" the tall, slick one said. "How the blazes do I know?" the other said. "Ah, hell," Slick said. "Burger said you was a tracker." He went on in his clipped tone, each word measured for its effect. "He might'n a gone up the crick we passed an hour ago. You wouldn't know. Might be anywheres by now." The short, thick man laughed and said I was still on the main river. "Isn't nuthin' up them smaller cricks 'cept mebbe Injuns. Be a matter of time afore we find him." The other replied, "We better find him, iffen you want any of Burger's money." He then asked could they winter in these parts, did they need to. "If that crazy Dutch kid can do it," Mike said, "I sure in hell can, but Burger don't pay 'nough for me to spend the winter freezin' up'n here." Slick agreed. "Be damned cold. We'll just learn his whereabouts and get ourselves back down to Saratoga. Spend the winter and come back early in the spring and knock him on the head. Let him do our winter's work for us."

I didn't know what to do. I damn sure couldn't lead them up the East Branch to Beaver Valley. And I didn't want to turn around and go home. I reckoned I'd let them get ahead of me on the main river, the West Branch, then follow them up. See where they went. Maybe they'd get tired of trying to find me. I chuckled to myself about this trick I would play on them. Even told it to the dog. Slept a few hours and followed after 'em and damn near got seen going 'round a bend. They were searching the shores for my campfire, which they figured must be a little way upstream of them. For two days they continued along the West Branch with me following a few hours behind and with them searching for my sign. Suppose I might a shot 'em from behind but didn't reckon myself a back shooter. I just watched. And learned. Mike was a woodsie, no mistakin' it. Whilst the other man stayed in the canoe, Mike checked the places where I might have set foot and he never left sign of his own.

My third morning trailing them I awoke before daylight to the dog barking loudly, something he never did. I had been tying him to a tree each night and now the two men was there with guns pointed at me and with me knowin' they'd shoot did I reach for my own gun. "How come ye been follerin' us, eh, chum?" Slick asked, in close now and with a pistol inches from my nose. I said I reckoned we was just all going the same way. The other man spoke. "I don't reckon nuthin. Ye been spookin' behind us two, three days. Did ye think ye'd fool me?" Slick pressed the tip of his pistol barrel against my nose. "Listen, Kuyler," he said. "I'll say 'er right out. We know who you be and what you be doing. All we wanna know is where the fur be growin'. Show us and we'll maybe let you go home. Don't show us or try'n shake us and I promise you'll be not dead when Mike takes your hair."

I figured he was bluffing and figured to do some bluffing of my own. "I reckon there be no money in it for you boys," I said, "lessen youse can go back and tell your boss where the fur come from, and how you gonna know iffen I'm dead? No, sir. There ain't gonna be no shootin' nor scalpin'. Not if fur is what you be wantin'. Iffen it ain't, why, go ahead and pull your trigger and go home and tell Burger the secret fur place is lost forever on account of you killed the only man who knowed where it be growing." Slick moved the muzzle of his gun away from my nose. I laughed for having gained a stand-off.

I said there was beaver enough for three and said I was willing to share, but not without a promise from them to not tell anybody else. They both swore they would never give away a secret beaver place. "And if I show you, you won't shoot me?" They promised. "Tell you what, boys," I said. "I ain't a gonna tell ya where the fur be. No, sir. You want fur, youse can spend the winter helpin' me roundin' her up. What I can tell you, it's one hell of a long ways." They looked at each other, and at me. "Follow along, partners, and you'll see some prime beavers." I knew damn well they wasn't intending to winter in the north but what I also knew, they couldn't kill me and go back down to Albany without knowing where the fur be.

Up the West Branch we went, them just a short way behind as I took 'em on a wander, my first time up this way, a chance for me to see the country, to learn it. We took side jaunts up some of the cricks which entered the main river, the waters clear and cold. My light canoe was perfect for traveling these smaller waterways. The rogues' heavy elm-bark was clumsy in fast waters, difficult to portage. My canoe floated in no more than three or four inches of water, theirs had to be dragged or carried. I left plenty of sign for 'em to follow. They had trouble keeping up and with them usually well behind, I some-times swung back on 'em to poke fun at their struggles. Even did I sometimes paddle along and converse with them. "How much farther, lad?" the thin one would ask at these times. He was more suited to barroom intrigues and games of chance than to the rigors of the woods. The other, Mike, was not fooled by my aimless wandering nor my claim I couldn't recall which stream had the fur. "I ain't seen no sign a beavers," he'd say. I'd say the streams all looked too much alike.

Other times, on warm sunny afternoons, I'd set up my writing and whilst I was penning inadequate descriptions of all I was seeing, along they'd come. How it did frustrate them to find me so! The second time they came upon me in this manner and damn sick of it all, they put their guns on me and demanded I give 'em my boat. I pointed out theirs was too big and heavy for me. The looks on their faces showed they might just shoot me, Burger's money be damned. But they let me keep my canoe and from then on, I mostly stayed away from 'em, trying to shake 'em yet not able to.

Came to a series of lakes and flows which, coming out of steep mountains, drew together to form the source of the mighty Hudson. I figured the mountains were those me and my companions had looked at from a distance, back when the Hurons was after us.

I skirted to the northwest, to where it was less mountainous though still rugged and where streams and creeks, lakes and ponds connected for miles of canoe travel. Spent a glorious October wandering new country. With so much fast water, I reckoned a man, was he intrepid enough and did he know the country, could travel forever without getting out of his canoe. Said man could go for miles up the little cricks, jump up deer and occasional moose, even elk, for I heard the elk bugle on a couple of occasions. Much faster than walking or going on a horse. Horses will never be feasible in the north. The brush is too thick, the way is too rough. There be no trails nor open country. The birch canoe is and shall remain the only way to traverse this land. It sometimes seemed I lived in mine.

One time I rounded the bend of a shallow creek, my canoe scraping the bottom and the dog gave a warning, too late, we was in the midst of a pack of wolves. They'd been feasting on a deer carcass and were on every side of us. I swung my paddle and hollered, the dog barked, the wolves spooked and run off. And lucky for the dog he knew better than to go after them.

On another occasion, sitting in the sun beside a delightful brook and eating fresh trout and a turkey drumstick, I noticed a number of tiny fish dancing along in the current. Curious, I caught one and put him in a small earthen jar. A hairsnake is what I called him, for such did he look. Not even an inch long and thin as a strand of hair, head no bigger'n the head of a pin. I could see right through him, like a small slip of water reed, so tiny and frail and yet vigorous with life. Kept him a day or so to puzzle over his size and to quench my curiosity for such a tiny living thing. Then let him go in another brook miles away and watched him take to this new home. In an instant he was bouncing along in the current. Sure as hell an interesting little critter. Made a man hanker to know what else was out here.

When the waters began to run down to the west, toward the Saint Lawrence, it was time for me to lose my shadows and get on with my winter's trapping. Trouble was, I didn't have no idea how to lose 'em. I had tried shakin' 'em along the different cricks. Get far enough out ahead and pull off and either wait for 'em to go by or portage around through the woods. Each time, when I thought I had maybe shook 'em, there they came behind me.

With them as determined to stay with me as I was to be rid of them and with me thinking hard on it, I damn near blundered a second time into a pack of wolves. These would surely have punished me for my carelessness as those others had not, for these wolves were of the two-legged sort. Fortunately, I seen their smoke from around a bend and wondering how in hell the two men had got ahead of me, for they had only recently been behind, I got off the stream and snuck up over the hill separating me from the smoke.

Where two rivers met, just back from a spit of sand, twenty or so Indian boys were camped, a fall hunting and fishing party. They had bark wigwams, and where the waters from one crick flowed into the other, nets stretched from shore to shore. They had fish drying and a couple of deer hanging on tripods. These were boys from one of the northern tribes, near to becoming men, just short of being old enough to go to war and no doubt anxious to get started. All consumed with thoughts of taking their first scalp and here it come damn near paddlin' right up to 'em.

I snuck back to my canoe, already well hidden, and along came Slick and Mike. They were moving fast and were excited for seeing the smoke. They hadn't laid eyes on me for a few days and now they must have figured they had me again and also maybe figured we'd come at last to where the beavers were. They were moving too fast for me to warn 'em and I wasn't sure I ought to risk my own hair for two men what was intending to kill me. Besides, it was past time I got up to Paradise Valley. As soon as they were gone around the bend, I shoved off and me and Blackie hauled our arses downriver, spurred by the shouts and whoops, the gunshots from the other side of the hill.

I suppose it was a mighty mean trick which might have caused me some consternation but I hadn't exactly tricked 'em and hadn't they asked for it by gettin' in with those crooked Albany fur buyers? Told myself I had just one fellow to worry about, a man in a canoe with a dog. I was afeared Slick or Mike might have told the Indians there was another scalp out there for 'em and I put as much river between me and them as I could. Aided by a following wind and a steady current, I paddled hard, spurred by the fear of my hair dangling from the belt of a fourteen-year-old buck.

I stopped nights for a few hours' sleep and when I did, I got the canoe under overhanging trees and slept in it. Made sure the dog did too. I never went ashore the whole way down, left not one track for the Indians, or for Mike, were he and Slick not already boiled and eaten.

At the fork of the Hudson, I turned up the East Branch toward my mountain fastness. This time of year, the river was slow and shallow and without much current to fight. Made for easy travel. Three days hardly stepping on shore and keeping the dog tied up in the canoe when I did. The days were pleasant, the bugs infrequent, and a few afternoons, late, came violent rainstorms. When the wind picked up and I seen the leaves of the birch trees turning their bottoms up, I'd go to shore, turn my boat over and get beneath it. When the rain abated but before it stopped entirely, I'd resume my journeying, the last of the rain serving to wash out my sign. The air fresh and clean smelling,

I often trolled a fishing line, a hook camouflaged with deer hairs. Caught trout after fat trout all the way up this wonderful stretch of water. Until they beat my few deer-fly baits to the dickens.

Up the East Branch and through Big Lake, I secured my canoe at the outlet of Second Lake. Left it hidden among rocks and covered with brush. A hard walk up to the Eagle's Lake and to my other canoe. I paddled east, a beautiful day, the sun bright along the far ledges.

I trudged up the cut and into my box canyon, still without sign of anyone. Nothing had been disturbed in the cabin, not even the spider webs. The same could not be said for my garden. Deer and smaller animals had finished off the squash and corn. I had hoped the lingering scent of man and dog around the canyon would have made the critters wary but not in the least. Even the few potatoes were dug up and eaten by coons and groundhogs.

My first full day back at the cabin I planted the four tiny apple saplings Mother had given me. The way she had instructed. Saplings of the famous French stock said to do so well in this climate. I put a concoction around the base of the trees to keep the mice from eating the bark under the snow. My first night, I listened as a pack of raccoons engaged in the most ferociously loud fight over some last morsels in the garden. "Welcome back to the north woods," I said to myself.

The gathering of firewood was my most immediate concern. The trees I had girdled before departing in the spring were about dead and were easily brought down with my hand ax and one-man saw. I was determined to start with more firewood this year than last.

I kept careful watch for French or Indians around the Eagle's Lake and promised myself I would depart at the first sign, although I did not expect to see them up here. The only trail near me was an old hunting path running east and west on the north side of the lake. Overgrown and more than a mile from the lake. I watched it for sign and never saw any.

I made some improvements on the cabin. I added an upper room and put a stouter roof over things. Still crude but better than last year. This upper room would be for storage and for working furs. At least now when I told Mother I lived in a cabin, it wouldn't be a lie. Or not so big a one. I maintained the trapdoor and ladder so I might still get onto the roof without leaving the cabin. This was advantageous for hunting and for defending against the wolves which were often driven by hunger into boldness.

Fresh deer rubbings on the trees around the canyon indicated a big old boy in the velvet had staked his claim as the biggest buck hereabouts. By the size of the tracks and the height of the rubbings, a real stag. When mating season began and he went into the rut, his neck would swell to immense size, the antlers he had worked so hard at sharpening through the fall would become deadly fighting weapons. Especially when in combination with lethal hooves. A buck his size could be dangerous did he choose to be. He could be aggressive and was capable of killing a man. In combat for territory and breeding rights most savagely contested, only the strongest got to mate. This is as it should be, ensuring the survival of the best stock for future generations of the herd. By the sign, he had spent most of the summer and fall there in the canyon. Now and with me and the dog present, he was scarce, though I saw sign indicating he had been watching us. Soon enough, when my rifle called out to him, we would see who was the biggest buck hereabouts. I decided to allow him one last breeding season before I took him. He was wily, as befits an old fellow. One afternoon as I sat in the sun, writing, he got in close, sniffing the air. Trying to figure me out, for I was probably the first man he had ever encountered. My eyes stayed on him as I reached ever so slowly for my bow and arrows. He was gone at the first movement, so sharp were his senses.

The bow and arrows I had added to my arsenal this year. A powerful weapon and invaluable, as it would be easier on my powder supply and would eliminate the musket booms which last year made me uneasy for fear said booms might betray my presence. I worked hard at mastering the bow for the advantages it would bestow upon me. Took practice to pull back the leather string and shoot with accuracy.

I purchased the bow and arrows from Trader Harrold, an agreeable old Mohawk who did his drinking in the Full Sail. Harrold and Pops had long been friends. They drank, swapped tall tales and laughed like hell at each other's stories, though, between Pops' Dutch-accented English and Harrold's attempts at the same language, I doubt they understood much of what the other was saying. For as long as I could remember, whenever Old Harrold came in, I had to watch the bar so the two old-timers could have their talks. Pops said Harrold was one Indian who could hold his liquor.

For a little money, almost anything the old savage had was for sale. He always packed a sackful of goods to catch the curiosity of a white man. Cornhusk dolls, silver bracelets, ornamental moccasins, bear-claw necklaces. Things in which Harrold put great store. He got mad if his prospective buyer did not concur in the value of the gee-gaws.

Harrold's main item in bartering for the things his overflowing longhouse of forty people of various ages needed was salt. Hard to come by in the colony and important for preserving meat and fish. Harrold said his salt was superior to all others, many in Albany would agree. He said his family had a magical spring deep in the woods out of which there arose salted water. The process of boiling off the water was difficult and tedious, which, he said, was why he never brought much at a time. I think he did it to maintain the stiff price but I never said so. He said the gods who watched over the spring had in ancient times chosen his family as guardians, allowing them to use it for their own benefit and for barter, but only for as long as the secret of the spring was kept. Harrold's people had never divulged said location, and so far as I knew, no English or Dutch had ever been so foolish as to go looking for it, or, if they had, they had not returned. Harrold and his kin promised death to whoever would seek to find it.

Harrold paid for his drinks with the salt. The night he sold me the bow, he and I sat up drinking and talking almost until dawn. Without telling him where I wintered, I got him to tell me about the lower Corlaer Valley, where he said he had taken many Algonquin scalps. He told me much I didn't know. Things to maybe save my life, such as certain trails and where they led.

He showed me how to notch arrow shafts and set the points, some for war, some for hunting. With both of us addled with drink, I bought the bow and quiver of arrows he was peddlin'. Thought I made a pretty good deal until later when I discovered the arrows had feathers but only those he had pulled from the quiver to show me had points attached.

Chapter XIV – A Regal Sense of Power

Me and the dog stood atop the easternmost ridgeback, the ground in front of us sloping down to Corlaer. The entirety of the low country, the Tyonderrogha Valley and a wide stretch along the east side of the lake, what the French called Verd Mont, lay before us.

With some time before the trapping started, I had decided to go down into the valley to collect flint and to spy on the French. And I figured to get some salmon, the Ti crick likely to be filled with them. Now, and seeing smoke emanating from the lower falls, I was going not for the salmon but to see what Frenchie was doing there. With the English unable or unwilling to counter the French encroachments, it wouldn't be no surprise were the French extending down to Ti from Crown Point.

A blockhouse at the falls would force the smugglers to take the more difficult route through the Drowned Lands. Still, I didn't figure the French was erecting anything permanent at the falls. Any fortification at Ti would be out on the point where the lake narrowed, same as it did at Scalp Point. Once established at the Ti point, they could cover both the Portage Crick and the Drowned Lands. Nobody, smugglers nor scouts nor armies could get past without their consent. Whatever they might be up to, we headed down to find out.

We got farther south along the ridgeback and went down through a narrow pass, following the brook which flowed out of one of my more easterly ponds and which, in its descent, dropped down over waterfalls and through rocky ravines. Where the land flattened, the brook settled and flowed into the Trout Brook, which we followed to Portage Crick, another wild flow over spews and foaming falls, loud, even from a distance.

We got down in close to the lower falls, this the place where Bill Morrissey had caught so many salmon the year we went smuggling with Hugh. The French were there for the fishing and hadn't erected nothing more than a smoke-house and huts. But with Frenchie present, there would be no fish for me. Not here, anyway, and I wasn't sure if I had ought to go for flint. Harrold's directions would make the beds easy enough to find but with the French so close, I maybe should have turned around and gone back up the mountain. I didn't though. This stubborn Dutchman wasn't going home without flint. And fish, too, which I still aimed to get.

I made a wide circle north and west of the falls and skirting the tiny pond which sits on a rise of ground to the east, I turned south. Then due east almost to the shores of Corlaer. I went slow and silent through the thick woods and soon found the trail which led to the flint beds. Got in close and stayed up high, observing the beds. Entire ledges chipped away and carried off by the Indians who had worked the beds for eons before the white race arrived on the continent. Indeed, with the coming of the white man and his guns, there was less need for the flint. I did a thorough scout and deciding it was safe enough, I went down. Working as quickly and as quietly as possible, I filled a bag and got to hell out of there.

Next order of business was spooking Scalp Point, to ascertain was it safe for me to spend the winter on my mountain, and to gather what information I could for taking to Albany in the spring. In deference to the French presence so far south as Ti, and not sure where else they might be along the lakeshore, I got back up into the mountains before heading north. Only as I got in close to Scalp Point did I work my way back toward the lake.

Extending around the tip of the Scalp Point peninsula and thus enclosing the stone fortress on three sides and with the straits on the water side, was a wooden palisade with three blockhouses manned by soldiers. Heard the sounds of axes, the French cutting down the trees 'round the castle. This was to provide fields of fire as well as wood for the garrison this winter. Once the land was cleared, it would be put into cultivation. The Scalp Point peninsula outside of the palisade and the shorelines along either side of the lake were dotted with peasant settlements. Fields, pastures, newly begun orchards of thin little trees in neat rows well-tended. Hovels not so sturdy as our colonials' cabins were boarded up tight for the winter. Once the fall harvest was in, the habitants got taken back to Canada for safety from our Iroquois and for watching over by the church. The winter garrison consisted of some few French regulars and Canadian militia. Along with the inevitable black-robes.

After dark, I got in past the palisade and up close to the fort, by the water's edge. This was my first close-up look at the castle. Heretofore

I had only seen it from a distance, from up in the mountains or from a canoe on the lake in the dark. The walls were made of thick blocks of limestone, squared off and mortared. The donjon, four-stories high, was a European castle. Cannon snouts protruded from the ports. The position of the castle, a way out on an open point and exposed to the north wind sure to be blowing down the hundred miles of wide-open lake, must a made for mighty cold times in winter. Must take a wood-pile near the size of the castle to keep 'er heated.

On my way out and still in darkness, I spooked the Indians' camp. Watched 'em performing a vile dance. Drinking, beating on tom-toms and no doubt boasting of all they would do when Onothio, the French King Louis, turned them loose on the English. The Indians knew war was coming and were anxious for it. The scene before me repugnant to a white man's senses. The drumming and howling brought remembrances of the awful things I had seen outside of Montreal when I was smuggling.

Not many Indians did I count, although it is hard to get a fix on their numbers with how they come and go. In the morning and with me backed away some and in thick cover, I watched as a flotilla of war canoes departed south. Riding in the canoes were a couple of Papist priests. Taking advantage of the peace and of English ineptitude to spread dissension amongst our Mohawks upon whom we counted for so much aid in time of war. The talk in the tavern this summer past was how something needed to be done to prevent further inroads into Iroquois support, else the balance of power between us and the French would tilt in their favor. Did the Mohawks swing decisively over to the French, Albany would not last an hour. From this evil donjon of Scalp Point came the rotten seed sown amongst our allies, dividing the Six Nations.

"Just one of those silver-tongued devils," Bill Johnson told me, "if given the time to build up Papist strength in a Mohawk castle, would become a formidable opponent, cause a hell of a lot of trouble." Bill told me the western Iroquois had already lost a considerable number of their best fighting men. The Jesuits had a camp for these Praying Indians, on the lower Saint Lawrence River, at the falls of the Saint Regis. Many of the smaller castles of the western Iroquois were said to have gone over. The Jesuits were untiring in their efforts for France and the Cross. The Iroquois complained the English did naught to counter the French. Other than Bill Johnson, only the Schuyler family had influence with the Iroquois and the Schuylers were most always distracted by political affairs in New York Town.

There was plenty at Scalp Point to interest the Albany politicians but nothing which couldn't wait until spring. This winter, the French and Indians were not likely to stir trouble to the south nor were they likely to come up to Paradise. Those French unfortunate enough to be stuck here for the winter would hunker down against the cold. The Indians, despite their eagerness for war, would all mostly return to their lodges or go north to hunt and trap.

Next, another try for salmon. With the French doing their fishing down to the Portage Crick, I figured to do mine on the Outlet Crick, which flowed down out of Paradise. Outlet Crick was nearer to their fort than was Portage Crick but the French, with their reluctance to venture into the mountains, either didn't know about the salmon in Outlet Crick or more likely were unwilling to follow the crick into the woods for fear of who they might meet in there.

Walking south, still well back in from the lakeshore, I came to the crick. I followed it west and uphill, again staying off it. Rough going through harsh country. Came to the high falls, the farthest point into the hills where the salmon runs could be found.

Even without having seen any sign of French or Indians, I debated the wisdom of fishing but I did truly love the taste of the salmon and I knew they could be taken here in abundance. Working quickly with my spear, I soon enough had plenty. I wrapped them in wet leaves and moss and set out for home with a bulging pack. Were the trip down not so dangerous, I would come back often. The French did not know what hardships they had created for me by getting themselves down to Tyonderrogha.

Again in deference to the French, I walked straight back into the mountains. Found a bit of old unused trail leading up along a strong-running brook. This I followed at a distance and farther on, just where the trail crossed the brook, I came to where steep cliffs blocked my way. Started to go around and saw there were foot and handholds straight up the rockface. Chiseled by wind and rain, or by men, it might be a way for me to get to the top without going around. I hesitated for the bareness of the cliffside and the lateness of the hour. I might be seen from far away, even from the French fort, did they have a particular-glass atop the castle roof, or I might get only partway up before full dark. A short search showed there was no easy way around and I decided, with how exactly cut and spaced were the holds, I could get to the top quickly.

As it was, it took but a few minutes and at the top, I found the resumption of the trail, which further verified the stiles were intended for climbing. Followed the trail to the north and settled for the night in a small glen beneath a thick grove of trees. A cold camp, for I dared no fire. The dog got in some time after, he having gone the long way around.

I was asleep early but was awake often during the night. Something was making both me and the dog nervous. Early next day we struck out north. Two hours along the trail, we walked up onto the source of our uneasiness, onto the most amazing damn thing I had ever seen or could have expected to see in the woods.

A magnificent throne carved in solid limestone high atop the east slope of the ridgeback. Perplexed by such a mysterious find and agitated for having walked right in close to it, I immediately drew back and moved around the hilltop to check for sign. There was none and I approached the chair. Certainly a wonder for it had enough of the right configuration to convince me it was the carved work of men, same as the handholds. Carved by men but not by ordinary workmen, for such a masterpiece, as big as it was and intended as a throne from which to command a view of the valley, could only have been carved by tools in the hands of master stonecutters. Any man who could have wielded the necessary tools, same as any man who could fit comfortably into the chair would be a big man, a Goliath.

I climbed up into the seat like a small boy into his daddy's lap, first getting onto a rock which was set before the throne. The rock was as a footstool and it too had a carved appearance. The chair had armrests intended for the majestic limbs of some vanished imperator, the seat smooth and comfortable for the sitting. The high rounded back was ornamented with a simple pattern repeated throughout and was marred but not erased by the ravages of time and weather. The ornamentation was as rays emanating from a sun and I further reckoned the rays, when the giant sat in his chair, would be positioned as a diadem on his head. No accident of nature, this chair, and I repeat, no ordinary men could have had sufficient skill, strength, nor years, to sculpt such a masterpiece. Surely an enchantment had presided here over a regal court of vanished Ancients.

The view from the throne was a grand one, the French carryings-on at the peninsula palisade and the castle all more or less visible from where I sat. I could see south almost to the portage; the view north down the lake a far distance, yet the throne was tucked into a small bench on the side of the mountain. Not an easy place to find.

Seated on this magnificent throne, high atop the eastern slope with its expansive view, gave me a regal sense of power. Still, I reckoned it unsafe to linger. The Indians, so close by, would know of it, and I was nagged by maybe having been seen in my climb of the day before. I started out for home and was it a fear of Indians driving me or was I spooked by this supernatural mystery of the deep woods? Told myself what was hastening me was my cargo of fish which was spoiling. I would soon have every damn polecat and red fox in the woods nosing after me. Soon as I got home, I would salt the fish. Roasted, salmon steaks are tasty.

****

I was faring better this winter than last. Better prepared and supplied, and with the weather not as bad, the trapping was good, and without the fear of my gunshots echoing down into the valley, the hunting, too, was good. Deer were easy to take using the dog and the bow.

Despite the hardships of winter, there was such wondrous beauty, I wanted nothing else. Even a snowstorm, I realized whilst running outside for another armful of wood to build up a dying fire, had its advantages. It covered tracks to and from my trapline, making it all but impossible for anyone to follow me back to my lair. I built a toboggan and pulled it with a tumpline; this took a burden off my shoulders and kept my arms free.

Last fall, just before I departed Albany and when the nail-maker came to the tavern to warn me about those men, he presented me with two pairs of ice-creepers. He said he didn't know where I was going but figured the creepers might be useful, as indeed they are. Wooden clogs with nails on the bottoms, the nails bent at the perfect angle for gripping the iced trails, especially right at home, in the cut which led up from the Eagle's Lake to my hideout. I always took along a set of the creepers when I set out on my rounds.

I made snowshoes from cedar boughs. Bending the fronts circular, I reinforced them with thin slats and wove in smaller, springier wood. The shoes were necessary for traipsing the deep snow and I seemed always to be breaking 'em or just wearing 'em out. Made five pairs and expected to use up all of them and then some, before winter was over.

I also spent nights chipping flint into arrowheads, trying to do it just as Trading Harrold had shown me. Harrold told me the Mohawks of bygone days came in early spring and whilst some of them gathered flint, others set ambushes along the shores of Corlaer for their Abenaki foes coming up the lake. Any Abenakis which got taken were pressed into carrying the heavy bags of flint back to Iroquoia. Harrold laughed, said once they got back, the captives were thanked for the work they'd done, then were tortured and burned alive.

I chipped my arrowheads in the gloom of my cabin, which gloom and my own ineptitude caused me to spoil as many as I made. Frustrating work but I persisted for the importance it had for my continued survival. To chip the flint into the desired shape, I first fashioned a piece of smoke-hardened deer bone and used it to sharpen and flake the point to a proper balance, a tedious, exacting task. An Indian can fashion a point in just a short time whilst for me, in the gloom of my cabin, it took much longer before the point was ready for mounting on a shaft. Whenever I shot at something and missed, I searched for my arrows, not anxious to have to go for more flint.

****

By spring I reckoned I had enough fur to make me rich. Which was in no way true but I had a better season than I could have hoped for. The beavers were thick in my Paradise, which was no more than five miles east to west by eight miles north to south. Outside of this area, there were no beavers 'cept a few small colonies on the East Branch, north of Big Lake. Nobody would believe where I was wintering and none would dare stay here, only a durn fool like me. But for two winters, it was as peaceful as any place on Earth.

****

First thing down in the spring I reported my findings of French doings to the authorities. They did not seem grateful for the information which they could not have gotten elsewhere, nor did they offer any money for my trouble. Instead, the sons-of-bitches accused me of wintering with the French at the Scalp Point castle, as if my information might not be factual and might even be a French ruse.

I found out, without appearing too curious, that my two shadows from last fall had not returned. Burger tried to have me arrested for murder but, Van Schaack pointed out, nothing could be proved, "For ver are der bodies?" I did not tell them what happened to those two, nor did I tell them how or where I had spent the winter. My evasions to their queries got me into trouble with the sheriff. Van Schaack, not for the first time, spoke up for me and saved worse trouble. Still and since then, an odor of taint seemed to follow me around. Decided from then on they would have to pay up front for the information I risked my life to bring 'em.

****

For years, the Spanish, perceiving England as weak, had stopped English merchantmen at sea and taken off British sailors. A sailor named Jenkins had his ear cut off by a saber-wielding Spaniard and in 1739, England declared war on Spain. In New York Town, defenses were getting built against an expected attack by the Spanish fleets. None of us in the north believed the city of New York had anything to fear from the Spanish. The real threat was the French coming in against us. The French are Papists as are the Spanish and iffen they joined together, it was the northern parts of our colony which would be in danger. "Money enough for preparing defenses at New York Town," was what everybody said, "but not a farthing for where it be needed." Even Van Schaack complained about the New York politicians. Certain of them were skimming money in the name of defense, was what the old hypocrite told me. There seemed to be more friction between the British and Dutch of New York than with the French.

Word came of fighting down in our southern colony of Georgia. An Englishman named Oglethorpe invaded Florida and was winning hard fights against the Spanish.

****

In 1740 there began in Europe what was called the War of the Austrian Succession. I was not sure exactly what the war was about, just it was somehow wrapped in with the problem with Mister Jenkin's ear and was getting fought in many places. All the world, it seemed, was a chess board, although our colony of New York, so far as we knew, was not at war with anyone. Just everywhere else, plain folks were dying for the folly of kings.

****

Over the years, I began seeing less of Albany. Seems I couldn't be there a month before I would have to leave. The people were friendly to my face but outside of my hearing, they said bad things about me. Especially the English.

I seemed to always be skirting serious trouble with the suspicions raised by my fur business and the lies I must tell. Yet, if I told the truth I would lose my good living, for I was making a small fortune. I would soon have sufficient money to retire but for me, the harsh side of life in the wilds had become preferable to the stinking towns. I had come to love my North Country. Life was arduous, I was always at the whim of the worst weather. Winters were truly awful, a land locked in wind, snow and ice. Summers were hot and muggy. Terrible mosquitoes and flies. Too much rain in the spring, not enough in the fall. But up north, the greed and gossip of the towns did not touch me.

The summers I used to prepare for the winter trapping season.

My dugout was nearly a proper cabin with all the improvements I had made and I had built a smaller cabin down on the lakeshore so I was not always going up and down the steep cut to the canyon. This little cabin, well-hidden, was for fair-weather use.

A bit surprised at having survived against the odds in the north but being always careful and staying away from Corlear was what made the difference. It seemed someone tried to follow me up most every year and they watched for me coming down in the spring but with tricks and wiles, it was not hard to elude them, not even in the spring, when I was burdened with my cache.

Eric showed me the plant called ginseng, which he thought might grow in the north. He asked had I seen it. I said there were patches and I said I had often wondered what this unusual plant was. He said it had medicinal properties beyond all others. I carried a sack in the summer and picked what I found. Eric was always eager for it. Though the price fluctuated, the market stayed good. Folks in New York and Philadelphia paid good money for it. Eric taught me when to pick it, how to cure it. The money I made for bringing it went against the purchase of my winter supplies. I use it some myself. It had an earthy taste unlike any other. As Eric said, "A little each day is good for you." I suppose it helped some.

Once I brought in a huge root. Eric said it was hundreds of years old and said I was wrong for having dug it entirely up. I laughed at him for saying the mandrake plant could be so ancient. We argued until he showed me in a book where it said so. Which little bet cost me a drink in the bar. I read and reread all of what the book had to say about the plant and from then on, whenever I found a patch, I never took it all, as the book advises to leave a little something for seed. I said to Eric, "Isn't it so with all things?"

Mostly I stayed in the north and often, when I made the trip down, it was for no particular reason except to satisfy the damn fool urge for female companionship. With most of the unmarried girls looking for husbands and with my reputation, few cared to waste their time on me.

If the river was low, I might travel at night but when the upper Hudson was high and wild, I dared not. Then I traveled by the light of day. "Never be in a rush, don' be 'fraid to stop when it be necessary, always be cautious." Hugh's words from years ago still showed the way to get by in this country.

The black dog padded along whilst I checked my traps or set my nets and bobbers for fishing. When we traveled, he sat in the front of the canoe, his nose in the air, sniffing the riverbanks for excitement. For him, excitement meant chasing something. Usually a deer. When a deer did not sense us and we spooked him, the dog was apt to go a flying and iffen he did, all hell broke loose. More than once he upset the canoe and put me into the water. In the bush his low growl usually meant a deer but I always treated it as trouble and worked my way from there. I could tell by how his ears pointed, deer or danger. He could be used to great advantage in hunting. Up here, away from the deer-reeves who were constantly on the lookout for deer-running dogs and who passed out stiff fines to anyone caught hunting with them, it was safe to use him. Around Albany he had to be kept close to avoid trouble with the game authorities.

In Albany he rarely left my side and drove off trouble a few times by his ferocious presence. Make no mistake, the man who jumped me got Blackie in the bargain. My dog licked every dog in town which would fight and more which would have rather not.

Best thing about the black dog, most times he would cease chasing and come back, did I whistle. A rarity in a good deer-runner. He could swim like an otter but would only retrieve ducks or geese if he was of a mind. Now and no longer a pup, he didn't care for cold water. He would fearlessly chase a bear and I nearly lost him the time a raccoon got him into deep water and was fixing to drown him. He hunted out the squirrels and rabbits around my camp so my garden fared better.

Together, me and Blackie wandered every ridge and hill, fished every brook in these mountains. So far as I knew, I was the only white man crazy enough to be up here. Mostly it was safe, almost never did I see sign of men anywhere close in to my valley and those few times when I did, they had passed too far to the north to stumble onto me or the beavers.

****

Arnold and Priscilla were prospering. Her tongue was as harsh as ever but she talked now with a certain more respect in her tone to him. She had lately employed two black servants, a husband and wife, and it was they who took the brunt of her prolix.

Priscilla hated Saratoga. She hated the smell of the town and hated the people. She and Arnold were putting aside money to build a house on the land they had initially purchased, a half day's walk from Saratoga, out at the healing springs. It was to be a real house, not a crude cabin. Hardwood floors, glass in the front windows, ornate furnishings in the parlor, things to set her above the rest of the folks so she could indulge herself with thinking she was gentry.

I advised them against this. I said did France come into the war on the side of Spain, the northern Indians would come raiding and any house off by itself would be an easy mark. Priscilla scoffed, said no Indians could cause her any trouble. "Not if they be like the wretches I am forever chasing off with my broom." I said those she chased were our friends. "Friends!" she said. "At this dismal backwater?"

Arnold, serene as always, "You are too nervous, my boy. There will not be any trouble. Look at how many new people we are bringing to the area." He and Lydia's husband, Richard, were running the land office for the younger man's father and were doing well. Arnold, so sure of his words, said no mere savages could destroy what they were building. "Friend," I said. "You don't know Indians. They might come at any time." Arnold did not agree, nor did Richard, who said it was bad for business to talk about the dangers. Richard thought only of profit; Arnold, despite whatever misgivings he might a had, dared not go against either his boss or his wife.

A few times I saw Lydia, either in the land office or whilst visiting with Arnold and Priscilla. She always gave me the feeling she hated Saratoga and would rather be anywhere else. And, I began to suspect, with anyone else other than her husband. She was a naturally refined woman, soft and beautiful, unfit for frontier life.

Despite the land business doing well, Lydia did not have all the fine things Richard promised her. I saw a deep-rooted dissatisfaction in her, not for the things she didn't have and not even because of how much of their money went for Richard's carousing. Her unease went deeper.

One warm evening, me and her talked on Arnold's porch. She sat in the rocking chair, I on the steps. The moon on her face made for an alluring combination of light and shadow. I had a hard time with my emotions and I strongly suspect she did too. She told me she was pregnant. I was happy for her and hoped she was happy too, and though it seemed she was, I sensed misgivings. For myself, there were the old regrets for the life I might have had with her. After that night, I stayed away from Saratoga. Distrustful of my feelings. Bill Johnson came through Albany often enough to allow me diversions.

Chapter XV – War Drums

This spring of 1743, when I came down from the north with fur, the talk was the troubles in Europe might be coming here. The first ships of the year from England were not yet in and I decided I better stay around and see what news fair weather might bring. With plenty of money stashed in a box in my room in the cabin behind the tavern and more money with Eric, I had no need to work and only hunted and fished when I was in the mood or when Pops insisted.

Before the shad flower was gone by, farmers outside the smaller settlements began to complain of missing cows and other farm stock. A fire mysteriously started in a barn and another in a haymow. Most of these incidents proved not to be instigated by Indians but they did serve to increase tensions. In late June, a Dutch tradesman was slain just outside the gates of Albany. By the brutality of the murder, the disfigurement and the lifted scalp, Indians were blamed. The alarm was raised throughout the colony. For a week, even behind the walls, men went about their business with loaded guns. More dangerous than Indians. The murderer turned out to be a local man. An Englishman! The victim's unmistakable red scalp was seen in the honey-wagon one morning and the perpetrator lately found out and hanged.

Rumors abounded, mostly false, but a little girl was snatched from a farmyard, and it did seem to be Indians. At the behest and in the pay of the Albany commissioners, I led a strong but ill-prepared posse to look for her. We searched along the river as far as the lower Great Carry for sign but found none. I sent the posse home and me and the dog searched farther up Saint Sacrement. Along the western shore, at an abandoned Indian camp, I found a tiny pink bonnet, so Indians had carried the child this way. Followed their sign a ways but they were well gone.

December was quiet and I decided to go north and finish out the trapping season. I didn't dare go up the river and so I walked instead, a hard trip. Saw no sign of any intruders in my mountains, at least not since the last snow. The rest of the winter I stayed entirely away from Corlaer and trapped only the waters which emptied to the west. One broken strap lost in the creek and drifting downstream might alert a sharp-eyed savage to my presence. Then it would be only a matter of time before they found me. I didn't once shoot my gun, yet I ate well, and was grateful for old Trading Harrold having counseled me to become proficient with bow and arrow.

I spent more time watching for trouble than in tending my traps. With the late start and with plenty of money already stashed at home, I felt no pressure to pile up the furs. I would stay alive no matter how overdone my precautions and besides, the easing would be good for the beavers. I was always mindful not to wipe out any of the colonies. Better it was to move around, take just a few from each pond. I had learned that after losing a few of his workers, the old boss wised up to my sets. If I didn't get him first, it became near impossible to catch any of his domain. Once the beavers saw another in a trap, they were much harder to take.

****

Springtime!

The weather warmed, the rain mostly stopped. The mud dried up. The biters began to hatch on ponds and creeks. I stayed north to spy on the French and for the fishing. The fast waters held large numbers of brightly speckled trout. The deeper waters held the bigger lake trout. These were gritty fighters, strong enough so if I did not pay strict attention, they would take not only bait but hook and line as well. I set out fishing lines anchored with heavy stones. Each morning nearly all my steel hooks held a fish. Mostly perch, with their black and yellow stripes and orange fins. And the ugly but delicious bullhead.

****

Got in to Albany to some good news from the south. Oglethorpe had ambushed a counter-attacking Spanish army and won a victory at a place now known as Bloody Swamp. The Spanish were driven back into Florida but the situation here in Albany was distressing. War was surely coming due to events in Europe over which we had no say nor much understanding. The common man was helpless to prepare whilst our leaders procrastinated. There was grumbling wherever men met. The Full Sail was afloat with rumors. Not having control over one's future was unsettling.

France was said to be readying a powerful war fleet for the Canadas. Then came rumor of a large war party of western Iroquois close in to Schenectady. Led by Mohawks. Next we heard the war party was down in the lower Hudson Valley, below Albany. Not even this stirred the politicians. Governor Clinton and the mostly Dutch legislature remained locked in a fight over money and control. A militia needed to be formed and drilled but nobody wanted to pay for it.

The rumors came and went, all mostly proved utterly false. I found it hard to understand most of what went on, just I knew enough to be afraid, with our town leaders unable to decide on how to organize for defense. The problem was, the seat of government, New York Town, was not threatened by the Indians. If our powdered wigs and stuffed shirts were up here or were the Indians down there, the politicians would think harder about all the things necessary for defense.

The talk in the Full Sail was something to hear. Grumbling and cursing with liquored-up men bragging on what they would do when war came. Others of them, especially from over east of the Hudson, were talking of moving out. Most folks wrung their hands in despair and pleaded, "What can I do? I am only one." And in truth, with how isolated were the farmsteads and without leadership, which was surely lacking, there was not much they could do.

A more regular watch was posted at Albany and if not for the precariousness of our situation, it would a been comical to see our men up on the walls, more scairt of the parapet collapsing beneath 'em than of Indian arrows. Or see them trying to open and close the gates, which, rotting and warped, didn't fit so well as they should. Palisade logs were only good for ten or so years, then they had to be replaced. Ours were more than twenty-years old.

A corps was set up to watch the river crossings and trails. I was asked to join and maybe I should of but the watch was commanded by men in whom I had so little faith, I would not be part of their doings. They could get a fellow killed. Their system was said to be haphazard.

A detachment of British soldiers, including engineers, arrived in Albany. They marshaled men and supplies and were headed up somewhere north of Saratoga, to build a fort. No one knew exactly where, though the obvious place was the Great Carry. Near Lydius' house.

The high sheriff came to the tavern. He asked me to lead a few of his men up north, show them around. Get 'em familiar with the up-country, "In case something bad happens to you." I said as how something would happen to me, did I take his men up there. Funny, lately I had heard nothing from the sheriff about me spying for the French or trading with them. Pops was thinking the same and became abusive in saying what he thought about the spy business and reminding the sheriff of all he, the sheriff, had said about me previously. I thought Pops would toss the sheriff into the street, just as well he didn't. Pops had enough problems without tangling with the law.

Raiding was occurring over in the lower Connecticut River Valley. The trouble was out of Scalp Point. Completely ruthless, according to all we heard. Then in July, some cabins across the Hudson from Saratoga got struck. Families killed or carried off, so it was coming our way.

Another month passed. Word of the troubles in New England came in increasing doses. A blockhouse burned. Ten people perished inside. An entire settlement on the Connecticut River in ashes, the folks killed or taken off to serve as slaves to the Indians. Few survivors. Bothered by the talk, I agreed to go up to Scalp Point for a look. A big raid in the Hudson Valley might a been in the offing. Our people, so unprepared, made a most inviting target. I would go with just the dog and travel light. Only Van Schaack and Johnson would know I was going. Before I went, I spoke with the alderman. "Vhen you comen back," he said, "I goes to der Mayor vor your moneys." He promised payment for my services out of his own pocket, if need be. When we were done talking over the possibilities, Schaack presented me with a far-seeing glass. A most wonderful instrument. And useless in the woods. The merest glint of sunlight off its shiny metal tube or glass lenses, even from a distant mountain, would put the Indians onto me. Still, it was kind of him, and whilst wrapping the glass in sheepskin for storing, I thought how good it would feel to unwrap it, when our troubles were past and a lone trapper could use such an instrument without fear.

I walked up along the Hudson, unsure what route I should take. Saint Sacrement or the lower Corlaer Valley by way of Wood Creek. Decided on Wood Creek and the Drowned Lands. It'd be harder going but would offer better cover for a man and a dog, and I figured the French and Indians wouldn't want to be in there no more than I would. Turned out I was wrong, as I spooked a party of Indians about as soon as I got in, and at a few more places in there, I saw where other parties had recently camped. Took four days cautious going for me to reach the north end of Saint Sacrement.

Everywhere, parties were out. On the summit of Bald Mountain was a lookout-post manned by bush-lopers and regulars, watchful for any movement on the part of the English on the lake. I seen the smokes

of other watch-posts along rocky ledges. The Indians, with their constant prowling, presented added danger to my spooking. There was
much drinking in the French camps. Passing the time with brandy and
cognac, the French were often more drunk than the Indians. The officers worst of all. Contemptuous of the English and so sure of their
grip on the lakes and of their Indians' control of the woods, the French
felt they held a strong hand. They wouldn't be content to sit for too
long.

I watched from cover a shooting match, three Frenchies and a pair
of drunken Indians engaged in a futile attempt to hit a target. Got so
disgusted with their ineptitude, I wanted to get out there and show 'em
how a woodsman did it with a rifle. Then I got mad for thinking about
the money the politicians would pay me for the dangerous work I was
doing. A paltry sum! They'd figure I could be bought cheap. I shook
my head. As the only white man who dared scout this far north for the
English, my information must be valuable.

I spooked the fort peninsula for three days. The Canadian habitants
were working their fields and I saw plenty of French regulars, woods-
lopers and Indians. The woods-lopers were shaggily bearded men in
buckskins. They moved lightning-quick through the woods and had to
be respected, same as Indians.

I seen a war party of twenty Indians going south down the lake for
the Otter Creek trail, which followed said creek southeast, almost to
its source, a gap high atop the eastern mountains. Once up on this
height of ground, the raiders would be within striking distance of the
Connecticut River Valley from where they could penetrate deep into
Massachusetts.

I watched another party come across the lake. Screeching what
could only be scalp yells and all firing their guns and waving scalps.
They had a white prisoner, hands bound behind his back, head down
and looking to have already suffered much. They paraded him around
before tying him to a post just outside the stockade. The tortures they
inflicted were so awful, the sentries went inside the castle, raised the
drawbridge and bolted the gate. Why Indians commit such foul deeds,
I do not know. Hoped for a quick end for the wretch but knew such
was not to be. From my hidden place, I could not leave until night and
had to listen as they bedeviled their man in the most fiendish of ways.
The older Indians was showing the youngsters how to carve a man for
the cookpot. The more unspeakable the inflicted horrors, the more the

man cried out, the more exuberantly the Indians clapped and hooted. I left after dark, sickened by it.

I decided it would be unwise to traverse the Drowned Lands or the lakes, or even the wooded shores along the lakes. I headed west for the cabin and by nightfall, I was paddling close to the southern shore of the first of the Twin Lakes, aboard the canoe I kept stashed there, and taking advantage of the evening shadows. Whippoorwills called out as I moved easily into the narrow channel between the lakes. High ledges hung close overhead on either side. Got into the open waters of Second Lake, the night clear and bright and with plenty of stars. The Milky Way always a bright source of light in the blue-black sky. The mosquitoes and the rest of the flying biters were bad on the water, even with a light breeze blowing. Wanted for the wind to blow up a gale, to drive away the bloodsucking varmints. The light of the rising moon grew bright behind the eastern mountains. Another half-hour paddling and the upper rim of the moon peered over the tops of the hills. Big and bright. Soon the full moon was up in a cloudless sky, shining bright upon the water. A dangerous time to travel! The moon would show me like a beacon.

Paddled along quiet, listening to the sounds of the night. The ever-present buzz of the mosquitoes in my ears, the jumps of big fishes, the hooting of an owl. The splash of a large animal. Was he going to water or was he run there? Did something spook him? The yip of a young coyote learning to hunt with his whelp-mates sounded loud on the side of a mountain. A wolf answered the coyote call, close by and sharp. All others went stone silent with mute respect to the lord over these parts, as did I, my paddle out of the water. I reckoned if it be an Indian making the wolf call, he was good enough to fool the coyotes. That one was four-legged.

Got through Twin Lakes and coming to the outlet creek, I pondered the unique occurrence which existed here. Twin Lakes emptied into a creek which flowed into another and down to Big Lake. Sometimes in the spring, the rush of snowmelt down out of the higher peaks brought so much water into the second creek, the flow out of Twin Lakes was pushed back against itself. This reversed the creek into a west to east flow. Thus, the other name I have given to this lake, the Paradox.

The creek was low and sluggish this time of year, the water black and murky. Had a hard time getting through. Downed trees conspired to stop me. The sting of branches across my face, the canopy of leaves so thick overhead, the moon could scarce penetrate. Fingers of moonlight poked through the clouds. Spooky as hell, and I not able to be as cautious as I should have wanted. With so much of my attention on getting through the obstructions, I put all reliance for sensing trouble on the dog.

The flow opened into Big Lake. To the west, sandy shores. I stayed along the east side, more shadows, less moonlight. I needed all the darkness there was. Once the moon got higher up and did the clouds move off, the entire lake would be lit. I would be an easy mark for any what was watching. Told myself there'd be no French or Indians, there never were, this far out. Partway down, the lake opened to a mile or so wide. Stayed to the easternmost side, which still seemed to hold the most shadows.

The full moon on the water, the bite in the air warm yet brisk, the wind gentle and steady, I felt my blood stirring. Got to thinking, as I so often did, of Lydia and of the life I might a had with her. Dangerous to think about her now, I tried to push the thoughts away. They are a deadly distraction from the total awareness a woodsman needs to stay alive. Told myself Lydia was unobtainable and there came thoughts of Anneke, the serving girl. Remembered warm nights with her, which thoughts inflamed my breast to a wildfire. Anneke, run off last spring with Bill Johnson. That now-infamous baird who was cutting such a wide swath through the lady folk of the colony. Just before I left town, I heard Johnson had discarded Anneke in favor of the daughter of a Mohawk chief. Anneke would be too scared of her uncle to go to him and would come to the Full Sail seeking her old job. Hoped she might be there when I got in but Mother does not give second chances. It has always been so with her and what would Anneke do then?

Passed between the big island and the shore, a spooky passage. The wind helped me steadily along. The mountains in the full bloom of summer were alive and loud. Bullfrogs croaked and were answered. Moths, insects, a whippoorwill. Off to the west a loon's mournful cry, so clear she sounded much closer than she was, her cries echoing off the mountains.

Got to the south end of the lake where the outlet drained through channels, small islands and old beaver workings. Got past there and downstream to where the flows all came together into the East Branch for its thirty-mile run to a joining with the Hudson. The river was narrow and overhung with trees, it was much darker here than what it'd been on the lake. When the moon reached its high point, there'd be fewer shadows for the hiding.

I was well down along the East Branch by the time the sun was coming up and I decided it would be unwise to continue in the daylight. I got off the water, got my canoe into the brush and me and the dog spent the day hidden a little way up from the river. Soon's it got dark, we were back on the water. Pitch dark and nearly to the confluence with the Hudson, the dog started his warning growls, definite signs of trouble, and with the wind having shifted so it was coming now out of the south, I figured the trouble was still ahead of us.

I stopped paddling and sat quietly, hidden in shadows, listening. Straining for sounds of danger. We were on the lower part of the river, on the flats where the river meandered, and best I could figure our location, we was just around a bend from what I called Burl Pond, or Odd Pond. Odd because rather than having an inlet at the top and an outlet at the bottom, this pond was a bulge on the west side of the river, which put the inlet and outlet close together and with naught but a rise in the land between them. Figured the danger might be down there and thought I better have a look. I tied the dog to a tree and got down to where I could look out across the pond from the northeast. On the far shore, in the darkness beneath the trees, I saw the glow of a campfire.

I sat in keen study of the shoreline and the fire. I strained to hear voices. Might be English or Dutch. Or Iroquois, which could mean a friendly reception or death. Wasn't nothing for me 'cept to proceed. Might be able to get away with it. There was only the one fire and it was more than fifty yards out. Did I hug the side opposite the fire, I'd be screened by the shadows of the trees over my head, and with the pond situated as an appendage to the river, like a burl on a tree, I'd exit the pond about as soon as I entered. If whoever was over there wasn't prowling, and why would they be, this far out from anywhere, I figured to sneak on by.

Went back to the boat and let the current take us to where the creek entered the pond and we stayed there, listening as much as watching. The dog's wetted nose sniffed, alert, and with the look he gave me, he was saying we better not go any farther. My look back to him said we didn't have no choice. I listened some more, voices carry over water, and the talk I was hearing sounded to be French, though I couldn't say for certain.

I entered the pond and turned sharply to hug the hill along the shore to my left. I went slow and quiet, to ease my way past. From overhead came the cock of a gun hammer! Whoever was over by the fire had posted a watch at the outlet. "Que vive," came a voice from just above me, then a moment of deep silence. I held my paddle out of the water. Did whoever was up there hear the swish of the paddle or see me outlined in the moonlight, they'd pick me off easily enough.

No shot came, it might a been the outward curve of the rise was preventing him from getting a clear look down at me, at least until I got around the bend and showed my back to him. Or was he sneaking down to the outlet to blast me from hiding as I re-entered the river? He mighten be already down there. If he was, and as narrow as was the river, his gun, when he fired, wouldn't be more'n a few feet from the back of my head. I moved farther along with the current. The dog, bless him, stayed quiet. The voice challenged again, behind me now, still up on the rock, so he hadn't come down for a closer look. I dug my paddle deep and silent, a powerful thrust, there wasn't nothing else for me 'cept to go faster. The canoe leaped ahead, which leap probably saved my life for out of the darkness behind me came the abrupt flash of fire in the pan and the discharge of a musket. Heard a French curse. I maybe should a been boilin' down the river now but with a chance Frenchie wasn't entirely sure he'd heard or seen something, I did not want to dispel any doubts in his mind. Heard shouts from the men over by the fire. The man up on the rise shouted back. I didn't understand their words but it seemed the men by the fire were chiding the posted man for firing at ghosts. His tone, protesting back at them, said he wasn't entirely convinced there'd been something.

When I figured to be far enough down so the man wouldn't hear me nor see my churning wake in the moonlight, and still not making any noise, I commenced paddling hard. Hoped they weren't coming for me, but iffen they was, they'd have to go like hell to catch me.

I kept at it, the water bubbling past the sides of my boat. I shot over rapids in the dark, some I hardly saw until I was into them and fighting for control as the canoe banged into rocks and logs. Had to get out and drag over some places and portage around the worst of the rapids. Fear kept me going.

Those times when I stopped to look back upriver, I didn't see anybody coming fer me and I tried to convince myself the French must not have been sure enough of what they'd heard to think pursuit be worthwhile. Yet, if they were a raiding party, or scouts for a party, and what else could they be, stealth for them was paramount and they couldn't allow word of them to be brought downriver. Besides, and if there were Indians with the French, one or more of 'em might decide it was worth a look, to see if there be a scalp in it. The dog's chin was on the floor of the boat, his butt in the air. "If they get me, pard," I said, "it be the stewpot for you."

Daylight came before I reached the Hudson. I could hear the rapids ahead. Had to jump out to guide the canoe over the rocks near the mouth of the East Branch and damn near ran with my canoe whilst portaging the hill around the falls and getting back onto the water. Pushed down the main river still without any pursuit, best I could tell.

Even low this time of year, the current of the Hudson was strong and I made good progress. I eased my tired body some by letting the current do more of the work. Just before the big falls at the Great Carry and with still a ways to go to safety at Saratoga, there suddenly in front of me along the north shore was a clearing with more than a hundred men and with boats seemingly pulled up everywhere along the shore. If this was a French incursion, there was no way out fer me. I was in plain sight on the water and heading straight fer 'em. Might be the end of my road but there couldn't be so many French this far south and as it was, the men, unloading boats and cutting down trees and erecting tents were English fort-builders just arrived. A welcome sight. A fort at the Great Carry to protect our frontier and a place for me to run to, did I get into trouble.

I eased on in, a crowd of men come running down to the shore. Colonials with axes and shovels, British with raised muskets. A lieutenant in a red uniform jacket with gold braid, white pants, high black boots and leading a detachment of soldiers, came up. He ordered the men back to work and looked me over suspiciously for my having come from upriver. He demanded my name. I told him who I was and said I had news from the north.

He bade me follow him and we crossed the clearing, me behind him, British pigstickers behind me. Past rows of tents and the stumps of trees newly felled and to a marquee tent. The officer went in and when he came back out, he told me the North Fort commander would see me.

Inside the tent was sparse. A small portable writing desk, a bunk. Uniform parts and linens hanging from tent poles; a trunk on the floor beneath the clothes. The commander was standing, and before he sat down behind his desk and even with me taller than him, the twerp managed to look down his nose at me. "Kuyler," he said, smiling. "Consorting with the French?" I couldn't believe it, and with him saying he had been advised by his superiors to watch for me, it seemed he was going to arrest me as a spy. He said he was a lieutenant and his name was McMillian. "In command of North Fort. What is your business here? Answer quick and get your damn cur out of my tent." Ol' Blackie was about to lift his leg against the center post. I put the dog out.

I told McMillian I had been spooking around Scalp Point. He asked questions one after another and I could not help but ask, during a lull and whilst he was writing things down, how soon he was planning on gettin' after Indians. He looked up from his writing and said military information was not for civilians. "All the same," I said, "if you be goin' into the woods, you and your men need to shuck them red coats you be wearing." He said the coats were symbols of British power. I told him to get shuck of them, did he want to go on living. "Mister Kuyler," he said, and thinking about what he wanted to say and deciding not to say anything, he turned back to scribbling more of what I had told him. I stared down at him.

He was obviously new to the frontier. Same as the officer who had led me to the tent, they with their shiny buttons and fancy epaulets on coats so bright. Nary a spot. Like they was going to a military ball! Unfit for soldiering in the woods. When I again tried to warn him of the danger of those red coats, he got livid. Damn near jumped out of his chair, face as red as the coat he wore. Thought he might slap my face. I'd have put a knife into him iffen he did, and maybe he read my look because he didn't raise his hand and instead he sat back down, muttering about colonial clods, by which I reckoned he meant me. He said if I had no more information, I should get on with myself.

"Matter a fact," I said, "I do have something more." I told him of my encounter with the French out along the East Branch. He asked how many Frenchmen and when I told him I couldn't say for sure but said it was probably no more than a few, he shrugged. French voices and a shot in the dark didn't impress him. "His Majesty's troops," he said, "have little to fear from a mere hunting party out from Crown Point." I told him it was too far out and too close to Iroquoia for them to be hunting. And yes, it was maybe just a few but a few might be more trouble than what he thought. He looked up at me. I said the only reason the French could have for gettin' so far west was to agitate the Mohawks. "Stir 'em up against us." His thin smile said it amused him to think a provincial could have deduced something on his own, but he was at least willing to listen.

I repeated saying there weren't no reason for the French to be out there 'cept for a palaver intended to turn our Iroquois away from us. McMillian said it all had to do with diplomacy, not war, and fell outside of what he called my purview. "Maybe," I said, "but the higherups and the Albany politicians need to know about it. William Johnson too." Johnson had just recently been appointed as an agent for the Colony of New York, in charge of Indian Affairs. McMillian asked did I have anything more to report. I said I reckoned not, just I said something snide about tall pointed hats, such as some few of his men, his grenadiers, was wearing, and about fancified wigs which were naught but other men's hair. "Or a woman's hair," I said. He looked up sharply at this. He angrily dismissed me and as I was going out, he said I was not to bother his fort builders.

****

I walked the camp, looking for something to eat. Asked around of the colonials. Found a sergeant of provincials I knew from Albany. Michael Bowman. An Englishman, but a tough one, a man who drank in Pops' tavern. We talked some. He grumbled, said breakfast was at sunrise, supper at the end of a long workday and with naught but sips of water between. "Now you gots ta wait for supper," he said, "which isn't no damn good no how. The British want us up here buildin' a fort but they c'aint nor won't feed us decent and what we're hearing now, it might be there won't be no pay, neither. The men are talkin' about vamoosin', and if enough of 'em do, this fort ain't gonna be ready this year and if it ain't, it'll be overgrown by the time they gets back to finishin' 'er. Hafta do 'er all over again, mos' likely." I asked what was the problem. "Cain't neither king nor colony find money 'nough fer this year." His voice rising, Bowman was working into a tirade. "The gov'nor an' his henchmen only send supplies and pay in dribs'n drabs. Lots a men is upset 'bout it. Some is fixin' ta leave already and they all will, once it gets toward the harvest. You can bet your last shilling the gov'nor set aside money for his own self." He cursed, spit. I looked around and thought on it. "To tell you the truth," I said, "I wouldn't want to be stuck here in a winter's post." He agreed.

"I ain't gonna be, ye kin bet on thet." Told Bowman of the trouble I had with those Frenchies on the river and told him to be on the lookout for prowlers, and if he saw Iroquois in the bushes, I said he ought not to assume they be friendly. I asked him to watch my canoe. "Be back for it tomorrow."

I headed for the downstream side of the falls. Along the narrow, rock-strewn path to the lower falls, a small doe was drinking from a brook. I shot her and laughed to think of the alarm the musket shot must a throwed into the English camp. Gutted the deer, hung her in a tree and cut out a few steaks. Then part of the front shoulder for the dog. The rest of the meat I left hanging a short way from the path but hidden so no damn soldier would find it. If they would not feed me, I damn sure wasn't going to feed them. Off the trail, I built a fire behind some rocks and cooked the meat. When it was done, I moved camp and ate under a wonderful old oak tree. Slept the night on a bed of leaves. Awoke before first light feeling great. Glad I had not eaten army fare. I went back to the camp for my canoe, the soldiers was hard at work, the camp a noisy one. Men felling trees without seeming to know where they would hit, horses and oxen dragging logs. A dangerous place to linger! The dog stayed close to me, watching all 'round.

A buzz was going through the camp. I asked Bowman about it, he said a courier had come in during the night with news of a raid somewhere out along the Mohawk River and a lesser raid around Saratoga. I asked about Saratoga. Was the names Langston or Baldwin heard? Bowman couldn't recall hearing any names. I told him where I had hung the deer, said the rest of it was his, did he want it. "Keep your nose into the wind," I said, and soon after, I departed, to the relief of Blackie.

I stopped in Saratoga and spent a night with Arnold and Priscilla. I asked about the raid, they brushed it off, all they could talk about was the country house they were going to build, out by the healing springs. I exploded. "Outliers burnt out not three days ago," I said, "and you're wantin' to move out there? What the hell is wrong with you?"

Figuring it was Priscilla who most wanted to go, for Arnold much enjoyed the conviviality of town, I told Priscilla the gentry spent their winters in New York Town. Hoped flattery might convince her, since common sense hadn't. She replied, "If it is so dangerous just a few miles outside of Saratoga, my young bumpkin friend, why are you so often gone off into the woods?" I reminded her I was a scout. She gave me a sly sort of smile. "And a trapper," she said. The woman is far too clever for me. "You make good money at it," she said, "but what good is money if the savages lay their hands on you, eh, ducky?" She always had the last word. When I could get Arnold aside, I told him if he was ever going to say no to his woman, this was the time. He smiled and asked did I think she ever listened to him.

I departed soon after. Priscilla's airs get to me sometimes. First stop, Van Schaack's. He thanked me for the information I brought and asked me to come back in the morning. Said he'd have money for me and I could give another report to the town officials. I agreed and then I was walking through the door of the crowded tavern and elbowing my way to the bar. The greetings from family and friends warm. Pops poured me a tankard of beer and pointed to a table in the corner by the hearth. I looked over. It was none other than Bill Johnson, sitting as a beam of light. He and Pops had become good friends. Bill was fond of Pops' beer; he taking a keg or two home any time he was in Albany. Johnson lived to the west, amongst his Mohawks. He was a big man. Tall, wide of shoulder, a giant bear 'cept always well cultivated, never shaggy. Well over six feet of him. Dressed in sky-blue Indian leggings cut from the best cloth, buckskin gaiters over leather-fringed moccasins. A soft leather jacket of the same buckskin, highly decorated with bright, dyed quills, red, blue and white. The jacket no doubt the handiwork of some nubile Indian girl. Under the jacket he wore a silk shirt, white as snow; ruffled baubles hung around his neck. A frontier dandy but I was not fooled, he was a most powerful man. One cannot be in his presence and not feel both intimidated and fascinated. He commanded all within his sight.

I carried my drink over and sat down. "Ken, how was it?" His grin infectious. "How was what?" I would be vague until I knew what he wanted. "Scalp Point. What are the French up to?" I told him the situation, and when I told him about my encounter with the French out on the East Branch, he considered it gravely, even admitting it might be the most important piece of information I had brought. I asked what he was doing in town.

"Beer and females, the more of each the better, my friend." His smile said he would not fail. Then, holding his tankard high and with his voice melodious in a rough sort of way, "Best beer brewed in New York Colony. Lures me like a moth to the flame."

We talked whilst drinking my old man's good West Indies rum and chasing it with the beer. Our conversation was mostly about women but did keep swinging back around to the affairs of the colony and of Bill's duties as Commissioner of Indian Affairs.

When I was well-soused, he asked did I want to go to work for him. "You son-of-a-bitch," I said, and with my face getting red, "No! I won't go to work for you nor anybody." Which I thought closed the matter but he persisted. His fancy elbows resting on the wooden table between us, his eyes locked most savagely into mine, hard to say no to this powerful man. His force was strong. He grinned wickedly and said I would be well paid. "Johnson," I said, "I don't care if they dub you the bloody king and you offer me the royal trove. I won't work for you. Last time we partnered, I almost got killed. And cost me a fortune besides, which, as I recall, you neglected to help pay off. To hell with you and your chances to make money. Let's chase women and drop the subject, eh?" He, in his Irish brogue, kept on, as though he hadn't heard me. "You will scout the North Country for me, won't you? You are the only white man who knows the way around up there and who can be trusted. Nobody else dares go up, except my Mohawks. Damn it, I need your eyes and your savvy. What do you say? Is there any reason for you to say no?" I had no chance to answer for he kept right on, and the truth was, I didn't know how I would answer. He was right for insisting we needed somebody besides the Mohawks scouting the north. Still, I kept on shaking my head.

"You don't have any other work for now, do you?" he said. "What will you do if you stay here? I can tell you. Nothing! There is nothing here for a man of your experience." His eyes, strong presence, and the booze made it hard for me to think straight. Bill is a most forceful man. I tried to collect my thoughts before answering, so not to trap myself. "Why do you think I'm here now?" I said. "It's too dangerous up there. French and Abenakis crawling all over the woods. Shut the hell up and drink your beer." Even then he was not convinced and kept pestering. I blew up, about ready to fight just to shut him up. "Damn you for a drunken Indian lover," I said. "Why can't you understand what I just goddamn said? Go up and look your damn self if you want to see so bad. Or send some of your prize Mohawks." I pounded my fist on the table. The pints of beer jumping and spilling drew the attention of the entire common room. When things settled down, we got back into it. "Sooner or later, Ottawas or Hurons would get on my tail and where would you or your fat-assed king or your Mohawks be to help me then, eh? Besides, I already been insulted enough for stopping in up to the fort to tell the commander what I knowed and what he should a been grateful to hear. The little martinet son-of-a-bitch of a lieutenant said I was a spy for the French!" My voice getting louder again, I realized I might maybe a had more to drink than was necessary but I kept on anyway. "No, dammit! I am not going to work for you."

Johnson is a hard man to go against but he laid off and we talked about women. He did most of the talking, then plates of steaming stew and a slowdown on the rum. I told him I only spied on Frenchie for my own preservation but would let him know whenever there was something he should hear about. "Provided I go back up and provided I get paid for my trouble. Otherwise, you get nothing more from me." Told him I had made a report to Schaack and was to make another report to the mayor and the sheriff, at Schaack's office in the morning.

We drank and argued all evening. My old man threatened to throw us into the street. Just when I figured to drop from all the drinking, Bill decided it was time we went in search of female company. I had my doubts, given the lateness but off we went.

One thing about carousing with Bill, he knows all the right doors to knock on. Albany is a fair-sized city with three-thousand souls inside the palisade and Bill soon had us fixed up in a place I would never have dared to try. A most amazing man!

First thing next morning, I went up the hill to Van Schaack's house, to report my findings to the alderman and the others of the authorities. Bill was already there, showing no trace of our carousing, as if he'd slept the night through. I was hung over, sick as blazes. Schaack asked why I looked so bad. I turned toward Johnson. He was staring at something out the window, as if what I had come to talk about could have naught to do with him. Schaack and them others asked questions, I answered as best I could. They offered me a paltry sum for the information I had brought and another paltry sum if I would scout for them. It wasn't near enough for the danger, and the truth was, I didn't care to work for them. An argument ensued. I insisted on more money although this was because I didn't want anything to do with them and so asked a price I knew they would not meet. Johnson turned from the window and faced us, his elbows leaned now on the high sill behind him. "Don't give him a damn farthing," he said. "Until he agrees to work for us." I told him to go to hell. Schaack argued with the mayor and aldermen to get them to pay me more. Schaack pointed out they had no other way to get information. They said my price was too high, I said I valued my scalp. The mayor harangued me about men needing to band together in defense of the colony. Even though I didn't disagree, I laughed at him.

I finally agreed to do some scouting, not because of any pressure I felt but because if we ever expected to beat the French, we had to know what they were doing. I said it would be on my terms. I wouldn't work for 'em directly, just they could pay me for what I brought, and if it wasn't fair payment, they'd get nothing more. Johnson left town two days later. Mad at me. Not accustomed to not getting his way.

Chapter XVI – Easy Shootin', Hoss

"What's the news?" I asked the sentries at the gates of Albany and as I was getting in from one of my scouting forays. "War!" they said. "So she's opened," I said, and for the rest of the summer I mostly stayed around town, waiting to see what might transpire. There were plenty of rumors and a grave uncertainty. A bit of trouble, but such goes on even in times of peace. Seems the perpetrators of evil deeds were often not enemies from the north but our own folks, who used the troubled times for their own ends. I think this happens more than is commonly known.

Weakness will always draw trouble but it stayed peaceful, although the time granted us was wasted as the defense of our part of the colony was in no way advanced. With summer turning to fall, and even with the war, I decided to go north for the trapping. I didn't tell anybody, not even Pops and Mother. To most folks I said nothing at all, to those I could not say nothing, I said I'd be scouting and didn't say where. If I had said I was going to winter so close to the French, they'd have thought I was crazy but they didn't any of them know the lay of the situation up there. In my figuring, the war made things more safe, not more dangerous. The French and Indians, busy with preparing for war, would be even less likely to come out of the Valley of the Corlaer and anyway and in all the years I had survived in the north, war or peace hadn't mattered. French or Indian would a killed me, sure as hell.

What did bother me was the right or wrong of going trapping with a war on and I reasoned I could do more good scouting out of Paradise than I could out of Albany or Saratoga. Besides, going up there was what the politicians had been wanting me to do. Did I see anything which they needed to know at once, I could go down with a warning.

With some time before I would go north, I scouted around Saratoga and the Kaydeross. There was a small garrison at Saratoga, in regular contact with their headquarters in Albany and I sent regular dispatches down with their couriers.

Spent some nights with Arnold, he helping me with my writing. Priscilla was furious for the war news scaring the workmen so none of 'em were willing to go out and start on her country house. She said they were cowards and she insisted work would begin in the spring.

They told me Lydia had her baby, a girl. I stayed away from Lydia for the regret seeing her with another man's baby might bring me and instead, I got close to a young lady five years my junior. The daughter of the commander of the militia posted at the fort. We got intimate until her pa learned who I was and forbade the romance. The girl then pledged to a British officer passing through on an inspection tour.

The time came for trapping and I got started up the Hudson. The leaves had not yet turned their fall colors, the forest lush and green. Farther up, the leaves would be as colorful as the coats of the British. I arrived at the Great Carry fort about sunset on a fine evening with a heavy sack of winter possibles over my shoulder. I was surprised at how far the fort was from completion but not surprised with how few men was still there. The militia had all mostly gone home, their enlistments expired, or maybe they had deserted, as Bowman had said they would. Lack of pay and of supply and the harvest season at home. The British were preparing to break camp and go to their winter quarters in New York.

The British sergeants, of whom there were six, were friendly for thinking I was a curiosity. One even tried to apologize for the previous rude behavior of Lieutenant McMillian. They seemed more relaxed and more at their ease with me than when last I had come upon them. This, I found out, was because Bowman had shared with them the deer I had shot when last I was passing through. The only fresh meat they got in all the time they were up here. About dark they bid me join them for supper. We retired to the non-coms' mess and I was vexed to see the sergeants stacking their rifles as they went into the mess tent. Kept mine with me at all times.

Dinner manners, even in the bush, are most strictly observed and amusing to see. The steel-rod discipline obvious. These men would be worthy opponents in a fight if properly led. Lions led by fools. Supper was a stew of salted meat, carrots and peas, all in a broth and with black bread for the dipping. They had an ample supply of rum which, even sloshed with a little water, was enough to set one's brain on fire.

We sat inside the crowded tent, sharing a jug, and as the jug kept on its rounds, I asked did it ever go empty. "Nay, lad," one of the sergeants said, "and there be more jugs iffen it do." Laughed to myself for how these men, even after a hard day's work, were impeccably dressed. I asked had they seen any hostiles. They hadn't, and one of them, in his odd-sounding accent, hard to follow the Cockney tongue, said Indians wouldn't dare come 'round His Majesty's forces. "We 'ave sat in perfect 'armony all bloomin' summer," he said, and he started to call me bumpkin but stopped himself. "We keep close watch 'ere'bouts," a short man, Wilson, chimed in. Impossible not to wonder what he meant, with the woods so near and they not ever venturing out, from what I could see. They assured me no Indians could get up close to their camp. "The guards would surely see them." Unanimous they were in the belief their safety was complete. "I am no' afraid a any skulkin' savages whi' might be a prowlin' 'round 'bout. British steel would make short work a them did they show their bleedin' arses." Too sure of themselves, I thought. But did not say so.

Two colonial sergeants were with us. One of 'em, Bowman, didn't concur with the British opinion of their safety. "I've lived along the frontier long enough to believe most anything of Indians," Bowman said. "Most likely they have been around. If McMillian would let us scout a little, mighten be sure. He acts as if he don' want to know." I agreed but again said nothing, not wanting the British mad at me for it being their jug what was going unabated around our circle.

McMillian came by briefly. He glared at me and after listening to some of the sergeants' remarks about Indians, he said forcefully, "No damn savages will ever be a match for the mighty British army." Then, and directly to me, as if he were speaking a truth I refused to acknowledge, or daring me to challenge him, "We'll give them massed firepower followed by a crushing bayonet charge." His arrogance comical to anyone who knew the woods. He reckoned did he line up his men, the Indians would faint from fright.

McMillian knew he was not welcome here. The sergeants, all much older than the lieutenant, were deferential as rank demanded but the way they all looked down silently as he went through detail lists said plenty about what they really thought of him. After he left, I tried to get the sergeants to say bad things about him but they wouldn't. They were professional soldiers.

Another sergeant came late to dinner. "You heathen slackers," he said loudly as he came in. "There better be the king's share of supper, for I be hungrier'n a Scottish tax collector and I'll kick the arse of the man who ate mine." He squinted at me. "An' that means you, bucko." The others told him my name and said I was an esteemed trapper and woodsman. A visitor to their mess and entitled to the respect of all. "Well, pox on me wicked manners," the just-arrived sergeant said, whilst another said of him, "Sergeant-Major Thomas O'Brien, top sergeant of our band of fort-makers. A soldier twenty years and more. Tell just by looking at his face. No civilian could look that mad all the time and not get killed for it. Tom can both cuss his men and laugh at himself. Loved by all for his kindly temperament and saintly words of compassion."

O'Brien stuck out his hand. "Hello there, Mister Kuyler," he said. We shook and I felt as if my own hand was locked in a vise. "Good handshake, Kuyler," he said. "Been in the woods, eh?" Before I could answer, he was back scowling at his men. "Not one o' you kin stand the amount of work I do in a day. Who is to check the guard tonight? Wilson? Get your arse out there, see what's doin'. An'gimme your cup." He grabbed the cup; Wilson went quickly out of the tent. This Sergeant Tom was bigger than most men. Well over six foot. Not as tall as Bill Johnson, but close. Rough and heavyset, the marks of multiple campaigns etched on his hard-set face. Sandy red hair and long since faded freckles. Rough and boisterous.

"We shall see about you, Mister Kuyler," O'Brien said. "We shall see." He dug into his peas and bully beef and he groused at the other men, who he considered to be of a lesser make than himself. We kept on drinking whilst O'Brien had his dinner, and after eating his fill and cleaning his mess kit, this big man showed what a prodigious drinker he was. With him refilling his cup more often than any of the rest of us, I thought he must keel over, yet he did not seem affected. The big ox showed sign of brains by pointedly getting into the conversation on my side. "Laddies, we be in trouble if we try an' fight the way we be used ta. There is no ruddy sense linin' up and firing volleys aginst a foe is 'iding in the bloody trees. I 'ave fought guerillas in the mountains a Spain, lads, an' I kin tell ya 'tis no' a picnic. They don' sit long enough to get 'emselves shot nor stuck wi' bayonets."

I was surprised he was honest enough to admit they needed to make changes. One of the other sergeants, a good-size man, didn't think so. "Rubbish, O'Brien!" he said. "You 'ave been spoutin' naught but your malarkey since Albany. The same discipline what 'as seen us through everywhere else will see us trou'h 'ere as well. The bloody savages be no better than others we 'ave done ba'tle wi'. Is all thee bloody same."

"Malarky, eh? The ruddy devil you say!" O'Brien was on his feet, fists balled for fighting. I was excited to see such a fight, it would be a good one, for these were rugged men, although I hoped we'd go outside less they bring the tent down on us. Some of the sergeants got between O'Brien and the other man. "Won't do, buckos," one said, "to have our sergeants fightin' amongst themselves. 'Specially our top man, the one we counts on the most fer steadiness." O'Brien replied, calm as could be, "The toughest too, an' I'd be most willing to demonstrate if the three of these fine chaps would be so kind as to let go of me. I won't hurt him. Wouldn't harm a puppy. Just let go my arms." The others knew better and held on. And began to razz O'Brien until he calmed down. In a few minutes they all laughed it off and resumed their places, and their drinking. I figured there were plenty of fistfights in British camps.

"The Indians, aye. We kin lick 'em." Tom spoke thoughtfully now. "Tis the countryside I fear. This land be naught like any we've experienced." He spoke to me. "How cold does it get here in winter, laddie?" I told them about the cold and the snow, and with me going on and him nodding and getting impatient, he talked over me. "It's all a what I 'av bin saying, buckos. We're not prepared for thee likes a' it."

Sometime later, all of us well-soused, we went outside and got 'round a fire built up too high. Made me uneasy to sit in the bright light of such a blaze. We stayed there most of the night. Drinking and swapping stories. I told them of my life in the mountains, the solitary ways of the fur trapper, the cold, the deep snow, the winter wolves.

They spoke of their service to their king. These were veterans of countless campaigns on the continent and had long experience with the army camps of Europe. One had been long enough in the ranks to have been present at the Battle of Blenheim where twenty-thousand Frenchies died, most of 'em drowned when the lines of redcoat bayonets pushed 'em into the swift-flowing Danube River. The sergeants, for as many times as they had probably heard the story, laughed now to hear it. The French begging for mercy as the relentless lines of pig-sticking British infantry pushed them into the swift current.

The sergeants recalled the cities of Europe, opportunities squandered, sweethearts left behind. Families half-remembered, wives and wars come and gone. They spoke with resignation about themselves. Some was counting the time to retirement, others would never retire for having signed on as lads for a lifetime of service. This, whilst not unusual in the British ranks, was beyond belief to colonials such as me. Yet, and as I listened, it was the lifers around our fire pitying the termed-men. Said they'd be sad puppies pining to crawl back into the ranks once they had experienced life on the outside.

They queried me plenty. O'Brien asked so many damn fool things, I, as I slipped under from the rum, told him to go to hell and shut up and leave me alone. Spent the night wrapped in my bearskin, outside, on the ground and away from the still-roaring fire. It's a wonder they didn't burn up the camp, with embers blowing in the wind and dry brush piles everywhere.

****

Before first light, the camp was astir. The sergeants were up and buzzing, impossible for me to sleep. I went to the mess tent and got some coffee, to clear my head. By my second cup I was awake. It was just coming light. The air was crisp and cool. Cup in hand, and with the dog running ahead, I found Sergeant O'Brien. I pointed to a knoll outside the perimeter of the camp. I had been eyeing it the entire time I had been drinking my coffee. I asked why it was not posted, since it clearly dominated the camp. Tom said the lieutenant would not permit it. Said there was no need.

I asked O'Brien to walk up there with me. We crossed the clearing and got up onto the knoll. From the camp below it maybe looked insignificant but from the top, it presented an altogether different aspect. Screened in front by a line of trees and impossible to reach quickly from the camp for the ravine behind the trees, it loomed a perfect spy post. I walked around some, bent down here and there, and touching the tall grass, I pushed it aside to inspect the dirt underneath. The sergeant looked on, unsure what I was searching for, or finding. Showed him the grass where the Indians had lain, how it had been pressed down and raised up again. At the back of the knoll where it was more dirt than grass, I showed him the faint traces of moccasin tracks and how branches had been used to feather-swish the tracks. O'Brien whistled softly, seeing, now it was pointed out to him, how the Indians had watched the camp from the knoll. "Why, laddie," he said, "this spies' lair 'as lain 'ere all bloomin' summer, no' a hundred yards from the bloody camp." He looked down on his men as they went about their duties, their bright uniforms presenting easy targets in the early morning sun. "If they wanted to, they cudda shot us all on just such a fine morning as this. Right from 'ere. Damn their souls to perdition, we wudda no had a chance." He shook his head. "Not a bloomin' chance." I told him the Indians had come for spying, not for fighting, and there was never more'n a few at a time. "Aye, an' a good thing." His eyes searched the woods around us. "Tis a sorry state we 'ave come to 'ere. Like this they will 'urt us bloody awful. I don' mind tellin' ya, I'll be powerful glad to see the last a this bloody land. The mountains give me the shivers." He was looking north and contemplating what sort of heathens was up there. "I keep s'pecting 'em to come down. Tis for bloody certain we're n'ready ta fight 'em." We looked somberly down on the camp. The pickets was posted no farther out than the perimeter and the men rarely ventured past them. The Indians had done their spying amid perfect security all summer.

"Damn lucky they didn't try something on their own reckoning and without French permission," I said, "but now the war has commenced, you can bet your arse they'll not be content with watching." Sobering thoughts for both Tom and me as we watched the soldiers lining up for roll call amid the rows of white canvas tents, laid out symmetrical between the stumps and cleared brush. "Easy shooting, hoss," I said, "when they do come back." Tom's face furrowed with concern. "Don' wanna think about it," he said and he went to find his lieutenant.

I looked around some more whilst he was gone, then him and the lieutenant crossed the clearing and ascended the hill. Took them time enough to get up, the lieutenant's heavy boots made for hard walking. They arrived, the lieutenant red-faced and puffing from the climb. A camp soldier. As I pointed out all of what had been going on there on the hill, the lieutenant wore an expression of denial and disdain across his skinny young face. So obvious his annoyance, as if it were painted on, same as on an actor's face in a play. I savored punching holes in his imperiousness with all I showed him. It was rubbing hard on him; the crow he was tasting a tough swallow. A bitter taste but not so bitter as what the Indians was surely intending.

McMillian tried to remain skeptical as I pointed out the presence of a spy camp, all of what I had shown Sergeant Tom and the piece of French leather I had picked up out of the grass. "Damn provincials see a red devil hiding behind every bloody bush," McMillian said. "You might have built this camp yourself. You certainly knew right where to look." Anger rose in my throat. How could an officer be so stupid as to deny what was in his face and with the awful potential consequences? I thought how Johnson ought to come here to see for himself what I meant by British officers getting men killed.

I told McMillian what I had told the sergeant, how there were never more than a few Indians here at a time but one fine morning he'd get awakened by a sizeable war party come for easy scalps. "Then what?" Still he would rebut the evidence, his face as red as his coat. "I will have no such impertinence in my command, bumpkin. Depart at once or I will have you flogged. I believe this skulkers' camp is your handi- work. You and your Indian friends." I was ready to fight, he didn't back down, seemed to want to goad me. "I may yet arrest you as a spy for the French, you Dutch turncoat." I told him to say it again and I'd have his damn scalp. He drew his sword, bringing it loud out of his scabbard. The dog was growling, his upper lip curled back. I reckoned the officer's sword arm would not be worth much with my partner's teeth sunk into it. I also knew the sharp saber could take off Blackie's head with a single swipe. O'Brien took hold of me roughly, and with a look to singe the hair off a cat, he pulled me aside, the lieutenant smirking for having known O'Brien would intercede. O'Brien told me to hold still and he made it clear if there was a fight, he'd be against me. The lieutenant uttered another threat. "Don't ever come back to this fort. I don't care how many goddamn Indians are after you. Take them elsewhere." He laughed, high-pitched and nervous, like a horse's whinny, then he spun around and stalked off, still cackling as he went down the hill. Sergeant Tom held onto me until McMillian was gone. "He means it, Kenny. Do as he says, at once. Don' push him. He is law and lord here. I'll arrest you myself if you disobey his order." Tom gave me a hard look. "I'll bring your pack 'round to the south end of camp." He walked back down the hill, I went around the outside of the camp and waited at the south end until Tom, escorted by two bayonet-wielding privates, came back with my things. "Sorry I am, Kenny boy," he said, "but an officer is used to bein' talked to in a cert'n way." Uh, huh. Don't make a fool of him even if he be a fool. I apologized for the trouble and thanked Tom for his help. "I'll try an' keep an eye on the hill for so long as we're here," he said. "Maybe get provincials posted up there." Then he bade me to go. Said his orders, if I didn't leave immediately, was to arrest me as a spy. They'd flog me and put me in irons. Tom finished with a pained look. He knew better but he meant it. A British soldier follows orders. "Flee, laddie!" I grabbed my gear and vamoosed.

Chapter XVII – Intruders in Paradise

I waited out the daylight hours at the upper end of the portage. These waters were dangerous. Indians might be anywhere. None but a fool would take the chance. I carved two more paddles whilst I waited and watched the upriver and the banks.

I had decided to take a more westerly route than my usual way, an extra precaution. Upriver from me, the Sacandaga flowed into the Hudson from the west. I would go up the Sacandaga and somewhere along the Great Bend, I would strike northeast, into the back country. Use the portages I have heard tell of, some few of which I was already familiar with. I believed it would be possible to get up to Paradise Valley this way. It would be an adventure, with or without Indians but I felt I would be less likely to encounter trouble out here than closer in. Plenty of extra work, though.

After dark, I started up. Hard paddling in the narrow waters where the current was swift. This part of the Hudson was never easy. After a hard go upstream, I came to the mouth of the Sacandaga. High water-falls blocked the confluence, a tough, uphill portage the only way to get around them. In the early morning light and before moving my canoe and gear, I studied the ground, saw Indian sign, no more'n a few days old. A dangerous reminder. The portage is not long but with the cautions I took, it was two days before I was through.

The Sacandaga is not very high in the fall of the year. I had to walk often, sloshing the many riffles, towing the canoe at the end of a rope. Slipping and sliding on rocks and hidden snags, often falling into holes and receiving a thorough dousing. Soaked clear through. A hard pull with the feeling not much was accomplished for the amount of work. The creek bed narrowed, the way became rougher. Stonier. I felt as if I had made a mistake coming this way until I realized there had been no hostile sign since I'd got past the confluence.

The river turned to the southwest. The Great Bend. As I persevered onward, I happily realized being so far from anyone or anything can be a soothing elixir on the mind. The old feeling from my youth, to see what is over the next hill, or find where does a certain cold brook come from. Can't help it, my heart opens up when I am heading along an unknown path. My vision and horizons widen. A wonderful set of eyes through which to look forward. Makes wet moccasins and leggings less of a burden. My legs and shoulders ached. Slept a cold camp in the rain.

Next morning, I started out early. The river turned north, another hard go against the current and with snags and boulders blocking the way. Followed the river through upsloping country so peaceful one might almost forget there was the threat of danger. Up in this colder country, autumn had faded. The yellows and golds were gone out of the hardwoods; the scarlet of the oaks had browned; the ground maple yet held some faint color.

To cross over to the West Branch from the Sacandaga, I had to find the right creek amongst several coming in from the north. Follow it farther up into the hills. I found it after a couple of frustrating false starts. This creek was low enough in some places so my canoe could not support the weight of me and my gear. I had to drag the boat, and in the worst places, I had to empty the canoe, carry it, then go back for my gear. Kept trying to convince myself the extra work was what was keeping the hair on my head. The dog, bored with such slow progress, prowled the shoreline.

I followed the creek to its source, a small pond full of big trout. I spent a day spearing fish and come the night, I rested on a bed of pine needles, ate fish and drank the rum I had found in my pack, snuck in there by Sergeant O'Brien when his lieutenant ran me out of the camp.

I stayed awake, studying the stars. How far away might they be? Pondered the nature of things until the mist lifting off the pond and the canopy of trees blotted out the lights. A chilling dampness crept over the land. I had not often heard mention of this route. The scant pages upon which I had it written down were with Eric in Albany. After Arnold checks over the pages, I stash them with Eric for safekeeping at his apothecary. Hid my canoe, and pretty sure the trail I wanted was close by, I spent half the day searching and finally found an old blaze on a tree. The trail was easy enough to follow though it was much overgrown, the walking rough. Drug the canoe on a travois, my possibles bag over my shoulder. I crested the height of ground and came out on the river I had hoped for. The waters flowed east. An hour's rest whilst I searched the banks for sign. Found plenty! Indians, more likely Iroquois than Hurons or Abenakis. Hunters, not raiders.

A week or more old. I boarded the boat, thankful for putting an end to the worst of the portaging. Headed downstream, skirting the numerous small waterfalls when I could, exhilarating when I couldn't. Came to a long lake and started down. A cold wind whipped up waves which threatened to sink me. I went ashore for the worst of it. When the wind died enough to resume, I paddled ten or fifteen miles, made another short portage and arrived along the northerly reaches of the Hudson, country I knew. And realized how far I had still to go. My usual route from the Hudson, the East Branch, took only a couple of days to reach the cabin. This time and venturing overland from the West Branch to the East, I was days finding my way. Truth was, and even with hard going through the mountains, I was glad for the chance to explore this sightful land at its most spectacular time of year. Surely pleasing to the eye. Highlands opening onto views of beautiful country, the splash of color against a backdrop of evergreen mountains. Words woefully inadequate for so much pleasant seeing.

The nights turned colder fast, I needed my blanket, though the days stayed sunny and warm. A beautiful time of year in the high mountains, with the mosquitoes and blackflies gone by. The higher into the hills I got, the frostier the nights. Filled with the promise of another early and hard winter, I pushed on, eager to get to my cabin. Had to find just the right creek to turn up, get farther north. Crest one more mountain range. I found the creek, followed it to its source, a small pond. Someone had been here within the past year. The blazes on the trees fresh cut, plainly visible. Then a portage to a creek. Through the trees and whilst portaging, I got glimpses of a mountain range to the east. My mountains, the last before Corlaer.

After two miles this gentle creek began to roil as it descended a series of steep grades. Rapids, and ahead, by the sounds, a waterfall. My boat dropped suddenly into a rocky gorge, the water got wilder, and first chance, I got off this crazy ride. Named it Suicide Creek. Blazes on the trees showed where a trail led around the dangerous falls. Skirting the precipitous chasm on spray-dampened rocks made for cautious going. Might fall a long way off those slippery heights, hit my head and die quickly. Or snap an ankle bone and die slowly.

Got down below the falls and the damn dog took off after a blackie, howling in a beeline up the steepest slope they could find. I spent hours in pursuit. Finally, the dog treed the bruin. I ran like hell to get there but whilst I was still a hundred yards off, the bear come down out of the tree and off they went again. The dog was having a hell of a time, with him chasing the bear and me coming behind, trying to get to him before he forgot he wasn't supposed to catch the bruin.

High atop the mountain where the chase had taken us and with the bear vamoosed and the dog having returned, proud of hisself, we bedded down for the night. Next morning, I watched as the light came up over a misty dawn. The sun over the Pharaoh's Peak, what a sight! The big mountain like a pyramid. I had stood up there on just such a morning as this. Remembered shooting a big buck up there. Remembered dragging him home, too.

Came down to the base of the mountain and back onto the stream. The bed flattened out to good canoeing, winding around sandy curves. Below me was yet another set of rapids. Too late to avoid them, over the rough spots I went, bare rocks showing all-round. Broke a paddle and had holes punched in the canoe. Glad I was when the waters calmed and I came to the west shore of Big Lake, somewhere around its midpoint. I made camp. I would not get onto the lake in the daylight and waited for the dark. Another night paddling under the stars and noon of the next day, my eleventh, I reckoned, since gettin' tossed out of the British camp, I was home in my canyon.

Got up to the rim of the cliffs and searched for sign, found none. The only intruder was the big buck. He'd spent the summer feasting on the remains of my garden, his track plain in the potato mounds. I have been told a deer will not eat potato leaves but this one sure as hell did. And my groundnut eaten down to the nub. In some, even the roots were dug up by coons and groundhogs, the remains trampled by the deer and finished off by the mice. After this, I doubted I would try again to grow a garden. Not worth the effort. Not for the few ears of corn I managed to save.

Before I could start trapping, I went to see about the French. Being careful to leave no sign, I followed Outlet Creek down into the Corlaer Valley. I cut away whilst still on the higher ground, a good walk, and crested the rugged hills high above the French fort. The castle and blockhouses were garrisoned and alert, the fort imposing and sinister. The peasant huts looked to be shut up for the winter. Indians came and went. As always, it was not possible to tell how many were present at any one time. I also saw plenty of the dangerously-adept woodsmen, the Canadian-born woods-lopers.

After dark and with the drums from the Indian camp beating, I went in for a closer look. I stayed back from the outermost palisade, in the orchards, close enough to hear the melodic tongue of the French sentries as they called out their cadences. Snuck through a hole in the palisade and on the inside, I got close enough up to one of the blockhouses to hear the French fiddles and squeezeboxes and the lonely lament of their songs as they drank and sang away the lengthening nights until spring.

The French were secure and would take the offensive when they were so ordered, but with them settled in, I figured there wouldn't be anything big before spring. Nothing for me to forgo my trapping and go south at once with a warning. I laughed for what good a warning would do. The English could not even set a proper watch, how in the hell could they stop an incursion? Nothing in northern New York was safe and there was naught I could do to make it otherwise.

I fished for salmon on the way home.

****

Preparing for winter kept me busy. I repaired my traps and soaked them in a concoction of water and sumac bark to get the rust and the man odor off them. I cut firewood, hunted and fished and salted the meat. And spent a few enjoyable afternoons writing in the sun outside the cabin or up on the ledges overlooking the lake. The big buck came in close a few times. He was crafty, a superior animal with a regal rack and I decided to let him live. He had become a sort of companion, despite his devastation of my garden. Besides, he looked to be getting on past his prime. The meat would be tough. Rather shoot young ones.

My second winter in the woods, I had discovered a small cave behind a waterfall partway up the cut where the creek came down off the cliffs. The cave went in just a short way and had a low ceiling which didn't allow me to stand upright, just there was sufficient room for stooping. I decided it would be my icehouse. That winter and every year since, I have loaded ice into the cave. The ice, covered with dirt and woodchips, is slow to melt, the cave stays cool most all summer. I take what ice I can from right there in the cut. For bigger chunks, I go down to the lake. The lake freezes to great thickness in winter, two feet or more by March. I cut squares out of the ice with my ax and drag the chunks by toboggan up into the cut. Getting the ice up there is terribly hard work but is worth the effort. I keep this natural locker as stocked as I can. Fish, venison and potatoes will keep until almost the next ice season. This enables me to go for longer stretches without hunting and still eat good. On the hottest days of summer, when the mosquitoes and flies are at their worst, the dog keeps cool in the cave. I sometimes join him in there, to escape the bugs and to cool off whilst having my iced rum and birch tea, mixed.

****

The winter was hard upon me as I sat writing in my snug cabin.

The trapping was good. I checked as many sets as possible each day. A tough task to keep up with the demands of the work. Many a night was spent away from home, in bark shelters, and hard it was on a man in the vigor of youth to come home to a lonely cabin with the inside colder than the out. A struggle to rescue a spark from the ashes in the fireplace with fingers frozen nearly stiff. Once I got a fire going, the cabin thawed quickly enough but the existence was a miserable one. This year the weather was worse than my first year, which I had thought was as bad as a winter could be. The miles of trudging through deep snow on snowshoes took its toll. At night my back ached fierce. Only thing keeping me going was the fur. And plenty of it. Wished I had more traps to put out, except it would lengthen my already too-long days. Nights I worked the fur and mended snowshoes. The shoes took a beating from the miles and from the brush under the snow. Each pair wore out after only a short while.

Three months I plodded my wintery solitude with just the sounds of the forest around me. The thud of fresh snow falling from the trees when the wind did not blow. It never blew, it only howled, and when it did, I heard the clicking of the ice-encrusted branches of the more-slender trees as they swayed overhead. Limbs cracking and sometimes falling, entire trees, big ones, pulled out by the roots and blown over. Scary to be in the woods when it was like this. Dangerous, for there was never a warning. The fierce north wind pounded wicked hard on my door at night. The winter wore on, the snow piled up. The waterfall froze solid and for two weeks I was not able to get into the cave where I kept my food. I had to spend time ice fishing instead of trapping. I subsisted on fish and turkeys. Turkeys were usually in abundance although even they were scarce this winter. Some days I had naught to eat but thin soup made of the inner layers of birchbark and balsam. Ran out of coffee and rum before Christmas.

The deer used the high cliff walls for sheltering against the bitter winds and the deepest snows. Probably they had wintered in my canyon for years, nay, centuries, and when they came, I left them alone for they too were having a hard time in the deep snow. So weak, they barely moved. Especially toward the end of the winter and with the females growing heavy with their fawns. The pitiful things hardly had strength enough to bound away when I passed. I didn't shoot or spook 'em if it could be avoided and I didn't let the dog run loose. Unchecked, he could do plenty of damage to the herd. I would not give him the chance. The deer were necessary for his survival too.

The deer fed on the cedar behind my cabin, around the pond where the water collected as it came off the ledges. The cedar soured the taste of the meat, unlike the good meat of the fall hunt. In past years, the deer seemed to understand our truce, and I suppose they understood it this year as well, because, and so desperate was I for meat and just as I had resolved to break the truce, they stopped coming around.

The wolves preyed on the deer and when the deer, late in the winter, did finally get around my cabin, the wolves came too, often taking the deer almost on my doorstep. With the snow crusted over thick, the wolves ran across the top whilst the deer, with their sharp hooves, broke through and floundered helplessly. I heard it at night, and come morning, I'd see the bloody remains on the snow.

I set traps around the fresh kills. Caught foxes and fisher-cat, a big owl, so even the owls were stressed by the winter, else they would not investigate something already dead. But no wolf or coyote did I snare. Too smart they were. From the sign and the individuals I had come to recognize, three distinct wolfpacks, each of ten or more, shared my canyon. I was at the intersection of the boundaries of the packs, in a sort of neutral ground for them, as if a treaty of understanding existed between the different family-groups. This grand show of mutual respect did the deer herd little good. The wolves made two or three fresh kills every week.

The wolfpacks never seemed to converge on the area at the same time. They hunted in wide circles, each returning here at certain intervals, staying a few days then moving on, with one pack or the other close by and making noise most any night. Though they were always hovering and even did they sometimes sniff around my cabin, they feared and respected me, our own uneasy treaty. They hadn't ever made an attempt at me until this winter. With the deer herd reduced, one of the packs became more bold, howling in close, circling. I stayed home and did not check traps but when they began scratching at my door one night, I reasserted myself. First thing next morning, I got up onto the roof and wiped out nearly the entire pack with my bow. Another pack came in and feasted on the meat, so their treaty did not extend to the dead. Glad my cabin walls were stout!

The only good thing about the cold weather was the quality of the fur. The pelts got thicker as the harsh winter wore on. Even better than last year. Not just the beaver but the mink and otter, coon, fisher-cat, and the few coyotes I shot. I didn't set traps for coyotes, they were too clever a critter for me.

****

Oh, but it was cold! Wrapped in bearskins, I was spared the worst of it except for my face, which froze, even wrapped in skins which I secured with leather straps. When I walked my trapline and the wolves hovered, the dog stayed close alongside me.

Keeping enough wood was a problem; I burned great amounts. I thought I had put by enough to get me through but there was never enough. And when the woodpile was caught up, there were traps to repair, furs to be worked. Prime fur can be ruined by improper treatment. Long hours spent by candlelight. And trying to rub feeling back into stiff fingers. Through it all, I trudged along, followed everywhere by the dog. He was forever on the lookout for excitement.

One time, unable to resist one of the big cats we jumped, he took off after it. Gone for three days, I gave him up for lost. Then it snowed for two days. I figured the wolves got him, if nothing else. After the storm passed, I went west to check traps. Hadn't gone far when here came Blackie, limping along, near frozen stiff and tore up wicked. All cut and bleeding, his neck in shreds. Left ear chewed about off and one foot broken. After looking him over, I decided he had no chance and I lined up to shoot him. Really didn't seem to be much choice. He knew what was intended. I cocked the hammer and sighted down on him. Those big gold eyes looked back at me. Sad, pleading. I remembered all the times we roamed and the long winters spent in the cabin and how, when meat was scarce, he accepted without complaint what little I could give him.

His eyes closed, I lowered my gun, figuring he was dead but when I checked him, he yet lived. I lifted him onto my sled and wrapped him in furs. Reckoned if he lived to get home, he might recover. That must a been some fight with the cat. Whilst he was laid up, I stayed close to home and kept a fire going and with him up close to it. Moved my trapline in closer to the cabin so I could get home every night. His leg was not broken, only badly ripped up. Time, a little attention and he was up, though gimpy. And very chastened.

****

I had often considered the eventuality of being discovered. Thus it was no surprise when it happened. One day there they were, fresh man-tracks in an inch of new snow on top of the old and no more than a mile from my cabin. Two men, and with their unfamiliarity with their snowshoes, they were fouled in the brush frequently. The signs of clumsiness evident, they were not Indians or Canada-born French. Must be French regulars but if they were, what were they doing up out of their valley? Deserters? Had they come all the way from France in their majesty's service, only to desert when war came? More likely they were on a lark, driven by boredom into some harmless hunting or exploring.

The reality of what I had to do was stark. I had to kill them. They had crossed my sign and one of my beaver sets was missing. I was found out and must take action against the pair at the risk of my own life. Them or me. My survival, my life's work, was at stake. Kill them or give it all up and flee. In a cowardly way.

They were following my old tracks, visible under the newer snow, and were heading directly along my main route, probably intent on robbing more of my sets. Doing pretty well for themselves too, the dirty skunks!

I always carried my bow on the sled. It is as handy as the rifle. I reckoned it would do as the weapon of their demise. Most of my arrows were for hunting but I carried a few which was made in the Indian war manner, the heads sideways from the hunting shafts. Made to slide between a man's ribs, which lay opposite to a deer. Arrows made for one did not work well for the other, something Old Harrold had taught me. Strung the bow and flexed it.

I followed after 'em, studying the woods ahead at every step. They might a been watching their backtrack and I would not be ambushed. Late in the day they turned directly for my cabin. They could not be allowed to plunder and get away to tell their story. A drastic end awaited them, or me.

The light failed early this time of year, it was getting on toward full dark and I moved slowly in the fast-coming gloom. I lost their sign and despaired of finding them. I backtracked some and found where they had gone off. They'd done a fair job disguising their sign but only for a short distance and their trail became plain again in the snow. I followed, afeared of getting bushwhacked, then it came to me, a whiff of smoke. The fools had lit a fire. Cold camps are not pleasant. Neither is death. I stood still, not daring to take another step until I could locate the pair. For a long time I couldn't, then I heard low voices. French. Crept up on 'em and saw they had built a shelter, and in the gloom and with the shelter disguised, I had damn near walked right up to it. Their shelter was no more'n four-feet tall, scooped-out snow packed into walls and with brush for a roof and for shrouding around the sides. They were hunkered down in there. I could see their silhouettes behind their wall of snow.

These were brave men, adventurous but foolish, for in coming up out of the valley, they had stepped out of their world and into mine. The fire was plenty reckless for them knowing somebody was around. The night was turning bitterly cold, their need for warmth had over-ridden their caution. They must have figured who was up here was a French trapper who wouldn't dare take offense at regulars raiding his traps. It wouldn't have occurred to them there could be an Englishman with the fortitude to be so far from home, so close to the enemy.

The woods were entirely peaceful, as they are when the snow falls without there being any wind and I decided not to risk shooting 'em through their wall of snow. I'd draw them out and kill them as they emerged. I readied my dragoon pistol, slid it into my belt, rechecked the priming of my rifle and replaced the buckskin covering over the lock. I moved step by careful step, easing around until I was square to the open front of the shelter. I could make them out on the other side of their snow wall, reflected by the light of the blaze. I leaned my rifle against a tree, still in its case but with the case opened, the gun cocked. I set two arrows against the tree, a third arrow I nocked. Arrows with war notches.

The thought struck me, was this an act of war or murder? Seemed like murder but surely these men would kill me did I not kill them. Besides, it was they who had created the circumstances of their deaths. I could have holed up until they went back down to the Point, thus sparing their lives, but they would tell their superiors what they had found and it would be the end of Paradise for me, the ruination of all I had ever worked for. Pointless to consider any further. Either do the deed or slink off into the dark night, like the coyote before the wolf. The terrible cold of the night took control of my heart.

I knew if they doused their fire before coming out, which I doubted they would, it'd be more difficult for me. Might be scuffling in the snow with two Frenchies. I felt around in the darkness and touching a branch, I took hold of a twig and snapped it. Loud! The noise alerted the pair. They came cautiously out of their shelter, one in front of the other and without dousing their fire. My eyes were adjusted to the dark, theirs were not, and as they stood up, I shot the first one with an arrow, the second with my pistol, which I fired as soon as the first man fell out of the way. My gun roared, his did too, my bullet tearing into his chest, his zapping into the trees well away from me.

I rushed over to them, my breath heavy, not from exertion but from excitement, or fear. I stabbed 'em both in the chest with my knife, then went inside their shelter and grabbing a burning stick from their fire, I went back outside and used the light to check 'em over more closely. They were regulars, officers by their uniforms, and by their faces, they were young, very young. Come all the way from France in search of glory and finding only death.

I went through their pockets and packs, found good possibles and a healthy portion of smoked meat. I would take their guns too, the French military model, fairly-new issue. Dragged both bodies farther away from the hut. I went inside and built up the fire. Wrapped myself in one of their bearskins and kept the fire going hot. I ate the meat and shortly, I had to pry open a hole in the roof for the smoke to escape. Among the things I had found in their pockets was a letter. It was in the French language, I could not read it, I only sniffed it, for it had the enchanting whiff of a mademoiselle's perfume. I put it on the fire and watched it crinkle and burn. I went to sleep after once more making sure of the two outside. The snow continued hard. By the time the sun came up, so much snow had fallen, the bodies were but lumps in the snow. The foxes and mice would clean them up.

Recovered my stolen traps and furs and trudged back to check any sets the Frenchies might have disturbed, a job lasting the morning. The beavers they robbed they had skinned, a poor job done of it. The pelts had to be cleaned if they would be worth anything. Gained two pair of French military snowshoes. Superior to my own, these might last the rest of the winter. To the victor belongs the spoils! I was nagged for thinking myself a murderer yet what was I to do? They were robbing my traps and heading straight for my hideout and would have killed me as soon as they seen I was English. I had reason enough to kill them and expected not to be bothered long by it. Luck had been kind to me, not to them. Before the snow was gone, all trace of them would have vanished except bleached bones and even the bones would be gnawed.

****

Spring was overdue. Three weeks earlier, a thaw convinced me winter's grip was broken and it was time for me to see about Scalp Point, but following a deceptive interlude, two days of warm rain, winter resumed its hold with a fury seldom seen even here. The heavy rain turned back to snow. In the paths around the cabin, the snow had melted but the cold refroze the mud. I could not see the ice underneath and I slipped and fell often, taking some nasty bruises. A continuous run of the coldest weather against which no fire could warm a body. I was angry for the winter not going away. And was despondent for the time I had to stay in the cabin. Hard to keep my mind on the work. I was more than ready to get the hell out. Some Paradise!

Even when I was able to work my trapline, the wind shrieked with a violence, the more-slender hardwoods waving and snapping. So many lost their tops, I was constantly fearful of them coming down on me. In some places they looked as if they'd been felled by a scythe. Blowdowns impossible to get through. I began to find deer carcasses around the canyon and under the ledges. Dead in droves. The wolves got sated for feasting on the carcasses and stopped hunting, as if they knew how close they were to the complete destruction of the herd.

Finally, the winter released its death grip on the north woods. Good thing, for me and the dog was about to go raving mad for being stuck inside for so long. Nature seemed reluctant, so not to get fooled again, but the buds opened on the trees, the nights shed their bitterness. The first flocks of geese returning north were certainly a joy. Large V-shaped flights, all honking with their own exuberance a way up high. I figured no false thaw could fool them. My furs, packed into tight bales, so much weight per bale, were all prime blanket.

Problem was how to get it home. With the rivers opened for travel, the way would also be open for bandits and Indians. Either would kill me for my furs, this was as it had always been, but this year, farther down, I would have another worry. The British. I'd look mighty suspicious, coming down from enemy country in wartime in a boat piled high with furs.

Chapter XVIII – Joe the Grinder

I spooked Scalp Point and was on my way home, out along the East Branch, itchy as a dog full of fleas, hoping to steal a march on any trouble. Tried to be careful despite my eagerness. My canoe loaded to the gunwales, I traveled only at night until I came to the Hudson. I decided it would be too dangerous to traverse the big river in the dark. A strong current with snags and logs enough to sink even the stoutest of canoes. Huge ice chunks sweeping along, some driven by the current onto the banks, a mad torrent of whitewater boilin', frothin' and stained brown from all the dirt it carried.

I made the dog walk most of the way. He gets too excited when the going is wild. He yips and gets in my way, alerting me to every danger, as if I am unaware of them. He seemed glad to be out of the boat, for which I couldn't blame him, it being a wild ride. Waves and current threatened to tip and wreck the boat but she was sturdy, the load stable, and down toward the Great Carry, I got ashore just above the English clearing. The dog was glad to see me.

I snuck down the shore and saw work on the fort, closed down over the winter, had resumed. A large party of men and with no indication they had seen me. Good. I didn't need 'em nosin' around my business. I moved my cache around the cataracts in three loads. Hid them within a mile of the lower landing and went to see if Lydius' house was occupied this early. It was and I thought about peddling my cache there. It would save me traversing the stretch of the river from the Great Carry to Albany, where I would be most likely to encounter the British.

Lydius was no more crooked nor honest than the Albany fur-buyers and he asked no questions of prime fur but did I go to him, he would know it was because I did not want to risk taking my cache to Albany. This would drive down the price and would embolden the hangers-on at his place, most all of whom were pirates always on the lookout for a mark.

I did some spooking and got back to my canoe. I carried the heavy boat over my shoulders. A travois arrangement would have made for easier going but would leave drag marks. Then and during darkness, I crossed over the river in the calmer waters below the falls. Hid my boat, slept some, and in the morning, I walked over to the fort clearing. Work parties were busy, the sound of axes and of trees falling.

A British sentry challenged me. Told him I was a scout, which I supposed was true enough, and he allowed me in. I walked through the camp unnoticed amidst the bedlam; non-coms shouting orders, ax-men and saw-men in teams at work everywhere, clearing and burning away brush and tops, stripping the trunks clean and cutting them into eighteen-foot lengths and sharpening the tops. Squads of men digging trenches for the stockade logs. Raising the trunks and holding them in place whilst others shoveled dirt in around the bottoms. Redcoat officers strode importantly, slow-moving horses and oxen strained with the loads they pulled.

I looked for any familiar faces. Not having spoken to anyone other than the dog for months, I was ready for some real talk. Went over to the colonial camp and ran into men from Albany. I didn't really know 'em but for now, they seemed like cousins. Afraid my mouth ran like a babbling brook. Asked them the news and never gave 'em a chance to answer. They had a good laugh, and I calmed down. I looked around some. "Shapes up to be a mighty isolated post," I said. "Long ways from anywhere." A man agreed harshly, "I ain't a staying once she's built, I kin tell ya." The others around us agreed. With strong emotions. They said they had a new commander, a British engineer, older and more experienced than last year's brash twerp but who, same as the twerp, didn't much like Americans.

A colonial sergeant led me to the British officer of the day, who was standing, arms crossed, in the middle of the work. After a flurry of sharp questions, most of which concerned me and not the French, and which I mostly evaded, he, with a few of his men, escorted me through the camp. We arrived at the command tent and with the officer holding the flap open, he announced me by name and just down from the North Country. The commander, from inside the tent, "Come in, Mister Kuyler."

The officer was still holding the tent flap. For me, I supposed, and as I was going in, he let go, so the flap hit me. The commander didn't seem to notice although he had been watching. "Let us have a spot of rum," he said. "You look a bit thirsty, eh?" He meant ragged, by the way he wrinkled his nose at my appearance. As he got the rum bottle out and fumbled for glasses, I couldn't help notice his unsteady hands.

"Fort building is bloody, dusty work," he said. "A spot of rum is good for a man." He said his name was Steele, a captain of foot. The rum he poured was no more than a thimble's worth. I guzzled it. He didn't offer a refill.

"Tell me the news of the north. Eh? What are the French up to?" He said this chuckling, and whilst I told him what I knew, he kept interrupting. Seemed he was more interested in talking than hearing and he poured out scorn for the American forest, colonials, Indians, and the French. For men such as him, a British victory was inevitable. He had harsh words for the Dutch aldermen of Albany. He accused them of pushing for neutrality to keep their fur market open, and he asked was I in cahoots with them.

I tried interjecting my own thoughts about the war and when I said he could save plenty of settlers' lives by going north with his men before the French came down, he sneered. A colonial with an opinion. He told me not to worry myself over it. Said he knew from having battled the French on the continent how slowly they moved. I told him we wasn't on the continent and the French we were battlin' was Canadian French and their red friends, all of whom moved lightning-quick. He reminded me of the alarm I had brought last year, about those French out along the East Branch. "As even you can see," he said, "nothing has come of it."

He then shared with me what he thought was an amusing story concerning my earlier alarm about those Frenchies out to Odd Pond. McMillian had not written it up in any of his reports. Bill Johnson knew about it from me and with Bill seeing it had not got reported, he had railed at McMillian's superiors. Bill said it was information of great import and said the wilderness was no place for an officer who neglected to pass along what Johnson's scouts risked their lives to bring 'em. McMillian had been reprimanded and when the British higher-ups learned about the other thing, the knoll from whence the Indians had watched the fort builders, McMillian had been removed from his command. Steele maybe didn't agree with Bill Johnson and me about the importance of the French out to the East Branch or of the Indians spying on the camp but it didn't keep him, Steele, from relishing the rebuke handed down to McMillian. Steele's mirthful face and tone turned abruptly cold and he warned me not to start trouble with him, as I had with McMillian.

Not caring to suffer any more of Steele's belittling and figuring he wasn't going to give me any more of his rum, I was glad when he indicated my interview was over. I left the tent mad for his disrespecting me. I wandered the camp in search of a drink. The taste of rum Steele had given me had wakened a powerful thirst. Surely there must be someone with a jug.

Walked over to where the noise and commotion was the loudest. Just about what I figured, who should be there, bawling like a fat cow at a group of clumsy redcoats and too-slow colonials, the top sergeant, Tom O'Brien. Showing the men how to position a tall tree-trunk into a trench. A delicate and dangerous job, aligning the ponderous trunk for the stockade. With the log situated to his satisfaction and with men holding it upright whilst dirt was shoveled into the hole, Tom came over. He pulled off his heavy work gloves, we shook hands warmly.

"How's the fur trade, Kenny?"

"Don't talk about it with so many around," I warned him. He said he could not get away until work was over for the day but answering my unasked question, he said there was rum to be had. Told me where it was and to help myself. "If ye stand around blatherin', I'll put ye to work." He grinned. I left at once! Found his stash. He certainly kept a plentiful supply of thirst quencher.

By the time Tom came in, I had one of his jugs on toward bottom and I was feeling comfortable. "Ave ye got a lots a fur?" Tom's eyes said he was eager to know. I said I had plenty. "Tomorrow," he said, "I kin get ye a couple a buckos to help with the portaging." I told him it was already moved. He showed his usual curiosity for my sojourning in the mountains. I told him I had brought him something and I handed him an otter-skin pouch I had worked on over the winter. He expressed his thanks as he fingered the soft, fine-worked pelt. I asked where had he wintered. "New York, bucko. Thick-legged women and tasty grog but you colonials know naught of building towns! A stinkhole!" I said our politicians wouldn't spend the money. They'd rather put it in their pockets. "An' women what don't bathe," Tom said, and when I said that wouldn't stop him, he laughed. "Aye, there's only so much time in a man's life, an' so many lassies."

I told him about the two Frenchies I had killed. He was glad for it and said at least somebody on our side was doing some killing. He then warned me not to tell it around, or I might get arrested. "War is declared," I said, "and your British would arrest me for killing Frenchmen?" He said as how his superiors might want to arrest me for some other reason and would use the killings as an excuse, maybe say I'd done it before war was declared, although I clearly had not. And just as clearly would have.

We went over to the sergeants' mess and after dinner we were once again outside, around a fire with more of the sergeants, as was the custom of these hard-working men. We got deep into the rum, another of their customs. The last glow of the sun cast a shadow over the foothills to the north and tinted the mountains behind the hills with a reddish hue. "Now the mountains move in," Tom said, in what was almost a whisper. He said he always felt the mountains shouldering in on him when the light failed, and I thought he said it not fearfully, just he was resigned. "Aye," he said. "Here they move the mountains in at night." Bill Morrissey had expressed the same thought back on Portage Crick, when we were smuggling with Hugh.

We talked and drank. I spun tales of the solitary mountain man. How it could snow a foot in a night and about the troublesome thaws. Told them about the wolves, how their growling and scratching at my door woke me up some nights.

The sergeants talked about the war as part of a greater conflict in far-off places I knew naught of, except what Pops had told me. Said there was fighting in Europe and India, in the Caribbean and on the open sea. "Tis a world war we be waging, laddie," Tom said. "Princes and armies. Starvation and pestilence. This new world of yours is but a part of it." Another sergeant brought us back around to our American troubles by saying the French had turned loose their savages out west. Tom agreed. "The frontiers," he said, "be a smoldering. This is not rumor, t'is the truth. Aye." I knew it was all too true, and in the silence which followed, I sipped from the tin cup I was holding. Our frontier and the New England settlements were in for a hard go. Folks with the courage to tame the wilderness, to gamble their all, would lose the most. "Like your man, Lydius," one of the sergeants said. "With his stone trading house at the lower end of these clamorous falls." The sergeant had a better opinion of John Henry than I did, and I didn't say what I thought of Lydius and his place and of the hangers-on there. "The politicians in New York and London," Tom said, "sit on their fat arses arguing what is to be done whilst the simple folks be a burnin'. Between the gov'nor and his Dutch Assembly, there is naught being done to prevent a great tragedy from occurring."

We talked about the rush of settlers up along the Battenkill River, across the Hudson from Saratoga. Farms and blockhouses burnt, folks holding tenuously to their scant clearings. I asked was anything being done to strengthen Saratoga fort. Tom said the colonials were to post a stronger detachment. "And repair the walls." He shook his head with disgust for knowing the colonials would do a poor job of it.

The stars shone bright, the night clear and fresh. The Aurora Borealis flashed across the northern sky. We mused at the possible origins of this wonder of nature. One of the sergeants asked were the lights more brilliant farther north. This I confirmed.

We toasted each other, fine women, and victory in the war. Drank our fill of rum and spruce beer and toward morning the men drifted off to their quarters. I slept on the wood floor of Tom's tent, wrapped in my bearskin and with bad dreams of Tom's words about the mountains moving in on a man.

I was awoken way too soon by the sounds of an army camp stirring. Sergeant Tom was up and in uniform. Slick, as befitted the top sergeant of an outfit. "You don't show a bit of it this morning," I said, marveling at his steady hand. "Practice, laddie, practice," and in his top sergeant's voice, "There's naught else fer entertainment here."

After breakfast I walked to the lower end of the falls and gathered my furs. Saw tracks fresh-made, someone had been prowling in the brush. Most likely looking for my furs. Someone from the army camp or from Lydius' post? No telling. I boarded my canoe, wary of trouble on the river and I didn't get far before the trouble came 'round the bend. Five whaleboats lined up one behind another and fightin' the current. Four of the boats were crammed with lobsterback redcoats. The last boat, getting towed and slowing the progress of the others, held three small swivel cannons and some few soldiers, one of whom worked the rudder. In the lead boat, officers watched me through far-seeing glasses. Nervous for my furs, I raised my paddle in greeting and kept going, and as I went past, an officer shouted and pointed for me to go ashore. I did, and waited as they came ponderously in behind me. When the boat with the officers came in, a shave-tail ensign gave orders to the rowers and they put the boat crosswise to the current. A hard job and only so their commander, a skinny man with gold lace all over a spotless uniform, could step ashore without getting his fancy boots wet.

I was up a little on the bank and whilst the soldiers, about thirty of 'em, disembarked and got lined up, the commander ignored me and inspected my furs, touching, lifting, sniffing. Only when the men were arrayed did he look to where I was, the butt of my rifle on the ground between my feet, my hands gripping the barrel. He made a flicking motion with his fingers, which meant I was to walk down to him. I hesitated, to make my own point, and one of the soldiers who'd got behind me gave me a nudge with a bayonet.

I went, and whilst the commander looked me up and down, I stared at the gorget hanging around his neck. No ordinary piece of jewelry. He got his chin up close to my face. "What is your name and what is your business here? What is a lone white man doing in these parts and with fur?" Before I could say I was a trapper who did some scouting for him, he asked more questions, one after the other, and with me not replying for how rapidly he was spewing, he took a step back and had another look at me. He asked did I not speak English. I said I spoke 'er well enough. "Answer me, then," he said. "Who are you and where are you come from? Why are you here? Answer quickly. I am Colonel Hubbard."

I didn't flinch. "Hubbard," I said, "I'm Kuyler."

"Kuyler, h'mm. Yes. I have read reports about you." His face became thoughtful and he glanced some more at my furs. He said smuggling was against the law. "Prove it," I said, angry with his attitude. The dog did not care for it either and was growling. Hubbard, his hand on his sword hilt, eyed Blackie warily. I gave the dog a kick, for not wanting to pay for the pants' seat to get put back into the colonel's fancy uniform. Hubbard's face, set so hard, looked frozen in stone. "I know about your spy camp overlooking the fort," he said. I said it weren't my camp. It were the hostiles. "Come, come, man," he said. "Do you really think the savages were up so close and watching us?" I said they surely were, and said British denials only showed how unfit they were for woods' warfare. He bade me to answer properly or he would investigate me as a smuggler and a spy. I backed off some on account of my furs.

I asked was Scalp Point where he was heading with his cannons. He said whether or not he was going to Crown Point was not my concern. I was a civilian. I said it looked to be a civilian's concern to me. "I have not come to fight," he said and he smirked. "Not yet, anyway. I am on my way to inspect the progress of the fort builders and to deliver cannons, to teach the savage beggars to keep their distance."

Inspect your fort and parade around in it, I might have said, before

213

the hostiles burned it down. "I am displeased to find a civilian so far north," he said. "I did not believe the Albany authorities who said you wintered up here. Where?" I said it would do him no good iffen I told him. "Near the French at Crown Point?" Again, and before I could reply, he advised me to answer properly. "Few miles west of Scalp Point," I said. He asked was I the only one of ours up there. I said yes, so far as I knew. He asked if I had ever been inside the Crown Point fort. I said I had not been inside but had been up close. "Then I need to have a further talk with you," he said, he clearly not relishing more talk but he likely got to be a colonel by being thorough. He asked more questions, mostly about the French regulars, not so much about the Canadians or Indians, those most likely to hit him. He asked about the approaches and outer defenses at Crown Point. He surely reckoned hisself a mighty tough bird. Ready to go up and take Scalp Point any time his superiors said so. I told him did he want to go to Scalp Point, I could show him the way. He ignored this and fired more questions. Terrain and routes. Places for encampments. "Is the water bad?" He had heard stories. "Cavalry can get there?" I said he would need a road for horses and there weren't none. I warned him about his men's uniforms and boots. "Wrong for the woods. Best is buckskins for hiding, moccasins for walking." He brushed aside my cautions and persisted. "What are the grounds around Crown Point like? Are there other posts around?" When he asked could I draw him a map, I said a map would do him no good because his men would never get close enough to use it. "The Indians will get you afore you gets near the fort." He seemed to consider this, then, dismissively and by way of closing our interview, "I will be back in Albany in three days' time. You will report to me as soon as I am back. We will talk further. As of now, you are not to be up here without a pass from the military authorities, which means me. Anyone north of Saratoga without a pass signed by me will be arrested as a spy and dealt with accordingly. If you want to go up for the trapping, you need come to me. If I deem it advisable, I may allow it. This is your warning." There was plenty I wanted to say back to him. How I went where I damn well pleased and how no goddamn two-bit peacock was going to push me around nor keep me from trapping next winter iffen it was what I wanted. "We shall see, we shall see," he said, which I wasn't sure what he meant. He again reminded me I could be arrested for insubordination or treason, and he said it with his hand back on the hilt of his wicked saber. He was looking at my furs some more, he knowing I was fearful he'd confiscate them did I not show the proper deference. Much as it galled me, I kept my mouth shut. He laughed for knowing why I dared not say much but he did admit my information had value for I being one of the few Englishmen to know the far country.

I, just as haughty, told him I was no damn Englishman. "More's the pity," he said. I repeated my earlier caution. "Your bright coats make for poor fightin' in these parts for your men will be plain seen, even in shadows." He said the British army didn't hide in shadows nor anywhere else. And said not all his men wore red coats. "These here do," I said and I persisted, not to win an argument but to make a point which might save lives. He became irate. "That's enough, you impertinent bumpkin son-of-a-bitch. I will have you arrested." It was a more serious threat this time but he got back to asking about the layout of the Scalp Point forts. How high were the walls of the castle and what was they made of. "The inner castle," I said, "is four stories. The outer walls and bastions are twenty-feet high and plenty thick. All are made of limestone slabs kilned on the grounds. South of the castle and up close to the water is a windmill for grinding and which serves as a redoubt. Of the same stone as the fort. Holds a few cannons, mostly swivels. Boats has to pass by the windmill to get to the castle."

An officer came up, saluted smartly and asked about feeding the men. Almost without shifting his eyes from his superior, the officer managed to give me a look to say I was a colonial ruffian. "Fall them out, Lieutenant," Hubbard said, "and see they are fed. We have all worked hard this day." I wondered how hard could it be to sit in a boat whilst other men rowed but Hubbard at least showed his men some consideration. Not typical of what I knew of these officers. The lieutenant saluted and went off.

Hubbard then saw I was eyeballing the few small cannons he had brought along. He boasted about scattering the Indians with artillery. And once the Indians were dealt with, he said, his guns would knock down the walls of Crown Point. "And Montreal and Quebec," I said, a veiled barb. He dismissed me with yet another warning. "You may go now. I am finished with you, but do you fail to report to me when I am back in Albany, I promise I will have you arrested." I bade him good luck with his cannons. "Hope you can use 'em to put the Ottawas and them others to sleep." Doubted it. It surely took a brave man to charge into the mouths of cannons, and Indians could be the bravest of the brave, but they were never stupid.

I pushed off, relieved to still be in possession of my cache, and a little way farther downriver, I overtook a slow-moving dispatch boat with four British privates bound for Albany. All four were supposed to row in unison but if any two had their oars in the water at the same time it was a wonder. The current was doing most of their work for them, they were drinking rum. Warned them of the dangers they might face afore Albany was reached. "Even in supposedly safe waters, take no chances. You'll live longer." They laughed and passed their bottle to me. I drank, just not much. The current was swift and with logs and debris from spring runoff, but I did slow my own pace to stay with them, for the protection their company afforded.

At the small palisade at the upper Saratoga landing, the colonial soldiers admired my furs and offered me and the redcoats the use of a wagon for portaging furs and boats. We accepted and walked behind the wagon, through town in broad daylight, something I never done before with a cache of furs. In the company of armed redcoats, I had no fears.

The people came out to watch, as if we were a parade. I saw Lydia. She saw me and come running across the muddy street, her babe in her arms. I was moved beyond reason by the gladness and by the dig of her fingernails into my arm. The crowd hooted at her open display of affection and she pulled back some. We talked briefly, she proudly showed off her baby, Desiree. My British friends waited, amused, and when Lydia made me promise to visit soon, they erupted with hoots and jibes. After we got past town, they got on me pretty good. They insisted the babe was mine. They made jokes and roared at my denials. They dubbed me Joe the Grinder. Pretty rough talk but they were good fellows and didn't mean anything by it.

We launched at the lower end of the portage and getting to Albany, they escorted me to the fur buyers' wharf and amidst their raucous goodbyes, I told them I was mighty grateful for their company. And was quite happy with the money received for my winter labors. Went to the tavern, the folks was glad to see me. Pops poured me a beer. A wonderful taste! Worth coming home for just the first sip.

****

Nearly a year into the war, the rumors were terrifying for anyone who believed them, and added to the rumors was the rancor between the different colonies. So much discord, it was impossible to keep straight the arguments. How many troops must each colony provide, which colony would bear what part of the cost of the campaigning and why should one colony defend another. The only thing for sure, the farther a colony was from the French threat, which was mostly out of the north, the less-inclined were they to pledge money and troops. Our inability to work together increased the danger for all of us.

What was not rumor, an expedition was forming for a great task. Speculation was rife. Montreal by way of the Corlaer Valley was most hoped for, but the troop movements soon put the lie to the Corlaer route. Troops were heading for Boston. Boston! Part of a great expedition to go by sea to the Canadas. To attack Louisbourg, a most impregnable fortress. The New York Assembly, which couldn't find money to pay us, pledged a large sum in support of the campaign. The fleet would be Old England, led by Bill Johnson's uncle, Peter Warren. The troops would be entirely from New England.

Also, some New York militia was gathering in a camp outside our north gate and would soon be on its way to strengthen Fort Oswego, at the western end of the Mohawk Trail. From there, the army was to advance on the French posts of the Great Lakes, to sever their lifeline to the Ohio. This, said the politician whose idea it was, "will drive them from our western frontiers." A big undertaking for an untrained army. "What about our own frontier?" asked the commoners, who were never listened to. There was loud grumbling against sending our best men off to far places.

One thing for certain, Bill Johnson, in his office of Indian Affairs, had so far kept the Iroquois on our side. He had them in a solid grip. May he never let go! Bill claimed to have persuaded large numbers of Mohawks to take up the war hatchet and go with our army to Oswego. Which would make a difference. I wasn't sure how many Mohawks would muster on the appointed day but it was reassuring to hear. Others of the Mohawks were raiding the French around Scalp Point and along the northerly reaches of Corlaer. I had seen evidence of this. Johnson and the Mohawks were surely exaggerating their deeds, they always did, but the French settlements on northern Corlaer were said to be mostly abandoned, which would be the result of Iroquois raids, or the fear of them.

According to Pops, Johnson came by the inn whenever he was in town. Bill always asked about me but was mostly interested in good beer. Bill had not lost his eye nor his appetite for the ladies. He never passed up the chance to chase, and with his good looks, size and demeanor, it was the women who were often doing the chasing, or who were at least eager to get caught. Father said Johnson had earned his diversions. Said Bill had done more in Indian matters than anyone and more than could have been expected. Bill told Pops and Mother his Mohawks were in a turmoil. Said they and their brother tribes might all go over to the French in a body and attack Albany some fine night.

The first week I was home, a party of Indians was sighted on the east side of the Hudson and a militia detachment was sent to have a look. Turned out the Indians were of the Stockbridge Mohicans, our friends. A tragic encounter narrowly averted. Arrangements needed to be devised to keep friends from shooting each other.

I decided I'd summer over in town and maybe make some money hunting but with an army present, game was scarce. I mostly worked for Pops. He was grateful for the help. The Full Sail was busy from noon, when we opened, until late at night, when Pops tossed the last of the drunks into the street.

I marveled at Pops' appetite for work. No other man could cope with such a staggering amount of business. He kept running short of beer and sent me around town to secure all of what was necessary for brewing new batches. He was showing me how to do it. It is a precise, frustrating business which reminded me why I had chosen the north woods over a life in Albany.

Word came of trouble encountered by Colonel Hubbard on his way back to Albany. Seems he was coming downriver in just two boats, he having left some of his men and boats and the cannons at the fort. After spending the night at Saratoga, he had gone ashore around noontime, so his officers could stretch their legs and have lunch and tea. With his detachment a short way up from shore in a clearing, Indians got up on the few men guarding the boats, killed and scalped 'em and got the boats into the current and away. In broad daylight and all because of goddamn teatime. Then, Hubbard, fool that he was and forced to trek to Albany, couldn't manage to follow the river. He and his men got lost in the woods. Took 'em three days to get in and with militia out tryin' to find 'em before Indians did. When they finally came in, mud-splattered and bedraggled, the Albany folks were lined up along Yonkers Street laughing and jeering. The trail along the west side of the river was well-marked and the folks was givin' it to Hubbard, to think he couldn't find the trail once he'd got off it. I was there on the street and same as some others, I didn't see the humor.

A few days later, when I reported to Hubbard, he was still steaming mad over it. He said there'd been a lot of Indians and he'd have fought 'em if they'd showed themselves like men. I didn't believe him. The theft and destruction of his boats had been done by just a few Indians or we'd never a seen him again. Wonder the Indians didn't trail him in and pick off his men a few at a time. Them Indians didn't realize how big a fool they was dealing with. Reckon they'd know next time.

I asked him about the rumor he was moving his headquarters out of Albany and up to Stillwater. He said he was moving so's to get up closer to the troubles. Folks said it was because of the ribbing him and his men were taking in Albany for having lost their boats.

****

One of the first nights I was home, Mother told me Lydia's husband, Richard, was in Albany assisting immigrants just in on ships. She said he had been in the Full Sail many nights this spring. The look she gave me when she said it meant something bad was afoot. She would not say anything more about it, and in the time since I had been home, Richard had not come around.

Until one night he came in, drunk and with a lass on each arm. One a frowzy German, I couldn't follow her words, the other a mousy, red-headed English gal, couldn't follow her either, her words thick with drink. Trollops! Richard got up close to my face, his breath reeking, and said I had maybe heard he was drunk every night, which I had, and he warned me not to tell Lydia. Then, and sneering, he said he reckoned I'd tell her. "Know you want her, Kuyler, but she's too good for the likes of you." I grabbed him, dragged him to the door and threw him into the street. Not because of the women, who was only trying to survive in a harsh foreign land but because of his neglecting Lydia and the baby. Wanted to kill him and likely would have, had not Pops and some others grabbed me after I had tossed him and afore I could get on him. They held me whilst Richard stumbled drunkenly down the street, looking over his shoulder to see was I in pursuit.

Rumors hardened about Indians and we heard of more trouble. A couple of strikes across the river from Saratoga. Two men working in a field got killed, then another, his scalped body tossed into his barn, then the barn was burned. T'was the work of small parties scouting for those who would soon come in greater numbers. They took advantage of situations and with how scattered were our farms and towns,

219

it was not possible to maintain a proper defense.

****

One night when I was well soused, I got to thinking about Lydia. I had heard Richard had been hanging around the Bloody Bucket, a squalid, disreputable alehouse down a back alley, and I went to see for myself. The debauchery I saw him indulging in made me think he was probably not going home again. Least not right away. Wondered what made a man behave in such a way. Reckoned to punch him up, could I get ahold of him without the interference of friends, mine nor his, but what would be the use?

Feeling aggrieved for Lydia, I went up the next day to Saratoga. I did not tell this kindest of women about her husband. Figured she knew anyway. I wondered how a man could stay away from a house which held his wife and little baby girl. I stayed the night with Arnold, he asked if Richard was misbehaving in Albany. I confirmed Arnold's suspicions; the little man shook his head. "There has always been trouble," he said, "with the lad's roving eye." Priscilla of course had much to say about it and not all of what she said was for Richard. "I have watched you and her, friend. You can't fool me! Not with the way you two have made eyes at each other for years." She gleamed when I flinched, for knowing she had caught me square. "Do you think her drunken sot of a husband doesn't know? Lydia would rather have you than ten of him, if you would but settle down and do something with your misspent life." I had no answer. She cackled like a harpy who had won at cards for the misery on my face. With how precariously Lydia was situated, and whenever I could get away from the tavern, I went up to scout around Saratoga. And to do whatever I could to make her safe and comfortable. Priscilla, ever the catty one, "My, my, don't we see a lot of you these days."

I found fresh hostile sign around Saratoga every time I went up. Abenakis prowling the woods. Lone men slain and mutilated along the roads and in their fields. "There is going to be big trouble one of these days," is what all were saying. Tried to convince Lydia to move to Albany at least temporarily, same as I had tried with Arnold. Lydia appreciated my concern and the fresh meat I always brung but she said Saratoga was her home and there she would stay until her husband moved her. Useless to argue with a woman whose mind was made up. She held my hand so tight. "Oh, Kenneth," she said in a whisper. "I wish so very much it were different." She and I had been alone a few times. Dangerously close. She asked, "What will Richard say when he comes home?" My heart squeezed so tight I could hardly breathe but I dared not answer.

****

The army marched for Oswego, business at the tavern slowed and in the second week of July came news which no one could believe. Our Canadian expedition, which all had thought was a waste of men and money and which Arnold called quixotic, had succeeded! The mighty French fortress had fallen to us. This Louisbourg was said to have cost the French a huge sum of money and thirty years labor to build and now it was ours. Our losses were said to be not severe. Bill Pepperrell and his Massachusetts men had done it! Johnson's uncle, Peter Warren, had been there with a British fleet so Johnson's boast of his uncle accomplishing great things had proven true. In the raucous celebration in the tavern, I heard men proclaim our troubles were over. I reminded them it was the French what surrendered at Louisbourg, not the Indians. Still, there was great advantage in it for us. With British warships now to be sailing out of the captured port and seizing French supply convoys, the French would struggle to feed and supply themselves. And were the French unable to meet the Indians' incessant demands for gifts, the Indians might lose their stomach for the fight. So men said, but as tightly bound as the Indians' fortunes were to the French, they would have no recourse but to stay with them, as much as they might grouse over it.

****

Soon after came rumors, yet another army was forming, to march against Scalp Point. I didn't believe it but in August an army did begin to gather outside town. Business at the tavern picked up. The soldiers were mostly Massachusetts men, a rougher cut than our New Yorkers. Some of 'em had been with Bill Pepperell and their success at Louisbourg had made them most obnoxious. I was asked to join as a scout. I refused, but if an expedition went for Scalp Point, I would go. Just I would not offer my services until I seen the army moving. No sense spending my summer getting harassed by Hurons and blackflies for no good purpose. No sense being the only one up there.

****

When I had first come down in the spring, I had used some of my fur money to partner with a farmer. We purchased a herd of cattle to fatten until fall when we would make a nice profit. I was not surprised when my partner told me one of our beeves was missing, then two more. Indians were blamed but I was inclined to think it was soldiers doing the poaching. We sold our herd to the army before the soldiers could steal it all. Turned a small profit. Not enough for the headaches and worries.

****

Into September and the army had not moved. Disgruntlement was rife with the soldiers. They were undisciplined and surly, slow getting in and unprepared when they arrived. Many came without guns and as soon as a gun was issued to 'em, they vamoosed. They idled in their camps, drinking, shouting down their officers, refusing orders they did not care for, more rabble than army. They complained of spoiled meat and fish. I have smelled the rot which comes out of the barrels when they are opened.

This ugly situation persisted as did the Indian raids. None of our big towns had been hit, nor had the growing settlements across the river but outlying farms were burning. The New England frontier was getting hit hard. Before long, the enemy would move into the void which should have been occupied by our own men and the raids would not be so small. Then what would we do?

Many of the soldiers at both Albany and Oswego, New Englanders, went home to defend against the Indians. Hard to sit idle whilst raids on their homes occurred with more regularity and ferocity. Families and friends burned out, slain. Too much for the soldiers to bear, and if they didn't get their crops harvested, their families would starve come winter. So they departed in droves and who could blame 'em?

The locals were glad to see them go, so boisterous and demanding were they. Those still encamped around Albany became even more unruly. Poor Pops! Drunken soldiers in the tavern all day and most of the night. The common room seemed more dangerous than the north woods. The fights were of big proportions and of a peculiar hardness. Pops, sick of it all, declared I'd had my sojourn in the north woods and said it was time for me to settle down. He offered me the tavern at a price much reduced from his previous offers. I wanted nothing to do with the rowdy soldiers and the troubles they caused. I told Pops I would not spend the rest of my life dealing with drunken sots, no matter how much did they spend. Besides, the war was making prime fur even more dear; my last cache had fetched a goodly sum. Once a man's appetite is whetted, who can say what he might do?

The situation with the army got so bad, the Albany council barred the soldiers from town. The Full Sail was empty most nights. The New Englanders threatened to storm Albany and hang the politicians for not releasing them so they might go home. Van Schaack, one of the detested politicians, feared for his life and tried to hire me as a body-guard. I told him I must protect family first. There was more than a little sympathy in town for the mutineers and few able-bodied men to oppose 'em. The only regulars available in the colony, forty British, were at the fort up to the Great Carry. These, men said, should be brought down to quell the trouble. Others boasted the militia would rout the British. They were wrong. No militia could stand up to British steel. The redcoats would be ruthless in settling matters. The more sober-minded were repulsed by the notion of Englishmen fighting Englishmen. Although the lobsterbacks were of the Old World and we of the New, and though many Yorkers such as myself were of Dutch origin, we were all Englishmen. And with a war on against the French!

Finally, the army was disbanded, the mutinous soldiers were told to go home and for a few days, there was a fear the army, a mob now, might storm and loot the city. In the end, the soldiers simply departed. Business picked up at the tavern, the regular patrons drifted back in, much to Pops' relief. He kept me hard at work, it was impossible to get away. I feared I might after all be stuck there forever.

Chapter XIX – Blanchard's Rangers

I was in the Full Sail, at a table by the fire and watched as a big, rough-looking man dressed in buckskins came in. He looked around, his glance seeming to stay on me. His chin bobbed slightly with what might have been a greeting, or just a nod for him seeing I was watchin' him. He walked to the bar, got two tankards of beer and came over. Couldn't help but notice the confidence in the lengthy strides he took. He, towering over me, asked was I Kuyler. I said I might be. "Name's Blanchard," he said. "Joe. Wanna talk." I looked him over some more. A most capable-looking giant of a man. Light complexion, reddish tints in his blonde beard. Broad of shoulder, thick of girth. His size and the fullness of his beard reminded me of Hugh McChesney. When I first seen him come in and with what he wore on his head, a leather slouch cap with gold threads and with the sides curled up, I took him for a river sailor. Now and up close to the smell of him, I knew he was a woodsie, same as me.

Just as he was setting down the beers, a drunkard bumped into the corner of our table and toppled toward the fire in the hearth. Blanchard, quicker'n any man, caught the drunk with one hand and pulled him back. This Blanchard moved quick! He sat down as if nothing had happened and said he was a sergeant of New Hampshire Foot, recently discharged from militia service.

He said Colonel Hubbard had given him my name and told him I spent time up to the lakes. I didn't say anything, I just looked at him. "Me an some others," he said, "is fixin' to go for scouts for the army." I said he was too late, the army was gone home. "For the British up to North Fort," he said. "A ranging company to help with the war, iffen we can get funded. What me and you both know, we ain't goin' to lick the French and Indians nor put a stop to their raiding 'til somebody learns our boys how to bushwhack. They don't know shit. Get into trouble iffen they go into the woods, most of 'em."

"All I got so far," he said, "is ten half-arsed woodsmen. You should see 'em, Kuyler." I made the mistake of asking why I'd want to see 'em. "Cause you's gonna assist me in schoolin' 'em," he said. "Oh, no," I said. "Oh, no!" I told him I was no schoolmaster and I didn't go into the woods with green men. "Besides," I said, "we got Mohawks for scouting." Blanchard was scathing in saying the Mohawks was in it for their own purposes and for Bill Johnson's purposes.

"Hubbard won't say it out loud," Blanchard said, "but when he lost his boats to the Indians back in the spring and had to walk down here, it taught him the value of getting around in the woods." I again said I didn't go out with greenhorns. "The colonel," Blanchard said, as if I hadn't said anything at all, "don' 'preciate gettin' whupped and he'll do whatever it takes to prevent it from hap'nin' again. I'm hopeful he can find money enough to pay fer us." I interjected, said the British weren't going to succeed until they changed how they felt about us and neither Hubbard nor any of the other ratfaces was going to change. Blanchard again kept on as if he hadn't heard me, or as if he'd finish having his say afore I had mine. He laid out more of what he intended and when he was done, finally, he stared at me. Reading me; then, and still looking me in the eye, "Hubbard says you mighten be a spy for the French."

Here it was again; English persecution. The old insinuation the French had a spy amongst the Albany Dutch so's to blame us when things didn't go well, and who was more likely to be the spy than me? Blanchard's face, a wide grin now, said he didn't believe it. I took a sip of beer and with him silent, I reckoned it was my turn to speak. I was cautious, but curious too for it being clear to me the truth of what this big lug across the table was saying. How stumbling through the woods was all we could expect from the British unless and until we showed 'em how to get around up there.

Blanchard knew what I was thinking. "If the French and Indians don' start finding us to be wilier than what we've shown 'em so far," he said, "we're going to lose this war, and the only way for us to do it is with rangers leading our men."

Even though I couldn't disagree, I insisted I wouldn't work for the British. We argued back and forth over this and with me going on about how horribly the British had treated me and with Blanchard nodding along, I seen he was getting exasperated. He said he understood how I felt, it was how he felt, most times, but, he said, every man must do his duty. This got me hot for I having done more than just about any man. He said my already having done more than most didn't mean there wasn't more for me to do, and when I, in my own

225

exasperation, said I'd as soon go fishing, it was him who exploded. "Fishing! Whilst all around you is up in smoke? I ought to punch you in your big fat nose for saying such a damn fool thing!" Never seen a man get so roaring mad. Got the attention of the entire room, including Pops, who was near ready to come over and toss both me and Blanchard into the street. Then Blanchard must have remembered what it was he'd come for, me, for he calmed down and it was as if he hadn't been mad at all.

I let him go on some, then, and tired of hearing about all the big plans which was fermentin' inside his head, I asked about the rumor which had come in a few days before, the Indians' hitting a wood-cutting party from out of the fort. The army wasn't saying much about it and with Blanchard not saying anything either, I gave him a nudge. "Heard our boys got treated kinda rough." He still didn't say anything and I figured the soldiers had been warned not to talk about it.

Turned out Blanchard wasn't against telling, he was just sorting the words in his mind, and when he did finally speak, it was with disgust. "Ottawas jumped our woodcutters in a clearing a quarter-mile from the fort," he said. "The boys had done with cutting and stacking their wood and was getting ready to head in. The Injuns waited until the woodcutters and the lobsterbacks was bunched up and having a drink, all of 'em thinking the day was over and there came a volley from outta the trees. Indians a whoopin' and a hollering in there. Our boys ran for holy hell before they even seen an Injun. Left the shot men behind." He became rueful. "The Indians fight from hiding, I don' have to tell you, but this time I think they was hiding so our men didn't see how few they was. Only when our men commenced high-tailin' did the Injuns show themselves. Got more scalps than they could a hoped for, and guns too, which our men throwed down when they ran. Doubt there be twenty Indians in all, yet they scared off an entire troop." He shook his head. "The British had two dead, four hurt. Six colonials killed, five wounded, and two of the wounded got taken on account of they got left behind by the gutless others." My bile rose for it being as bad as the rumors. "Them Indians," I said, "is finding out just what easy pickings we be. Won't be long afore they come down with lots more men."

We talked long into the night. I opened up more than usual for it was plain, listening, and with him having been born and raised along the New England frontier, here was a man much like myself. Surely no stranger to Indians and their ways and with him running an outfit, there'd be no fiascos in the woods. Leastways and iffen there was, it wouldn't be on account of him.

I told him about the lakes and for as long as we talked and whenever our beers got low, our serving girl came over with more. Each time she came, Blanchard, without looking up or stopping talking, nor listening if I was talking, reached for the leather purse on a string around his neck. And each time, the girl smiled and shook her head. Pops was buying tonight.

"I have never been to the North Country," Blanchard said. "Never seen Saint Sacrement nor Corlaer. I need you to take me up there." I told him I'd draw him a map. "I ain't wantin' a goddamn map," he said. Irritable sort, I thought. He said North Fort was nearly complete except for sheds and barracks and he was going up with whosoever would go with him and for as long as the British or the colony agreed to feed and pay 'em.

****

It was past midnight, the common room had cleared out 'cept for me and this Blanchard and a few other stragglers. Tired as I was and with my head heavy enough with drink so's I thought it might crash down on the table, Blanchard urged me, and not for the first time, to join up. "Don't mind admittin' I need the help." The look in his eyes begging or threatening, I could not say. He got quiet, watching me. Quiet but about ready to bust loose again. Like a tea kettle fixin' to rattle and boil. Or explode, if I did not assent. Thought if I wasn't careful with what I said, I might be fighting him. Not something I cared to do. He was too big and fast. I reckoned to push the table over on him and get ready for the fight of my life. Or run like hell. Blanchard knew what I was thinking and said did I try to fight, he'd beat me, and did I run, he'd catch me and drag me in. Leastways he was still talking, and I eased up some. "Mister," I said, "there's no call for us ta fight over it." He agreed. "My whipping you," he said, "nor you whipping me is gonna fix our problems." He grinned. "Hubbard weren't lying when he said you was a hard-headed Dutchman." Grinning in appreciation for hard-headedness. I conceded I might be willing to help, iffen I could, but I remained adamant against serving directly under the British. For iffen I did, every shavetail lieutenant would have the authority to have me nine-tailed for refusing stupid orders or maybe just for saying what was on my mind. "The thing is," I said, "I'll take the army's shilling and do their dirty work for 'em but I won't take their orders. Too many of 'em already got it out for me." He said my cussedness would not sit well with the British, then he asked would I join did he fix it so's I'd be working only for him and not for the ratfaces. "They won't go for it," I said. He agreed, said the British were too by the book. Called them martinets. "All of 'em," and said it was too bad, for I had much to offer, for knowing the country. I said I was the only one fool enough to have been up there. "Well, you have survived it," he said, and he offered to go back to the colonel to see about getting me taken as an attached. Before I could say no, he stood up, offered his hand and said, "Do I have your word on it?" I shook my head. I still wasn't on board, just I was maybe leaning his way, and because what I most wanted was to go to bed, I again conceded I could maybe help some. I said I'd go north with him but only to see how it looked before I decided. That was enough for him, for now, and with me joined up, in his mind, if not in mine, he was out the door. Seemed he had further business this night, late as it was.

I got into bed but couldn't sleep with all the thoughts which were in my head. Hoped the British would refuse to take me under the terms I had laid out. This would rid me of them and of Blanchard. Trouble was, much as I wanted to wash my hands of 'em, it didn't sit well with me. Stayin' home whilst all them Indians came down and Blanchard trying to stop 'em with naught but greenhorns. Which didn't mean I was ready to tie in with him. He was a New Englander and them Yankees could be as stiff-necked as the British. Told myself the British wouldn't take me as an attached, which would put it on them, not me, for me not getting in.

I did finally fall asleep and my nightmares came back only now it wasn't me gettin' chased by Indians. It was Mother and Pops, Lydia and Arnold and all the rest of the Albany folks who depended on men such as myself. I awoke, my bed was soaked with sweat, the knife which I always kept at my bedside was in my hand. I said the hell with it. Went into the darkened bar and pondered whilst getting even more drunk. Convinced myself Blanchard had laid a trap for me. Knowing I wouldn't serve under the British, he had arranged it with them aforehand for me to serve as an attached. Getting me in under a condition which was already made.

I stayed there in the dark, drinking, pondering.

****

A few days later, I was behind the bar, pushing beer. Blanchard came in and said he was still waiting for his outfit to get funded. Hubbard was saying he didn't have the authority to recognize us and had passed the decision to his superiors in New York Town. Blanchard said Hubbard was posting letters down to New York in support of us whilst Captain Steele, in his own missives, was arguing against us.

Blanchard said he wasn't going to wait any longer for the slow-moving British. He was taking his men up to the fort to get started on all of what he intended. I agreed to go, to have a look at things.

A couple nights later, on the eve of our departure out of Albany, Blanchard gathered us in the Full Sail. He bought us supper; ham-steaks, cheese, bread and beer, and whilst we ate, he told us of the increased Indian troubles up at the fort. Two teamsters picked off, their wagon plundered and burnt, a sentry on the wall taking an arrow in his chest. When Blanchard got talking about the tortures Indians inflicted on white men, did they catch 'em, he was winnowing out the faint-hearted amongst us and the next morning, when we assembled for departure, more than a few of the men didn't show.

We went up along the river with Blanchard cobbling maneuvers. Using the trek to instill some rudiments of woods' lore. Single file on hard ground. Flankers out. Lines abreast in swampy goin'. "You hunts Injuns quiet, same's you hunt deer," Blanchard said. One of our few woodsmen, John Scott, who'd come over from New Hampshire with Blanchard, said, "Hell, Blanch, most a these fellows ain't never kilt no deer." With all of what I seen, John Scott was right about the poor quality of our men. They made plenty of noise and showed themselves openly when secrecy was called for. Lost or late at rendezvous points. If there had been Indians, most of our boys would a been minus their hair. Blanchard was all mad for trying to keep things in hand.

Finally got in to the fort, the garrison was less than we had been told. There were just twenty British and an undermanned company of thirty-five New Jersey militia. We asked about the men from the other colonies who were supposed to be there. Gone home or never arrived.

Steele, for as long as we weren't official, would not supply us nor even allow our staying in his fort. We built huts outside the walls, our men griping for there were plenty of empty bunks in the barracks. Once our huts were completed, we constructed elm-bark canoes. One of our men, with second thoughts for having joined and figuring to go home and too scairt to go by himself, tried riling up the rest of us. Told us with how shabbily we was getting treated by the British, we had all ought to vamoose. Blanchard beat the hell out of him and sent him back to Albany. Alone.

Tom O'Brien was still at the fort and was no longer a sergeant. He had got busted down in rank for his actions with the woodcutting party when it got jumped. He told me and Blanch about it. Said the day had passed quietly. Bright and sunny. No sign of trouble. At the end of the day, with the sun setting low, the men got lined up for a drink of water and an issue of rum before going back to the fort, a quarter-mile away. A sudden trap was sprung. "We never suspected." Tom's respect for the red devils' ability for trickery and his warnings had been vindicated. He said our militia fled at once. "Colonials," he said, "will not stand in the open whilst getting shot down and without somebody to shoot back at." The British had stood up stoutly to the sniping fire of the well-hidden Indians but lines of men volley-firing in the open cannot prevail against arrows from the woods. Tom spoke proudly for his lads holding their ground long enough to save many lives and they did it in a most astounding way for redcoats. Tom put them behind rocks and trees. The British officers ordered the men to fight the way they was trained. Tom told them to stay behind cover. The contradictory orders maybe caused further casualties but without Tom's actions, the entire troop might a got wiped out. Tom said his lads, trained for volley fire and not for sharpshooting, couldn't have been expected to hit any Indians but, and pausing for the pride coming into his voice, he said they drove the Indians back into the woods, which enabled most of our men to get out.

Captain Steele was furious when he was told what Tom had done and he busted Tom down in rank. Then, and on the insistence of some of his officers, Steele demanded a court martial. Tom told me he didn't care, for his actions had saved lives. The next I seen Tom, a few days later, he was again wearing his sergeant's sash and lacings. He told me Hubbard had tore up Steele's report and told Steele to return Tom to his rank.

Blanchard tried to get us supplies and equipment with chits payable after we got authorized. Most of what we needed was there at the fort but Steele wouldn't provision us without written orders. More of our men talked about going home. A frustrating time. Blanchard refused to do any scouting until he was sure his men would get paid. We'd a gone hungry except for hunting and fishing. Whilst hunting, we used the time in the woods to instruct the men.

Two weeks after we arrived and having just met with the captain, Blanchard came into the hut I shared with him and John Scott. Blanchard was whistling, unusual for him. I asked, "What bit you?" He said we were official. "Funded for up to twenty men. Posted here. Captain Steele don't like it but we got permission to draw equipment and pay." Blanchard's New Hampshire accent stands out when he is excited. "I'm sergeant, we are to have one corporal, Scott, and one scout." He paused, grinned, said, "Attached." He said I got mentioned by name. "The British," he said, "think more of you than they'll admit. Some of 'em, at least, appreciate your savvy. You'll draw corporal's pay, unofficially, for as long as you're contracting your services." Corporal's pay for officer's work but our way of fighting was deemed important, and not having expected to get paid, I was happy to get something, even if it be not much. Blanchard eased toward the door. I suppose I could have reminded him I still hadn't agreed to join up. "Oh yeh," he said, so casual it might a been an afterthought. "Stand by for a sashay afore first light. Be gone up to a week. Pick up your rations tonight. Don't eat 'em all ta once." I asked what was it about. "Small raiding party on the river," he said. "John says he knows where their camp is. We're gonna set an ambush for when they come back." I asked where on the river. Halfway down to the Sacandaga. Which side? North.

We were called out halfway through the night watch, and after a high-smelling breakfast, we picked up our rations. Bad powder, old flints. Men grumbled at the food. Poor quality and not enough to last a week. We mustered with our shivering breath showing in the cold morning air. Blanchard, always a bear for getting things right, checked the men's cartridge boxes, thirty rounds. My gun will not accommodate cartridges as the smoothbores do. This made for slower loading with a powder horn but with my rifled barrel, I could outshoot anybody, red or white. Any sharpshooting, Blanchard would be countin' on me. He inspected each man's bedroll for tightness, tin cups and other metal gear for noise. Wood canteens filled, water only, no rum or whiskey. He ordered each canteen opened for a sniff. He gave us instructions and warnings and we slid through the half-opened gate an hour before the first streaks of the dawn showed. We put our canoes on the water and moved upstream in a single file of boats. Even in the calm water, our men showed themselves as inexperienced in canoes as they were in the woods.

We disembarked on the north shore; the blue jays stopped their screeching to watch us. We hid the canoes. John Scott, me and the dog went ahead. Found the camp easily enough, a mile in from the river. We did not enter the camp and stayed on a hilltop looking down into it. Deserted, well-hidden.

We went back and I reported to Blanch in a low voice so the men didn't hear me. Told him there were many more Indians than what he had maybe thought there was. I said they'd outnumber us two to one iffen they came back. He shrugged and took us in and we hid where we figured the Indians would pass by, did they come back. We stayed in the brush two days, the men scared at the dangerous turn the episode had taken and hoping the raiders didn't return. Blanchard stayed calm, I challenged him. "This is exactly the sort of thing to get us all killed. You trying to build a reputation?" I asked what he was intending if the Indians came back. "Ken," he said. "They ain't comin'. I reckoned this to be as safe a place as any to spend a few days, give the men a feel of danger without being exposed to it. Thought you'd see it." He was smiling as he said this. Of course. Indians wouldn't return to an old camp, for fear of just such a trap as we had set for them. Blanch knew it, I should a knowed it, and our men didn't know it. Sly as a fox, this man. "Do you live long enough," I said, "you'll put together a solid company."

We stayed out six days. Moving men around, spooking trails and stream crossings. A dangerous time. Me and Blanchard showed the men how the Indians covered their passing, said we had to learn to do the same. Returning to the fort, I scouted ahead, jumpy as a weasel. Saw where Indians had gone to shore only a few days earlier. Tried to find their canoes but no luck. We got in tired and hungry, food and supplies used up. This foray showed how much work we had to do before we would have ourselves a trustworthy force. Too often did we have to search for our wandering lads.

We rested and refit a few days and went out again. Another week of hard scouting through the Kaydeross. We saw plenty of sign, war parties were around. Lurking. They vanished whenever we got after 'em. Captain Steele considered our forays to be useless and he used 'em as an excuse to downplay the importance of what we were doing. Instead of giving Blanchard credit for hard work performed, Steele berated him, often in front of our men.

A half dozen badly needed recruits for our ranging service came in and two more men were lost. These we found. At least their mutilated remains. Two scalped heads mounted to a post at a deserted Indian camp, one head belonging to John Scott. "We need us a new corporal," someone said. Indeed, the loss of John was a heavy blow for Blanchard, although he did not speak of it. He and Scott had been together a long time. By the look of the hastily abandoned camp, the cut-up body parts and the stewpot a boilin', we had interrupted a feast getting started.

Our encounters, such as they were, provided plenty of anxiousness and little enough to shoot at 'cept for patches of movement. We were fortunate for not shooting any of our own. Usually nobody killed on our side and maybe not on theirs neither, though a few times after we ran 'em off, we found drips of blood on the leaves where they'd been.

One of our sashays turned into a fiasco when we were coming in and were almost back at the fort. We landed on the south shore, more for training than for scouting, there didn't seem to be much sign around, and when we got back to our boats, which we thought well-stashed, the bottoms was chopped out. The aspect of our foray had changed. We were three-miles upstream from the fort and on the wrong side of the river without boats. We needed rescuing but had no way to let the fort know of our situation.

Our men were scared. Eyes darted fearfully around, searching the shadows, expecting an attack from any direction. "If there be a war party around, we're gonna be foxbait," somebody whined in a high, trembling voice. Blanchard chewed him out for a coward. We moved trepidaciously along the riverbank, toward the fort. We came to a crick which we would cross over one man at a time. The dog gave his low warning growl. We all looked at him and at each other. He was froze. Nothing did we hear, the woods deathly silent around us. I nudged Blackie with my foot, he snarled without looking back at me. Some of the men, scared, were for hightailin'. Still the dog would not move. I clumb a short way up a tree and came back down fast. "Dog's right, Blanch," I said, short of breath. "They's waitin' for us on the other side of the brook." He asked how many. "I seen at least ten," I said. "No telling how many I didn't see. They're behind a log barricade." Some of the men laughed, scared. Said I must be wrong, the dog too. They didn't maybe disbelieve it, but with as near as they were to panic, they were denying what they didn't want to be true. Blanch settled them with a look.

We backed off, clumb a ridge and set a trap of our own. A good position on the Indians' flank. A height we could defend. If they tried us, we might hurt 'em. They declined to cross the brook, same as us.

We endured a long afternoon of watching for any movement of the Indians and sometime whilst we were watching, they slipped away. Once we were sure they were gone, we moved downriver and got in contact with the fort. The redcoats got us out, and gave us a ribbing for the loss of our boats. Especially did we hear it from the lieutenant who'd been with Hubbard when he lost his own boats and got jeered by the Albany folks. At least we didn't have to walk all the way down to Albany. Or swim across the Hudson to the fort.

After this, Blackie received a lot of attention from our boys. Everybody wanted him along when they went on patrol and he stayed well fed. I made a number of lone scouts, accompanied only by the dog. He was the one I trusted the most. There was nobody in the company I dared partner with in the bush, except Blackie and Blanch.

****

North Fort was intended to stop the enemy depredations. It had so far not done much good. Sign right outside the gates attested to the Indians maintaining a watch on us as they came and went from their raiding. And raiding they were! Our northern frontier was aflame. Most of the settlers had departed, those who stayed got swept up by the violence, so many slain and a bloody procession of captives going north through Scalp Point. Fated to spend the rest of their short lives as camp drudges. Homesteads burned out; pigs with bellies slashed; hamstrung bovines bellowing piteously; crops rotting in the fields.

The trail to Scalp Point ran red with English blood.

Our work was unabating. The woods were full of Indians, by the sign, but we mostly chased shadows. We set traps for them, same as they did for us and whenever we got 'em at a disadvantage, they melted away. When they set their own traps, it was most often Blackie who sniffed 'em out. Enough so Blanchard relied heavily on the dog. He said without Blackie's nose and ears, we'd a been wiped out many times over.

We had our first real fight when we jumped Indians in a clearing. Ten or so men to a side, tomahawk against gun-butt and knife. Plenty of yelling. One of theirs fell, we cheered. One of ours went down and the cheering was from them. They broke first and ran, a victory for us.

Our ranks down to nine exhausted effectives, we had a desperate need for men. Blanch refused the help of the New Jersey men. He declared them not good enough. Captain Steele admitted the value of our work and leaned on Blanchard for information yet he only grudgingly supplied us and did little with the information we brought him.

Sergeant Tom was keen on our ranging. He had seen enough of the wilderness to know it was necessary. "The whole damn army ought to be trained same as Joe's men," he often said. He had been asking to get himself temporarily attached to our company; each time he asked, Steele refused him. This was for Hubbard having backed Tom against Steele in the court-martial business. Tom persisted and Steele finally assented, probably on Hubbard's orders. What I think Hubbard and his higher-ups envisioned was a soldier who combined the battlefield acumen of the regular with the woods' skills of the frontiersman. This would be a most formidable man. He would also be British. Easier to discipline and order around.

Blanch had Tom shed his red coat and clumsy shoes and get into a hunting shirt and moccasins. A buckskin shirt didn't catch on the brush, moccasins made for quieter walking and the marks they left didn't gouge so deep down into the dirt. Harder to see and faster to wash away. Out of his uniform and into stiff new buckskins, poor Tom looked damn uncomfortable. Blanchard was glad to have him along. Tom paid attention to everything we showed him, trying to learn as much as possible. The written report Tom turned in upon our return was not detailed enough for the prickly-tempered Steele. He badgered Tom which caused the sergeant much agony over quill and paper. I helped him with the writing.

A few days after Tom's first affair with us, Steele asked for volunteers from amongst the other sergeants. They signed on, guided by Tom's words and his pressure. And boredom. Steele sent his men with us a few at a time. All the sergeants, then an ensign, a junior lieutenant, a midshipman. They were enthusiastic, though somewhat clumsy, and nervous in the woods. We lost one of the sergeants to a gun accident.

We scouted around the settlements and along the Hudson and the Sacandaga. I took a few of our best men up along the Great Carry to the south end of Saint Sacrement and to the borders of the Drowned Lands, by the ruins of old Fort Anne. I told the men they were fortunate the nights had turned cold for otherwise the rattlesnakes in the Drowned Lands would be moving and would be in foul humor. Come summer in those parts, the snakes would strike at anything. They were good eatin' but deadly for the man who knew not how to approach 'em.

Steele decided the surest way to keep watch on the Indians was with permanent watch-posts at Saint Sacrement and the Drowned Lands. Him and Blanch had a fierce argument over this. Blanch said leaving men in any one place for too long and too far out from the fort was suicidal. Once discovered, they were sure to die. Steele went ahead with it anyway, with our men getting rotated out and back. One of the men sent to a lonely watch-post didn't come back. The next day, another sent to find him was also missing. No sign of 'em did we find. Steele said our boys had deserted. We didn't think so, they were good men and wouldn't have absconded and iffen they did, it was not likely they'd have made it home with so many savages around. Blanch finally convinced the captain to abandon the idea, no more men were sent and nothing more was said about it.

****

Fall came in cold and wet, then it warmed up and dried out. Indian Summer, our men called the dreaded late-season fair weather, for it brought the raiders down out of the north in greater numbers. Our men went about their dangerous duties in bad humor. Always out chasing Indians and trying to convince the settlers to leave. Those which agreed to go we shepherded in to Saratoga and Albany. Even with the imminent danger, many refused to depart. They were afraid to stay but feared they'd lose their houses and crops did they go, and with winter coming. Cruel winter, sure to be a hungry time.

Some nights the Indians were right outside the fort. No man dared leave through the front gate, even in darkness. We used the newly constructed sally port, a low door on the palisade wall opposite the gate and disguised to look like no more than a part of the wall. We only used it after dark or when we were certain Indians weren't lurking. So far they had not discovered it.

Us rangers were fortunate we were not required to stand guard on the ramparts. This was a most dangerous duty. Never knew when one of the devils would get in close and put an arrow into the man who showed himself. One Indian was so bold as to come over the wall one night in quest of a scalp. And almost got away with one. Steele tried posting the sentries in pairs and he had sentry boxes constructed. The boxes gave protection but limited a man's vision.

The Indians from the far western country of the Great Lakes were around sometimes. These westerners, more savage than the Indians which lived closer to white civilization, used stone arrowheads which were heavy and left gaping wounds. The New Jersey men told the British the western Indians dipped their points in human excreta. This spooked the British. The wounds from these arrows often festered into foul infections and worsened until death resulted.

****

I made a trip down to Saratoga, to see were my friends safe. On the way in and knowing Arnold had begun work on his new house, out by the healing springs, I went for a look. The house was untouched, the work had barely commenced. Hoped the Indians might burn it before it was completed. Thought about torching it but couldn't bring myself to doing it.

Got to Saratoga, the garrison had been strengthened. Many burned-out folks was refuging there. Priscilla told me the men building her house had got scared off by a rumor. Cowards, she called them, for refusing to go back, even for the extra pay she offered. I told her the workmen had more sense than she did and I again tried to convince her and Arnold to move temporarily to Albany. They were not entirely dismissive of my arguments, or maybe they went along to shut me up.

When Priscilla was not within hearing, I asked Arnold about Lydia. "Richard," Arnold said, "has accused you of vile sins. He says it is all your fault their marriage is in trouble. He says you have done them wrong. I am afraid my partner means you harm." Lies, but I felt bad. Arnold suspected Richard was beating Lydia, making her sick. "Lydia wants to move to Albany," Arnold said, "but Richard will not hear of it because he does his carousing down there. He is rarely here to help with the land business."

I went to see Lydia of an evening. I knocked on the door, she came and seemed glad at the first to see me but quickly turned cold. She said I couldn't come in, the baby was sleeping. I asked could we speak on the porch. She stepped outside. She was troubled and I realized she was sick. Puffy eyes. Had she been crying? And was I seeing bruises? "I am Richard's wife and must stand by him," she said. She drew her breath in sharply and gathered strength for something she had been wanting to say to me. "Why did you jump Richard in such a cowardly way?" Before I could answer, she kept on. "Why have you caused me so much grief? Oh! He told me what you did to him. He says those mountains have made you into a man most wicked and I feel he is right. I feel I no longer know you. Nor do I think I want to know you." The look in her eyes said she knew it was all lies, and when she said I was not to come around anymore, I got hot and asked, nay, demanded, did she truly not want to see me or did my presence mean more beatings for her. She became jumbled and emotional and shook her head as she backed toward the partially-opened door. Her shaking her head was not a denial of what I had asked, it was for her not wanting to be asked what she could not truthfully answer. She went inside. I stayed on the porch a moment. Convinced she didn't believe the lies her husband told but powerless to do anything about it, for the trouble it might cause her, I went back to the fort with a hollow feeling.

****

We always knew when our supply boats were coming up the river by the increase in the number of Indians around the fort. The Indians intent on grabbing the supplies, us intent on keeping them. Barrels of worm-infested meat, rotten fish, corn with the color leached out of it. Should let the Indians have it, yet and did the boats not make it in, we had naught to eat. The boatmen told of arrows and muskets fired from shore.

A road needed to be cut from the lower landing to the fort, a widening and smoothing of the rough path so ox-drawn wagons could use it. For now, supplies which came off the boats had to be loaded onto men's backs for carrying around the falls. We had just a few oxen and no horses. We tried using hand carts with large wheels but the rock-strewn trail was rough on wheeled traffic. Breakdowns were frequent and time consuming. Did one cart in ten break an axle or drop a wheel, the entire load had to be transferred to another cart or all the men had to remain there whilst the cart was repaired. Too few men left to themselves was sure to lose their hair. Travois were tried but the trail was too rough for much to be hauled in this way.

A large supply of wood was needed for cooking and for warmth. The wood-cutting parties were constantly out, always escorted by a large force. Along with their axes and two-man saws, the workers carried their muskets. Even with rangers covering the flanks, the parties got jumped. Tough to counter every skulking warrior armed with hatchet and knife. The man who wandered away from his party, if only for a moment, lost his scalp.

****

An ensign of artillery mounted a small swivel cannon on a cart. It carried all the accouterments for firing. Powder and shot, buckets, ramrods, swabs, matches. It was drawn along by men in harness. When Steele told Blanch us rangers was to take a turn in the harnesses, Blanch said we were men, not mules, and said he'd take us back to Albany and disband us afore he'd subject us to the indignity.

The ensign, enamored with his own idea, convinced his superiors of the cart's effectiveness. Clever as hell, this contraption, and useless, unless what the ensign intended was for the Indians to laugh themselves to death. The cart was better suited for hauling firewood, the cannon was naught but a pop-gun, though it did make a loud enough boom when it went off. In a fight, the cart would tie up five or six men who might be put to other purposes.

****

Blanchard and me had been wanting to find time to go up to the lakes. He had never been up, only had he been to the south shore of Saint Sacrement. During a lull in Indian presence, we went. Just the two of us and the dog. We would not risk getting onto the water, even did we have a boat, which we did not, and we walked the mountains along the west side.

I showed him the old Mohawk trail from Saint Sacrement to the East Branch, the trail I had sought when I fled from the Hurons who had attacked my smuggling party and which seeking brought me to the discovery of my Paradise Valley. The trail started along the west shore and made a long climb out of the valley and into the mountains to the west.

All the way up the lake, Blanch thrilled to the sights below us in the early-winter sunlight. I enjoyed seeing a man gazing for the first time at Saint Sacrement. Its clarity and beauty never failed to delight. Sky Waters. Showed him Portage Crick and when we got up onto the top of Rattlesnake Mountain, from where we could look down on the Valley of Corlear and over to Verd Mont and beyond, indeed, all the way to New Hampshire, he grasped at once the strategic importance of Tyonderrogha. The invasion route, us into Canada or the French down to New York, was along these two lakes to the Great Carry and south along the Hudson. Tyonderrogha, situated at the junction of the lakes and overlooking the Portage Crick outlet, was the key to controlling the route.

Blanch said something about the French not having yet fortified Ti and we agreed the French would get there afore we did. I told him my reasons for thinking the French had built their fort at Crown Point instead of Ti, they not wanting to provoke us by getting too far south. Blanch looked around some, at the valley, and looking down on the Ti Point, which seemed close enough below us so we could have spit on it with a favorable wind, he said a couple of cannons situated where we was standing could blast any fort built down there. I asked, with the ruggedness of the mountain, would it be possible to get cannons up where we were. "Dunno," he said.

****

We spooked Scalp Point, a cold, cheerless place soon to be buried in ice and snow. Blanch, seeing Corlear for the first time, said it maybe lacked the mountain fastness of Saint Sacrement but had a majesty of its own. We stayed on the station five days. The French were masters hereabouts and Blanch was disgusted with how the French, without fear of the English, shot off their guns and hunted and fished around the lake. We checked the gaps leading into the mountains on the east side of Corlear.

On our way up to the lakes, I had offered to take Blanch up to Paradise, eager to show him all I had done there. He'd said there wouldn't be time for it but with us back over on the west side and with me showing him Outlet Crick, he asked did my offer still stand. It did, and we went up for a few days.

****

The Indians had been around in bigger numbers than usual and we got called to alarm late one night and as I scrambled out of my bedroll and grabbed my gun, I was sure we was under attack. Turned out the Indians had set fire to unfinished barns and sheds outside the fort. The fire was bait intended to draw us out from behind our walls. Steele and Blanchard were not fooled and we stayed inside. The red men hooted out of the darkness as the fires burned. We couldn't understand their words but it was clear what was in their voices. Mockery for us cowards.

Men said afterward we should a slipped out the sally port and snuck around to where we could jump the Indians from behind. Blanch said it was what the Indians was waiting for us to do. They'd have jumped us sooner than we could have jumped them. The next day Steele assembled the men and in a defiant speech, he told us we were going to rebuild all of what got destroyed. Said it would show the Indians our determination. I think Steele expected the men would cheer for hearing it, they didn't, and our rangers laughed afterward. Show 'em our determination since we hadn't shown 'em any courage. I reckoned the rebuilding was just something to keep the Jersey boys busy. Without cattle or horses, we didn't have much need for barns.

With this humiliation and with the Indians still trying to draw us out, the British lieutenants hatched a plan. A decoy wood-cutting party to lure in the Indians and with rangers positioned to hold 'em whilst the cart-cannon and the regulars emerged from the fort. Blanch spoke against it, said it was too complicated an undertaking. Too much could go wrong. Besides which, he said, "My ranger company is not strong enough to hold a large force of Indians whilst your too-slow men and too-slow plan is put into effect. We'll be more than a mile from the rest of youse." The officers said the rangers could be augmented by militia. Blanch protested further but as a colonial and a non-com, he was silenced by the regular officers, eager for action. The ordinarily cautious Steele agreed to it, maybe feeling he had to, to make up for his not having gone out when the Indians burned the outbuildings. And to put a stop to the Indians' near-constant nighttime drumming which he always complained kept him awake.

The night before we went out, a light snow fell. No more'n an inch, it'd be gone by mid-morning but the British were gleeful. Said it'd make for easier tracking and the savages could not conceal themselves against the backdrop of white. Blanch said Indians were plenty capable of hiding in snow-shrouded woods and he repeated what he'd said when the plan had been proposed. The war party was too large and Indians too wily to be taken the way we intended. Steele said we were going out and said it as if it were the last word, which it was not, as Blanch retorted, "With them Injuns scheming on a way to get us to come out, here we go marching into their fondest hopes."

Our rangers snuck out whilst it was still dark and at dawn, out came the woodcutters, then the British with their cannon-cart. The cart slid on the snow and went into a ditch and whilst the British extricated it, us rangers and our too-few militia were outmanned and hard-pressed to hold off the Indians. The fighting was brisk with the Indians trying to close a circle around us and iffen they had, it'd a been the end of Blanchard's Rangers. Only just in time did we find a gap in their lines and get through it. We snuck out along a deer run through a cedar swamp and heard the rattle of muskets and finally, the boom of the cannon. The Indians was vexed for us getting out and they sniped the wood-cutting party. The belated arrival of the British got 'em out.

The aftermath was disgraceful. The British put the entire blame for the failure on Blanch. They claimed they would have destroyed the Indians if only we'd held our ground long enough for the regulars to get up with their cannon. They said our withdrawal was abject flight when in truth it was a masterly performance by Blanch. Abject flight would have finished us. The accusations were not worthy of comment, except it made affairs more difficult for our bedeviled leader.

Late October, the raiding slowed. There were no Indians around. With the weather turning colder, they had seemingly all gone home, which didn't mean at least some of them wouldn't be around for the cold months ahead. We scouted farther afield and not finding much sign, I decided my stint with the rangers was up. There was still time to get north and do some trapping. I'd be safe in my Paradise, could I get there. With luck and with the supply of pelts from Oswego about dried up by the war, this old hoss might be the only one with fur come spring.

I went to see Blanchard and when I told him my plans, he rose up over me. "Kuyler," he said. "Are you plumb nuts? No! You ain't a goin! I order you not to go!" I told him I had been cooped up long enough. "And since I am unattached, I am either going north to trap or south to Albany for women and rum. Ain't much of neither here." He, exasperated, again ordered me not to go. I told him I didn't know for certain were the Indians all coming down Saint Sacrement and through the Drowned Lands. "Some," I said, "might be comin' through my valley and along the East Branch and iffen they are, I need to know about it." Blanch didn't believe this was my reason for going. He said if the Indians had discovered my valley, there was naught I could do about it. "Knowin'," I said, "would mean I didn't have to keep worrying over it. Besides, last winter I brung up a load a new traps. Special made and cost me a lot of money. I got to make sure I still own 'em."

"Blast it!" Blanch said. "I ought'n to whip your'n ass." His voice held its usual authority but we both knew there was naught he could do to stop me.

I had to wait two days before I could get a chit from Steele for money owed and whilst I waited, I spent time with Sergeant Tom. He had done well in getting our rangers and regulars working together. He always gave as good as he got. Tom had strong objections to my going. He didn't know where I was headed but he knew it was toward the wilderness, not away from it, and he said I was crazy.

Steele finally paid up and I used the money to outfit myself at the sutler's store. On my way out of the fort, I stopped to see Blanch again. He poured us glasses of rum and whilst we talked, him telling his plans for what was next, I was mindful of all the good work he had done. Given a couple more years, he'd mold himself a useful company of bush rangers. I was also mindful of how much I had come to respect him and how joining up had been the right thing for me. A pleasure to share a fire with a man who understood the woods so well and who always pulled more than his own weight. I learnt from Blanch every day, same as I had with Hugh McChesney.

When Blanch reached for the bottle, to refill our glasses, I waved him off. It was time to go. "I 'preciate your help, Ken," he said. "Wish you'd reconsider. I could use you here this winter. Damn, but you are a hard man to convince." I told him I'd check Scalp Point as soon as I got up there and did I see anything big, I'd turn around and come right back down again. Blanch said he'd see me in the spring. "Keep your nose into the wind," he said.

Chapter XX – River of Danger

Four days later and looking down at Scalp Point, one thing was for certain. There wouldn't be no trapping for me. My string was played out afore I had even commenced unraveling it. More goings-on down there than I ever saw before. Bateaux and whaleboats drawn up along the shore and swinging supplies over the sides on booms for stacking on the wharves and carrying into the castle and with more boats waitin' to unload. A sloop of two masts, from the Imperial French Navy, by the uniforms of the crew, bobbed like a fat duck in the open waters. Indian-filled canoes surrounded it and each time the ship fired off its cannons, seven or eight guns on each broadside, the Indians whooped and fired their own guns.

Indian encampments were spread out on both shores. With as many camps as there were and with the different Indian nations all tending to stay to their own, even when they were in alliance with others, it was more than just the usual Abenakis and Hurons. Must have been five or six different tribes, some had probably come long distances and had maybe never before been so far east. There was plenty of woods-lopers too, and in a cleared field outside the stockade fence, white-coated French officers drilled what looked to be a full company of Canadian regulars.

I returned to my cabin and whilst I was hastily making ready to depart, they came up from Corlaer. I heard shots somewhere north of the Eagle's Lake. Deer hunters, and by nightfall, I was gone. Worried they might find my cabin and destroy all I had worked at for so long. If they should find my beavers, it would be the end of my Paradise. They would wipe me out in a season.

****

Late afternoon the next day, rain was coming hard, soaking me and the dog. Snow would have been better. We arrived at the confluence of the east and west branches of the Hudson and I figured to spend the night. Hunker down somewhere along the portage trail and hope the rain stopped by morning.

I made two trips along the trail, up the hill by the falls and a short way down the other side, first with my gear then with my boat. Just a short way into the woods and with the boat leaned against a tree and with my gear underneath, me and the dog got under for the little protection there was from the weather. A cold, wet camp. Feeling lonely and miserable, I got wrapped in my bearskin.

The hound got up close for warmth. And awoke me sometime during the night with a low growl. I reached out, still more asleep than awake, and touching his ears, I felt as how they was pointed forward, a sure sign of trouble. A further sign was how stiff he was and how he wasn't looking up at me, the way he usually did when something had alerted him. He was sulking, his head and neck lowered. I moved my hand along the back of his neck. Never felt so much tension there. He turned his nose to the trail, down toward the river. I slid out of my wraps, ax and knife at the ready. Hard to hear anything for the rumble of the falls and the pounding of the rain, which had turned to sleet. The wind howled through the trees. Hoped what Blackie had heard or smelled was an animal or something he'd dreamed. Then I heard footfalls. Men coming up the trail from the downriver side, enough of 'em so they weren't taking much care for quiet. I heard low talk, didn't know who it might be, hoped they be friendly, then a Frenchie broke into song, a voyageur tune about paddling the Saint Lawrence.

T'was French and Indians and what the hell was I to do? Best thing for now, I figured, was to not do anything. If I stayed where I was, they'd maybe not see me and they'd portage around and get out ahead of me on the river. The tramping of feet got louder, closer, and I heard hatchets banging against tree limbs. They were getting into the woods, putting up crude shelters against the rain. They'd be spending the rest of the night with me, and with how they were dispersing as they came up and with a few at a time going into the woods to the left and the right, it was possible some of them, maybe the last of 'em, would walk right in on me.

Couldn't tell how many they were, maybe fifteen or twenty, and there wasn't nothing I could think to do. Stay where I was and get found out or flee and get chased and caught. Either way they'd have me. Decided to stay, or maybe I was too scared to go but it turned out to be the right thing, at least for the moment, as the last of 'em got into the woods no more'n twenty feet from where I was. Close enough so if they moved around much in collecting branches for their shelter, they might see I was there with them. Close enough for their Indian noses to sniff me, or more likely sniff the wet dog, and close enough so a fire might throw light on me and my boat.

Things quieted without them seein' nor smellin' us and I figured to back away from the trail. Get far enough and I could run. Trouble was, they'd find my canoe and gear at daylight, just a few hours away, and it'd be a long way to the fort without a boat and with all them Indians chasing me through the woods.

The only thing for me was what I least wanted to do. Walk right down through the middle of 'em, down the trail and hope none of 'em was still there by the water. And hope there be a boat for grabbing. Didn't think much of my chances but couldn't see no other way. Only good thing, so far out from anywhere and on such a miserable night, they wouldn't be expecting company.

And what if I did manage to steal a boat and get away, then what? These were northern Indians, not Iroquois, best I could tell, and what the hell were northerners doing so far out to the west of everything? Whatever it was, they most surely wouldn't want someone such as me to know about it. Soon as they found my boat and gear and with one of their own boats missing, they'd figure whoever took theirs was hightailin' down the Hudson and they'd get after me. I decided I better trick 'em. Steal a boat, get downriver a ways, sink the boat and walk to the fort. Long walk but safer. They wouldn't expect it, and once they got onto the Hudson, they'd likely keep on, figuring to catch me.

Before I could go one way or the other, I had to first get me a boat and before I stepped out, I looked down at the dog and thought about cutting his throat. He was more likely to give us away than I was but he'd give one last yelp afore he died and anyway, I reckoned me and him was in it together, for better or worse.

I picked up paddle and rifle and stepped out onto the trail, worried the Indians farthest up the hill and closest to me might get curious did they hear a man moving around above them and maybe knowing there wasn't none of their own up there. I started down. I couldn't see much for the darkness and went with a boldness I didn't feel.

Some few of 'em was still gettin' settled, making it more likely I'd bump into 'em but which would also make my own movements less suspicious. Anybody asked questions, I'd bluff 'em with what little French I knew or put a knife into 'em afore they called out a warning.

I was seeing a little better in the dark and looking straight ahead whilst walking as if I was going back to my boat for tobacco or something to eat. I heard low talk to the sides and some snoring. The dog stayed at my heels. He was slouching to make himself seem smaller, his tail between his legs, and he kept tangling under my feet. My body shivered with the cold and with the near certainty I mightn't be getting out with my hair this time.

Hoped nobody was watching the boats. That was possible. Indians and woods-lopers, despite their savvy, were often negligent in posting a watch. If French regulars were along, the boats would be guarded. The rain did not seem inclined to let up, this hid me, as did the cold mist coming up off the water. It'd hide them too, if they be down there. Wouldn't be no way to tell for sure. Got down to the water and saw their boats was pulled up on shore and didn't look to be guarded.

I heard voices above, on the trail. Indians coming down. Me and Blackie slipped into the trees, just a few steps, for fear of stepping on somebody already in there. Hoped those coming hadn't seen Blackie. If they'd seen me, and with as dark as it was, they might have assumed I was one of them but sure in hell Blackie would give us away. There were no dogs along on this war party. The Indians was coming as if nothing was amiss, they might a been a decoy for others sneaking on me through the woods. No way to know but they went on past, seven or eight of 'em, more than I could a got my knife into. They got down to the shore and stood there in the rain. I couldn't figure what the hell they were doing. Or what the hell I should do. Couldn't steal a boat whilst they was there. Weren't nothing for me 'cept to wait 'em out.

I heard noises on the water, a whole 'nother flotilla was coming in. I couldn't tell how many boats or men but as the arriving Indians disembarked, their greetings with those already there were in a mix of Indian tongues, some Mohawk, some I figured for northern lingo. The Mohawk talk was from those arriving. They all went up the trail, damn near brushing elbows with me as they went past my hiding place. Another ten or so had come in, which made for around thirty, all told.

When they was all gone up into their shelters, me and Blackie gave 'em a few minutes to get settled and with no more coming, we stepped back onto the trail. Got down to the water and with nobody there, we got into the first boat which looked a size one man could handle, an elm-bark, and pushed off. I thought us most fortunate to have got out though I understood we was a long way from safe.

****

The rapids, usually low this time of year, were swollen with the rain and I was going like hell, staying as best I could to the middle of the river. It made for a most exhilarating ride with the current lurching us forward, out of control sometimes, the water and foam flying but it was faster going than it would have been closer to either shore and with fewer rocks and snags. The rain was thick, the river high, the night shrouded in fog. Hard to see in the gloom. Penetrating cold. Got to shivering and couldn't make it stop.

Hadn't gone far before the dawn began showing in the eastern sky. Thought how an Indian hunkered down close to where I had been might open his eyes at first light and see my boat propped against a tree. Or maybe one of 'em had crawled out from beneath his shelter for one reason or another and whilst it was still dark and had bumped into my boat. Could be they was already right close behind, riding the rapids as fast as me.

Managed to stay afloat through the worst of the river, and farther down, where the roiling of the rapids eased some, I got thinking about how poor were my chances of making it to the fort. Seemed did I want to go on living, the best thing, maybe the only thing, would be to sink the canoe and trek back on up to Paradise. Fool 'em, not outrun 'em, and I might maybe have done it 'cept I couldn't, on account of those Mohawks. The northerners had been expecting the Mohawks, so the two sides, age-old enemies, was meeting in secret council. Weren't no other way to see it, and with how it was getting conducted, away from the villages and not in regular Indian fashion, they was cooking up something between 'em. It weren't hard to figure what it was they was cooking.

The Iroquois were officially on our side or neutral but with something big coming out of Canada, these northerners were an advance party come ahead to secure allies from amongst the Mohawks. There were plenty of Iroquois, including Mohawks, who had gone north to join up with the French. Caughnawagas, we called 'em, and they, with cousins amongst our Mohawks, might be seeing about getting the cousins joined up to fight us. And if the northern Indians were looking for Mohawk assistance, it'd be for something bigger than just ordinary raiding. More likely a hit on one of our major towns, Schenectady, Saratoga, Albany. Or, and did the Mohawks go over in big enough numbers, they might wipe out the entire damn colony. The Mohawk Council and the older warriors wouldn't go for it but for the younger bucks, eager to prove themselves, the chance to make war on close-by, easy prey, might prove irresistible.

Whatever they was intending, I had stumbled upon them, or rather, they had stumbled on me, and the fort needed to be alerted. Trouble was, going for the fort, I'd have to out-paddle any Indians which was in pursuit and there'd likely be more Indians watching the river, and with twenty-five miles of hard going between me and the fort. I'd be throwing my life away trying to bring to the British a warning they'd most likely ignore. I thought some more about just getting myself away. Uh-huh. Spend the winter up to Paradise and come down in the spring to see everything in a smoking ruin, my friends all dead for me taking the coward's way.

****

Went hard, spurred by the fear of Indians coming after me and with my determination to take a warning to the fort. I passed through more swollen rapids, and seen now in the light of day, I knew I'd been damn lucky in the dark. Rocks, roiling water, snags to knock me out of my boat. A few times I got into backwaters for a rest, I had to, and only for a moment and only for my arms and shoulders aching fiercely, my breathing labored, my heart a tom-tom in my chest.

With daylight, the chances of meeting a war party on the water or of getting picked off from shore increased. Wouldn't be no warning, not even from the dog, he was curled under the nose of the prow, out of the rain. In the gloom and with the fog not dissipating, I couldn't see nor hear much, and other than ax and knife, I had no weapon of any use. My rifle was too wet to fire, even wrapped in deerskin, and anyway, there wasn't no sense thinkin' about fightin' or eludin'. Only thing was to go like hell and trust to luck.

Watching behind me as best I could, which is to say hardly at all, just some scared glances over my shoulder, I didn't see any pursuit. The elm-bark was built more for sturdiness than speed, which was both a good thing and bad. It wasn't so fast as a birch-bark but a birch-bark could not have endured the jolting this boat was taking against rocks and logs unseen in dreary mists.

The rain was in cold sheets, big frozen drops driven by the wind, which had shifted to the northeast. I about dozed off a few times and was brought back by a bump against a rock or the cold spray of a whitewater turbulence. My arms and shoulders ached, my legs was cramped, stiff, the urge to pull in to shore and rest was overpowering.

Shaking, wet and chilled, I kept on.

****

Late morning, my tired muscles screaming for rest and still with a ways to go, the rain eased and stopped, the fog lifted. The wind stayed strong and shifted again, to the northwest, a sign the storm was passed, not a good thing. The hard rain might a been keeping prowling Indians off the river and they'd be eager now to get back on. Down this far was the added danger of getting shot by one of Blanch's patrols. They might not recognize me until too late.

****

It was dark 'ere I seen the walls of North Fort. I called out as I came in, to avoid getting shot. The sentries on the walls, colonials this night, called back, "Who goes there!" I seen torches and heard men scurrying. The challenge was repeated. Damn near impossible for me to bring the boat in with the current drawing me on but I managed to get in toward the skinny between the palisade wall and the river. Heard hammer clicks and a voice. "State your business and be quick about it, eh?" Certain they'd fire did I not say fast enough who I be and with the canoe getting pushed hard by the current, I struggled to ground 'er. I thought I was gonna get shot by my own side. I shouted into the wind, "Don't shoot, goddamn it! It's Kuyler with news from upriver!" A shot rang out, smacked into the side of the boat. My voice pleading, a sense of futility came onto me. I screamed again. "Kuyler!"

Now they seemed to understand I was one of 'em. "Come on in," they called. "Quick'n easy." Their voices out of the darkness told me they were still up behind their wall. Suspicious and scairt, they wasn't coming out to help and I seen their guns pointing down at me from up over the rampart, a most unpleasant feeling. With them plenty excited, any one of 'em might a shot first and asked questions of a corpse.

I got my boat onto the rocks where the bottom of the river came up sharply to meet the shoreline. The canoe hung there just long enough for me to grab my gun and for me and the dog to get out and splash to shore. The blasted dog had to shake himself before he would proceed. A backward glance showed me the canoe was gone in the current. I ran on stiff legs the short distance to the gate. The sentries held one gate a little way open to let us in, then shut the gate and barred it.

I faced gun barrels and hard faces in the torchlight. "Sorry we pegged at ya," said a young New Jersey lad. "Glad I missed," claimed another. Sheepishly. The officer of the guard took me in to see Steele. He was at his desk, writing. He looked up, annoyed. "Good god, man.

You are soaking wet. And making a terrible mess. Whatever you want, it best be important." I started to tell him all of what I had seen, both at Scalp Point and out at the confluence. I was trying to tell too much at once and he held up his hand to stop me. He asked was I sure. I said I was, he got up out of his chair and called for an orderly. "Fetch dry clothes and coffee. And wood." The captain sent another orderly to summon his officers and sergeants. "Sit down, Kuyler," he said and he built up the fire himself.

He ordered stew warmed up and poured me a stiff rum. Having heard the rudiments of my story and by the questions he asked, it was clear he was more concerned with the Mohawks than with them northerners. Same as me. He asked about the doings at Scalp Point and I kept bringing him back around to my encounter at the confluence. Asked how many Indians had I seen there. I said I didn't take the time to count heads but it seemed there were at least twenty in the first party and another ten in what come later. Thirty in all. He suggested it was a raiding party with some having got out ahead and the rest catching up later. I said they was too far west for raiding down into the settlements and said the second bunch wasn't laggards. They was our own Mohawks. Steele doubted I could tell the difference in the dark between Iroquois and northern Indians. I told him the elm-bark I came down in was Mohawk. The markings on the canoe would be my proof against his doubts, until I remembered the canoe had washed away. He asked was I aware how easy it was to get confused in the dark. "Yes, damn it," I said, "but I wasn't." He said we were too close to winter for a big raid out of Crown Point and reminded me this was not the first time I had reported seeing the enemy out to the west. The last time, nothing came of it. Besides, there had been no hostile activity for some time. Maybe, but there sure as hell was now. Hard to make a believer out of this man. With the fire built up, the room warmed and I felt drowsy. "Damn rangers see a skulker behind every tree," he said, "and now you are reporting a conspiracy when what you probably saw at Crown Point was them bringing in their winter supplies." His insistence riled me and when he again dismissed those out to the confluence as a hunting party, I snapped back at him. "The only thing they be huntin'," I said, "is scalps." The look on his face showed how much he wanted me to be wrong. "Hell, you know I'm right," I said. "I have survived here too long to mistake what I seen. Them at Scalp Point was coming, not goin', and if what I seen at the confluence was somethin' other than a palaver, you tell me what the hell it was." He said whether he believed me or not, it was his duty to separate the facts from the fancy.

An orderly returned with a British uniform for me to put on. The only clothes available. The officers and sergeants were arriving and not too long after I put on the uniform, Blanch came in, saw me, and laughed. "What'd you do, sign up? Is this why we're called out? To see Kuyler the lobsterback?" He laughed again and was about the only man I knew who'd use the lobsterback slur in a roomful of British. They didn't any of them say anything about it.

My too-long exposure to the weather had me sneezing and coughing. My body racked with the shakes, I had been wet and cold for so long, I knew I was going to be sick. An orderly gave me a sutler's blanket. Too thin, not near as good as a bearskin but better'n nothing. Sergeant Tom came in, gave a surprised look at my uniform but didn't say anything, nor laugh, neither. I asked him to get the dog something to eat, dry him off and get him up to a fire. "He saved my bacon, Tom. Treat him well." Tom scratched Blackie on the head. The dog looked at me searchingly, then followed Tom out.

Steele told the men what I had told him and what I surmised, and he said they were to talk it over, "As if it were true." The son-of-a-bitch still refused to believe me. Why did I risk my life to come down and warn him? Someone said the Indians, "Assuming they were out there," would have found my boat and gear. I spoke to Blanch. "The canoe I came down in was Mohawk," to which Steele replied, "The canoe which so conveniently kept on down the river." After all I had been through, the sneer in his words caused me to lurch toward him. Blanchard, as big and strong as he was, blocked me with his body, and without even looking at me and whilst speaking in a level voice to Steele, "If Kenny says they was Mohawk, they was Mohawk."

"Since it appears you are fully backing Mister Kuyler," Steele said to Blanch, "I shall, for prudence's sake and for now, take him at his word. This doesn't mean I believe what he has told us. It only means I am willing to consider it." Blanchard gave Steele a hard look and gave the same to me, for iffen I was intendin' to go again for Steele. I was, but I didn't.

The room filling now with officers, whale-oil lamps were lit, and with all the officers assembled, I told them more of what I had seen, then Blanch spoke about the seriousness of our Mohawks palavering with their Canadian cousins and with Hurons and Abenakis, both of which tribes were eternal foes of the Mohawks.

"The Mohawks bring us nothing but trouble," a British officer said. This was answered by grumbles of assent around the room. Those conniving Mohawks. It seemed to me premature to condemn the Mohawks. They had probably not gone over yet to the enemy and might not ever go, 'cepting maybe a few. Hell, and for all we knew, the Mohawks had maybe been laying a trap so's to kill the northerners and collect their hair. Whilst we were talking it over, the Hudson confluence might be littered with the corpses of scalped Indians.

Blanch assured the British how, even did some of the younger Mohawks go over to the French, the bulk of the tribe would still be allied with us. Blanch also pointed out the bigger reason for not condemning the Mohawks. The tribesmen were the only Indian allies we had and were crucial to our success, nay, our survival, at least until Blanchard's Rangers could hold their own in the woods. The British would be mighty foolish to do or say anything to turn the Mohawks against us. "You fellows forget," Blanch pointed out. "So far the Iroquois are the only ones doing any fightin' fer us. Bill Johnson has them raiding Scalp Point and all up along Corlaer." This was greeted with derision from the British. If the Mohawks were raiding Corlaer, what the hell were they doing west along the Hudson? Probably getting drunk with their supposed enemies, and after they sobered up, they'd come in and tell us how hard they was fighting fer us and show us scalps boughten off the northerners.

Blanch backed up what I said was the real danger with what I had seen. "The Mohawks isn't likely to go over to the French, least not in any numbers. But the thing is, and Kenny's right about this too, the French and their Canadian Indians wouldn't be looking to bring in the Mohawks less'n there was something bigger brewin' than just hittin' cabins. Something big like we ain't seen yet."

A British officer suggested the purpose of what I had seen might have been the Canadian Indians seeking to secure permission from the Mohawks to raid farther west, closer to Iroquoia than previously. The officer said how, with the white settlements encroaching on Mohawk territory, particularly their Kaydeross hunting grounds, and with the Mohawks not able to hit the settlers and still maintain peace with the English, they, the Mohawks, might not be averse to the northerners doing some raiding. This might have seemed plausible but Blanch was scathing in dismissing it. He conceded the Mohawks were not happy with the encroachments but said such permission could only be given by the entire tribe in grand council, or the entire league of tribes, certainly not by a small band of warriors. Further, for the Six Nations, as the Iroquois constituted themselves, to assent to such an arrangement would be a humiliation for making 'em look unable to take care of affairs around their home fires.

An officer said if the Mohawks were throwing in with the enemy, then goddamn it, it was time we wiped out Iroquoia. I sneered for thinking it would take a hell of a lot more men than what we had to put a dent in Iroquois power. The British groused about the fecklessness of our Iroquois allies. Steele allowed them to go on, frustrating Blanch, and me too, and with Blanch trying to explain to them and to some of the Americans, who should a knowed better, the difference between allies in Europe and in America.

In Europe, a king or prince could commit his military to one side or another in a war which maybe didn't concern his people and the men would obey, even did their officers order them to march into the mouths of cannons, which they often did. Europeans called it valor. The Indians called it stupidity. Indian warriors mostly went along with tribal decisions with regard to all things, even war, but the decision to fight or not was left to each man and there were always young bucks who'd defy tribal dictates for a chance for glory and spoils. Blanch explained the divisions roiling the Iroquois Confederacy, with some on our side, some gone off to Canada, most staying neutral. He further conceded the words of any Canadian Mohawks accompanying the northern Indians might carry weight with the local Mohawks, eager as they might be for war, but said it would mean little to the sachems.

An officer speculated the discovery of my canoe and gear in the morning might have spooked the Mohawks sufficiently for them to abandon thoughts of joining the northerners. "Indeed," Steele said, fixing me in a cold stare. "Our bumpkin may have just saved the entire damn colony." Then adding pointedly, "Unwittingly."

My least-favorite ensign, the cannon-rigger, demanded we go out at once, before the Indians could get away. Chastise them. The ensign was sufficiently stupid enough to head up the river in search of an unknown number of hostiles with a cannon mounted to the front of a goddamn whaleboat. Another redcoat officer repeated what had been said earlier. "Seems to me what Kuyler saw were Johnson's tame Mohawks skulking when they should have been raiding. Indians all look the same." I looked helplessly over at Blanch, who fastened his coldest, hardest stare on the officer. "Don't all of 'em look the same," Blanch said. "Nor smell the same, neither, and there ain't a man on this frontier knows better than Kenny what's a northern Indian and what's a Mohawk."

Steele then asked what he should have asked at the start, for me to go to the map on the wall, to better illustrate the situation. The map was a poor one, especially the way it portrayed the Indian trails out where I had been. An orderly held a candle up to the map and I, with quill and ink, began filling in the trails which led from the rivers down into the settlements. None of the men present, British nor American, were familiar with the country. A big mystery to them all. Blanch explained the importance of the warriors' trails as I drew 'em in and it was clear, for all the trails I was adding, how broad were the possibilities for the Indians. "Just give me a whack at them," the cannon-ensign said. "Catch them on the river and blast the hell out of them." The captain turned slowly toward the ensign. "Mister Upton," Steele said. "I am not going to commit my troops to chasing Indians without first ascertaining where they are and what they are intending."

A New Jersey captain spoke. "Could be the work of Blanchard's Rangers is making 'em think they has to get help from the Mohawks to keep themselves from gettin' destroyed when they come down, and iffen they don't get the help, they might go home or not come at all, if they ain't already here." Nobody believed this, or bothered refuting it.

"Maybe what the northern Indians are looking for," an officer said, "is permission from the Mohawks to go home through Iroquoia after they do their raiding, since we would have their way back to the lakes blocked off." Blanch said it was a long ways down the Mohawk and up the Saint Lawrence. "And they'd need the permission of all the Iroquois tribes, not just the Mohawks. They'd hafta bring the chiefs from all the tribes into a big council to talk 'er over." A colonial lieutenant spoke next. "Ain't a part of the New York militia still out there somewheres?" Steele sneered at the notion of militia accomplishing anything without British regulars to stiffen them. "Too many places fer'm to cover," Blanch said in defense of the militia, to which an officer said, "If they were any good."

Blanch repeated saying I had it pegged right, the Indians were planning something big, but exactly what it was, he nor nobody could say.

When he added as how the Indians might not decide until they got here, one young British officer scoffed. Surely the Indians would have decided on their objective before coming down. "Sonny," Blanch said, "you don't know nuthin' 'bout Indians. They be different from me and you, and from Frenchie too. Sometimes the only thing what saves us is some of the Indians goin' for one thing and others of 'em goin' for another and them arguing so much about it, they end up not doin' anything." Blanch said the only thing for sure, did a large force, or forces, come down, they wouldn't be hitting isolated cabins. They would aim big. Saratoga or Albany. "Or it might be they converge right here." He slapped his palm loud against the wall map. North Fort.

Blanch allowed the silence which followed to hang there, then he got back to business. "We can't assume the main party, if there be one, is out to the west. Ain't no good reason for 'em to be out there. With the run the northern Indians have of Saint Sacrement and South Bay, and with how goddamn blind we are to their movements, ceptin' for when they got their noses up to the walls of the fort or when they burn down a cabin and we get there too late to do anything 'cept bury the dead, they could bring as many men as they wanted right down the lakes and we wouldn't be the wiser 'til we woke up to 'em pounding down your gate." Blanch let another silence hang whilst he looked into the faces of the officers. "What we are up against," he said, "is a large force, or possibly two large forces intending to crush us between 'em. Even with as little as we've done so far to protect the settlers, it'll be plenty worse for 'em does your fort get taken. Make no mistake. The Indians is coming and we're in a hell of a fix."

More silence, an orderly re-lit some few of the lamps, which had gone out. "Assuming the veracity of Kuyler's report, which for now we must," Steele said to Blanch, "your men will have to go out at once. Tonight, to see what might be developing. Get down into the settlements to see are Kuyler's Indians down there and watch the rivers and as many of the trails as you can. Send men up the Hudson to the junction with the Sacandaga and up to Saint Sacrement and the lower Corlaer. Locate the Indians and get word to me at once." Steele was sure'n hell askin' a lot. With just fifteen men, Blanch would be stretched mighty thin. Steele asked Blanch did he have men he could trust for the work. Blanch said he trusted all his men. "Very good," Steele said. "Get them ready for action tonight."

Steele got behind his desk and ignoring the talk around him, he began writing. When he put aside quill and pen, he asked for a courier to go to Stillwater, to carry dispatches, to request reinforcements and to advise Colonel Hubbard to alert the countryside.

"And to get word to New England," Blanch said, "and to Bill Johnson. If any of the Mohawks is for goin' over, Johnson's the one who can persuade 'em otherwise, or warn the chiefs so they can put a stop to it." Steele looked up, another cold glare toward Blanch. In British thinking, Johnson was an upstart with more power and influence than what any colonial merited. And Bill was Irish born. "It is for Colonel Hubbard to alert Johnson," Steele said. "If he deems it necessary."

The ranger Blanchard chose to carry the message to Hubbard was John Robbins, known for his integrity and for his considerable ability to accomplish any task. Blanch asked Robbins what route he would take. Robbins pointed it out on the map. Blanch said, "It's not likely them Indians is south of us yet so you may not have a hard time of it." Robbins grinned, as if he wouldn't mind if some of the Indians got between him and where he was heading.

The captain repeated saying Blanch would have to watch all the overland trails from the Sacandaga and the Hudson, down into the settlements. "Two rivers and lots of trails," Blanch said. "Lots a possibilities." Steele told him to do the best he could. "Once them Indians get off the rivers and into the woods," I said, "we'll have the devil's own time finding 'em." Steele sneered. "If there be so many as you seem to think, you'll find them soon enough." Then and to Blanch, "Should you succeed, send word to me and follow them. To discern where they are headed, and as soon as I have solid information, by god, I'll get after them." This brought loud assents from the British. Steele said he'd need two rangers to serve as runners between Hubbard and him. "Won't leave me many," Blanch said. He would have liked to disagree more strongly. A captain of the Jersey militia offered his men to be used as runners. Steele said no. He wanted rangers.

The conference went on, no longer centered around the map board and devolving into blathering on the part of the officers. Blanch still had more to say and he had to keep raising his voice up over the jabber, to keep the officers on what it was they yet needed to hear. I edged up nearer to the fire. I was feeling the further effects of exhaustion and of the dousing I'd taken from the rain and from all the cold river water splashed into the canoe. Sickness and drowsiness drawing down on me, I was annoyed by so much useless talk and by the formality so strictly adhered to between officers and sergeants. A few good ideas from the sergeants got dismissed; bad ideas from officers were treated with more respect than what the ideas, or the officers, deserved. Steele said little, keeping any thoughts to himself. He only commented on what was getting said, good or bad. Most of it bad. Too many of the officers were for marching out at once and heading up the river without solid intelligence. Despite the enthusiasm of his younger officers, Steele had sense enough to not commit to going blindly out. I hoped the eager fools were not able to convince him otherwise. He didn't have men enough for it. I slipped out before the meeting broke up, to get some rest, certain it would be my last chance for a while.

Chapter XXI – River of Danger Continued

First thing for me, after the conference broke up, was to get to hell out of the lobsterback clothes I was wearing. I scrounged homespuns, pants and a shirt from the rangers and a pair of high-topped moccasins. Back at my hut and hunkered down by the fire, wrapped in a too-thin blanket, I worked on my rifle. If wet powder be not removed promptly, it rots the barrel. I needed my piece ready for the morning, so's to go with Blanch. He would be taking the rangers out and would need help. I slept some, until Blanch came in. "I'm powerful sorry," he said, "for Steele challenging you as harshly as he did." I said Steele had a duty to ask the right questions but said I was more disgusted now with how the British treated us than I'd ever been. "Well," Blanch said, and he was placating me. "Steele at least seems to be going about it in the right way. He's not gonna sit and wait for them Indians to come down, nor will he go blustering out before he gets an idea of what's out there." I asked was it caution or cowardice. Blanch said he reckoned it was a little bit of both.

Took another short sleep and awoke feeling even more poorly. Sniffling and sneezing. Hot coffee and a fire in the guard shack, an hour spent talking with the men and I prepared to go. Before first light, Blanch left the fort with ten men, me included, and the dog. Blanch was uneasy about having to post men all over the countryside where he could not watch over 'em. He is grouchy and hard to deal with when he gets this way. He first dispatched two men to go north, one to watch Wood Creek, the other to the portage trail to Saint Sacrement. "Good luck," Blanch said to the two men, "and for the love of Jesus, be careful." Easy to understand his bein' so worried. Either of the men, or both, might have been heading into plenty of Indians.

The others of us walked west along the north bank of the Hudson under clearing skies, the weather cold and blowy. Light snowflakes danced in the air, mixed with sunshine. Four miles out and not having seen sign of anything big and coming to where the river curled south into a horseshoe bend, Blanch posted a man. We then cut across the top of the shoe and regaining the river, we followed its wide sweep to the south and came north again, a fifteen-mile loop to the Sacandaga confluence. Blanch posted men as we went and when we got to where we kept stashed canoes, Blanch sent the remaining men across the river, to watch the trails down into the settlements, likely places for findin' Indians. Blanch told the men same as what he told the others. Soon as they seen redskins, they was to hightail for the fort. "Don' fight 'em less'n you has to and don't come lookin' to tell me 'bout it. Just get the hell in with word of 'em."

"If them northern Injuns have Mohawks joined up and guiding 'em," he said, "they'll know the trails as well as you. Don't move too fast and once you get settled, stay put and chances are they'll come to you. Keep your eyes open and your powder dry, and soon's you locate 'em and can get a fix on where they might be going, get back in." One of the men said with all the rain, most any sign would be washed out. Blanch agreed. "Have a look anyway," he said. I was not alone in thinking how poor were their chances. Any of 'em what found Indians might die for it and did none of us find 'em, we might all die. Blanch told them to watch three days and if they didn't see anything, they were to get back in.

The man tasked with watching the trail leading in from Johnson's holdings, which was thirty miles southeast of the Sacandaga confluence with the Hudson, said, "It be a long way from anywhere." Blanch agreed. The man would be well out from the others of us. Blanch told the scout he was more likely to find Mohawks than northerners. "If any Mohawks is coming," Blanch said, "it's the way they'll come. They'll sneak past Johnson's place at night and once they get rendezvoused with the others, it mighten be you can follow 'em, see are they headed for the fort or down into the towns, and though they be our Mohawks, don' s'pect 'em to be friendly."

Blanch, me and the dog headed up toward the confluence of the East and West Branches and got there late the next day for a close-in look at the Indian encampment which I had snuck away from. Along the way, we seen plenty of sign. Indians in canoes had come ashore often and hadn't stayed long. "Looking for you," Blanch said. He said they had probably been close behind the entire time I was gettin' away from 'em. And what else he said, the Indians must a figured I wouldn't be stupid enough to just keep on down the river and would instead get off into the woods. Blanch laughed, said stupid or not, my staying on the river was probably what saved my life. We got to the confluence and poked around some. Sure as hell there'd been a lot of Indians. My canoe and gear were gone.

The next morning, we started back down the Hudson. We got to a place where we could watch not only the river but some of the trails which led south. We camped in thick brush. Blanchard prowled, I tried to sleep, but with how poorly I felt, I tossed fitfully. When he got back, he told me he hadn't seen much, just some old sign. We sat the rest of the day in watchful anticipation. Blanch did most of the watching. All through a cold day and into a night with a blanket and no fire, I got to hacking and sneezing and couldn't stop. "Look," Blanch finally said, exasperated. "With the shape you're in, you ain't worth two dead flies to me. I want you out of here afore dawn." That was still three or four hours away. "Any Injuns come by, you'll sure as hell give us away. I got me enough sleep. Get goin' and be as far down the river as you can afore daylight." I was so damn sick, I didn't know could I make it in. My head was hot and I got dizzy did I move too fast. I stumbled around for hours like a city boy. Lost my way a time or two, gave up and spent the rest of the night huddled over a small fire under my blanket, sick enough to risk Indians smelling my smoke.

Early the next morning I resumed my stumbling around. Got in at dusk, about at the end of my strength. I made a report to the captain, told him what we found, nothing, and showed him on the map where Blanch had posted the men. Steele used pins to indicate the locations. I showed him where our man was situated to watch for Mohawks. "Blanch," I said, "don't 'spect we'll have trouble with the Mohawks but figures the best way of findin' the northerners is for the Mohawks to lead us to 'em. He figures you're who they be after and thinks they might feint toward Schenectady or Saratoga as a way of drawing you out." Steele's face, when I said this, showed fear. Then came denial and he asked how many Indians did we actually see. "None we laid eyes on, damn it, but if they's out there, we'll be seein' plenty, soon enough." Steele didn't say much, 'cept to tell me none of the other scouts had come in so it was likely they hadn't seen anything either. He scribbled another message to the colonel and ordered me to bed, under the care of the fort surgeon. I did as he said, and mad I was for him mistrusting the information we was risking our lives for.

The sawbones took a liking to me. A stern old Scotsman. Tall, stiff, and very straight standing. His most prominent features, besides his gruff nature, were bushy eyebrows and thick gray hair. Doc believed the occasional dram of whiskey good for the body. I agreed when he offered me a drink. So did Tom O'Brien agree, when he came to see me late of an afternoon. Tom, bless him, sneaked in a bottle of West Indies rum under his coat. By next afternoon, when Tom came again and with me having finished off the bottle, I was more numb than sick. Doc got mad for my abusing the privilege. He was stern, not prone to bending. "Doc," I said, unintentionally getting myself in deeper, "it was your idea, and surely a good one. The rum worked wonders. I feel much better." He saw no humor in it, his scathing look saying he did not much care what I thought. I tried to soothe him but anything I said just seemed to make him madder. He gave Tom and me stern tongue-lashings. Tom retreated and did not come back. Another day and I was up and around though I was still coughing and wheezing. Should have stayed in bed but had to get away from the cranky old sawbones.

****

The tension in the fort was growing each hour. The men were kept ready to march out on just a few minutes' notice and with everybody speculating and arguing where the blow would fall and wondering what might have happened to our scouts. None had got back in, 'cept me and Robbins, he coming in from Stillwater with dispatches from Colonel Hubbard. The woods stayed silent. More days with no news and with nobody in or out of the fort, no word from the towns or settlements. We were an island in the sea, cut off from the outside world. The entire New York Colony might a been on fire and we who were to protect it would have been the last to know.

The militia and even some British began mocking me for the bother I was causing. I had aroused the entire colony and for what? The men were convinced the hostiles would have shown themselves by now, and so thought what I reported was something conjured out of fear. Those who believed me, and there were not many, said the Indians would hit one of the big towns whilst we sat and did nothing.

My sickness took a turn for the better but I was not yet ready for active work. Blanch must have desperately needed relief. "Think he's still alive?" someone said, and it was what we was all thinking. He had been out a long time. Over the next couple days, all our scouts got in 'cept the boss and the ranger posted up to the Drowned Lands. The scouts reported Indians but no sign of anything big. Volunteers from the colonial ranks were formed to help our depleted, exhausted ranger force in scouting. The colonials only watched in close to the fort. The grumbling grew louder with men saying we should split into detachments and go to the relief of the towns; others said it was all a useless bother.

****

I was in the small shed which John Robbins, Blanch and me called home. I was on my stump seat, writing at my makeshift desk, a board set between two barrels, and I heard the evening gun. Wait a little bit longer and I could go out. I was going looking for Blanch and would leave after dark so's not to be seen, either from outside or from within. Steele was restricting our patrolling, we couldn't hardly do nothing without his approval, and I couldn't leave Blanch out any longer on the orders of some damn Britisher.

Got started half an hour after full dark. In my pocket was a forged pass to show the militia at the sally port but just when I got there, they were opening the door and in come Blanch. I gripped one of his hands with both of mine, so glad was I to see him. "Just on my way out to check on you, pard," I said. He was silent, grim. I followed him back to our hut. In the dim light I seen his face. Haggard. His body sagging, voice hoarse. Too exhausted to say much but the haunted look in his eyes said it for him. "Found 'em, eh?" I said. Blanch, warming himself by the fire, nodded slightly. I asked had the Indians hit anywhere yet. Blanch said he didn't know. Robbins had just brewed some tea and gave his cup to Blanch. Joe drank gratefully and closed his eyes for a moment. When he opened 'em, what I seen was sorrow for all the suffering which lay ahead. He took a few more sips and asked about the scout up at Anne. We told him the scout had not got back, which seemed to confirm something in Blanch's mind. He asked about the man sent up to Saint Sacrement. That man had got in. "Just in time," Blanch said. We waited for what he meant by this. He didn't say and instead, he went to report to Steele. I and Robbins followed along.

Blanch told Steele how he had stayed in the brush for a day and a night after I had departed and hadn't seen anything. Said he couldn't stop worrying the whole time about the scouts sent to watch Wood Creek and Saint Sacrement. Convinced the bigger threat was what was coming down the lakes, not what might a been brewing out to the west, Blanch had crossed over to the north side of the river and walked almost to the ruins of Anne. He saw no sign of Indians having come down through the Drowned Lands. I asked about Saint Sacrement. Silence from Joe and the look on his face told us there were Indians.

Lots of 'em. Steele knew better than to ask Blanch had he seen 'em or only seen sign. Steele asked how many. "Three hundred French and Indians," Blanch said, "including French regulars." What else Blanch said, the Indians had come down between the time he went up to the Drowned Lands and the time he came back down. Two days ago. The room got quiet. "They cut west," Blanch said, "and stayed above the river, on the trails up there." Blanch traced on the map the route the Indians had taken and said they hadn't done much to cover their sign. As if they had no worries. "Walked away from your fort," he said. Steele pondered the Indians not having come for him. "Think they will?" he said. Rare for him to ask a colonial's opinion. "They ain't much for hittin' forts," Blanch said. "Especially forts what has cannons. More likely they'll try to draw you out from behind your walls, see can they catch you in an ambush."

A knock on the door, an orderly toting a bowl of stew and a bottle of wine. Blanch ate nor drank little. Too tired. He looked some beat. His sandy hair stuck out from under his leather sailor's cap in wet, stringy lines. I looked over at Steele. The skinny man with long nose sticking so far in front of his face stared stonily into the fire. Worry etched across his forehead. "Reckon the bush-lopers and their Indians is moving fast," I said, trying to draw the captain out. "By now they could be in position to raid most anywhere in New York Colony, even south of Albany."

Steele, ignoring me, scratched out a message and gave it to Robbins to deliver to Colonel Hubbard. Blanch finished reporting and went off for some sleep. Militia patrols were put out close around the fort. I went to position them, then came in and slept. At dawn, I went out again. The woods woke up quiet. Too quiet. Even the blue jays. Checked the watch-posts, there'd been no incidents through the night.

Spent the next few days with the patrols, an anxious time for us not knowing when or where the Indians would strike. Captain Steele, despite prodding from his officers, refused to budge without orders from higher-ups. One of our patrols reported a hundred Indians had been in close to the fort. Intending something or just wanting us to over-think what they were up to? No telling. Then, and during a midnight watch, Robbins came tippy-toeing in with dispatches from the colonel, and with Robbin's arrival, the rumors swept through the fort. It was something to hear. One rumor said five-hundred Indians was on their way to surround us. The militia was certain of the truth of this and could do naught but talk about the need to get to hell out before all those Indians arrived. Robbins, preparing to go down again to Stillwater, laughed and said he'd have to be a pretty good spook to get past so many of 'em. He then turned serious, unusual for him, and said when he was in the woods now, he had a feeling there were plenty of Indians out there with him. Me and Blanch felt it too, and we were wondering why the Indians hadn't hit anything yet. At least so far as we knew. "Them devils," Blanch said, "cain't stay down here forever without their provisions running out." We agreed. Whatever the Indians were intending, they'd have to do it soon. "If the Mohawks is still on our side," Blanch said, "and iffen they can work something out with their brother Mohawks so they don' have to fight agin one another, they'll maybe have a whack at the northerners." How I seen it, the Indians already had us in a fix. If we didn't get out after 'em, they'd hit one or more of our big towns. And if we did go, they'd swarm us soon as we left the fort.

Our scouts reported more sign than usual around the fort so the Indians were watching for our next move, whatever it be. We pulled our patrols in closer. We kept 'em moving and didn't leave 'em out too long. Whenever we reported to Steele, he didn't react much, which had become his way. No one knew what he was thinking or what he might do. He had his orders and would follow 'em, or had not received orders and would do nothing without them. Hardly anybody left the fort. Even walking up the hill to the blockhouse was dangerous.

The rumors said Colonel Hubbard's dispatches contained strong reprimands for Steele. Hubbard was livid for us reporting so many Indians and Steele not having done anything about it. Hubbard was heedless of the facts. Or the numbers! And worse!

Finally, Robbins came in and told us the New York militia, in from Oswego, was on the way up. Hubbard was coming too, with his red-coats. Steele's orders were to get out after the Indians as soon as the militia arrived. Find the Indians and block their withdrawal until Hubbard could get up with his force. The colonel did not believe the large number of Indians reported and would disprove the notion, galling to the British, of a single Indian worth two or three redcoats in the woods. Hubbard was convinced the Indians would withdraw as soon as they seen he was coming and he was determined to punish them for their incursion, as bloodless as it had so far been.

****

The militia came in, a hundred men. With the way they stumbled out of the woods and into the fort, we were grateful they made it without getting annihilated. A few of us were standing by the gate as the mostly youngish lads arrived. Sergeant Tom shook his head for the sloppiness of their formations. Robbins at least saw some humor in it. "With them steppin' out to Oswego and back agin," he said, "you'd a thunk they'd at least knowed how ta march." To Oswego and back again for nothing.

That same day, whaleboats came with more reinforcements, forty redcoats and more militia, which brought us up to two hundred and fifty men. What else they brought was further orders from Hubbard. The towns and settlements had been reinforced; the Indians, thought to be somewhere to the west or south of us, could do naught but withdraw and their only routes were Saint Sacrement or the Drowned Lands. Either way, they must come east, toward us. They had been thwarted in whatever mischief they had been intending and now it was us who would strike. The newly arrived redcoats and militia were to make up the bulk of our force. Our rangers were to find the enemy so Steele could engage and wipe them out. The fort was spurred to action, the officers were ecstatic and shouted encouragements to the men.

"We are going after hostiles, by thunder!"

"We'll find them and give them a whacking!"

None was more eager than Sergeant Tom. He liked action but he understood better than his officers how it might be we were giving the Indians what they wanted. Then Tom got word he would not be going with us. He was livid. I think Steele had spitefully disallowed Tom on account of Tom's actions at the blockhouse fight, when he saved lives by disobeying orders and putting men behind trees and rocks. Steele was still angry for the rebuke Hubbard had given him when he tried to have Tom court martialed. I didn't say anything to Tom, I just stayed away from him, he was so mad. Blanch said it was going to be a fiasco but he too felt we must do something.

Some colonials deserted during the night and come the dawn, we left fifty men at the fort and marched out, two-hundred strong, slightly less than what we figured the Indians had, not accounting for any Mohawks which might have joined up with them. We went west along the north shore of the Hudson. Rangers prowled ahead on both banks. Small parties of Indians were about. They showed themselves, always at a distance. Blanch warned Steele about the danger to stragglers but we moved so slowly, there wasn't much straggling.

It was hard going, there were short stretches of road around the fort, trails through thick woods farther out, and mostly woods without trails. There was scant sign of hostiles, men were asking what the hell we would do when we reached the Sacandaga. Continue up one river or the other or go south along the trails. I figured Steele would turn around and go home as soon as he'd made enough of a show of lookin' for Indians. One ranger said Steele might take us all the way to the Hudson confluence and sit us there so the Indians could slip around and get on toward home. Uh-huh. And maybe hit our undermanned fort whilst going by.

The next day when we halted, we was still on the Hudson, six miles from the Sacandaga. One more day would get us there. We felled trees to form three squares, two facing the river, one behind. We covered the fronts with brush. Inside the squares we built crude bark lean-tos and covered the whole thing as best we could with brush. An ambush not even a blind Indian could miss. Had to laugh when I overheard a British officer, "All we need is for the rat to stick his nose in the trap."

With nothing big having got hit to the south of us and with scant sign of Indians down there, so far as we knew, the British were more certain the Indians were somewhere to the west. There was no good reason for 'em to be out there but the British could not be convinced otherwise. They said it was the direction the Indians had fled when they seen us coming and now we had 'em backed up against Iroquoia.

The British said with no place for the Indians to run, they were sure to get bloodied, either by us or by the Mohawks, or maybe in a vise between us. The British said we should push the northern Indians until they bumped into the Mohawks, then the two sides could rip into each other whilst we stood aside. The British weren't concerned with the possibility the two sides might join up and all come against us.

The way Blanch saw it, Steele had got a wildcat by the tail. Blanch said the Indians' strategy was always the same. Get the white men thinking they had the Indians in a box when the whole time it was the white men who was in there. Blanchard kept scouts out, watching all sides. Men grumbled it was all a waste of time, some was still jeering me for it being my fault. Whenever me and the dog came in or out from scouting, the men asked with ill-humor was I gonna tell Steele more lies about Injuns so's we could all stay in the rain. I seethed but said nothing. What we were doing was not a waste of time. Them

Indians was out there and were going to hit something. Maybe they'd attack the undermanned fort and once it was taken and us with no-where to run, they'd come for us. Or they'd hit one of the bigger towns whilst we were out looking. I couldn't stop worrying about Saratoga.

During the night a light snow fell, and in the morning and with the men speculating our next move, a runner came up along the river. He said Colonel Hubbard had arrived at the Great Carry with a flotilla of bateaux and whaleboats, four companies of militia, one of regulars. Hubbard and Steele each had about the same number of men; each, alone, had nearly as many as did the Indians.

Hubbard was portaging his boats around the falls of the Hudson and would soon be up with us but as the day wore on and with no further word from him, our men started grumbling. They said Hubbard was coming upriver in a grand procession; officers in their finest and with flags flying, drums beating, fifes tootin', the way it was done in Europe. The pageantry of war, 'cept this wasn't Europe and wasn't no pageant.

Meantime, the hostiles had vanished. Where before there had been plenty of sign and occasional sightings, now there was none. Not even footprints in fresh snow. Blanch and me figured the Indians wouldn't allow our two forces to get joined up. They'd hit both of us, one after the other, and from the abrupt lack of sign around us, it looked as if it would be Hubbard first, then us. Blanch told Steele a warning should be taken to Hubbard. "The colonel," Steele said, "knows his chances." As if he didn't care if the colonel got into trouble. We went out for another look. A half day's prowl provided no answers. Two more cold, wet days in camp with failing rations, the men miserable from sleeping on the frozen ground and bitching for all the tents and food they figured Hubbard had. Many of our less-hardy men took sick.

Just before dark of the second day, a Jersey Blue came up from Hubbard and reported the colonel's flotilla had got around the falls and had so far had no contact with the savages nor seen much sign, not surprising, considering none of his scouts were rangers. He was camped three miles below us, on the river. Word went 'round the squares, the men cheered. Food and reinforcements were at hand. The Indians, our men said, would not dare hit us once our forces were com-bined. The colonel would come up in the morning, the Indians would run for home, our futile, dangerous endeavor would be concluded and we would all be heroes for having chased off the savages. Such was the change of mood in what had been an otherwise cheerless camp.

We waited one more cold night, lightened by the expectation of succor and the lack of trouble so far. "The Indians probably turned tail and ran soon's they saw us out," one New York volunteer said cheerfully to Blanch, and thinking Blanch would just as cheerfully agree. Instead, Blanchard's temper flared wickedly. He got on the man for uttering the careless remark. "We ain't outta this yet, you young fool," he said. "Not by a damn long shot." He got more worried with each passing hour. The night was cold, sleep impossible. We were called out early. Before daybreak and before what the men thought necessary on such a blustery morning. The wind was strong out of the north. Our men were posted around the squares, arms at readiness, and as the sun came up, we heard a few shots, faint in the distance, then an eruption of noise; volleys followed by a sustained shooting, a battle. For two hours we heard it, furious at times, slackening, then resuming again. Steele, meantime, didn't say hardly anything. He just stared straight ahead, into the woods and across the river. Blanch kept wanting to send out men, to see what the hell was going on. Steele refused. Our men were so taken with the cold, it was doubtful they could have shot straight did anything happen. Breakfast was dried corn. The men had been anticipating a cooked breakfast when Hubbard arrived, now we didn't know what to expect, the distant sounds ominous as we waited.

The shooting died out mid-morning, the silent forest giving up no secrets. Around noon a militiaman come runnin' up along the side of the river, hollering bloody hell. We watched him from behind our log barriers; lucky we didn't shoot the fool. He stumbled, fell, got up, and when he stumbled again, some of our men ran down, grabbed him and brought him in. With his stammering, it was hard to make out what he was saying. Blanch had to slap his face to startle him to his senses. He reeled from the blow but it settled him enough so we could understand him. "We been hit," he said. "Gettin' wiped out." He became incoherent again and this time Blanch belted him. The stinging sound of the open-handed smack to the face had me wincing in the cold. The man repeated what he'd said, about getting wiped out.

"Jesus Christ!" Blanch said, and to the closest ranger, "Get Steele. Hurry!" Steele was already there, having just come up, his sword in one hand, flintlock pistol in the other. He asked the red-faced man what happened. "First thing this morning, sir." The man saluted, a raggedy attempt at soldiering. His whole body shaking with the fear

269

and the cold. "Just as we was putting the boats in, Injuns and French on t'other side of the river started shooting. Peppering our boys, they wuz. Didn't hit so many of us but they had us pinned. The colonel ordered the men who was already in the boats, two companies of Yorker militia and some British, to go across and get 'em." A trap. Blanch knew the place where Hubbard had camped for the night and already had it figured out. "Aye," the man said. "Our lads wuz game." Tears filled his eyes, ran down his cheeks, he was unable to continue. "Well, damn it, man," Steele said. "Out with it! And quit blubbering, you colonial bastard!" The man got ahold of himself. "Our boatmen was pulling hard on their oars, the soldiers in the boats was hunkered down and was answerin' the Indian war cries with their own oaths and with tellin' what they was goin' to do once they got over. Then came a barrage from our side of the water."

Blanch asked, "The north bank? The man said, "Aye. They was on the same side of the river as us, upriver and close, along a point jutting out, and from where they could give our men in the boats a close-up broadside, same as they gave to us what was still on the shore." The man's eyes grew big and round, he repeated himself, as if still not believing it. "They wuz on the same shore and laying a barrage on us and with how they was hidden, we had nothin' to shoot at 'ceptin puffs of smoke, and the colonel wouldn't let us get into cover." The man's eyes darted from one to the others of us. "We was tryin' to form up and the whole time, they was firing. Our men was falling as they was gettin' into line. Finally got men enough to advance with bayonets and when we got to the woods, the Indians was gone."

"Meantime, our boats got in close to the south shore but not before catching holy hell from all them Indians hidden over there. Some of our boats turned around, some kept going and got to the other side and whilst the men was getting out of the boats, more'n a hundred Indians come chargin' out of the woods a whoopin' and shakin' their tommy-hawks. Put our men into a panic, and with no place to run and with the Indians all over 'em, some of ours was surrendering and whilst they was at it, the Indians was tying 'em up and dragging 'em away. The colonel sent me and some others to bring you fellows down. Got chased damn near the entire way. Reckon none of the others made it. You got to come quick, it be just a few miles." He was shaking so hard, I thought he might collapse. "Quick, hell," Blanch said. "Quick is what the Indians want and it's how come they let you get through

270

to us. To get us running down there so they can hit us too." He spoke to Steele. "Somewheres between us and Hubbard, the Injuns is sittin' in ambush. They'll wipe out Hubbard first, then us. Sounds like they got him, now it be our turn. Well, I ain't surprised. Damn it all to hell!" His voice so harsh it startled me. "Them Indians is going to hit us next, to do to us what they done to Hubbard." Then, and to me, "Ken, take two rangers and get down there. Tell Hubbard it ain't wise for him to go chasin' after the Indians until we get joined up. Send back word of the situation, iffen you can."

I and my rangers was gone at once. We went fast yet heedful, and instead of staying back from the river, away from where the Indians was most likely to have set their ambush, we went right into it. How I figured it from knowing Indians, once they had an ambush prepared, they wouldn't expose it for three scalps. The woods, murky and silent, didn't fool us into thinking we wasn't walking through hundreds of Indians but they let us pass.

We got down to where Hubbard was and seen the carnage on both shores, the signs of disaster everywhere. Five or six beached whale-boats on the south shore and with so many sprawled bodies over there, the entire force sent across looked to have got wiped out. Plenty of dead on the north shore too. The sound of the river rushing by mingled with the sounds from the other side. Indian whoops, screams and pleas of terrified white men getting scalped. Scattered shots. Most of the Indians were back in the trees, some was in the open, gathering scalps along the shore and ignoring the shots our men was taking at 'em. I raised up Nitpicker, took aim on an Indian, squeezed my trigger and the Indian fell. The others scampered back into the woods.

I reported in to Hubbard, told him what Blanch said about not goin' after the Indians, then there wasn't anything much for us rangers to do 'cept organize a perimeter, which should have already been done but wasn't, and wait for Steele. Meantime the soldiers was tending to the wounded. They told us Hubbard had fought smartly and bravely, once he got into his fix. He and his officers held his sorely pressed men together and returned fire with at least some effect. The boatmen began on their own to pick up guns from the dead and wounded. This staved off an even worse bloodying.

The way we put it all together, it became clear not too many Indians had shown themselves on the south shore. The bait, to split the English forces and draw our boys onto the water. Hubbard hadn't known most of the foe was right there with him on the north side, hidden upstream. They didn't start firing until our boys were more than halfway across and with some of the boats keeping on and others trying to turn around and all of 'em gettin' in the way of the others, it was easy shootin' for the savages.

Two hours after we got there, a barrage of gunfire came from up-river. Steele was engaging the enemy, and had Blanch and the rangers failed to keep him from stumbling into the ambush once he got going? It seemed so, and when I offered to lead a detachment, to try to hit the Indians unawares, and with the officers for it too, Hubbard refused. He told his officers to prepare to get attacked. "It won't be our turn again," one of 'em said bitterly, "until the Indians are done with Steele." We got behind the barricade where Hubbard's men had spent the night. The firing stopped, there hadn't been much following the initial barrage, and we waited, the woods deathly silent around us.

A runner came in, exultant. Steele had driven off the Indians. "Smashed 'em!" The man shook his fist, oblivious to the death and carnage around him. He said how the sight of Steele's redcoats lined up with gleaming bayonets had put the fear of Hell into the Indians.

When Steele came marching proudly in, Hubbard reprimanded him harshly in front of the men, Hubbard already trying to shift the blame for his own defeat onto his subordinate. Hubbard said if Steele had come back down the river first thing, instead of cowering behind his barricade whilst he, Hubbard, was getting hit, their combined force could have thrashed the Indians. This greatly agitated Steele, who was reveling in what he considered his finest moment.

Blanch told me Steele's driving off the Indians wasn't so big a deal as what the captain was saying. Said it had been nearly bloodless despite all the noise. The Indians had shown few enough of themselves to entice our men into chasing them. Steele might have gone for it had not Blanch convinced him otherwise. Robbins asked did Steele refrain from going after the Indians on Blanch's say so or did Steele not have the guts for it. Blanch gave Robbins a look; Robbins laughed. The feeling amongst the men now was mostly relief. With our forces combined and with the Indians having got scalps and plunder, the men figured the Indians would go home. One of the militia officers told his men the Indians was already well gone. Us rangers knew better what was the truth of our situation. The Indians would try again to draw us into something before they departed.

Steele was sulking for his victory having been denigrated. Hubbard's aspersions had the normally reticent captain demanding we go after the Indians. The officers was clamoring for it too. Blanch said to us, "Reckon we'll give them Indians what they want." Steele was adamant the Indians had fled in terror when they seen the gleam of British bayonets advancing on them. An officer said he had heard the terror in the Indians' shrieks as they fled. We figured what the officer heard was Indians trying not to laugh for pretendin' to be scairt. Robbins thought so too. Blanch told the commanders what the Indians would do next. Even with our forces combined and with the Indians already having bloodied us, they'd try to draw us away from the river and into the woods, where our superior numbers would avail us naught. Blanch said the best thing now was to let the Indians go home. It was galling but they'd whupped on us once and did we go after 'em, they'd do it again. The indignation of the British made it plain Blanch had little chance of convincing them; still, he tried. He said our duty was to protect the settlements, and if none of the big towns had got hit, which was how it looked, and with the Mohawks not having joined up with the northerners, for there were no Mohawks amongst the dead, we had succeeded. "Our purpose," Hubbard replied coldly, "is to win a war." The British cheered.

Meantime, we did what we could for the hurt men and gathered our dead. Bodies were floating the river, hung up on rocks and logs. Many had already got washed away on the current. The bodies we brought in were mostly scalped and mutilated. Ears and eyeballs, fingers, even entire hands, were missing. We had lost a fearful amount of men and were sorely affected for knowing not all those sent across the river had died. Many had got taken and Hubbard was determined to get them back.

The men commenced scrounging food and fresh powder. Most of the supplies had got spilled into the river with the shooting and with the bateaux overturning and the men scrambling for cover. The boats which had gone to the other shore had obligingly carried supplies over to the Indians, who took what they could of the kegs and boxes, the rest they smashed and dumped into the river.

On the south shore, and as we started getting men over, the carnage was grim, nearly a full company wiped out, and with half as many taken away. The bateaux-men had suffered hard losses, first from getting fired upon whilst crossing, then whilst picking up weapons and getting into the fight.

One Albany lad, a boatman with the ferrying operation, told of militia surrendering to the few French regulars present. The French promised to protect our men from the Indians and after our men gave over their guns, the French betrayed them. "Who did the militia think they was surrendering to," I said, sneering. "The Dutch?" The lad said, "Our own men tried to get me to give up but I run to the woods where others of ours had got dug in and I loaded for 'em. The few of us who got back across the river is the only survivors from all those who went over."

Robbins and me and two rangers made a scout in the direction the Indians had gone. We quickly determined the Indians were heading north, their trail easy enough to follow. Too easy. They were headed overland to Saint Sacrement, where their boats was stashed but we didn't believe they were going for their boats. Not yet.

We returned to a most melancholy bivouac. Fires blazed, the men sulked in their squares and huts. Beaten in spirit and angry for all of what had been done to 'em and for the Indians having got away.

Our combined troops spent the rest of the day and the night to arms. The Indians, up close and unseen in the dark, whooped to draw us out. We heard taunts in French-accented English. By the next morning, the colonel and Captain Steele had organized a pursuit. A half company would be left back to protect the wounded, the rest would go after the Indians. Blanch told Hubbard the Indians had already had plenty of time to get themselves gone. If they were still around, which he was certain they would be, it meant they were hankering for another fight. Blanch might as well have saved himself from saying it. The officers and men were angry for having got whipped and were determined to put things right. This the Indians were counting on.

We rangers ate salted pork and drank coffee, scrounged from the boats and hastily cooked. We then got around Blanch whilst he gave a short talk. "Men, you all know what's waitin' fer us out there. Still, I reckon if we pay attention and do this thing right, we can give back to the Indians some of what they gave us, and we can save some of the men what got taken. God help them, and us, if youse do not pay strict attention."

The colonel ordered the men who were staying behind to bury our dead. But without shovels and with the ground froze, he changed his mind and ordered the dead and wounded to be loaded onto the boats and taken back to the fort. When it was pointed out to him the danger of sending boats down the river lightly-guarded, he ordered the men to build another funeral pyre.

We commenced pursuit. The way led through thick forest. Blanchard kept us rangers moving slow, wary of ambush. We passed where the Indians had camped the night before, a grove of pines in a ravine. Some militia broke ranks and got into the camp to see was there any plunder.

Blanch sent me back to tell Hubbard it was plain we were moving faster than the Indians and would soon be up with them. This was meant as a caution to go more slowly but its effect on Hubbard was opposite to what was intended. "Faster!" Hubbard said, and on he went, followed by the captain and the men. Charging through the woods along the plainly marked route of the retreating Indians. Over hills and through swamps and with the British officers exhorting the rangers to stay in front. Blanch bade us ignore the orders and he kept us to our own pace despite the soldiers rushing by and cussing us for not getting out front where they said we belonged. Another hour and all control over the pursuit was lost. A dangerous situation developing. Plain it was the Indians was preparing something with how their main force stayed just ahead yet close enough to make us think we was about up on 'em. They had sniping parties on our flanks which drove us back in whenever we leaked out of what was looking like a box. Herding us, sure as hell. Hubbard called a halt, to regroup his men. Blanch and me caught up. Hubbard was sitting on a downed log, giving orders, wiping sweat from his brow, his wig askew, his three-cornered hat in his hand. Blanch barged in, broke up the polite conversation. He said we could yet punish the Indians but not by going in disorder. Our advance needed to be better thought out. Hubbard insisted the Indians' fleeing was proof of just how scared they were. Abject panic, he called it. "Somewhere up ahead," Blanch said, "them Injuns is gonna make a stand." His voice sounded from the depths of exhaustion and for him knowing he was wasting his time. "Precisely what I intend them to do, Mister Blanchard," Hubbard said. Blanch looked Hubbard in the eye. Hard. A look of disgust. "They are gonna beat up on you again. You are taking us into a trap." The colonel, same as his officers, could think only of recovering men, and so clearly, honor.

Another hour and we was still close to getting up with the Indians. We heard plainly the screams of those of our men who were getting

Francis J. Smith

taken along. A loud whoop followed by the terrified cry of a soldier, the men induced to scream, to goad us on faster. Hard it was to see Indians in the thick brush but there were more of 'em along our flanks now than what there'd been and yet our men was mostly shooting at shadows. Bullets and arrows knocked down branches, thwacked into trees. Musket balls hum like angry bees. The more angry they whiz, the nearer they be.

The fighting got closer up, the Indians jumped lone men and found out British infantry was goddamn good with cold steel. Our colonials did not fare as well. Knife and gun-butt proved inferior against nimble-footed foes wielding tomahawks. I seen plenty of our men go down. The sneaking enemy grabbed any of us which got separated, the screams of the men caught thusly were most awful to hear. Some of ours, again too quick to surrender, paid dearly for their cowardice.

I seen an Indian rise up in the face of a colonial soldier and cleave his head with a tomahawk. Before I could get the Indian in my sights, he leaned down and brazen almost beyond belief, he took the man's scalp, shook it at us, whooped and run off. A soldier asked how the hell did the Indian get so close without being seen.

****

We got up to a skirmish, the firing abated, the Indians fled. Dead Americans lay in the snow. At another place, it was British regulars with bayonets dripping red and with Indian corpses around them. Farther along, Robbins got locked up with a tall, buckskin-clad Indian. Robbins was getting the better of it, I was trying to get in a whack with my hatchet. They whirled away from me, the redskin broke and run off. "Why the hell'd you let him get away?" Robbins screamed. "Too goddamn fast, pard," I said, and we got back in pursuit. The colonel and his officers, certain we was closing in on the main party of Indians and would soon have them, demanded all ahead faster. The chase continued with our troops refracturing into smaller groups, out of breath and not able to keep up.

Misfires were frequent, our powder of poor quality and wet, still we pushed forward. The firing was heavier now along both flanks. The Indians, still mostly unseen, had us on three sides. Blanch knew what the Indians were intending and having got our rangers back out front and when we got atop a wooded ridge with a creek down at the bottom on the other side, he stopped us. He spread us out along the ridge and we began stopping the men as they came up. We put them behind trees and rocks and told them to stay hidden. One of the men, hearing the screams for help from our captured men on the other side of the creek, asked wasn't we going to do anything for them. Blanch said no. Any men out there would have to get themselves back as best they could. The Indians' firing slackened then stopped. One of the militia said the fighting was done. Blanch said not by a longshot and he dispatched rangers to locate Hubbard and Steele, both of whom were somewhere behind us. Our men were saying we had to pull back afore we got surrounded. Blanch said we was already surrounded.

Up came a British lieutenant named Clark. He asked who was in command of us. We said Blanch was. Clark told Blanch he was taking charge and plainly misreading our situation, Clark told Blanch to pre-pare his rangers for leading the men across the creek. Blanch told him we was staying where we was. Clark reminded Blanch he, Clark, was now in command. Blanch said crossing the creek would get us wiped out. Clark said he'd be damned if he'd let fleeing Indians get away. Blanch cursed him and to the men, "Don't nobody listen to the fool. Stay here! Don't goddamn show yourselves and don't shoot less you got something to shoot at." With Blanch telling the men one thing and Clark telling 'em another, some of the men got lined up, some didn't.

The lieutenant, with two lines of men and with his sword raised, talked about duty, honor and the king, all the things which was going to get 'em killed. Blanch interrupted the lieutenant, loud enough for some, at least, of the men, to hear him. "I can tell you without sending men over there to die," Blanch said. "Sure in hell the Indians are there in numbers. Waitin' for just what you be orderin'. They'll blast us when we try to get across and when we turn around and try to come back, others of 'em will be up here on the hill, right where we're standing now. We'll be fish in a barrel and all those men who aren't up yet, as strung out as they are behind us, won't have anywhere to run to. They'll come up in dribs and drabs and those which make it will die when they get here." Hold the hill else our entire force might get wiped out. The lieutenant swore he'd see Blanch court martialed; Blanch told him to go to hell. The lieutenant ordered the few regulars who were there to get around Blanch. They backed us rangers off with their pig-stickers.

Clark sneered at Blanch and marched his two lines, one behind the other, seventy men, down the slope and into the crick. The men pushed through the water, it not rising much above their knees. The brush and trees on the other side exploded in a fusillade of bullets, arrows and spears. Our men recoiled at the fury and closeness of the firing. Those of us yet up on the hill directed our own heavy fire over the heads of our men, who were splashing and scrambling to get back to shore and up the hill. They fell in swathes. Not many got back; most, including the lieutenant, lay dead and wounded.

Heavy white smoke drifted over the creek and over the stinking woods on the other side. There were the cries of the wounded and the fading ululations of departing Indians, exultant, unseen. Those men still coming up behind us a few at a time either cussed for seeing so many corpses in the crick and along the slope or stared in mute silence. Hubbard and Steele got up and the argument now was whether to continue pursuit or go back to the Hudson. Blanch was for neither. He said did we go forward it'd be into another trap and did we turn 'round and with as beat up as we were and with so many wounded, the Indians would pick us off as we went. Best thing was to fortify ourselves along the hill. With as many of us as the Indians had killed, with all the scalps and loot they'd got, Blanch said they wouldn't hit us did we get forted up. Hubbard sided with Blanch and we began downing trees for forming squares along the ridge. Darkness came, Hubbard wanted big fires to draw in the men but there were too many Indians around for us to illuminate ourselves in this manner.

****

Me and Blanch was out putting a night watch along the perimeter, a soldier came and told Blanch he was to report to Hubbard at once. I went too, to try and keep Blanch out of more trouble, iffen I could. Steele was there, as were some British and colonials. The colonials had been with us on the hill and the British were interrogating them. Neither Hubbard or Steele was saying much, they only listened whilst the different men told what they had seen and heard. The British were making it clear we'd have wiped out the Indians had Blanch not held so many men back. Most of our colonials agreed but they didn't mean it. The British fired questions at Blanch, more accusations than questions, he not saying much. Truth was, and most of us who'd been up on the hill knew it, Blanch had shown what sort of man he was by defying orders which had got so many men killed. When the British demanded Blanch get arrested, Hubbard told him to get back to whatever it was he had been doing.

****

Our defenses erected, our mood sullen, a cold night to be endured. Wisps of smoke emanated from bark shelters inside the squares. There was little enough to eat and with darkness, the fear of another attack was in the eyes of the men. Wore out, they'd had a bellyful of chasing Indians and wouldn't be so eager next time.

A most melancholy night with men coming in and the wounded asking for help, of which there was little to give. We lay through the night, listening to the exultant savages looting corpses. Steele was giving the orders. Hubbard was whipped, it was plain. His usually dancing eyes were dull. His face an ashen hue. Not much left in him for chasing Indians. With no more illusions about victory, or even of saving men, he would gather his dead and wounded and get out of the woods.

More men died during the night, adding to the downcast, and come daylight, our rangers went out with militia to fetch men still adrift. Lone Indians and small parties were around, intent on getting to our stragglers afore we did. Me and Robbins ran into two of the devils. They, by their whoops when they seen us, mistook us for lost men. Easy prey, until we shot 'em. Robbins took their scalps and strung 'em with the topknots which was already dangling off his belt. Another buck we came upon was carving one of our men with a knife. The Indian should a done his deed on the quiet but he couldn't stifle his high spirits. I shot him, too, though too late to save our man.

Corpses were everywhere, the charred remains of men tortured, burnt alive, hacked apart. Ghastly, the work of the fiends. The survivors we found were hiding or stumbling and were scared, hungry, cold. Many were wounded. One we saw was on his hands and knees with six or seven arrows in him, another was blubbering for having got scalped alive.

A funeral pyre was built, more wood stacked, bodies thrown on. The flames licked high, the smell of burning flesh awful to the senses. Strong men had tears in their eyes; tears as much for rage and frustration as for grief. We made stretchers of cedar poles and blankets for our more severely wounded.

The sun shone bright as we trekked back to the river, flankers on every side. We picked up a few men along the way and when we got back to the river, fifty just-arrived New York militia awaited us. Their captain, in a loud voice which heretofore no man could have used with Hubbard, demanded to be allowed to take his men out after Indians.

Francis J. Smith

A ranger named Grant spit tobacco, his entire plug, onto the ground with a loud splat. Some of which caught in his beard. We laughed. "S'cuse me, your lordships," Grant said with a low bow to the officers, and as he cleaned his mess with his fingers, he laughed along with us, the officers not amused.

Whilst Hubbard and Steele conferred with the captain, our rangers was telling the militia the Indians was close by and waiting for 'em. The raw men didn't know enough to not believe it. They was scairt certain they was heading into a one-sided fight.

The captain came back to his militia wild with enthusiasm and told 'em they was going after Indians. Hubbard, or Steele, had given the go-ahead. The men mustered trepidaciously whilst the militia captain tried rousing a fervor which none of the men was buying.

Grant, in a loud voice which all could hear, asked the captain who was gonna scout for 'em. The captain said he expected the rangers would. "We may be squirrelly," Grant said, "but we ain't nuts." Our men laughed but with bitterness for knowing if the militia was going after Indians, we was going too.

Robbins interjected, "Chasin' Injuns for the dang officer to make his reputation on." Then, to the Westchester men and whilst grinning and nodding toward the stacks of wood from the burning of our dead, "Leastways we won't be fetching wood for any of youse who don't get back alive." The truth was, and maybe some, at least, of the Westchester boys knew it, they wouldn't encounter Indians. Just they'd have to endure a futile trek through the cold woods, which was better than fighting Indians but wasn't something to look forward to.

Blanch, in the meantime, had gone after Hubbard and Steele and not politely. With how Blanch was railing, we figured he was gettin' in deeper but when they finished and it was announced the order was rescinded, the Westchester men gived three cheers for Blanch. The captain cursed Blanch for a coward. Blanch swore back a terrible epithet and drew his knife. The captain demanded Hubbard arrest Blanch. John Robbins lifted his skunk-hat off his head and sweeping the hat and bowing to the British, he said for all those wanting to court martial Blanch to please get into a line. Through it all, Hubbard stayed silent and it was Steele coldly silencing the militia captain. "All will move toward the fort." Daring the captain to challenge him, which he didn't. Seemed as though Hubbard and Steele had a bellyful, too, and with a long way to the fort still in front of us, what we needed was to get the hell away from this cold and bloody place. All of us, at once.

With not nearly enough boats to carry us all, the wounded were put on board the bateaux, the able-bodied would have to walk, and whilst we were doing the loading, two rangers sent to spook the Indians came in and reported the Indians was moving northeast toward Saint Sacrement. Just not all of 'em. Some were headed down river, toward our undermanned fort.

Chapter XXII – North Fort

We began our return march with leaden legs and hearts, the foulness of our mood obvious in the talk and in the silences. The ease with which the savages had outplayed us was galling to officers and men. We were whipped and carried a trepidation for whatever lay ahead.

We had expectation of making the fort before nightfall but not long after we got going, it started snowing. The wind-driven snow was in our faces as we trudged. Hubbard ordered the boats to shore and had the men fell trees for squares. Hubbard sent for Blanch and with no word having come to us from the fort and with the rumor which was going through the ranks, the Indians having gone there and massacred the garrison, I was afeared Hubbard might have got talked into a hard push to catch the Indians before they got away. Blanch would have spoken against this but as it was, Hubbard was too whipped for any more action and told Blanch to get out ahead and scout the situation.

Me and the dog and some few rangers went with Blanch and as we neared the fort, we seen smoke but heard nothing. Blanch sent me ahead with a few men. We got within fifty yards of the walls. The blockhouse on the hill was burnt, smoldering, the fort looked to not have got hit, just we couldn't see who was in there, us or Indians. With so few men holding the place, a war party might a got in; the British flag snapping in a stiff wind over the bastions might have been a trick. With the rangers covering me from the brush, I went to try and discern the situation. I dared not show myself to anyone on the walls. A strong possibility I might get shot, no matter who was there.

Militia was walking the ramparts. I eased up under the wall and called to 'em. They called back, asked was I from the colonel. I said who I was and asked had they see any Indians. "Here and gone," they said. I asked did much happen. "Nah," a man said. "They made noise enough to try and convince us they was the entire war party but we knowed they wasn't. They burnt the blockhouse." I asked did all our boys get out, he said yes. They asked how it had been with us. "Not good," I said and I told them part of our story. One of 'em finally said, "You comin' in 'er ya gonna stand there jabberin?" I said I was going to report their situation back to the colonel.

Hubbard decided to keep us where we were for the night and next morning, three hours after first light, the entirety of our army was back inside the fort. Hubbard went straight away into Steele's office, closed the door and didn't hardly come out at all. Crushed by the mauling the Indians gave him. Outfoxed by Stone Age warriors and with naught to show for his efforts 'cept wrecked boats, lost supplies and a lengthy casualty report.

The posted numbers were grim. As roughly as the enemy treated Hubbard, he was sure to lose his command. Seventy militia dead or wounded; fifty missing, dead in the woods, slunk off for home or dragged off to Canada. The regulars had twenty-five dead and plenty in hospital. The bateaux-men lost more than thirty. We were downcast at this severe loss of life. The pallor of defeat. So much needed to be corrected before we could venture forth with any hope of success.

Our rangers had six dead, three hurt, two missing. We had been augmented just a few short weeks before, now we were back down to fifteen. Bloodied, but we held together. The losses of our foe impossible to determine, they take their dead and wounded with them when they can, or hide them, but I reckon they didn't lose half of what we did. Certain it was they would have plenty of scalps for the dancing come winter. And when word of their great success spread up north, their forays would become even more aggressive. Especially did they figure a way to supply themselves down here. What was most worrisome was their victory might turn the heads of our Iroquois allies. Not even New York Town would be safe.

The men told us the raid had been a severe test of their mettle with Indians shootin' and carryin' on. A Frenchman waving a white flag had asked for a parlay. Insisting the others, meaning us, were wiped out and saying they had the garrison outnumbered ten to one, Frenchie demanded our men surrender. The officers and non-coms debated the proposition. Many of 'em were too scared to disbelieve the Frenchman and was for giving up. Sergeant Tom interrupted such talk by saying naught but cowards gave in to mere words. Said to make 'em show how many they were. Their gambit failing, the Indians burned and looted what they could on the outside and shot flaming arrows over the walls before departing. I recalled how mad Tom had been when we marched without him. This act of spite on Steele's part probably saved his fort from destruction.

Tom told me about the loss of the blockhouse. Indians got around it and a buck got up on the roof and plugged the chimney. The inside filled with smoke, the men panicked, and instead of putting out the fire, they ran out the door and down to the fort, the Indians in pursuit. A few men got killed and scalped in sight of the men on the walls, others got led away by the Indians.

Days following our return, Sergeant Tom was still fuming for not having got into the fight and for the arrogance of the Frenchie who had demanded the surrender. To calm Tom and get fresh meat for the rangers, we went on a deer hunt. Me, Robbins, Tom, Grant and some few others. Using the dog as a driver, we pushed hard and killed six deer. And missed as many more. Tom shot a doe at a hundred yards using my rifle. "I shot at a buck," he angrily spouted. "It was way up on the hill." He pointed. Indeed, it was a long shot. "The damn doe walked in front, just as I shot. A big buck! But I never could a hit either at such a distance with a Brown Bess. That's some gun ye got, laddie."

****

The infighting between the factions of our colonial government worsened our already bad situation. The politicians all schemed to put men they could control at the head of our forces. Then we heard New York Colony was out of money. Army pay had always been poor and most infrequent, now the rumor was the legislature had pocketed our money. Again! We were not to be paid for our work and North Fort might be shut down. Despite everything, this would be a mistake, and what was clear, our first need was for a better system of government. This we must have before we could expect to win. I did not care to put much faith in the words of the politicians. Too many selfish interests at heart.

****

Blanch summoned me. He was in hospital. Long had I marveled at how hard he pushed himself, now he was showing the effects. Bedridden, bloodshot eyes. He spoke in a voice so low, I had to lean in to hear him, and it was as if he was speaking to himself, not to me. "The day is coming," he said, "when we'll take this war to the enemy and when we do, we're going to need men who know their way around up north." He looked up, and for a moment, he was his old self. Defiant in the face of defeat. Then he wilted again. "Take either Grant or Robbins up to the lakes. Don't take 'em both. Christ knows I can't afford to lose all three of you ta once."

I asked Robbins to go. "Long walk," was all he said. He had been setting and overseeing the patrols whilst Blanch rested. We organized the men for the time we would be gone and talked to Grant about it.

****

Winter lay heavy on us as we traveled Saint Sacrement on skates. The ice for long stretches was smooth and bare, the fierce gale winds having swept off the snow. The dog, as he often did, was mostly out following scents, on the lookout for excitement, just he'd come in to check on us and go out again and he always got back for supper and for bedding down. Despite the cold and the wind, it was a spectacular trip. The beauty of this lake always filled me with vigor and stirred my senses, the views especially sharp with the leaves gone out of the hardwoods. We slept nights in bark shelters we found on the wooded islands.

We scouted around Portage Crick and Scalp Point. There weren't many French and Indians, they were mostly gone home for the winter, the French to Montreal and Quebec, the Indians to their lodges. What we mostly saw were small raiding parties going out and coming back. I showed Robbins trails and watch-posts. Caves, some to be avoided for being known to the enemy, some lesser known and useable for caching or for holing up. If a polecat or catamount be not already in there.

I took him up along Outlet Brook, the snows getting deeper, the air colder as we got up toward the Eagle's Lake, my Paradise lying under a blanket of white. Saw no sign of Indians having come this way so's to go down the East Branch, which anyway I had thought unlikely.

Robbins was leery of entering into the cut which led up to the canyon and he went with his hatchet in his hand. Nothing had got touched in my absence. Robbins was delighted with the canyon and the cabin and with all I had done here, the life I had made for myself under such harsh conditions. We got up onto the rim of the canyon for the view over and beyond the lake.

I took him to the top of the Pharaoh's Mountain, the wind wicked cold up there, and we trudged around to some of the ponds. Robbins gaped at all the beaver sign, the lodges and dams and all the timber the beavers had brought down. One old boss beaver smacked his tail about where we were standing and Robbins, delighted, slapped his knee with his cap.

We finished off my rum at night, my supply not inconsiderable, or so I had thought, until Robbins got into it. We talked about how brazen were the northern Indians for having sent a delegation to meet with the Mohawks. Damn good thing the Mohawks decided to stay out of it. So far, anyway. As bad as we'd got whipped, we'd at least survived, which we would not have, had the Mohawks been in with them others. Robbins snorted his disgust for so many Indians coming down all to once and we not able to punish them for it. Hell, we wouldn't even of knowed about 'em until they hit us if I hadn't stumbled onto them, or them onto me. Such was our ignorance and lack of control over the lakes' country.

When it was time to head back, I told Robbins he was the only one besides Blanch who I had shown my secret valley and I told him not to speak of it when we got back. "I won't spill your beans," he said. "So's you won't have to spill my guts. Only beaver enough for one." He took one last look at my valley, shook his head and off we went.

****

Blanch's condition worsened and he decided to go down to Albany to recuperate. At his behest and as a favor to him, I agreed to stay the winter at the fort with the much-reduced, much-maligned army of northern New York. To assist Robbins, who was to lead us in Blanch's absence. And unsaid by Blanch but understood by me, to keep an eye on Robbins for what he might otherwise do.

With the Jersey men and most of the redcoats gone, we had just two undersized companies of Yorker militia. Our too-few rangers prowled the frozen woods, tracking the movements of the elusive foe, trying to divert the devils from their intentions. Giving warning when we could. With Robbins and me having reported decreased goings-on at Scalp Point and with so much snow and cold, the militia said we were fools to go out. They said the routes from the north were locked up. No large movements of Indians was possible.

When the snowdrifts began piling up around the walls, shoulder-high and driven by the ever-fierce winds, Steele ordered out shoveling details to clear it away. Shepherded by rangers. At least we didn't have to shovel. Men grumbled but Indian raiders in other places along the frontiers were said to run right up the snowdrifts and leap over the walls and into the forts, and there were enough Indians around to keep the pot, if not exactly boiling, then plenty hot.

North Fort had become little more than a frontier outpost for the rangers. We carried warnings to the towns when trouble was around; the Indians often kept us cooped up in the fort whilst they raided over the northern frontier. They were ever more bold. For them, the more daring the feat, the bigger the boasting. Our patrols went in and out only through the sally port and only by dark. The Indians had not yet discovered the port. When they did, we would be shut in even tighter.

The Indians sometimes brought their captives here for torturing and burning alive in our full view, on a hill within sight of us and just beyond musket range. The Indians were often led by Canadian-born French officers. Hard to imagine Indians torturing white men whilst other civilized men looked on.

Around dusk, when the drums started and the Indians got their fire going, our men commenced to grimace and curse. Dread for the night to follow. The Indians caressed and whooped all night, sleep for us was impossible. Sorties were hotly discussed, even demanded, but Steele refused in most stern terms.

Any of our men who got taken by the Indians ended up on the hill. The Indians used the captives to try and goad us into coming out. The captives' blubbering whilst they got worked on, their pleas for help, hard to ignore, but with Indians lurking in the woods, there was naught we could do except try to shoot the man who was tied to the stake. Put him out of his misery. Only my rifle would reach up there with accuracy and I was often called out to finish off men or to shoot at those Indians which couldn't never seem to shut their damn mouths. At the sharp crack of my rifle, the Indians scattered for knowing who spoke to them.

Despite strict orders to the contrary and out of a deepening sense of frustration, our men sometimes fired round shot from the cannons. The Indians, hearing the loud boom, fell on their bellies and howled in mock terror. They learnt to judge the trajectory of the cannonballs, how long it took to reach 'em. An Indian seeing the ball in flight would give a telltale screech and point skyward. They'd carry on derisively as the slowly arcing missile approached. The heavy ball would land with a thud and roll through the grass and with the Indians running alongside until it came to a stop. Then they'd taunt us to fire again by exposing and slapping their backsides.

One time, a young buck, either inexperienced, or drunk, or both, tried grabbing a rolling cannonball. Because it rumbled along slowly, he thought it could be grabbed. We cheered for it taking off his leg.

Any ambitions the young savage had for a warrior's life dashed in an instant of rashness. He'd spend the rest of his life as a camp cripple, watching the war parties coming home wrapped in a glory he would never know.

The war of nerves went on through the winter. Many of our militia and even a few rangers broke under the strain. Some foolishly went over the walls and into the woods. Heading for home but more likely going north into slavery. Or up onto the hill. Others went out to try and rescue kin or friend staked up there. Our sentries had to watch the inside as well as the out. One soldier we locked up for a week until he calmed down. His brother was up there.

Discipline was harsh, whippings were frequent, morale was low. Our militia lads were sullen. The English regulars, inured to the hardships and boredom of camp life, sneered at us. A severe split existed.

In January came welcome news. All our back wages would be paid and we were to receive a belated Christmas bonus. Also, we were to be upgraded to a battalion. Two companies, a hundred men if we could find 'em. One company to be led by Theodore Chester, an experienced woodsman from south of Albany. The other to be led by Robbins. The First New York Mountain Rangers, paid for by the New York legislature, now sitting. Blanch was made a lieutenant, Robbins and Chester got elevated to ensign.

In February and with the pressure around the fort eased considerably with most of the Indians going home on account of it was so cold, I decided to run a small trapline close to the fort. One morning when I went out to check my traps, Indians was hiding around one of my sets. I would a walked right into 'em had not Blackie smelled 'em in time for us to sneak away. After this, I gave it up and left my traps for the Indians. A few bales of fox and fisher pelts wasn't enough to justify the danger and besides, the quality of the fur wasn't near to what I was used to and there was little enough of it.

****

Springtime, Blanchard was back from Albany. He was still weak and had to lean on a stout hardwood stick to get around. Yet he was strong-minded, and with a will to carry on the fight, he refused to step down. His courage and strength an example to all, colonial and British alike.

Colonel Hubbard was relieved of command of our northern department. Captain Steele remained at the fort, the only British officer north of New York with a rank above lieutenant. Then Steele and the last of the redcoats were withdrawn. Said goodbye to Sergeant Tom. He did not know where he was headed but was glad to be away. His parting words, "I hope it be someplace warm, laddie." He left his supply of rum with me and Robbins.

What followed the departure of the British was a succession of incompetent colonial commanders. The rapid replacement of one for another due to the political infighting in Albany and New York. Each new commander made a further mess of the situation.

With Blanch gone off again, recruiting for all the new men we would need, Robbins once again led our forays. John was much more aggressive than Blanch and was as fearless and as wily as any Indian. He had us setting ambushes. Our first few tries went badly, we were still getting out-snuck but we were getting better and began hitting the Indians from directions they did not anticipate. Just as they had been doing to us. Often when we got the better of the sneaking and before we could get our firepower concentrated, the Indians melted into the forest. Without the advantage of terrain or numbers, they wouldn't fight.

One time when we hurt 'em bad and as we were coming in to the fort, Robbins and some others raised up scalps on sticks. "Hair!" John shouted, which brung a cheer from the men on the walls, pent-up frustrations let go all to once. One thing for certain, the Indians were not going to whip us forever, if we could hold out.

****

On Blanch's orders, I spent time writing of our exploits in a manner as if I were writing home to the folks. Our rangers, when they read out loud my letters, which were for posting in the newspapers and broadsides, laughed for it seeming as if our work was romantic, not deadly, but Blanch said it helped bring in men. Replacements arrived steadily although some, upon gettin' a whiff of our fort or stalked by Indians, vamoosed. Still, we were gaining strength and numbers and were becoming a mixed brew from five or six colonies.

We had two men from the Carolinas. Their drawls a curiosity to many, though not to me. I had often heard such in the Full Sail. I think they were fugitives from justice but they were woodsmen, which was what mattered. We also had some Stockbridge Indians, Mohicans, a once-powerful tribe much reduced through white-man's diseases and the depredations of the Mohawks. We had Mohawks and two rented slaves. The slaveowner, a Dutchman, had been lauded for his benev-olence in leasing his slaves. I was comfortable with the Negroes, they were solid men, but I did not care to be in the woods with the Mo-hawks. Captured as young boys and adopted into the tribe, they were not blood Iroquois. They seemed in every way to be Mohawks, yet they were of a people which was against us. This made me nervous. Robbins said if they wasn't all right, Blanch wouldn't have accepted 'em. I, too, trusted Blanch's judgment but the two Indians didn't speak English so it was hard to get to know them.

Summer and fall, our Mohawks raided up north. Their war parties often passed by the fort and haughtily demanded supplies and rum. They made a profane show of their disgust for how poorly we lived.

The Mohawks, home from successful raids, showed us their prow-ess. Scalps by the handfuls, though many were halved. Loot carried by captured men, women, even children. The Mohawks sometimes tortured and burned captives on the hill where last winter the hostiles had burnt our men. The Mohawks did it here for the same reason as had our foe, to make us endure it. Our own allies so fiendish it escaped the civilized man's ability to comprehend, and we made no attempt to stop it. Indeed, some of our militia went up onto the hill when the Mo-hawks had captives up there. Were we then no better than the French? The men who went up told us the Mohawks felt cheated when a pris-oner died too soon and thus robbed them of sport. Once, the men told of the Mohawks cussing and kicking the burnt corpse of a Huron war-rior who sobbed and begged whilst gettin' caressed. Bad manners, the Huron, not the Iroquois.

With the coming of another cold season, our militia settled into a winter routine of collecting pay whilst staying close to their fires. They did not believe the Indians would come down. "The snow's too deep, the nights are too cold." They scoffed when we said there could be something big this winter in reprisal for the Mohawks' sacking of Indian towns along the Saint Lawrence. Still, the woods stayed quiet. And the longer nothing happened, the more complacency set in. Hard to keep our militia at their work when trouble was not about. They grumbled for what they considered unnecessary vigilance.

Chapter XXIII – Acrid Smell of Smoke

Late November, me and the dog were out with seven men. Two rangers, Abner Brown and Grant, and five militia. We were prowling south of the fort, east of the Hudson. Already out four days and not having seen anything and with snow starting, we decided to get back to the fort. First, though, I would go to Saratoga, to have a look at the situation. The men were for going straight in to the fort. "Hot food and a hearth at Saratoga," I said.

We headed back toward the river, and where a good-sized creek crossed our trail, we found fresh tracks, five or six Indians. One of 'em had fallen through the ice. The sign showed his struggles to get out of the water. "Been in the past two hours," Grant said. "Hole ain't refrozen." He had been poking around in the snow and picked something up. "Fella dropped his knife." He tossed it to me. Huron.

Just over the creek, we discovered a bark shelter. We spread out and approached with guns full cocked. Grant and me investigated, the other men covered us from the brush. Nobody home. The fire inside still held some heat. The wet one, with one or two others, had stayed just long enough to dry out. Left not an hour ago. "Hurryin', waren't they?" Grant said. I built up the fire with what little wood was there and we spent a few minutes warming ourselves, half of us inside the shelter at a time, the others standing watch outside.

We moved out and coming to where our canoes was stashed, we crossed the Hudson to the west side and got on the military road which followed the river north to Saratoga. We smelled smoke and came to a burned-out homestead. A cabin smoldering from inside, gutted; the barn and sheds burning. In the front yard were four bodies, the farmer and his wife, a Dutch peddler and a black man. Bound and tortured afore they was killed.

We followed the road along the shore and with so much fresh snow falling, we had a time staying with the narrow track. Cold and wet, our snowshoe-laden legs doing poorly, we seen from the sign where more Indians had joined up, and with us figuring 'em to be watching their backtrail, our pace slowed.

Darkness was settling in on us when we came to a glen and made an ominous find. "Kuyler!" Abner Brown called to me. "Come look at this." Oh, Lord! One sweeping glance around the glen at so many wood and bark shelters and I knew. A major force, hundreds of French and Indians. The sons-of-bitches had got down on us in force again and without us having known they were coming. Hours ahead of us and going straight for the town. A numbing chill went through me for Lydia, Arnold and Priscilla, the chill making the snow and cold of the night seem like nothing.

I sent Grant to North Fort, Abner down to Stillwater. This left me with my five militia. Their sergeant, Benson, said there was no point getting closer in toward Saratoga and said we ought to hightail instead. Wasn't nothing we could do against so many Indians. The other men said so too. Said the town had more'n likely already got hit. "Ain't you supposed to be men?" I said. "Act more like dandies. There might be folks we can help. Just has ta be careful." They remained dubious. "I'm in charge," I said, my voice turned cold. "Any of youse want ta argue?" None did.

After midnight, careful not to blunder into something and afraid for what might be in front of us, we came to a sawmill on a creek. The mill and sheds was burning and as we got closer in to the town, the wafting smoke and acrid stench came thick through the trees and we seen an orange glow in the sky ahead. We strained for the sound of firing which might mean someone holding out. There was just silence.

We worked to within a musket shot of town, close enough in for a look. From the glow in the sky, I expected Saratoga to be engulfed in flames. Instead, it was many small fires which had looked from a distance to have been a single conflagration. Some of the fires still raged, others smoldered or had gone out, dampened by the falling snow or having consumed house or shop.

We went in trepidaciously, the town deathly quiet 'cept for the snap and roar of the flames and the sounds of collapsing buildings. I sent my men to the Schuyler house, the one place where there might have been survivors. I had often told my friends to go to Schuyler's if there was trouble. The house, brick and stone, was defensible, more so if Schuyler, a military man, was there.

I set off running for Lydia's. Got there, the land office was aflame. So was the house behind the shop. I found her. Dead. Scalped. Hard to recognize the pretty lady with so many cuts from knives and tomahawks. It pains me to write this. Her little Desiree lay next to her. Scalped, her angelic face, so much like her mother's, turned up to the sky, to the falling snow which gently shrouded her. Alongside was a swaddle with blood on it, and recalling Lydia had been pregnant again, last I heard, I lifted the cloth. Underneath, half buried in the snow was her naked infant. With so little hair for the taking, the savage who'd lifted it had taken a share of skin and bone too. I cursed the monster who would display the tresses of a babe as proof of his manhood. How I put it all together, the Indians had killed the babes for knowing they couldn't survive a trek north, and Lydia, having witnessed the deaths, wasn't going either.

Arnold's house, close by, was a smoldering wreck. Three sides fallen in. Just the front wall and the porch yet standing. Priscilla's rocking chair was on its side on the porch. Looked to have got thrown through the glass window from the inside. The fire too hot to go in and search for bodies but no blood on the porch nor on the snow did I find. Hoped my friends might somehow have been spared. If they had finished their new house, out by the healing springs, and if it hadn't been hit, maybe. Doubted it. With so many Indians, everything within miles of Saratoga must surely be aflame this night. If Arnold and his wife were out there, they were dead and had they heeded my warnings and stayed in town, they were dead.

The footprints led out toward the main avenue, where I figured the Indians had assembled their captives afore leading them off. I headed out, past corpses in the streets. Some were nailed to the sides of houses.

I came to where the snow was trampled and bloodied and with corpses, pieces of clothing, shoes. I went from one dead body to the next, looking at the faces. The savages had been thorough in their butchery. It is fiendish what they do to people who come under their power, though here, and with the need to be away, their foul deeds had been hastened. In the sanctuary of their deep north woods, they would perform prolonged acts of torture meant to mightily grieve the tormented yet keep them alive for as long as possible.

I found Arnold or what was left of the little schoolteacher. Scalped, a poor job done. The top of his skull showed through a tangle of hair, of blood and brains caked and frozen. Besides the scalping and whatever else, I seen his face had been cratered, as with the back end of an ax. His nose and mouth were crushed, one eye hung by a thread down onto his cheek. Killed by the violent acts of Indians or frozen to death afterward but with the dog tugging on his sleeve, Arnold stirred. A little. It'd been a few hours since the Indians departed and Arnold must have lain in the snow in his bedclothes. On his feet were thin bedroom slippers which gave no protection against the awful cold. I wrapped him in my bearskin, dug into my pack for spare moccasins and put them on his feet. I rubbed his arms and chest, to put warmth into him, if I could. He opened his one eye and spoke, I leaned in close. He said the Indians had carried away his wife, and said most pitifully, "Cannot you bring her back, cannot you put things awright?"

Benson come running. He said Schuyler's brick house, where I had hoped there might be survivors, had been breached. The inside was blackened, smoldering. The smell of roasted flesh, people burned alive in there. Benson said the Indians appeared to be gone. So too the folks, slain or carried off to the north. A slushy path, the footprints of many feet, led out of town. Some was barefoot. A trail of blood. And tears. Saratoga was destroyed.

Another of my men came up and said there was a family of survivors. At the south end of town, house and family spared by the grace of God. A man and wife, two young sons and a daughter of ten. I told the ranger to take me to them, and picking up Arnold, I carried him over my shoulder along the burning streets, all darkness and light, fire and shadow. A strong wind blew the flames around. Arnold revived some and struggled feebly against getting carried. He insisted he could walk. I put him on his feet. He stumbled and pitched forward into the snow. I picked him up again.

The farmer was a Dutchman, Vorhees. He sat numb whilst his wife tended to their children, who were wrapped in silence from their night spent in the cold and with all else they had endured. The wife made a place for Arnold by the fire.

Benson, meanwhile, got me aside and said he and my other men had talked it over and decided we had ought to get to hell out of town. Go for help. I reminded him Grant and Abner had already been sent. Benson said if we were going to stay, we should at least make camp outside of town. Just a short way. He said how after a raid, Indians often stayed around, some of 'em, on the lookout for the chance to hit the relief columns. I said I was aware of how Indians did things and I said it'd be a cold camp in the woods. The town was at least warm, with so much of it burning. He started to say something more, I told him to shut the hell up. Told him to post a watch at each end of town and to rotate the men every half-hour.

Voorhes' wife gave me coffee. I drank gratefully whilst Voorhes told me what he'd seen. Indians creeping silently through the town. Two warriors coming up to his door. He and his family got out a back window, hid in the brush and watched. The Indians spread out through the sleeping town, posting men at every door until all were set. Then they commenced yelling and crashing in, catching the folks in their beds. Any who resisted got killed at once. Vorhees' house had got ransacked and set on fire though the fire had gone out before much had burned.

Vorhees must have read my look because he began blubbering and nodding. He said if he wasn't such a damn coward, he'd have given an alarm instead of slinking off into the woods. Some folks might have been saved. I let him blubber, even with his wife looking for me to speak words to soothe him. I had naught for him, though it was not likely he could have done anything 'cept get his family killed. Which didn't mean he shouldn't have done something.

****

A long night endured, then the sun came up, the start of a gray, uneasy day filled with terrible cold and the sure expectation of more snow. Sometime during the night, Benson and the others vamoosed, either camped outside of town or gone home, I didn't give a damn which. Now it was just me and the dog waiting for help to come.

By noontime, the ruins of Arnold's house had cooled enough so I could go inside and search for Priscilla's body. I did not find her, so Arnold was probably right in saying she'd got carried off. I returned to Vorhees' house. Arnold told us, feebly, about getting awakened by crashing noises at the door. He got up thinking it was the blasting of the wind and when he lifted the latch to re-set the door, Indians pushed it open from the other side. Said he fought them until he got knocked on the head.

"Friend," Arnold reached out to me from where he lay. "They have taken my wife. You must help me bring her back. I am so afraid for her." The damage to his head had surely affected his brain but not so much he didn't understand all was lost. He, sobbing, called out for his wife and he tried to get up, to go for her. I put a hand on his chest to keep him down. "Go back into the cold," I said, "and you won't be looking for nobody." He demanded I bring his woman back and began

295

struggling against me. If I wouldn't get after his woman, he'd go. I held him down by his arms, the Voorhes woman, big and fat, sat on his legs. He got the shakes and ceased struggling against us. I feared he was in his death spell with how bad he was trembling.

I told him if Priscilla was among the captives, we might be able to ransom her come summer. I said this to lift his spirits, which it didn't, though it was true enough. Many captives perished along the trail but the Indians had learned the value of ransoming instead of braining and the old tradition of adoption into the tribe remained. As did the other traditions, torture and death, and I had a bad notion of how the Indians would react to the shrill Priscilla calling them every bad name she could sputter. And even did she survive the trek into Canada, it was painful to envision her as a broken-spirited drudge or, God forbid, a submissive squaw in a buck's lodge. I don't know but those same horrors was conjured in Arnold's mind because whatever he was seeing, it was damn near the last blow. His sobs awful to hear, I had a time settling him. After he fell asleep, I went outside and searched around.

The gates of the stockade were crashed in; gray smoke wafted from barracks and sheds. Found no soldiers' corpses; Voorhes had told me the soldiers had departed no more'n a week before, the corporal and his few militia walking away for not having an oven for the baking of bread nor a well dug for them. Or some such things.

Late afternoon, Abner came in with ten men, Jersey rangers from Stillwater headquarters. Then, around dusk, Grant arrived with twenty rangers and militia and with more on the way. I was cheered for Abner and Grant having got through. They must a had some night, especially Grant, going north, same as the Indians.

The next morning, early, I got word of a little man in his bedclothes running screaming along the streets. Figuring it was Arnold, I took the dog and some men and hurried out to retrieve him. A Jersey man posted at the north end of town said he had seen the little man go by in his bedclothes. "Didn't you try to stop him?" I said angrily. He just shrugged.

The thought of Priscilla getting dragged off by the Indians was too much for Arnold to bear. Heedless of his own life he had gone to get her, or to be with her. We followed the trail but dared not move too fast. Snow covered most of the sign but so contemptuous were the Indians of pursuit, they had not split into smaller groups, their usual tactic. They just walked up the trail. We saw corpses in the snow, the old, the young, any who could not keep up. Brutally slain or froze to death. Mostly all in their bedclothes. We came to a creek, to the ford where the departing Indians had crossed. We walked on, and with no sign of Arnold, I figured he had wandered into the trees to die but up along Fish Creek, we found him.

Face down in the snow and even yet clinging to a spark of life. Poor man. He who had never harmed a soul in his life was now come to this. I built a fire, kept him up close to it and washed his wounds as best I could with melted snow. My men built a stretcher and we got him back in, he never uttering a moan of sorrow for himself, only for his lost woman.

Word came, Albany had got wiped out, same as Saratoga. I didn't believe it. With as many Indians as had struck Saratoga and with at least an equal amount or more needed to have hit Albany as well, it would have put their force near a thousand. They could not have gathered nor brought down so many without us knowing, nor could they have victualed so many for the time they were here. As it was, the rumor was false. Albany had not been attacked, though there were more Indians down there than usual prior to the hit on Saratoga. They had been probing, seeing who to hit, and must a decided Albany was too strong for the taking.

Everybody's nerves were shattered, the men jumpy, sentries firing at shadows. Spirits sunk to a level I had never seen before. Including my own. Seemed I walked with my head on the ground from grief and exhaustion. And anger, too, for knowing what would be the reaction to this tragedy. Many would be for giving up the fight. They'd demand we make any sort of peace with the French.

Blanch came with fifty men and I shall never forget, for as long as I might live, the look which passed between us. It was for our failure to take the war north to the French and Indians before they brought it down to us. Again. All our effort were for naught. Proof of our failure was all around us, the corpses in the snow, the burning town.

Blanch said the Indians took a hundred captives. I told him we had collected thirty dead; men, women and children, with probably more which we had not yet found or wouldn't ever find. He said the main body of Indians was gone, only a few prowlers were yet around. He said there'd been as many as five-hundred French and Indians and with them knowing we could in no way assemble forces enough to get after 'em, they had been stopping on the way home to torture captives and feast on the flesh.

I asked if the Indians made an attempt on North Fort. He said no. They'd had a look but daunted by the walls and cannons and already sated, they hadn't tried anything. Blanch said Lydius' trading post, up at the Great Carry, had been burned. "Anybody hurt there?" I asked. He shook his head. "Weren't nobody home," he said. "Injuns torched it and kept going."

Blanch had brought in a boy, Johnny, twelve years old. The lad had fled from the Indians and running through the woods, had blundered into a ranger patrol. Fortunate he was to find rangers afore the Indians found him because had he got retaken, he would have been beheaded, his head carried along on a stick as a warning to any others of the captives who was thinkin' of running. The boy said people had been killed for not keeping up or for no reason. Blanch confirmed there were plenty of dead along the trail. We questioned the boy closely; he kept his courage despite the sobs racking his slender frame. He said the Indians roasted a woman whilst she yet lived and made the other captives taste her flesh. The Indians considered this great sport, the kid wretched to think on it.

I asked did he know anything of Missus Baldwin. He nodded and told a troublesome story. He and his family had been taken to the place on the street where the folks was getting gathered and Missus Baldwin was there, screeching and spitting at the Indians and trying to bite 'em on account of her hands were tied.

When others of the Indians came in with Mister Baldwin, Missus Baldwin screeched at him even worse than she'd been going after the Indians. She called him an idiot, said it be all his fault and her with a rope around her neck and with the other end of the rope attached to an Indian's belt, "Mister Baldwin jumped on the Indian's back and commenced beating him on the head with his fists."

The Vorhees woman brought the kid a bowl of steaming soup. He took too big a swallow and scalded tongue and mouth. "Eat 'er slow," Blanch cautioned. The boy nodded. "The big Injun," he said, "was trying to shake Mister Baldwin off his back but he couldn't get loose of him." Johnny took a spoonful of soup and continued. "An Indian smashed Mister Baldwin in the face with the back end of a warclub and scalped 'im and when she seen this, Missus Baldwin got all tender and loving. She knelt down in the snow and was kissing Mister Baldwin all over and telling him how much she loved him. Then she became a wildcat with how she went after the Injuns, and the one which had aholt of the tether got his hand 'round her throat. He'd a strangled her for certain but for another putting a hand on her, and after the two Indians talked it over, the one gived the end of the tether to the other." Claimed her, sure, and as sad as I felt for Priscilla, I could not help but wonder why in the hell an Indian would want her. Johnny said the Indian dragged her away and with him pulling his end of the rope and her pulling hers, both of 'em using two hands with pulling, the Indians and even some of our own was laughing. "Couldn't help it, I reckon," Johnny said, "for it were comical to all." He said they got walking and the Indian who now owned Priscilla stuffed a rawhide gag into her mouth and raised his tommyhawk, which raising was ominous. The buck wouldn't tolerate her commotions. I have known of them, when confronted with just such a prisoner, to dig into the offender's mouth with a knife, cut out the tongue, skewer it on the knife, heat it over a fire, cut it up and jam the pieces back into their victim's mouth for swallowing. The best Priscilla could hope, for now, was to make it alive to her owner's northern lodge.

****

When folks showed up from Albany searching for kin, my friend Eric was among them. His father had been at Saratoga on business and was missing. I told Eric we had all taken a look at the faces of the dead before we burned 'em, to see could we identify any and I had not seen his father. Which didn't mean he hadn't been on the pyre; many of the faces were unrecognizable, some of the bodies were without heads. Eric and me checked the list of people dead and known to be missing. His father's name was not on the list.

I told Eric not to lose hope, his father might be yet alive, a captive on his way north. Trouble was, and Eric understood this, his father's age and citified ways were against him. The Indians would be most harsh on an old man of negligible use to them as a slave or an adopted tribesman, and same as what the Indians had done with Lydia's babes, did they judge the old man not capable of making the trek to Canada, they would take just his scalp. Or, and did he give out along the way, he'd get tomahawked.

We described Eric's father to Johnny. He shook his head, for not recalling having seen him. It would have been difficult for Johnny to remember, he'd been in so much danger himself and so scared, but he did say there were strangers among the prisoners.

Eric demanded I give him a gun, said he was going north to search for his father. This was impractical but he was adamant and I took him to see Blanch. Told Blanch I was taking Eric up for a look. Blanch didn't think I should do it but he understood I had to placate Eric and knew I would keep him away from trouble, best I could. Maybe Eric knew this as well. Blanch also knew I would scout for sign and report it to him. His parting words, "Goddamn it, watch yourselves."

We spent three days and nights in the woods following the way the Indians had gone. With so much sign and with Eric along, I didn't dare move too fast. Found the grisly remains of a few people but naught of Eric's father. When Eric was satisfied he'd done all he could, I guided him back to Stillwater, where Blanch was now headquartered. Blanch told me to take Eric down to Albany, get him in safely.

A few days later, Eric and me sat in the Full Sail. The place was somber. The men, mourning the loss of Saratoga, were silent or spoke in low tones. Except for one drunkard who put all the blame on me. Said I was paid to warn 'em when trouble was coming and I had failed. Maybe he was right but even iffen he was, I didn't need fer no city boy to be saying it and with him not shutting up and me feeling the way I did, I beat the hell out of him.

My thoughts kept going back with bitterness to Scalp Point, that damnable black-slate fort so far north. A noose around our necks. And tough it was to watch Eric mulling the fate of his poor father. Doubted he was yet alive, for how could he survive the trek north? The old storekeeper would have been at perilous disadvantage and even did he survive the trek, how long could he last up there in winter? He was not a woodsman and having spent his life in a shop, taking his comforts by the hearth, how could he stand up to being worked to death as a drudge slave? How the hell could anybody?

Chapter XXIV –Mutiny

The winter was cold and snowy. The Hudson River froze all the way south to New York Town, where the Hudson, which some of the older Dutch still called the North River, emptied into the ocean. The wolves, both two- and four-legged, prowled. The Canadian Indians were around on snowshoes, mostly in small parties and often right up to the very gates of our towns and forts. Patrols jumped, farms burned, people out on the ice of the lakes and even on the river near Albany were not safe.

Our wood parties went out armed and escorted. Any man alone in the forest risked a bold young Huron or Abenaki tryin' for his hair. They were daring in their attempts. Always were they confounding our men. No feat too risky for these devils. Through it all the governor and legislature, from the safety of New York, remained embroiled in their fights over money.

Supplies meant for the military garrisons were sold and resold, to the detriment of the men. As a result of these pecuniary shenanigans, food in camp was always scarce. And poor. Political favors got repaid by putting unqualified and often dishonest men in charge of the army. We saw this firsthand with some of the commanders we had, for with the British gone, we were led by colonial officers who were all mostly incompetent. The number of sick and starving folks crowding into the towns was increasing. We were a long way from a harvest, the future looked bleak.

In March we began hearing rumors of mutiny. At first it was only the mutterings of hotheads amongst the colonial companies stationed below Albany. Then the April supply column came in with reinforcements and within an hour of the column arriving, the garrison was buzzing with talk. Some of those who had come up brought word from the leaders of the mutiny in Stillwater. We must declare ourselves in their favor or suffer dire consequences. "More dire than staying here?" Grant said. Robbins laughed.

The reasons for the troubles were valid. With polecats in charge of supply, our meat was black and foul-smelling, there were weevils in the bread, our powder was of poor quality, the money our men depended upon for sending home was not forthcoming. Valid yet not valid, for revolt in the face of such dangers as we faced could never be justified. Not when our very existence was threatened.

The rebel leaders said we must hold an election for officers. The Albany garrison had chosen their own leaders and thrown out any who wouldn't support better conditions and now we must do the same. The mutinous troops would only follow men of their choosing. Told us to join or they would deal most harshly with us. I told them I would follow none except Blanchard. Robbins said, when they demanded he declare his loyalties, "Seems to me you's going aginst yourselves." They tried to bully him, he called them every sort of fool. He and Blanchard insisted there would be a fight before the rangers would go along with what he called a rabble. Robbins asked was any of 'em goddamn stupid enough to get into a fight with rangers. None were, and none dared say much when Blanch or Robbins was within earshot. Though we agreed conditions were wretched, our men remained stout for Blanch. Still, I wondered over our ability to overcome such hardships with the war sure to resume its fury with the coming of spring. Seemed it might be the end of us.

Another week without news and the rumors were rampant. Funny how they got going. Nobody had come into the fort from the outside, yet the words flew unhindered by reason or common sense. Must be they were carried by the birds of the forest or on the wind.

A dispatch rider came in with news the colonial troops from the army camp at Stillwater had marched into Albany with fixed bayonets and seized the town. Taken the reins of the government from the politicians. They promised change. The rider said he did not think there had been any bloodshed.

I was worried about my folks. Pops would be thundering at both sides. His contempt for the English would be running at fever pitch with every schnapps. Decided I better go down and see for myself. Told Blanch I would scalp any damn mutineer who touched my folks. Robbins, saying he hadn't got any scalps lately, came along with me.

We stopped at Stillwater on the way down to see Arnold who was surprisingly still alive and recovering from his wounds. I took heart from his refusal to die, as did others. Arnold had become a symbol of our determination. The woman who tended him made up a tray of tea and biscuits and took me in to see him. He was improved and sat up in bed like a prince of old Egypt, his horrific wounds covered over with bandages. The poor bugger was disfigured but at least he was alive. He got excited seeing me, certain I had brought joyous news of his wife, and when I said I had nothing, he cursed me most vilely, something the genial little man had never done before. He said if I had not insisted they stay in town, had they been out to their country house when the Indians struck, his wife would not have got taken. I did not argue, nor did I tell him I had checked on his house. It was burnt to the ground. I understood his ranting was the result of a fractured brain, still it saddened me. It was only his body recovering, not his mind. He had truly gone 'round the bend.

Got to Albany, the folks were fine, and whilst I was there, Eric and me went to see Schaack. The fat old Dutchman was said to hold contacts in Montreal. Perhaps a letter could be sent inquiring the fate of Eric's father. Schaack, without revealing much, cagily said he would do what he could. Eric was downcast at this but was placated some when I said it was just Schaack's way of doing things.

Our stay in town was short. The raiding had resumed and me and Robbins were back north with the rangers, spookin' and skirmishin'. Brutal fights with just a few men to a side. Tomahawks, knives and gun butts. No quarter asked nor given. Our militia drilled with the bayonet but was not very good with it. Never would be. I hoped Sergeant Tom O'Brien never saw us with the pig-stickers.

An uneasy time with Indians in the woods and dissension inside the fort. The mutiny got debated in the barracks, on the parade ground, even at the cook shack, where one of our cooks harangued every time we lined up for a dish of whatever slop was gettin' dispensed. A few hotheads were belligerent toward me for my refusal to get mixed up in their sordid business.

****

Springtime, the ice on the lakes would soon break up and with the fear the mutineers would seize the fort if too many rangers were gone into the woods, few patrols went out. Blanchard called me into his office one day and said the French would have heard by now of our troubles and might be intending a move to take advantage of it. He said he needed me to go up to Scalp Point and have a look. "I an' Robbins cain't go," he said, "for fear this damn insurrection might'n git outta hand but somebody's gotta do 'er. We talked 'er over and you're the only one we trust. Stay for as long's you kin. T'will be cold. An' plumb dangerous. Don't look fer relief. Isn't gonna be none. Just come in when you sees something or c'aint take no more. And don't say no, cuz I already heard you volunteer. Anybody ye wanna take along with you?" Nope. I left within the hour, me and the dog.

Got up there without any trouble. The snow was around in patches but the ice on the lakes was still thick enough to support the weight of men. An opportune time for a war party to come down on skates. I moved around atop the craggy peaks and even seeing plenty of sign, I found more peace and solitude in this dangerous country than amongst my peers, with all their squabbling.

Mostly, and same as always, I had to stay hidden but I did get one Indian with the thud of my hatchet against the back of his skull. The whole time I was stalking him, he thought it was him stalking me. I stayed until the lake ice softened and blackened, this would slow the raiders until the ice was more fully out. Coming back down, ice jams and high water made for difficulty getting across cricks and streams. Back at the fort, the mutiny was over though the disgruntlement lingered; the arrangement worked out was to the satisfaction of none.

We began hearing rumors of peace and of a better organized, better supplied and officered army for our frontier. Mere words meant to soothe the discontented, for the warmer weather brought Indian raids in full fury. Frustrating days spent pursuing and getting pursued. Often it was only our stashed canoes and knowledge of the trails keeping us from getting wiped out.

****

One of the militia officers put in command of the fort was a retired British officer who had chosen to stay in America when his enlistment was up. Unlike some of our other commanders, this man, from whom more was expected, did at least try to do something about the sickness and stink of the fort and tried to instill discipline such as was in the British ranks. He got little cooperation from the colonials, who preferred lazing about, and when he ordered a Massachusetts soldier to be flogged, our commander became the victim of his own mutiny.

The Massachusetts sergeants refused to pick up the nine-tails so the officer ordered the New Hampshire men to do it. They too refused. The commander decided to do it hisself but the sergeants dragged him out through the gates, dumped him in the river and told him if he came back in, it'd be him who got nine-tailed. He had sense enough to depart and was not seen again. Men laughed to think the Indians got him.

A half-company of British regulars arrived, a court of inquiry was held to deal with the perpetrators and what the British found, damn near the entire garrison was in on it so there wasn't much they could do.

****

Me and Robbins went up to the lakes. Robbins was a rascal who got quickly to the heart of a position. He grasped sharply the importance of terrain. I showed him shortcuts and landmarks which enabled us to get around smartly whilst stayin' off the main trails. Showed him the rock ledges from where it was safe to observe the portages and the fort without gettin' seen. I was not surprised at how fast he learned country new to him. He was as woods-wise as any. As good as Blanch. Or Hugh McChesney.

I took him to see the King's Chair. He sat in it one morning and watched the sunrise. He declared himself to be royalty on a throne of gold, and despite his shaggy look, he did have something of the regal lion about him.

At Scalp Point, we seen a party of Indians, bodies painted, crossing the lake. Headed for the Otter Creek Trail and the gaps through the eastern mountains. Off to raid the lower Connecticut Valley. Another party came in shaking bloody scalps and screeching the victory cry for their booty and bound captives. That night we listened to the pleas of the captives in the Indian camp. How could the French ignore it? Were they afraid to interfere? Or did they openly approve?

We got up close under the guns of the Scalp Point castle, to maybe hear loose talk. Spent a night hidden in the dry, grassy moat around the citadel. As the night wore on, I got edgy. "Goddamn it, let's get the hell out of here." Close to daylight, we watched the woodcutting parties going out with scant escorts, so confident were they.

"They ain't gonna be safe forever," Robbins said.

Robbins burned with the desire to bring the war to the French and Indians. He was certain we could bring up men in large numbers. His confidence I shared not, even with the heedlessness of the French. "Fine, Robbins," I said. "So you hit a column. Then what, fly home like a bird?" He grinned and shook his head. When the son-of-a-gun figured out how to do it, watch out! We stole a canoe and crossed over Corlaer so Robbins could study the palisade on the east shore. This post was little used. There was just a sutler's store surrounded by a rickety stockade fence in dire need of repair. Gaps in the walls. We counted a few dozen Canadians. Some farms and fields were scattered around.

Robbins decided to burn down the palisade, which notion scared me. I did not know my partner well enough. Had no idea just what bold really meant. To just what limits his daring would go. But I was fast learning. Never known such recklessness in a man, nor a man who was any better at surviving his own recklessness. "Be doin' the French a favor, burning those rotten old logs," I pointed out. He might yet have done it, had it not thankfully rained hard for two days, and whilst we was holed up, he seemed to forget about doing the burning.

A day or so before we planned to leave, Robbins decided we should take a prisoner home with us. He began looking for the right situation. Two more days we prowled but found no opportunity. I was impatient to be going. About the time I hoped he might have given up, we seen a lone Frenchie. Half out of his uniform, asleep in the moonlight under an oak tree. On the ground beside him lay a jug of brandy. We were in close to the outer palisade. It looked like a setup to me. "Ah," Robbins said. "They don't know we's anywhere around."

He crept up and with his musket butt, he hit Frenchie hard on the noggin. I figured the blow had ended Frenchie's life but we checked him, he wasn't dead, just knocked out. We bound his hands and feet, tied a rag over his eyes and gagged him. John raised the jug and took a swallow. Passed it to me. I drank but little. Robbins stuck the jug in his pack. He lifted Frenchie and with the unconscious little man over his shoulder, John took off at a fast pace. We were well away from the castle when the Frenchie began stirring and Robbins, coming to some rocks, dumped him. Almost as though John had looked for just such a place. John, huffing and snorting, said the carrying had made him thirsty and in one swig, he drank down most of the brandy. I told him I didn't intend carrying Frenchie all the way back to North Fort. "He might walk if we make him," I said, "and iffen he won't, I'm fer killin' him right here." Robbins removed the gags from Frenchie's mouth and eyes. "Anglais!" Frenchie said, looking up with disbelief and disgust. John asked him in the French tongue, with which John was well acquainted, if he was willin' to walk. Frenchie cussed and began tearing at the bonds which held him.

"You'se a viper, isn't you?" John said, and he began kicking the Frenchie, first on one side then going 'round to the other, and I said nothing for it was plain now John was in the right. Our Frenchman was an obstinate bugger and had to be learned not to resist. Still, I could only imagine his suffering, not only from the kicks but from what must a been an already ferocious headache from the rotgut swill. I saw no good in any further harshness but when I tried to intervene, John snorted like an old bull and pushed me aside. He got his foot on Frenchie's throat and pressed down. Frenchie made choking sounds, his legs flailing, his hands clutching John's foot, then he gradually ceased struggling and looked up at us with hatred and rage.

I told John to tell Frenchie we wouldn't beat on him anymore, did he walk, and if he didn't, we'd use him for tomahawk practice, right where we was. John spoke to him. Walk or get tommyhawked. We untied Frenchie's legs, his hands was still secured behind him, and with his mouth gagged again and his eyes covered, we got him to his feet. John drew a leather thong tight around Frenchie's neck so to walk him in front of us, the noose at short shank. Robbins got behind him and reached around and with a knife to Frenchie's throat, told him to get goin'. Frenchie started walking. Robbins checked the bonds often. Two days to get back to our canoe and we were on our way home. We traveled only at night, and when we seen the outline of the fort ahead, Robbins reminded our boy if he did not talk when we got there, it would be the tomahawk tree for him.

The fort was getting a thorough cleaning, which it sorely needed, and had been reinforced with about twenty redcoats. There was a new commander. A British captain of one of His Majesty's lightfoot brigades. I read the fancy sign on the door to his office. This smart officer acted surprised a bumpkin could read. Said so. His name was Philips, another martinet. He took our report hastily and made it plain he had more important duties, and without asking questions about what we had told him, he ushered us out. Acted squarely as though he did not want to be in the same room with us. John was fuming at the rebuff. "Must be you stink a little high, Robbins," I said but I too was angry for how we was treated and after such hard, dangerous work.

Our next report was to Blanchard. As we sat in the hut, sipping on rum, I reflected on this just concluded sojourn to the north. My compatriots' words slipped further from my mind, I having a little private mourning to do. This was the first time I had ventured north in years without my faithful dog at my side. Old Blackie and me shared many adventures. He saved my hide many a time with his warnings and I reckon I saved his a few times. His company kept me from going stir crazy when the harsh winters kept us bottled up in our cabin. A trusted partner, I missed his presence keenly. He was shot by an angry sheep farmer just outside the gates of Halfmoon, mistaken for a wolf after the man's flock got torn up in the field. I don't think the dog did it. At least not all of it. Local dogs formed a pack and he ran with them.

****

This summer, the rangers were called to Albany to form part of the escort for Governor Clinton at a major conference held out to the west of Schenectady, at the forest estate of William Johnson. I went along. In Albany, we were issued hats with large plumes and leather leggings as symbols of our unit. Silly, useless things.

At the conference, the Iroquois Confederacy, already splintered, declared to the consternation of all, that the League would henceforth stay out of the war. Those friendly to us would remain neutral. This neutrality was not shared by those more western Iroquois who had mostly gone over to the French. Until now, the Iroquois, especially Bill Johnson's Mohawks, had raided the French. This would cease. The sachems said they were done with being caught between two warring white-man nations, both of whom were interlopers on Indian lands. In the minds of the chiefs, the English were treacherous in their dealings. And what was maybe even more dangerous to us, in Iroquois eyes, the English appeared weak. One chief said, "You are open and defenseless, like women." The Iroquois were too proud to stand with the English, who, in the opinion of the Iroquois, either could not or would not fight like men. It was said, probably truthfully, that Albany existed only by the forbearance of the Mohawks. May it be they had come to regret English presence? The chiefs said they felt unsafe with the English as near neighbors. So much so, and this the chiefs left unsaid, they might have to strike us suddenly. Out of fear, the way a rattlesnake did. "Won't be no warning rattle iffen they do," Grant said.

Johnson, who, as Commissioner of Indian Affairs, conducted the meeting, had the respect of the Indians. He represented them fairly and strongly. He was more honest with them than was any other white man and the Indians knew it. He was their go-between in all matters dealing with the colonial governments. He was fervent, passionate in his defense of Indian rights against the land-grabbers and swindlers. His enemies, and he had many, said he took ruthless advantage of the red men. Robbins said the reason the Iroquois put much of their land in Johnson's name was to keep it from getting taken in white man's court by some other rascal of a speculator, of whom there were many in the safer parts of the colony.

Despite the Indian troubles, the speculators were always bringing in new settlers. The Iroquois were angry with the land-snatchers. "At least with Johnson," Robbins said, "the red men know who be cheatin' 'em." This, I think, was true. Bill must cheat them, for the land had made him wealthy beyond all imagining. For reasons of their own, the chiefs knew and allowed it. Maybe because Bill gave good service for the price exacted. He was fluent in the Iroquois tongues; he respected and observed their customs. We heard how he carried on worse than the most savage warriors when they got painted up and danced naked around their council fires. Yet a lion for their cause and for us too. He was steadfast in every way.

At the conference, the bombastic Governor Clinton, anxious to keep the Indians allied and active, made them many promises, which Johnson would have to keep. The governor's empty words did not fool the Iroquois. One tall speaker, King Hendrick, warrior and orator of renown and a sachem of the first importance, stood before the English and in what was termed a great speech, he harshly denounced them for stealing Indian lands. The sachem coyly asked Clinton how he could expect to give aid to the Iroquois when he could not provide for his own soldiers. "We have seen the weakness of your forts. A wind from the north will blow them over." We cheered these words of wisdom. Hendrick harangued the English for how poorly they fought. The governor retorted, "Louisbourg." Hendrick's sneer was the demeanor of a strong man. Of the wolf unimpressed by the snarling coyote.

"This French fort, Louisbourg, of which you speak," Hendrick said. "And this great battle you say you have won. How are we to know it is not just a story you tell? Where are your scalps? How can you show this poor old man the proof to make him say to his people, the English are great ones and their word can be trusted? We are many miles from this Louisbourg. I know just where it is. We Iroquois have raided in the far-away, cold country many times. The people there know the fear of our coming. If you have taken it, then where are your prisoners for the burning? Is your victory so barren you have neither scalps nor slaves to show me? Bah! Surely, Englishman, you can see my trouble. Your words are naught but another white man's boast, like the one last year. Then you told us your army would sweep the Great Lakes. Seize them. Yet you could not even find the lakes, big as they are. Your young men needed our help just to reach Oswego before the snow flew. Bah! Your stories are meant to stir the blood of our young men so we will do your fighting, which you are not able to do for yourselves. Bah!"

The English assured him Louisbourg was true. The chief remained unimpressed. Hendrick and Johnson were friends, so Hendrick surely knew Louisbourg was ours. Robbins laughed to hear Hendrick deny Louisbourg and speak to the governor with such scorn. When I heard Robbins, and with Blanch agreeing with him, I realized the shrewd Hendrick was putting on a show of disbelief to obtain more promises from the governor, who was desperate to keep the support of our wavering allies. Blanch thought Iroquois neutrality was smoke to cover their going over to the French. "This palavering is sure to stir their young men." He may be right.

When the council closed, a number of oxen were roasted, good rum broken out, a multitude of toasts drunk. To King George of England. The Indian chiefs. The commissioners. On they went. We returned to the fort, bitter at the lack of results. To us rangers, up on the frontier, chasing Indians and more often getting chased, the only result of the conference was money wasted. Our colony remained in consternation. If the Iroquois went entirely over to the French, not even New York Town would be safe.

Chapter XXV – 1748 – '53 – Mary

In June of 1748 came news of a peace treaty between England and France, to be signed in Europe this fall. The war was over! The peace would bring the frontier back to life. Our towns and farms would rise up out of the ashes, out of the weeds and brush where thriving settlements had once stood. The fields cleared with so much time and labor and now getting absorbed back into the forests would be reclaimed.

The army disbanded, we went down to Albany to get our money. Many of us had a goodly sum of back pay built up. We waited for it. And waited. One excuse followed another. We were a month getting paid. When we did, it was in useless script. The Full Sail was raucous with men celebrating the end of the war. Some fools were calling it a victory for our side. This was in no way true.

Robbins was headed west with trade goods and a new partner, Abner Brown. Blanch was headed home. They all promised to keep in touch through the Full Sail. Blanchard warned me how for the lone trapper the war was not over. Hostile Indians would yet prowl the hinterlands. He said they'd find my Beaver Valley, sooner or later. No peace treaty signed in Europe would have meaning for me then. The dangers would not go away until the French were driven from the continent. I agreed. "Watch your hair," I said.

I decided to stay home for the summer for an overdue rest. We soon learned the French had not relaxed their pressure on the frontiers. Not open warfare but troubles enough. Wherever Indians ranged or were said to be about, folks scurried for cover. Alarms came in to Albany. It was plain the war might reopen at any time. Hostility in New York Town between the English and Dutch politicians ran high. The land speculators were everywhere. More people flocked to the colony in the wake of peace.

The western Mohawk Valley and the Ohio country beckoned. Rich farmland. Seemed every day ships came to Albany carrying settlers from Europe. People of every language and skin shade. One watchful night spent in the Full Sail would open even the dullest eyes to the contrasts existing side by side in this world.

News traveled slowly. Only now did we hear details of the fighting in other parts of the world. The war had been fought on a much larger stage than just our own. Which fact did not help with so many dead and so much hard work gone up in flames. Cabins and barns was rising again in the clearings. Saratoga was getting rebuilt but too many of those going out to tame the wilderness were unprepared folks from settled Europe. They knew naught of forests or Indians and our politicians could not see one whit into the future. They did nothing to organize for protection. No new posts or military roads built nor even planned. For our Assembly it was business as usual, cheatin' and stealin' as much as could be got.

In August the authorities asked me to guide a delegation up the lakes to Montreal. They organized what is best described as a wishful try at discovering the fate of as many of our people taken from New York Colony as possible. The pay they offered was poor but I agreed to go. Schaack surprised me with a visit the night before we were to depart. He gave me a letter. Said could I get it to a Monseignor Wiseman in Montreal, Wiseman might help me find Arnold's wife or Eric's father. Schaack insisted I tell none of those I was traveling with about the letter.

The trip up, in a beautiful time of year, was hastily organized and poorly planned. Under the leadership of a pastor who knew nothing of travel in the woods. And, we discovered, nothing about people. But he had powerful influence through his church. The trials of journeying with Reverend Balcomb too clumsy and painful to write. Suffice to say it was a cumbersome affair. I caught pike in Corlaer and salmon and trout up the creeks. Our party stayed over at the castle at Scalp Point on the way north. First time I ever set foot inside those dreadful walls. Gave me an uneasy feeling. The place was haunted by all the good people who had died there. Tormented souls seeking resting places. My bad dreams were powerful, I could not sleep on the cot of filthy straw they offered. Lousy with lice. Tried to get up into the tower but was stopped by a bayonet-wielding sergeant. I was glad to leave this dragon's lair.

At the northern outlet of Corlaer, we were met by a delegation of Frenchmen. They were obviously not happy to have us there. Only one or two spoke English. They guided us around to a few tame Indian villages in search of people we could barter for or ransom. I believed the Indians had word of our coming and hid the captives they most wanted to keep. We did not find nearly so many as what had been taken. "All dead," the Indians said. The few we managed to buy back and who were able to tell us anything claimed there were plenty of others in the villages. Challenged with this, the Indians shrugged and walked away. A member of the delegation, Monsieur Montrain, spoke Dutch. I talked to him, he said he knew Wiseman and I entrusted Montrain with my letter.

We had a bad time when a little New Hampshire girl of six or seven years snuck away from her captors and begged us to take her along. Our pompous leader, the Word of God, so he thought, refused. "I am not authorized," he said, "to spend money on any other than Yorkers. Others would want to come along, too."

"What in the hell did we come for then, Reverend Balcomb?" I asked in disbelief. He insisted he would only barter for Yorkers. I said I remembered the little girl from Saratoga. He refused to believe me. Knew it was a lie. I tried to deal for her myself, he told me not to interfere, which made me the madder. Others of our party joined in against him and we offered to pay the child's ransom. I told Balcomb we were not leaving without her. He said he was in command and his word was final. "Lord sure'n hell works in funny ways, don't he?" my French friend said, not hiding his amusement. I said Balcomb was no Word of God. The poor child fretted whilst her fate was batted back and forth, her feelings of abandonment awful to witness. The argument continued, I threatened to knife Balcomb, more amusement for my French friend. Balcomb relented, we bartered for the girl and got her out. After this, I was so disgusted I gave Balcomb a hard time whenever I could find any kind of reason.

I found no sign of Priscilla or of Eric's father, though I searched where I could and asked many questions. Made a couple of short trips accompanied by Monsieur Montrain. He told me many of the Indians who took part in the Saratoga raid dwelt on the shores of the Ottawa River, which joined the Saint Lawrence upstream from Montreal. "A wild river, M'sieu, of many hundreds of miles. The Indians inhabiting its banks just as wild and impossible to control." I said I was prepared to go there and search, though I reckoned neither Priscilla nor Eric's father were still alive. "A perilous trip at best," Montrain said, concerned I might go despite his warnings. "Those Indians will not give up adopted family or slaves. Though it is true they have many. Your life would be in extreme jeopardy the first time you set foot in one of their camps." He then added with a warning shudder, "M'sieu, they are wild beyond imagination."

Monsieur Montrain brought back a response from Monsieur Wiseman. Wiseman knew men who had been upriver recently and he said he would make inquiries of them. In the meantime, would a friend of whom Van Schaack had spoken so highly do an old man the honor of a visit? I very much wanted to, but the French would not allow it. I corresponded with Wiseman, asked him to get me the names of any he could. He promised but said there was little hope of information.

All the way home, the little girl stayed away from the preacher, despite his attempts at befriending her. Balcomb got mad because she would only stay with me or with one of the women we brought back. We returned to Albany to a mostly disappointed crowd of tearful folks who had hoped for at least some word of their lost ones. I listened incredulously to the preacher tell, in front of the many folks gathered around, how he had saved the little girl from the Papists and Indians. "No Christian man," he said, "could have refused to bring her out." Then, and saying the little girl had won his heart, he announced he was going to adopt her, give her a pious upbringing. In a half-drunken nasty rebuttal, I told Schaack and the mayor the truth of Balcomb. Then, and with all of what the good reverend said about me, the mayor refused to pay me for my work, he citing my uncooperative attitude. He finally paid in useless script. I had to threaten to horsewhip a clerk before he paid up my chit in king's silver.

After a quiet fall in town, I decided to go north for the winter. On my way up, I stopped at North Fort. It was an abandoned, dilapidated ruin. The gates broken on their hinges, weeds growing on the parade ground. Fire had been set to the commander's office but had burned out afore it caught.

My cabin, when I got there, was untouched but for the ravages of time. I remained cautious as always. Kept close watch on my back-track and on the French garrison at Scalp Point. A few regulars, some Canadian militia, woods-lopers and Indians. Shepherded by the black-robes. Indians prowled the countryside from time to time. Care was a necessity, yet I loved my life of freedom and wild danger. The fur was good and with an insatiable demand in England and Europe for beaver hats, my furs, all of which came up prime, fetched high prices.

In the spring of 1749, when I returned from the north woods, there was word of the official signing of the peace treaty. Signed last fall and called the Treaty of Aix-la-Chapelle. As part of the agreement, the English gave Louisbourg back to the French! A battle won at so much cost in men and money and a position for blocking shipping into the Canadas lost at the stroke of a pen. Our people were furious. They condemned the English for giving away this great colonial gain for the sake of a French concession someplace far away and not known to us. Certainly a grand giveaway.

I discovered Arnold up and about, doing odd jobs for Mother and Pops, running errands, cleaning up the common room in the mornings. He was recovered enough from his wounds to get around, except he had just one eye. He wore a patch over his empty socket and a stocking cap low on his head to hide the disfigurement of having got scalped and bashed in the face. He walked stoop-shouldered and bickered with an imaginary someone at his side. Poor man, gone right 'round the bend! He could no longer teach school or cipher numbers and babbled incessantly, though his mind was not entirely gone. He had got into the habit of listening to the talk around town and repeating what he heard to any who would listen. He became an unofficial courier who could be counted on to have his stories straight. He sorted out the different pieces of what he heard and retained what was true. Anyone wanting news from around town or of the world needed only to ask Arnold. Better and more up to date than the newspapers and broadsides. He'd spend hours down to the docks or doing odd jobs up at army headquarters. Always alert for any bit of news from the sailors and British officers. "Oh, yes. Oh, yes. I see," he'd mumble to himself, putting it all together in his mind and arriving at a conclusion. Ship captains relied on him, or he might assist a newly arrived traveler or soldier about town, most often steering them to the Full Sail. Sailors learned that in return for tips and gossip he would wake them from a drunk in time to make a sailing board.

Arnold had learned a terrible ploy to quiet his tormenters, of whom existed a number. Get right up in their faces, pull the cap from his head and the patch from his eye socket, thus exposing his ghastly disfigurements. A most gruesome sight sure to make even strong men back off. Over his tea at night, the pathetic little man would get to remembering his wife and his former standing in the Saratoga community. Those were the worst times for him, and for those around him. He'd carry on so, laughing uproariously at the most insignificant event even whilst the tears flowed for his beloved Priscilla. Creating an obnoxious scene whilst he was about it. Then someone who did not know better would start in on him until he did his little scamp with his wounds. Still, and even with him occasionally most viciously blaming me for all his misfortune, I counted him my friend.

This spring I dallied too long in Albany and returned to my cabin with, of all things, a woman. The daughter of one of Bill Johnson's Mohawk drinking cronies. Her Iroquois name unpronounceable to my tongue. Thus, Mary. A beautiful teenager, with those wonderful high cheekbones and shiny black hair. The first time I set eyes on this tall, slender forest-vixen, she was standing in front of the fur-traders' shed, waiting for her father and brother. Dark flashing eyes set so piercingly in a beautifully chiseled face threw down a challenge I could not refuse. No picture could ever be so perfect. The dusky smoothness of her skin captivated me from the first moment. Almond eyes spoke volumes. Knew I must have her. Her father bartered a steep price. One I could scarce meet but was ready and most willing to pay. A shared jug and the deal was made. He told me she had seen sixteen summers. I met her mother. A tough old squaw if ever there was one and against the purchase from the start. She wanted a better match for her comely daughter. I believed Mama Bear had her sights set on Bill Johnson. The old man threatened to beat her if she did not acquiesce. She did, and I liked him from then on. I thought on Johnson, not sure he had not got there first. "Never known a man," her father assured me. I bought him another jug for telling me, true or not.

Mary wanted to get married right away. She, baptized in Johnson's Anglican Church, considered herself a Christian who was close to the church in her castle. I insisted we wait a year. See how it worked out. "I might want to sell you back," I said, mostly by signs and not realizing how insulting this was until she half-drew her knife. Her exciting eyes alive with feral anger.

I suffered much grief from my folks and friends. Mother declared herself most disappointed with how her only son had turned out. She threatened never to speak to me again. And might not! She would not allow us to stay at the tavern. Said it was because we were not married. Pops had never been so quiet. Eric called me a squawman, then he apologized.

I cared not for what anybody thought. Mary was the most exciting woman I had ever known, though I could barely make myself understood to her. The girl had me enthralled. She rebuffed my advances the short time we were in Albany, this I put off to the way my folks were treating her, and I thought to have her after we departed. As we approached Saratoga, on our way up to the cabin, I told her we would spend the night at an inn. Told her it was my right. She resisted, saying mostly by signs how a few days' tolerance was necessary so she might prepare herself. We argued. Figured I could wear her down until I realized she had kept the argument going until we had got past the town and to the upper end of the portage. She taunted me the entire time we were re-launching the canoe. I could see how challenging living with this lovely, strong-willed lass would be. Three nights in camp along the trail and the lake, and I was at fever pitch. But couldn't make her see reason. Being so close to this young beauty and knowing she was mine yet not partaking of her charms was frustrating. To distract myself, and annoy her, I dallied in the mornings and made camp too early in the afternoons. I'd set up my writing and spend hours with quill in hand. The first morning she sat in the canoe and waited. For two hours I enjoyed my leisurely writing and enjoyed too her annoyance. We argued, I won. But saw myself further from my intended goal. Then, and despite her anger, she could not help be curious about my writing and watched over my shoulder. I explained what it was, she understood. Some. Her nearness made matters worse, I started kissing her wonderful neck. Excitement rose within me. She broke free from my embrace and dashed into the woods. I waited an hour. She came back. Contrite. We pushed on.

The girl had been well trained. She knew how to keep a camp, to have the right things ready at the right times. She could paddle a canoe and make a smokeless cookfire. Once we got the newness worn off, she would make a fine partner, one to be counted on if I could swing her to my side. She was surprised a white man dared live so deep in the mountains. Her own prejudices did not allow her to believe a white man could do as well in the woods as an Indian. I think she was wary of where we were going. Even her father, an adventurous warrior in his day, did not know this country.

Arriving at the cabin on a beautiful summer day, mosquitoes and bees buzzing, we decided we would live in the cellar. It would be warmer than the upper room come winter. Within minutes of walking in, Mary was cleaning. The dirt was a flyin'. Down came the cobwebs. The mice droppings got whisked out the door. Once the floor was cleaned, she forbade me from wearing muddy moccasins inside. She chased me with her store-bought broom when I did. The second time she chased me it ended with the two of us in bed. At first, she stayed coy, not daring to reject me but keeping a distance. After a few days feeling each other out, both proceeding slowly, faster as we went, we began spending more time romping. She was a delightful, hot-blooded young wench. Our fires fueled by the waiting.

Mary knew few white man's words other than those learned from the prayers of her Anglican faith. I taught her English. In return, she learned me Mohawk. I had better luck with her as the pupil. She was smarter than the whites who thought all Indians were stupid. Her mind was a nimble thing indeed! Mary had brought along a heavy bag of seed. We cleared land for a garden. Iroquois women plant wherever they can. She worked the garden constantly.

During the hot months, we had got into the habit of going to the lake for a swim in the afternoons. Diving naked off the high places, like love-struck otters. Splashing and grabbing in the cool, refreshing waters. A thing of beauty to watch her half-woman, half-adolescent body in long graceful dives off the high ledges. Her lithe brown form straight as an arrow, long legs and slender hips cutting the water with just the merest of splashes. Disappearing underwater and not coming up for the longest time. Her head bobbing, a ways down from where she submerged, black hair glistening, pink nipples sparkling in the sunshine. Then was I in pursuit, eager for the taste. Mary was a fish in the water, too damn fast for this old man. But there are other ways. The race is almost never to the swiftest. The fish will always come to the right bait. I'd dive deep where she could not see me and come up under her in the clear blue waters to join in a frolicking, watery embrace until she'd break away and taunt me to chase her.

What a summer! The two of us alone in Paradise. Our blood ran hot. Time after delicious time did it reach fever pitch to be cooled one fine way. At night we lay out under the stars, wrapped in soft robes and light blankets, listening to the night sounds. The full moon shining on the water. A world at peace.

One night, as we lay on a ledge overlooking the water, our bedding underlined with soft pine boughs, a bear called out from across the lake. His barking caused Mary to move closer to me under the blanket. Wrapped tight, we lay still, holding each other, listening to Mister Bruin. His call might be mistaken for an owl, yet there is a difference. Only after the longest time did my woman break the silence. "Tis the sound yon boar makes when looking he is for a mate. Grunting and blowing across yon hills for his sow. As you the day you bought me. Oh, great huffer and snorter!" She giggled, I whispered, "Is that so? Are you such a sow to come running to the wild grunts of any boar? I suppose better it is to wait for some damn preacher to run his mouth over the words. Let him do the snorting, eh?" I tickled her ribs, hard. "White man's words," she said, squirming, laughing. "White man's religion, white man's world. White man's power. Poor Indian maiden has no chance." She was right, not one chance did she have. I started to take her again. And realized that as usual, she had found a way to get the last word. I could feel her mounting passion as we did some mating of our own.

"Never," I declared, when we had done and lay listening to each other's breathing, "will I have my fill of you, woman." She stroked my chin in a delightful way. "Nor I you, White-Eyes." She buried her head deep in my chest. Her loving drew me, as Bill Johnson was fond of saying, like a moth to the flame. She asked softly, "Did yon bear hark to the sounds of our coupling? Tell me, White-Eyes, ye who knows all, does ye think yon bruin is stirred by our sounds, as we were by his?" Teasing, yet innocent and coquettish, I had to laugh for the emotions she stirred within me. Oh sweet, sweet, ardor, there in the splendor of the wilds at their most beautiful. Feelings to fill a man's breast past the bursting point. I held her tight and squeezed for the shimmers of afterglow moving me. Already starting to rekindle the fires within. Mary kept me steaming for months. Never let me down. Tricks, games, words, tickling, touching, feeling, she had me chasing her all summer. And catching her.

****

Mary was a direct, simple-thinking woman, a bargain at any price. I could see through her tantrums and stubbornness and past her some-times flashing temper to all the strength and goodness within her. Still, I had to remember she was hardly more than a child.

Her garden produced a good amount of ground nut, potatoes and corn, and she made the cabin a warm, cheery place to live. With the coming of the colder weather, the field mice began to move inside the cabin. It had always been thus. I could never beat them and they were always gnawing at my food and furs. The dog had sometimes chased and ate them when he was hungry or bored. Mary set clever traps and within two months we were entirely rid of the rodents.

She tended to all the necessary work around the cabin, even the woodpile, leaving me free for trapping. She was the big chief around the place and had it feeling like a proper home. It seemed so fresh and clean. And her, too. She wore the prettiest things all seemingly created out of nothing. A garland of wildflowers in her shiny raven hair became a crown of jewels.

At the height of autumn of the year 1750 and with the leaves of the trees at their most spectacular, we canoed to Lydius' trading post by way of Saint Sacrement for our winter supplies. Bought her ribbons, a comb and a small mirror. The store-bought combs were easier for her to use than the bone combs she made herself, and she did not spend much time gazing into the mirror, as many white women do. Just she had to check herself from time to time. She was inexpensive to keep.

We met a cousin of hers at the store. A bad-tempered fellow she had not seen in some years. He was a Praying Indian residing outside of Montreal and had fought on the other side from me in the late war. I couldn't help wondering had I crossed paths with him, me stalking him or him me. He was maybe thinking the same thing as he was most hostile toward me. Thought I might have to fight him.

I thought I knew how to fish, my woman taught me plenty. With the ice thick on the lake, she'd set up her ice house, old blankets propped on sticks and arranged to keep the sun's glare from going directly into the hole whilst still allowing the light to penetrate down through the surrounding ice. She'd tie a shiny, fish-shaped ornament on a string and dangle it down into the water. With spear at the ready, she'd jiggle the lure close to the surface and when the bigger fish came for a look-see, she'd thrust the spear with amazing dexterity. My own winter fishing had always been with hook and line, long cold days often garnering naught whilst Mary never seemed to come home without a full basket. I tried her method and was not very good at it. She laughed at my efforts.

Adept at finding things to eat, regardless the season, she taught me about foraging in the woods. The snowshoes she made were better than mine. Lasted longer. The quality of my fur improved with her working it instead of me. I was getting better prices than ever despite renewed competition from Oswego and Lydius' smugglers. We had a satchel full of silver and copper coins. A few years of peace in the north would see us rich.

Slowly, one by one, she washed away all the hurts in my memory.

All the horrible things I witnessed in the late war. She got through the surface and down to the deepest hurts. Cut by cut. Scar by scar. Day by day they healed. She was responsible for the upswing my life took. We were comfortable though the living was mighty rough.

Mother eased some in her attitude toward me and my woman. She even conspired with Mary to see us wed. Surprising myself, I agreed. We married in the Dutch Church. Then my wife and me took a canoe west to William Johnson's castle where she announced our status to my in-laws. Her mother became easier to get along with. I enjoyed the stay, even with the stiff formalities of their brand of religious living. Quite a strong influence. Her father and me snuck 'round back of the cabin whenever we could, to drink from a bottle he kept hidden there. Spent a day with Johnson, who admired what he called my good catch. I warned him to watch where his eye roamed. He laughed.

Mary's mother told her, when I was not around, about a black-robe who had come to the Mohawks with an offer to buy up all the land at the south end of Saint Sacrement. "Even Warrigueghey does not know about it," Mary whispered to me late one night, using the name the Mohawks gave to Johnson when they made him a member of their tribe. Mary said her mother did not believe her people would sell any land to the French.

My wife quickly learned to speak English. And a fair amount of Dutch. She constantly amazed me with the rapidity with which she seemed able to say the words as well as grasp the meanings. She laughed whenever I tried to speak her native tongue. She'd pretend to be upset with her lout of a husband. She'd declare I was dumber than an Algonquin. Another season and she had grown taller. A lanky Indian lady. Just starting to fill out. There was something different about her, I did not know what until she told me she was a month or two along with a child.

I, too, changed. Distracted from my work. Worried whenever I had to be away. Hurrying home too early each day, not spending enough time trapping. I needn't have worried; she was a strong girl versed in the ways of a woman. She would not allow me to do her work for her. That hurt Mary worse than the child-bearing. I saw the pain in her eyes when I did the things she thought she should be doing, such as carrying in wood from the woodpile. I stopped getting in her way. And had more peace. She made me a beautiful ceremonial coat entirely of the skins of white mice, each worked carefully and all sewn together.

Decorated with dyed stick-piggy quills. An otter-skin collar and buck-horn buttons. A wonderful gift of love for her Chief. One over which she had spent much time and effort. And kept hidden from me until it was finished.

Mother, admitting to herself the changes Mary had brought in me and realizing she was to be a grandmother, had a change of heart. A big one! Father razzed her about it but she did not care. The baby was most important to her.

I had a letter from Robbins, now a trader on the Ohio. Settled in at a large Indian town. A palisaded post for trading with the Indians. He urged us to join him. Mary's father warned us against going. Trouble, he said, was brewing out there.

Late one afternoon, in the fall of the year, I got in from hunting and there sat Mary, on a stump in the yard, proud as can be, nursing her baby. Named him Thomas Kenneth and loved him dearly from the first moment I laid eyes on him. A joy to behold. I was happier than a man had a right to be. And prayed life could go on this way forever.

The baby drew Mary and me even closer together. Life was both wonderful and meaningful. A private affair, deep in the harsh north woods. Paradise. With her beside me and with no one to interfere with our happiness. But, alas. Smoke is always on the horizon. The English Colonies were getting crowded and people felt hemmed in to the west and north by the French. We were down to Albany in the summer of '52 when came the news, danger again threatened us. The western Indians, at the instigation of the French, destroyed the trading town of Pickawillany. Put it to the torch. The defenders said to be all dead. This would include Robbins and Abner. No way to know. The French were said to be building a fort where ours had stood. Holding the west meant dominance. Each side aspired to grab the advantage. Caught in the middle were the tribes, used by both sides and certainly capable of playing their own ends. By treaty, no white men from any colony were allowed to settle the far country. Yet who was to stop them? We stayed the summer in town to see would the uprising become general. Mother fussed constantly over her grandson. I loved hearing their laughter and watching as his tiny little hands reached up and grabbed her nose.

Through these seasons, writing occupied a share of my time. I remained fascinated by the written word. How it could be fit together with patience to say exactly what one desired. Another year we lived content in our cabin. From what little we heard since Pickawillany, a tenuous peace seemed to be holding. There was scant sign of inter-lopers in our North Country. Surprisingly, my beautiful woodland valley remained a secret. I prospered; life held so much meaning for us, I reckoned it to go on unchanged.

Until Mary, pregnant again and with little Tommy strapped to her back, fell through weak ice on the lake. I warned her against going out there, the ice was only days old. But Mary wanted fresh fish and would not wait. A soft spot broke under her and they went in. I was on my way down the hill from the cabin and heard her screaming for me. I knew at once what had happened. I rushed down through the steep passage, slipping on the ice, and down to the shore, tossing gear, more scared for what I would find than is possible to write. Got out onto the lake but the darn fool was way far out. Her favorite spot. Saw her go under and come back up. She knew she could not save herself and struggled desperately to free the baby board from her back, to save our little boy. More than willing to sacrifice her own life if he might live. She had freed the board from her back and was trying to hold it up out of the freezing water long enough for me to get there. The baby was crying for being so cold and scared. I had about got to him and they slipped under and were gone. There was naught I could do except stare at the hole, the horrible jagged ice, the water bubbling up around the edges, the pieces of the shelter she had always erected around her fishing places. The ice collapsed beneath me and I was immersed in the cold water. The ice around the hole broke each time I tried to get up onto it. I was floundering and about done in with the terrible cold. One last effort got me out.

I dragged my frozen body home and built up the fire. As a result of the dousing I became quite sick and cared not whether I lived or not. Only wanted to be with my Mary and little Tommy. For days I could do naught but keep the fire going and the door shut against the wolves. They sensed my desperate straits. The rest of the winter was awful. The longest, coldest, most despairing of times. A week passed before I could rouse myself to retrieve my rifle and possibles, dropped when I'd heard Mary's screams. All I saw, awake or asleep, was her. And heard her voice. Stopped me cold. Her memory was everywhere. In everything her hand had ever touched. No heart for trapping had this lad. Just I grieved for my family.

Spring came. I did not want to go down to Albany. I did not have the courage or strength to face anyone. Poor Mother! She would be so heartbroken. I wandered the hills. Trying, I suppose, to flee from the despair, the horror I could never erase. In July I could no longer stand my own company. Had to go down. I carried nothing for trade. Told my story to Eric, and when I said I was only staying long enough to tell my folks, then I was going north to wander some more, he probably figured it would be a long time before he saw me again. If ever. The folks, of course, were much aggrieved. Mother took it especially hard, the loss of her grandson. "Two," I told her. "Mary was pregnant." Mother cried for the babes, and for Mary. Pops buried himself in a bottle of schnapps and stayed there. I took a slow, sad walk out to Mary's folks to inform them. They were grateful to me for coming and invited me to stay but I left within a few hours, staying only long enough for supper and to garner what comfort I could from them, and, I suppose, them from me. I did not stop to see Johnson. I refuged in an isolated frontier saloon for a month, drunk the entire time. Sobered up long enough to get back to Albany. Stayed drunk another month with Pops. Had to leave town before it killed us both.

For a year I wandered the north. Slowly started to write again. It provided comfort, a place to pour out my grief. I did no trapping. Just wandered. Learned more of the back country. Lived by a thread, full knowing I could not have them back, no matter how hard I might wish it. Stayed at the cabin sometimes, often gone for long periods at a time.

****

The French were engaged in strengthening their castle at Scalp Point. The palisade across the lake was rebuilt. More Canadian settlers moved into the area. They stayed down in the valley and didn't wander the surrounding hills. Did they begin to spread out from the shore, they might force me to abandon my cabin.

I explored the Connecticut River Valley and went on a smuggling expedition up along the Saint Lawrence, which venture did not work out for me though I stayed up there for some time afterward. It was the most incredible land of all. Out past the mountains, it flattened to a marked degree. Grassy valleys surrounded by oak and beech forests. Nuts by the hatful. The uplands full of game, good country to wander. To get lost in. To lose one's thoughts. The birch canoe was, as always, the key to passage through this western country. The portages between waters were short and safe. Well marked. The waters placid, the rapids not so steep nor so long. Everywhere the land gave the appearance of having never been trod upon. I got lost often but cared not. One direction same as another. Spent nights in solitary camps. Fished the ponds and brooks, hunted the hardwoods, paddled the rivers, clumb tall trees to see what was beyond. Sometimes just sat thinking of Mary and the babes. Wondered if the second one might have been a girl.

In the winter of 1753, I resumed my life's work, though I was devoid of fervor. The cabin got its first reworking since Mary's death. Anything to remind me of her I put into a box which I buried in the ground. The less I saw of her things, the better, yet I might someday regret it, did I get rid of them. Many years would have to pass before the sense of loss would go away, before the hurting would dim. Sometimes my thoughts wandered to Sergeant Tom O' Brien. Retired or yet a soldier? Thinking of him reminded me of the fighting. Fervently I prayed for no more war. No more suffering and sorrow so I could stay in this country forever to hunt and trap.

****

Thank you for reading The Great Carry. With Book Two of the Skywaters Series (due out Autumn, 2019) King George's War has ended, the future of North America remains undecided. The savagery and tempo of the Indian raids are unabated. No peace treaty between European nations can quell the violence in North America and there is a weary fatalism. The wars must continue until either the French or the English are driven from the continent.

Made in United States
North Haven, CT
16 September 2023

41637853R00185